The Wild Cards Universe

Card Sharks

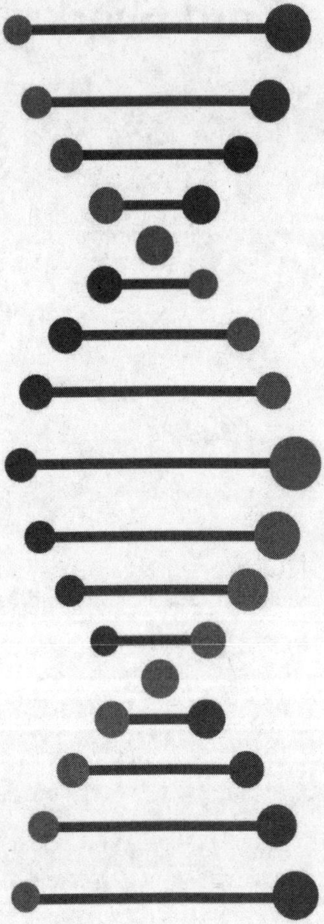

GEORGE R. R. MARTIN

Presents

Wild Cards: Card Sharks

A WILD CARDS MOSAIC NOVEL

EDITED BY GEORGE R. R. MARTIN

Assisted by Melinda M. Snodgrass

and written by

Stephen Leigh	Victor Milan
William F. Wu	Roger Zelazny
Gwenda Bond	Kevin Andrew Murphy
Melinda M. Snodgrass	Laura J. Mixon
Michael Cassutt	

Random House Worlds
New York

LIBRARY OF CONGRESS CATALOGING-IN-PUBLICATION DATA
Names: Martin, George R. R., editor. | Snodgrass, Melinda M., editor. |
Leigh, Stephen, author.
Title: Card sharks: a wild cards mosaic novel / edited by George R. R.
Martin; assistant editor, Melinda M. Snodgrass and written by Stephen
Leigh, and others.
Description: Bantam trade paperback edition. | New York: Bantam
Books, 2024.
Identifiers: LCCN 2023035736 (print) | LCCN 2023035737 (ebook) | ISBN
9780593357897 (trade paperback) | ISBN 9780593357903 (ebook)
Subjects: LCSH: Science fiction, American.
Classification: LCC PS648.S3 C3235 2024 (print) | LCC PS648.S3 (ebook) |
DDC 813/.0876208—dc23/eng/20230818
LC record available at https://lccn.loc.gov/2023035736
LC ebook record available at https://lccn.loc.gov/2023035737

Printed in the United States of America on acid-free paper

randomhousebooks.com

1st Printing

Book design by Virginia Norey
Helix art: Graficriver/stock.adobe.com

to Mary Wismer
always an ace

Wild Cards

The virus was created on TAKIS, hundreds of light-years from Earth. The ruling mentats of the great Takisian Houses were looking for a way to enhance their formidable psionic abilities, and augment them with physical powers. The retrovirus they devised showed enough promise that the psi lords decided to field-test it on Earth, whose inhabitants were genetically identical to Takisians.

Prince Tisianne of House Ilkazam opposed the experiment and raced to Earth in his own living starship to stop it. The alien ships fought high above the atmosphere. The ship carrying the virus was torn apart, the virus itself lost. Prince Tisianne landed his own damaged ship at White Sands, where his talk of tachyon drives prompted the military to dub him **DR. TACHYON.**

Across the continent, the virus fell into the hands of **DR. TOD,** a crime boss and war criminal, who resolved to use it to extort wealth and power from the cities of America. He lashed five blimps together and set out for New York City. President Harry S Truman reached out to Robert Tomlin, **JETBOY,** the teenaged fighter ace of World War II, to stop him. Flying his experimental jet, the JB-1, Jetboy reached Tod's blimps and crashed into the gondola. The young hero and his old foe met for the last time as the bomb containing the virus fell to Earth. *"Die, Jetboy, die,"* Tod shouted as he shot Tomlin again and again. "I can't die yet, I haven't seen *The Jolson Story*," Jetboy replied, as the bomb exploded.

Thousands of microscopic spores rained down upon Manhattan. Thousands more were dispersed into the atmosphere and swept up by the jet stream, to spread all over the Earth. But New York City got the worst of it.

It was **September 15, 1946.** The first Wild Card Day.

Ten thousand died that first day in Manhattan alone. Thousands more were transformed, their DNA rewritten in terrible and unpredictable ways. Every case was unique. No two victims were affected in the same way. For that reason, the press dubbed xenovirus *Takis-A* (its scientific name) the *wild card.*

Ninety percent of those infected died, unable to withstand the violent bodily changes the virus unleashed upon them. Those victims were said to have drawn the *black queen.*

Of those who survived, nine of every ten were twisted and mutated in ways great and small. They were called *jokers* (or *jacks*, *knaves*, or *joker-aces* if they also gained powers). Shunned, outcast, and feared, they began to gather in along the Bowery, in a neighborhood that soon became known as **Jokertown.**

Only one in a hundred of those infected emerged with superhuman powers: telepathy, telekinesis, enhanced strength, superspeed, invulnerability, flight, and a thousand other strange and wondrous abilities. These were the *aces*, the celebrities of the dawning new age. Unlike the heroes of the comic book, very few of them chose to don spandex costumes and fight crime, but they would soon begin to rewrite history all the same.

These are their stories.

Card Sharks

The Ashes of Memory

Stephen Leigh

1

How did I get involved in all this?

I'm not surprised at your question, given what I'm asking you to believe. Quasiman—you know him? He knows of you, but then I think everyone in Jokertown can say that. Anyway, Quasiman gave me his tale. That's the real beginning, after all. With that and my background, I can visualize that horrible moment, but I wasn't there. I wasn't part of it. Not yet, anyway.

But I can see it. I can . . .

Evening mass in Our Lady of Perpetual Misery on September 16, 1993, was packed. Christmas, Easter, and Black Queen Night: those were the three times each year that Father Squid could count on a full house. Half of Jokertown seemed to be pressed shoulder to shoulder in the pews or standing in the aisles, giving the interior a look not unlike that of a Bosch painting. Many of them were families, with children entirely normal or as misshapen as the parents. Imagine a shape, anything vaguely human or even not so human, and there it would be somewhere in the crowd; a lipless frog's mouth open in the group prayer, tentacles folded in some imitation of praying hands, slimy shoulders adorned with a new dress or faceted eyes gleaming as they watched Father Squid at the altar, raising a chalice to the congregation.

Swelling chords filled the nave, a subsonic bass trembling the floor: That was Mighty Wurlitzer. MW, as he was called, looked anything but human. He had once been the choir director for All Saints' parish in Brooklyn; now he was a ten-foot-long, thick tube of knobby, sand-colored exoskeleton from which dozens of hollow spines jutted out. A vestigial head capped one end of the tube: two frog-like bumps of eyes, a slit nose, but no mouth. Mighty Wurlitzer couldn't move, couldn't speak, but the bellows of his lungs inside that confining sheath were powerful and inexhaustible. He could vent air through the natural pipes of his immobile body, creating a sound like a demented bagpipe on steroids. Modifications had been added since MW had been "installed" in the choir loft. Flexible plastic tubing connected some of his spines to a rack of genuine organ pipes, allowing Mighty Wurlitzer to produce a truly awesome racket. It might not have been great music, but it was loud and energetic, and no joker in the congregation would ever fault another for doing the best he could with what the wild card had given him.

Mighty Wurlitzer trumpeted and a wild music sounded, a breathy orchestra. The jokers below joined in after the eight-bar introduction.

"Holy, holy, deformed Lord, God of Hosts . . ."

Afterward, no one was certain who first noticed. Someone in the congregation must have been gifted with a keen sense of smell in exchange for their warped body—the wild card virus had that kind of sick sense of humor. At least a few would have noticed that the odor of the votive candles seemed to be particularly intense, that there was a thin pall of acrid vapor wafting in, that the air was growing hazy and blue.

"Fire!" The word was shouted into the teeth of the song, the warning drowned out by Mighty Wurlitzer's crashing thunder. A few people heard the warning. Heads began to crane around curiously, the song faltered.

A bright yellow tongue licked at the crack between the side doors of the church, flickering in like a snake's tongue and then retreating. A child nestled in the multiple arms of his mother began to cry. The first tendrils of gray smoke began to writhe under the doorways.

A jet of blue flame hissed as it shot from under the side doors.

"Fire!"

This time the cry came from a dozen throats. Up in the loft, Mighty Wurlitzer coughed, and the bagpipe drone hiccuped in mid-melody. Like drawing the Black Queen from the deck of the wild card virus, the soaring paean to Christ metamorphosed into something far more chaotic, more human, and more deadly. The interior of the church echoed not to a hymn but to screams and shouts. Mighty Wurlitzer abandoned the song to coughing, barking discords like someone pounding on a keyboard with desperate fists.

The panic, the deadly fear, began its reign.

Father Squid shouted from the altar, his whispering, sibilant voice amplified by the microphone under the tentacles of his mouth. "Please! Don't shove! Everyone, let's move quickly to the nearest—"

The electronic voice went silent; at the same time, the lights inside the church died. In the sudden dark, the screams took on a new intensity. The surging, frightened congregation flailed and pushed and shoved toward the main doors at the rear.

There, the first people died.

Impossibly, the doors were locked or barred. Worse, the metal bands of the great wooden doors were searingly hot, and through the seams of the oak a threatening brightness flickered. Those in front shouted pleadingly, but they were crushed against the unyielding doors by the weight of those behind. The doors bulged outward and then held, and now those unlucky ones who had been first to the doors were suffocating, as smoke billowed black around them and the roaring voice of the blaze announced itself.

The mob tried to retreat back into the church, pushing now, heedless of those who slipped and fell and were trampled underneath, none of them thinking now of anything but their own survival. Breathing became impossible. There was no surcease in the superheated air around them, and the smoke flared in their lungs like acid.

"Oh, God, no!" Father Squid cried, but no one heard and God declined to intervene. The screaming had stopped out in the smoke-lost congregation. Those who could still breathe were saving that precious air for flight, for finding a way, any way, out from the relentless hell pit that now surrounded and pursued them. Flames crawled the west wall, at the ceiling of the east wall a Niagara of superheated air boiled. Yet the fire had sucked most of the oxygen out of the interior, and the blaze seemed almost sluggish. The flames subsided to a sullen orange glow.

Then the main doors went down—pushed open or unlocked—and the opening sent fresh air gushing in. The conflagration suddenly erupted with an audible *whoosh*, the inferno roaring higher and more searing than before. The walls re-ignited, a fireball rolled down the central aisle. As the stained glass windows shattered and rained bright knives, waves of fire leapt inward.

The heat puckered Father Squid's face, made the golden thread of his vestments burn through the surplice beneath them. He couldn't breathe, couldn't see. He knew he was going to die. Now. There was only the smoke and the leaping, triumphant glare of flame. "Mommy! Where are you?! Mommy!" a child screamed out in the roiling hell, and the sound caused Father Squid to take a staggering step toward the beckoning flames.

"Here!" he shouted into the roar. "Come over here, son!"

A hand grasped his shoulder, pulled him back. "Father— this way!"

"Quasiman . . ." Father Squid squinted at the hunchbacked figure through the smoke and coughed, pointing back into the inferno that was the church. "Save some of them. The children, the poor children . . ."

"Come!"

"Not me," Father Squid protested. "Them." But the hand was implacable and incredibly strong. Father Squid couldn't resist and—to his shame—he found that part of him didn't want to resist. The choir loft fell in an explosion of sparks, Mighty Wurlitzer giving a last scream like the final chord for Armageddon. The west wall sagged; part of the roof fell. Over the thunder of the flames, they could hear sirens, but out in the church there was only black silence.

Father Squid looked back once, then allowed Quasiman to drag him away: across the altar, into the sacristy to the side. That room was aflame, too, but Quasiman roared at the flames and leapt, gathering Father Squid in his arms. They crashed through the window in a cascade of glass, landing outside where suddenly there was air. Father Squid gasped and coughed, wheezing as he tried to drag some of that coolness into ravaged lungs. Half-conscious, he was aware of dark figures around him, faces peering worriedly at him through glass helmets. "Inside!" he tried to say, but his throat burned and all he could do was grunt. "For God's sake, please get them out!"

Someone murmured something, and he felt himself falling into arms. His head lolled back. Far above, a geyser of bright, whirling sparks spiraled heavenward around the steeple like burning prayers.

"Cassidy!"

At dawn, Hannah Davis stepped through the leaning, blackened timbers that had been a side entrance of the church. The wood steamed and fumed and hissed in the autumn drizzle. She noted immediately the black, rolling blisters on the wood—the fire had been unusually hot here. The floor had been burned entirely away in front of her; the undersloping angle of the char told her that the fire had communicated up from below. Someone had laid planks across the gap, and she walked carefully over into the church. The roofless shell of the building smoldered around her. Leo Cassidy, a lieutenant in the Jokertown fire division, straightened up from where he was kneeling near the front of the church and looked at her. His visor was up, and Hannah saw the scowl plainly. He turned back to what he was doing without a word.

Around the church's interior, department personnel were working, tearing down the walls as they searched out the remaining hot spots, or performing the grisly job of checking the soaked, black rubble for bodies. They were flagging the locations; there were far too many of the yellow triangles, more than seemed possible. The fire had come in as three alarms, had gone quickly to four and then five as soon as the first trucks had arrived on the scene. When Hannah had gotten the call to come down around midnight, the radio newscasters were already estimating that over a hundred jokers might have died. There'd been no hope of saving the building or getting anyone out—it had been all they could do to save as many of the surrounding buildings as they could. A strong wind had been blowing that night; the priest's cottage and two neighboring apartment houses had gone with the church. Burning ash had started several spot fires as far away as the East River. It had taken hours to get the fire under control.

The fire had been spectacular, fast, and extremely deadly. Even without the added interest of its location, the blaze would have made the national news. As it was, the torching of the Church of Jesus Christ, Joker, was the lead story everywhere this morning.

And it was, somehow, Hannah's fire. Her file. Her problem. She still wasn't sure how she felt about that.

Hannah picked her way carefully toward Cassidy. The rain made the fallen, scorched timbers slick and dangerous, and the smell of damp ash was overpowering. She slipped once, putting her hand out for support on one of the remaining pews and noting the capriciousness of fire—the wood under her hand was untouched: polished and golden and unblemished.

"Where'd the chief get to, Cassidy?"

Cassidy was putting a tarp over one of the corpses. Hannah forced herself to look. The body—too elongated, and with a neck as long as a small giraffe's—was on its side in the curled "fighting" position fire victims often assumed, as the intense heat caused the major muscle groups to contract. The abdomen gaped open in a long crease that almost looked like a cut, another legacy of the fire: with the heat, gas formed in the intestines, swelling them until they burst out from the weakened, seared skin. Unburnt, pink loops peeked from the slit. The corpse was badly damaged. Hannah couldn't even tell if it had once been male or female. The smell made Hannah want to gag.

"Funny, isn't it, that no matter how deformed they were before, they all look the same once they're crisped."

"The chief, Cassidy."

"Why you need the chief, Davis?" Cassidy grunted. He looked at Hannah, cocking his head as he noticed the leather apron stuffed with tools under her slicker. "Who you working under? Patton?" He put too much stress on the *under*.

"I'm not *under* anyone. This is my case."

Cassidy snorted. "Fuck," he said. "I wondered why the hell you were hanging around. Just what I need. I guess they thought this was a barn that burned down and they wanted you to count the dead cows."

Hannah ignored that, wishing she'd never mentioned that she'd grown up on the farm her parents still owned west of Cincinnati. She'd had to put up with the "country girl" jokes, with the sexual innuendos, with all the bullshit "we'll never let you be just one of the guys" snubbing, with the "just how the hell did you get this job" attitude. The first few months, she'd told herself that the abuse would ease up. It hadn't. It had gotten worse. "Stuff it, Cassidy. Where's Chief Reiger?"

Cassidy snorted. "In the basement."

"Fine. I'll be down there. I have Dr. Sheets coming in to coordinate the photographing and removal of the victims. Pete Harris from the bureau will be here anytime now. Let me know when he gets here; he's bringing the forensics team. Tell him to start on the entrances—all the reports from the survivors say they were blocked. And, Cassidy, give my people some cooperation, okay?"

Cassidy just looked at her, and she could almost hear his thoughts from the expression on his face. *Goddamn bossy bitch* . . . She also knew that if she'd been Patton or Myricks or any of the male long-term bureau agents, Cassidy would've happily nodded and said "Yes, sir." But Hannah was a newcomer, which was bad enough, and even worse, a woman. Hannah forced her anger down. "Any questions, Lieutenant?"

Cassidy sniffed again. Rain beaded on his black rubberized jacket, sliding down the yellow fluorescent stripes on the sleeves and waist. "No, ma'am," he said flatly. "No problem, ma'am. Cooperation is my middle name." A tic twitched the corner of his mouth as he stared at her, his face soot-stained. Hannah took a breath, making sure the anger was sealed in.

"Fine," she said. "I'll be down—"

She stopped. On the rear wall of the church where a crucifix would normally be placed, she saw something mounted. It was a wooden figure, blackened with smoke but unburned: a two-headed person, one head bearded, the other female. One set of hands were nailed to what looked to be a twisted wooden ladder behind it; another set of withered arms sprouted from the chest where three pairs of breasts ran down like the teats on a mother wolf. The feet were also nailed to the strange cross. Rain dripped from the feet, from the multiple breasts, from the faces. A chill went through Hannah, an unbidden outrage. Alongside her, Cassidy followed her gaze. He spat into the rubble; from the corner of her eyes, Hannah saw him make the sign of the cross. "Fucking blasphemy," he said.

"What *is* that?"

"Don't you hicks out in Ohio ever get papers?"

"Cassidy . . ."

"That's Jesus Christ the Joker, nailed to a DNA helix. This place is a joker's version of a Catholic church. Our Lady of Perpetual Misery, they call it. They even have a priest—guy looks like a squid. He went on that world tour five, six years ago, the one Senator Hartmann was on. You must've heard about that—the big dust-up in Syria with the Nur, Hartmann getting kidnapped in Berlin—or did that get crowded off the front page because of the Pig Festival?"

"Yeah, it did," Hannah replied. "And they ran your picture right above the goddamn blue ribbon."

Hannah walked away before Cassidy could reply.

In the basement, Chief Reiger was crouched in a puddle of water before an old porcelain-covered cast-iron sink. When the light of Hannah's helmet swept over him, the gray-haired man spoke without turning around. "Okay, Miss Davis, give me your evaluation of this."

"Chief, that's not fair. I'm a licensed—"

"Humor me, Miss Davis."

I shouldn't have to prove myself over and over again, not to you, not to anyone. Hannah stopped the protest before she vocalized it. She sighed, taking a quick inventory. "The porcelain's destroyed and the handles are melted off. There used to be a plywood wall behind here—nothing left now but the nails in the studs. The floor joists above are heavily damaged; so is the cabinet below the sink and the floor around it." Hannah paused, leaned over the sink. "I'd say that someone plugged the drain and poured a good quantity of liquid accelerant in the tub. Then they turned the water on and lit it somehow. The damage to the porcelain and the faucets means that we had one heck of a hot fire right here. The fire touched the wall and went up through it. When the sink overflowed, it spread the fire around the bottom of the sink and over the floor—you can see the trail following the slope of the floor. A definite torch, if we didn't already know that. No signs of a big explosion, so our friend didn't use gasoline."

Reiger was nodding. The condescension bothered her. He acted like a teacher acknowledging a student. "Gasoline and fuel oil mixture," he said.

Hannah shook her head. "Uh-uh. This was too hot a fire for

that, Chief. It *melted* the fixtures, and the ignition temperature of a gas/fuel oil mixture's too low for that. The fire went awful fast, too. When we get the results, we're going to find out it's JP-4: jet fuel. I'll bet on it—I worked on a job back"—*home,* she almost said—"in Cincinnati, where the stuff was used. And look here." She pointed to a corner of the sink, which had cracked off. "That's a concussion fracture, really clean. There was a little explosion here. Our torch used a device to set it off. He was already out of here when it went up."

Reiger scowled, and Hannah tried to keep the satisfaction from showing on her face. He'd missed the evidence of the fuse entirely, she realized. "You might be right," Reiger admitted grudgingly.

"So did I pass your little exam?"

Reiger grunted.

"I'll take that as a yes," she said.

"You know something, Miss Davis, you ought to leave that chip on your shoulder at home. I'm sorry if I've offended you, but I've never worked with you before."

"You do this field-testing with every new agent the bureau sends out, Chief?"

"Yeah, Miss Davis. As a matter of fact, I do." His dark eyes glared at her from under the rim of his helmet, challenging her. *You gotta work with him . . .* Hannah could feel the tension in her jaws. She relaxed the muscles, forced herself to give the man a half smile even though she didn't believe him. Reiger probably didn't call the other agents by their last name— they'd be "Pat" or "Hugh" or "Bob"—and she doubted that he called any woman "Ms."

"I'm sorry," she said, hating the words. "I guess I flew off the handle a little." She hated even more the fact that her apology and the smile—as she had known it would—melted the Chief's irritation.

"It's not a problem," he said. "I won't treat you any differently than anyone else. I just want you to understand that."

Right. "I understand, Chief." She smiled again to take the edge off the words, and the man nodded. He gave her a fatherly clap on the shoulder.

"Great. Then I think you should look over here. I think we've found where he broke in . . ."

"Here's some more tracks alongside the door."

"I'll be right there, Pete."

By late afternoon, the interior had been sketched and photographed. The victims had been tagged, field-examined, and removed. Evidence had been bagged and sealed and marked.

Everything about this fire was ugly. The fire setter, whoever it was, hadn't bothered to hide the arson. He—almost all arsonists were male—had entered through a basement window: Reiger had been right about that. All the windows were stained black with smoke except for one shattered pane on the floor. The glass was still clean, which meant that it was down before the fire. He'd set plants, material to start the initial fire, in the basement under each door of the church and in several other places along the walls. A trailer of oiled cotton rope had gone between each of the plants—Hannah had found an uncharred piece near the window where the torch had entered. The plants themselves were a potpourri of whatever the arsonist could find in the basement: votive candles, paper, cardboard boxes, all soaked in the same accelerant as had been in the sink. Hannah could guess at what had occurred: The fire setter had quickly heaped together the plants, linked them together with the rope, then soaked them all in the jet fuel. One end of the rope had been placed in the sink. Finally, he'd dumped the rest of the fuel in the sink, turned on the water, and placed his fuse on the side of the sink. He would have had ample time to leave the basement before the fuse set off the rising fuel in the sink, and the sound of the small initial explosion had been covered by the singing above.

Ten, maybe fifteen minutes' work. By the time the odor of the jet fuel had wafted upward, the fire would have been raging.

Hannah and Pete Harris were outside, to the rear of the church. The drizzle had stopped and the clouds had broken. The lowering sun touched the steeple, still standing over the roofless edifice, and threw a block of light on the wall in front of the two. A swirling path of darker black showed against the charred wood of the door, like a graffiti-scrawled name on a building: The arsonist, after setting the basement on fire, had gone to each of the entrances of the church and sprayed them with accelerant, also. When the fire climbed the walls, it found more fuel waiting for it.

What made Hannah sick was that he'd also blocked the doors. Here, on the rear sacristy door, a metal bar ran through the ornate curved handle, across the door, and behind the mounting for a lamp. Similar bars had been used on both side entrances and on the main doors in front, though they'd been broken or burned through eventually. As with the basement plants, no attempt had been made to even pretend this might be accidental. It was almost as if the torch was daring her to catch him.

Whoever he was, he'd wanted those inside to die. This wasn't just a pyro, someone setting a fire just so he could watch the building burn. It wasn't one of the repeat psychos who set a fire and then scurried around trying to help the smoke-eaters put it out.

This was someone who wanted to kill.

"Son of a bitch," she said. "No one saw anything?"

"We've talked to all the witnesses," Harris said. "No one's admitting it if they did. But then they're all jokers. They protect their own kind."

"If a joker did this, I don't think they'd protect him, no matter what."

"You don't know them, do you?" Harris answered. "I've had to do business in Jokertown before." His grimace told Hannah his opinion of the area and jokers in general. Hannah decided not to pursue it. Frankly, she didn't like what she'd seen of Jokertown herself.

"This was planned," she said. "Did you see the bar that he put on the front door? It was sleeved, so it could be expanded to fit yet not be too bulky to carry. Our guy had this all worked out, down to the last detail. Sick."

"This is the place for sick, if you haven't figured that out yet."

"Yeah. So I've been told." Hannah shook her head, staring at the door. *Ugly.* "I'll get the photos of this. Check the other entrances again; I'll bet we'll have the same pattern under the ash."

"You're the boss," Harris answered. Hannah decided that the tone was more tired than sarcastic.

As Harris walked away, Hannah took her char probe from her belt, jabbed the end of the stainless-steel rule into the wood, and recorded the depth of the burn. She did the same to the bottom of the door, then stepped back. She pulled her miniature tape recorder from her pocket and spoke into it. "Rear sacristy entrance. Same situation here: a plant in the basement beneath the door, accelerant sprayed on the door and surrounding structure afterward. Spray pattern on wall. Burn on door consistent with a fire communicated from below. Door barred with a steel rod that looks like the rebar used in concrete work. The sacristy window is broken out from inside—

that's how the priest made it out." Her head was pounding. With a sigh, she released the RECORD button.

Stretching, she leaned her head back, glancing up at the steeple. She thought for a moment that she saw someone up there, a figure staring down at her from one of the gargoyle-crowded ledges. She blinked and shaded her eyes against the sky-glare, but saw nothing. *Just tired. You've had about three hours' sleep in the last thirty-six hours.*

"You . . ."

Hannah whirled around with the word. A man, a thing, was standing behind her. He was humpbacked, deformed, a lump of twisted limbs. "Jesus!" she half-shouted involuntarily, then took a deep breath. "Listen, you aren't allowed here. This is a crime scene."

The creature took a limping step toward her. Hannah retreated. Back home, people touched by the wild card virus were almost unknown; in the few months she'd been in New York, she'd never had close contact with any of the jokers, the people altered by the virus. She found that she didn't like the experience much at all. A fear that this joker might infect her made Hannah shiver; she'd read the news stories about how, several years ago, one of them had run around New York unknowingly passing the virus. Almost worse, it was hard not to stare at the joker and that made her embarrassed, and she found herself covering the embarrassment with anger.

He took another step. Again, she gave ground, wondering whether she should call for Harris.

"Listen," she said. "I've already warned you."

"You," the apparition repeated again. His mouth twitched, and he seemed to look far away before his gaze focused on her. As Hannah watched, his right arm disappeared from hand to elbow, as if it had been wiped from existence by some cosmic eraser. There was no gush of blood; the arm just popped out of existence. The joker stared at the spot where it had been as if he were as surprised as Hannah. A few seconds later, the arm reappeared. The joker prodded it with a curious forefinger, as if to make sure it was really there, then turned back to Hannah.

"I'm sorry," the joker said, "but I belong here. I work here, and . . . I keep seeing you," he said. "Sometimes I remember, sometimes I don't. Right now I do, and I know that you will find out who did this." The joker's speech was ponderous, yet his intelligence wasn't in question. Rather, it seemed that he was receiving too much input, as if there was so much happening inside his head that it was difficult for him to maintain his train of thought. He seemed to be straining to remain coherent. When he did speak, the words were well articulated, but he frowned. He seemed to be listening to interior voices, scowling as he tried to keep his mind on what he was saying.

"You work here?" Hannah noticed now the telltale dark stains on his hands and the ash smeared into his clothing. A long fresh cut adorned his right cheek, the blood dried to a brown scab. Hannah remembered the reports of the first firefighters on the scene. "You're the one who pulled the priest out, aren't you? The one called Quasiman."

The being nodded, almost shyly, and gave her a fleeting, apologetic smile. "I did?" he answered, as if surprised. "Maybe. I think I might remember."

"You were lucky."

"No joker's exactly . . . *lucky.*" Again, that shy, quiet smile. There was an openness to the man, an odd friendliness belied by his deformed appearance and the strength evident in the knotted muscles of those arms and legs. Hannah waited for him to say something more, but for several seconds, Quasiman simply stared up at the steeple, as if he were standing there alone.

"Hey!" Hannah said. The ugly creature looked at her and

blinked as if he were seeing her for the first time. "I need to talk with you about the fire. Something you saw, something you heard, may give us a lead on who did this."

Quasiman suddenly looked grim and dangerous. "We'll find them," he said. "I saw us, you and me. There's more of them than you think." He stopped again, his gaze losing its focus.

"*Them?*" Hannah said. "Did you see something? Was there more than one fire setter?"

Quasiman didn't answer. He continued to stare past her at the burnt shell of the church, as if looking for answers in the charred ruin. Hannah shuddered—looking at the joker repulsed her, and he seemed half-insane.

"Hannah! The chief sent over some pizza—what's say we take a break?" Harris called from the side of the church. She turned, relieved and a little angry with herself for what she'd been thinking. "Half a second," she shouted, then looked back to the joker. "I'll need to—"

She stopped. Quasiman was gone. Vanished.

"It's after eleven. You're keeping later hours than me. That's not fair. Lawyers are supposed to be the overworked ones."

Hannah threw her coat and briefcase in the general direction of the rack, then closed the apartment door behind her. She unclasped the clip holding her hair and ran her fingers through the long, unbound strands. She heaved a deep sigh. "No kidding," she said. "That was the Jokertown church fire Malcolm threw my way last night. What a mess. The Reds still playing?"

Hannah's roommate, David Adderley, glanced up from the television, where the Brooklyn Dodgers were staging a late rally against the Cincinnati Reds. He set a bottle of Anchor Steam down on the coffee table next to the white cardboard container of Chinese food and came over to hug Hannah. "Sorry to hear that, kid. And no, they're not still playing. I had the timer set on the video, since I figured you'd want to see it: ol' thoughtful me. You're not going to be happy, though—the Dodgers come back big in the bottom of the ninth: so much for the Reds' one-game lead. This weekend the Dodgers are in Pittsburgh and the Reds have to play St. Louis, so chances are your Reds are soon going to be buried in second place. So why'd you get the freaks' fire?"

David didn't seem to be any more bigoted toward jokers than the rest of the people she'd met in New York; in fact, he'd worked a few cases for the city for joker causes. He wasn't one of the rabid fanatics, the ones who wanted to sterilize them all or worse, but he didn't hide his distaste. Normally she wouldn't have noticed or remarked on the "freaks" comment; tonight, the word made her knot her jaws. She'd seen the bodies of parents huddled over their dead children as if shielding them from the flames; she'd seen the desperate piles at the doors. *No one deserves to die like that. No one.* "Probably because no one else wants it."

"There's going to be some who think that the guy should probably get a medal for community service." David tried to soften the comment with a laugh.

"David—"

Releasing her, he held out his hands in apology. "Sorry. But you know that's how some people are going to feel. Hell, three years ago Manhattan was a war zone during the Rox crisis until the Turtle smashed Bloat and his damn fairyland to the bottom of the bay. How many bills have been introduced for mandatory blood tests since then?"

"Listen, I saw how ugly it is in Jokertown today," Hannah

interrupted. "Believe me, it's worse than I ever thought. But . . ." Hannah shivered, remembering the death she'd seen. "It's not their fault. None of them asked to be jokers."

On the TV, the camera was panning the crowd, picking out notables in the field seats. Hannah recognized ex-senator Gregg Hartmann, sitting alongside a woman whose skin might have been made from crumpled tinfoil. The commentator was saying something about Hartmann's efforts to achieve equality for all those afflicted by the wild card. David pointed at him.

"It's bleeding hearts like him who have been the problem," David said to the screen, then glanced back at Hannah. "I'm as sorry as anyone that these people were infected by the damn virus. None of them asked for it, sure, and probably none of them deserve the pain and disfigurement, but it happened. The best thing we can do is make sure it doesn't happen to anyone else. You've been here less than three months, Hannah. You don't know New York and you don't know jokers. I'm not the only one who feels that way. Ask any of our friends. Unfortunately, you get misguided people who think the answer is killing them all, like whoever torched your church. Talk to some of our friends."

"Your friends, David. Not our friends. I just adopted them. I'm still 'that new woman David's living with' to them." She wasn't sure why she said that—until she spoke, she hadn't even realized that the fact bothered her. She regretted the words instantly. David gave her his hurt puppy-dog look, his I'm-not-the-one-to-blame look, his why-can't-you-argue-logically look.

"Hannah, I didn't drag you out here. You wanted to come. You wanted to be with me, remember? I found you the job you wanted, pulled a few strings to get it for you."

"Yes, David. I remember." Hannah realized that they had

shifted from the muddy waters of wild card bigotry into the more familiar shallows of The Argument, the minor skirmishes in their relationship that seemed to taint their time together more and more often. *You shouldn't have come to New York this way. You should have waited, should have continued the long-distance romance, the weekend visits. Then you would have been sure. This is your fault. You feel guilty because you're afraid that if David wasn't friends with the mayor and half the city council you wouldn't even have been considered for your job. You feel guilty because you're not sure you like New York that much, because while David's a nice guy, somewhere in the last month the spark and heat and light went away and you were living with someone you really didn't know all that well.* "David, I appreciate all that. I do. It's just—"

"Just *what*, Hannah?" He sounded more annoyed than concerned now. "If you want off this stupid fire, I can understand that. Malcolm's just pissed that I forced his boss to hire you. You don't want to deal with jokers? Well, I'm not particularly comfortable with you prowling around in J-Town, either. I'll call Malcolm tomorrow."

"David . . ." Hannah began, wondering how he could be so blind as to say exactly the wrong thing. *Don't you understand? You pulled the strings and they all resent it. I can sympathize with that. I'm finding lately that I'm beginning to resent it, too. I hate that it's Jokertown. I hate that jokers are involved, but this one's mine and I need to show them that I'm competent. I should never have let you find me the job. I should have come to New York on my own, found my own place, found my own work instead of letting you arrange everything for me. But I was in love with you, and you were so convincing . . .*

But Hannah didn't say any of that. She tried to deflect the argument. "I don't want you to call Malcolm, David. Thanks, but I can handle this. This is going to be big news, even if it is in Jokertown. It'll be good for me." David shrugged at that; she'd known he would. A city attorney with political aspirations understood power, after all. He understood publicity and career moves. Hannah took David's arm and pulled him down on the couch, snuggling next to him. "Listen, I don't want to argue. I'm tired and beat and I'm saying things I don't really mean. I still smell like the inside of a chimney. I want to hug, cuddle a little, then take another shower and go to bed."

"To bed?"

"Yeah," she said. "I'm not too tired, if you're not."

The lines of David's thin face slowly softened.

"I love you," Hannah said.

"You don't mind, then, if I record this?"

"Not at all, Ms. Davis. Go ahead. Please, I want to help you in any way I can."

Hannah set the tape recorder down on the tray stand next to Father Squid's hospital bed. She checked the RECORD light. "Recording started on September 18, 1993, at 8:17 A.M.," she said and stepped back again. The priest watched her with something close to amusement in his watery green eyes. The oxygen tubing ran through the wriggling mass of tentacles that was his nose. His skin was a pale gray. He greeted her with a fleeting, almost sad smile. There was webbing between his long fingers and round vestigial suckers on his palms, and when he spoke, the scent wafting from him reminded Hannah of vacations in North Carolina, wandering through the tidal pools along the beach. Behind him, monitors ticked and whirred.

"I want you to know that we're talking to all survivors and witnesses, Mr. . . . Ummmm . . ." Hannah stopped. Her Catholic upbringing made it seem heretical to call him "Father."

"'Father Squid' is what most people call me," he said, and there was amusement under that voice. "Even those who aren't of my church. If you're not comfortable with that, I understand."

Hannah shrugged as if she didn't care. She didn't think the gesture convinced either of them. "Father, then," she said.

Father Squid coughed suddenly, sending the scent of tidal brine through the room. He wiped his mouth with a tissue. Hannah watched the tentacles wriggling around his fingers as he did so. "I'm sorry," he said afterward. "The smoke in the lungs . . . Tell me one thing, Ms. Davis—will you catch him?"

"I will try . . . Father." She stumbled over the word. "To do that, I need you to tell me everything you can."

"May I ask you a question first?"

Hannah shrugged.

"You're afraid of jokers, aren't you?" Father Squid held up a web-fingered hand, stopping her protest. His eyes, kindly and snagged in tidal ripples of skin, smiled gently at her. "Please don't take offense. You seem to find the curtains and the bedspread a lot more interesting than my poor face. The only time you've approached my bed was to put your tape recorder down, and now you're sitting all the way on the other side of the room. You held your breath when I coughed. My guess is that you're new to the city, and you don't know that the virus can't be passed by a joker's cough." Again, a soft, sad smile showed under the tentacles. "And the way you're blushing tells me that you're sensitive enough to care that I've noticed."

Hannah could feel the flush on her cheeks. "I've been here three months," she said. "I'll admit that my contact with jokers and aces has been, well, *limited*."

"Yet they gave you this assignment." The smile touched the lips again. "I suppose I shouldn't be surprised."

The words stung. "Father, I can assure you that I'm entirely capable of handling this. I was in charge of several arson investigations back in Cincinnati."

"Fires like this one?" Father Squid asked, but the smile took away some of the edge.

"No," Hannah admitted. "Father, I won't gild the truth; even when a fire is so obviously arson, proving a case against someone can be very difficult—your evidence tends to literally go up in smoke. But I have a good team of investigators working with me, and I have the cooperation of the fire and police departments. If your fire setter can be caught, I'll catch him."

He nodded, gently and sympathetically. "I'm sure you'll try. Yet . . ."

"Yet?"

His gaze held her softly; after his comments to her, Hannah could not look away. "Would your superiors have given this assignment to *you* if the Archdiocese of New York's cathedral had burned down, if the victims had included, let's say, a council member's family or two? What if a hundred of the Park Avenue wealthy had died instead of jokers? Do you think that you and your 'team' would be alone, or would the outraged hue and cry have mobilized every last department in the state, maybe even have brought in the Federal agencies? Would you be the one interviewing the archbishop in his hospital room?"

"I can't answer that," Hannah said, but the truth was that she could. *No, it wouldn't be me. It'd be Myricks, or probably Malcolm himself. Not me.*

"I know you can't," Father Squid was saying. "And it's not really fair of me to ask. I'm sure you'll do whatever you can. Behind your professional mask, you have a kind face."

"Father—"

"I know, that sounds trite. But it's true. Forgive me for my meanness and pettiness, but I think they chose you because they think a young, attractive, and relatively inexperienced woman will fail and they don't think that matters. I think it's because a fire in Jokertown isn't deemed to be worth the effort of the best people in your department, because they really don't care if a murderer of jokers is ever found as long as they can show that they made some effort. I also think that they made the wrong choice if that was their thought. So . . . where do I start, Ms. Davis? What can I tell you?"

Hannah wanted to respond angrily, but she had found herself nodding inside to each of his arguments. She retreated into routine. "Had you received any threats recently? Do you know of anyone with a grudge against you or your church?"

"My child," he said softly, sounding for all the world like Bing Crosby in *The Bells of Saint Mary's*, "I receive threats regularly, at least once or twice a month, and the list of those who might conceivably have reason to be annoyed with me is impossibly long. You don't have the manpower to check out each and every one of them. Besides, I'm a recognizable and easy target. I'm out in public every day. I never lock the doors to the church or to my house. If someone wanted to kill me, there were a thousand easier ways to do it. Ways that needn't . . . that needn't have killed—"

Father Squid's voice broke. Tears welled in his eyes, and he brought up a hand to wipe them away. "My dear God," he husked out, his voice quavering. "All those poor, poor people." He gave a great, gasping sob that pulled Hannah from her seat. She wanted to go to him, to comfort him, but she held back. She told herself it was only because she was being professional, not because she didn't want to touch a joker. After a few moments, Father Squid brought his hands up and knuckled his eyes with an embarrassed laugh. "I'm sorry. All last night and this morning . . . every so often I would remember

and find myself crying. Each time I think I've finally cried myself dry I find that there's still more grief underneath, layers
and layers of it." Father Squid looked at her with stricken eyes.
"Ms. Davis, what kind of monster would do a thing like this?
Those who died were all innocent." The tears began again; this
time he let them fall unashamedly down his face and into the
tentacles.

"Father, you said that you 'remember.' What do you remember?"

"It . . . it all happened so fast. It was Black Queen Night,
after all, and so the church was full."

"Black Queen Night?"

Father Squid smiled at that, briefly. "You are a newcomer,
aren't you? September 15 is Wild Card Day, ever since that day
in '46 when Jetboy failed us and let the alien virus loose. The
world remembers Jetboy on that day, but the 15th is the day for
the nats and the aces—the ones the virus left untouched or the
ones it made into something more than human. In a way, the
15th is a day of celebration. But the 16th, though, well, the 16th
is for Jokertown. The 16th is for sadness. The 16th is when we
remember the 90 percent of those who are forced to draw from
the wild card deck and get the Black Queen—the killer. And
we remember that in some ways they're the lucky ones, because almost all of the rest of us get the Joker, the bitter card.
We became freaks."

Father Squid spat out the last few sentences. His gaze had
gone distant. "When did you become aware of the fire?" Hannah asked, and that brought Father Squid's glance around to
her again.

"I noticed a haze about the time I was saying the benedic-
tion. I remember thinking that I should have turned on the
ceiling fans. Mighty Wurlitzer . . ." Father Squid stopped
again. Muscles knotted in his jaw. He swallowed hard.

". . . began playing and people started singing. There was a lot of coughing; I noticed that, too. I found myself clearing my throat. And then I saw a flame . . . at the side door."

His voice broke again. Hannah said nothing, letting Father Squid compose himself before proceeding. "Then it was just chaos," he said finally.

"You didn't see anyone, didn't hear anything from the basement, didn't smell anything?"

"No, I'm afraid not." Father Squid smiled apologetically. "I remember thinking that this was just like the movie. You know—*Jokertown*, with Jack Nicholson and Marilyn Monroe?"

"What do you mean, like the movie?"

"You've never seen it?"

"A long time ago. I remember something about a plot against the jokers, some rich guy." Hannah shrugged.

"They wanted to burn down Jokertown. They wanted to burn *everything*, all of us."

The slow voice came from Hannah's left, in the corner of the room. Hannah jumped, startled—she hadn't heard anyone enter and she couldn't imagine how anyone could have slipped behind her from the doorway.

Someone had. She recognized the humpbacked figure. "Quasiman," she said aloud, identifying him for the tape recorder. The joker glanced at her.

"Who are you?" he asked. "Do I know you?"

"Don't you remember? You talked to me yesterday. Your . . . your right arm was missing then."

"It was?" Quasiman shrugged as if he'd forgotten the entire incident, then went to Father Squid's side, looking down at the priest with an infinite tenderness on his strange, slack-muscled face.

"How are you, Father?" he asked. Then, without waiting

for an answer, "I'm sorry. I saw, but I didn't know . . . I couldn't get them all out. Only a few . . ."

Father Squid had reached up with his hand. He clasped the hunchback's shoulder. "You did more than anyone else could have. I owe you my life." Quasiman nodded, then he stiffened alongside the bed, looking off into distances only he could see.

"What's the matter with him?" Hannah asked. She hated looking at Quasiman even more than she did Father Squid. Something about him made her shudder in revulsion.

Father Squid shook his head. "Parts of him just go away at times. Sometimes parts of his body will simply vanish. Other times it's his mind or his memories. Often he doesn't remember me or what happened yesterday or where he is. Sometimes—like now—he just shuts down entirely."

"How long does it last?"

"A few seconds. Minutes. There's no way to tell."

Hannah started to ask another question, but Quasiman's eyes came back into focus then, and he was staring at her. "I remember you now," he said. "I needed to tell you: Father Squid is right. The fire was like the movie. You need to look into that. You ought to watch it."

"Why? How's a movie going to help me?"

"It was real," Quasiman insisted, and Father Squid's soft voice followed.

"Some of the events in the movie were based on facts," the priest said. "The script was written with the actual story in mind. There was a conspiracy, if not exactly the one in the movie, back in the late fifties. Fifty-nine, I think."

"Yes," Quasiman said. He was gripping the railing of the bed, and Hannah, fascinated, watched the metal bars bending under the pressure of the joker's fingers. Whatever Quasiman's other problems, he was incredibly strong. "There's a lot we need to know. Start with the movie," he said. "You have to."

"I don't think so," she told him. "I'm sorry, but we're not going to catch our torch by looking up a thirty-plus-year-old movie plot. I have a lot of leads to follow, good ones."

Quasiman was suddenly right in front of her, those horribly strong hands on either arm of her chair as he leaned in at her. Hannah could hear the wood-grained Formica of the handles cracking as she pressed her spine against the back of the chair. "Jesus, get away from me!" she shouted, but she couldn't escape. His breath touched her, warm and sweet, but it was the breath of a *joker*, of someone infected by that awful virus. She would have pushed at him, but she couldn't bring herself to touch him. Hannah started to shout once more, to call the nurses and security guards, but Quasiman's face stopped her. There was no menace there, only a soft, pleading concern. "This is very important, Hannah," he said, and the use of her name was startling. "I know. Please."

"Quasiman," Father Squid said from the bed. "You're frightening that young woman."

"Oh," the joker said, as if startled. "Sorry. It's just—" He lifted his hands up suddenly and gave Hannah an apologetic smile. He scuttled away from the chair and Hannah slowly relaxed.

"Just what?" Hannah asked shakily.

"I know that you need to start there. With the movie."

"You keep saying that," Hannah answered. "You 'know.' I don't understand." She looked from Quasiman to Father Squid; it was Father Squid who answered.

"Another by-product of Quasiman's affliction is limited precognition," he told her. "One of the places his awareness seems to go during his episodes is the future. The vision is very erratic, and he can't control it, but it's there. God has seen fit to grant my friend occasional glimpses of what is to be."

"Yes," Quasiman agreed. "I've seen you, Hannah. I've seen *us*. I've seen other faces. I'm going to try very hard to remember."

"Great. That all sounds very convenient. Now just tell me who started the fire and I'll have him arrested and we can all go home. In fact, with that kind of evidence, we can probably just do away with the trial, too." She wouldn't look at either of the jokers. She stared at the cracks Quasiman's fingers had left in the chair arms.

Father Squid's reply was as gentle as ever, and made Hannah's sarcasm seem even more vitriolic in comparison. "Ms. Davis, I wonder how many comments were made in your office yesterday?" he asked. "I wonder how many people said that there's no way you can find this murderer?"

"What's your point, Father?"

"I just wonder if you're letting your preconceptions blind you right now. After all, how much is Quasiman asking of you? An extra interview? An hour of your time?"

There'd been comments. Hannah had even half heard some of them. "Even granting that there's something to what you're saying, this supposed plot is ancient history. Half the people involved must be dead," Hannah said. "I don't know who to contact or where to start."

"I do," Father Squid answered. "If you're willing. If you can bring yourself to talk to another joker."

The priest's barbed comment brought up Hannah's eyes. She looked from Father Squid to the hunchback. She knew he was pushing all her buttons, but she wasn't going to be called a bigot. She sighed. "All right," she said. "I can give you an hour."

— — —

"Mr. Tanaka? Chuck Tanaka?"

Hannah had already decided that the atmosphere of the Four Seas Seafood Delivery Service, placed precariously between Chinatown and Jokertown, would probably put her off fish for months. The tiny office in the small warehouse was dingy, looking as if it had last been redecorated somewhere around World War II. From the look of the desk, the file cabinets, and each available horizontal surface in the place, every last scrap of paper that the business had generated had found a home here. On the wall were dusty, cheap frames holding faded prints that were just as cheap; behind the desk, a larger frame held a collection of baseball cards. They looked old, too, and there was a spot in the middle of the frame where a space had obviously been reserved for a card.

"You're the one called 'Chop-Chop'?" Hannah asked.

The joker behind the desk looked up, and from his appearance and the grimace on his face, Hannah realized that the question didn't need an answer. The joker was a walking cliché of every bad comic-book depiction of an Asian. He squinted at her from behind Coke-bottle bottom, black-rimmed glasses. His myopic eyes were almost comically slanted, the epicanthic folds stretched and exaggerated. He was horrendously bucktoothed, his upper front two teeth extending entirely over his bottom lip, and his ears stuck out from under jet-black hair like twin handles on a jug. His skin was a bright, chrome yellow.

I'd kill myself if I ever become a joker, she thought. *I wouldn't allow myself to be such a mockery of what I'd been.*

He sighed. "Yes, I'm called Chop-Chop. And you're . . . ?"

Hannah introduced herself and showed Tanaka her identification. "Father Squid gave me your name," she said as she took her tape recorder from her purse. "Do you mind?"

Tanaka shrugged, though he looked uneasily at the recorder as Hannah set it on a pile of old invoices. "Sit down," he said. "Just move those files off the chair. You know, I don't know anything about the fire. Just what was in the papers and on the tube. Why Father would send you to me, well . . ." He shrugged thin shoulders.

"It wasn't exactly this fire that he thought you might know about," Hannah said, and with the words, she saw something move in Tanaka's face, a twitch of muscles around his mouth and a slow blink of both eyes. She softened her voice, tried to smile at him. There was something there, and she didn't want him to think he had to hide it. "Father Squid said to tell you that you could trust me."

"How is he? I heard he got burned."

"He'll be fine. He's lucky—minor burns and some smoke inhalation. They'll release him from the hospital in a day or two."

Tanaka nodded. His skittish gaze moved away from her, as if he weren't comfortable looking at her. *Which is about the way I feel about you,* Hannah thought. "That's good. That's real good. I like the Father. I . . . I almost went to mass that night. Got stuck here instead; a problem with a shipment. I manage the place now. Have for a long time." His voice seemed to run down. He looked at the pictures on the wall, at the file cabinet.

"Father Squid said I should ask about a movie," she said, and that brought Tanaka's head around as if she'd reached out and turned it back herself. The eyes blinked again, like an owl's.

"*Jokertown,*" he said, flatly. It wasn't a question, but Hannah nodded anyway. "I don't know why you should be interested in that. It was just a movie."

"Exactly what I said. But Quasiman insisted that I ask. He seems to think that the fire wasn't just a random hate crime."

Hannah bit her lip, drumming her fingers on the arms of the chair. "Look, I think this is probably just a dead end. Thank you for your time, and I'm sorry to have interrupted your busy day . . ." She started to reach for the tape recorder.

"They were really all wrong, you know," Tanaka said.

"I'm sorry?"

"About the movie. They were all wrong." Tanaka looked at her through the thick windows of his glasses. "I was there. I know the truth. Did you see it? Did you see the movie?"

"'Til I Kissed You"

William F. Wu

I was working for the Four Seas Seafood
Delivery Service. On a very hot, humid day, I remember taking
a breather at the rear doors of the refrigerated delivery truck I
was unloading. I was working at a corner bay near the fence
that separated the yard from the street.

A beat-up old radio blared from a shelf inside the bay. A
news item about Bobby Fischer, the new US chess champion,
was followed by the melodic voice of Paul Anka singing
"Lonely Boy": *"I'm just a lonely boy, lonely and blue—ooh. I'm all
alone, with nothing to do . . ."* Out where I was, the music
sounded thin.

It didn't matter. I hated Paul Anka.

I had one more undelivered wooden crate to return to the
freezers in the back of the warehouse. Full of frozen shrimp,
and caked with bits of ice, it weighed only twenty pounds, but
these last few had felt like a ton. I put my arms around it, but
motion on the sidewalk caught my eye, and I turned to look.

A teenaged girl, a nat, had stopped on the sidewalk. She
was looking at me through the gate of the chain-link fence.

I usually turned away from strange nats, being deeply embarrassed by my appearance. As you can see, it's a racial caricature of both the Japanese and the Chinese from World War II. I had stopped growing during the previous year at five feet in height, and was kind of chubby. The only choice I had about my appearance was my haircut, which was a bristly flattop.

This time, I forgot about the crate. She was one of the most stunning girls I had ever seen. I just stared.

She looked like she was about my age. Rich sable hair was drawn back from her face in a ponytail, tied with a pink ribbon. Her skin was pale, flawless, and slightly flushed from the heat. Brown eyes studied me carefully from under long lashes. A short string of pearls lay on the swell of breasts that were unusually full, especially for a teenager; they strained against a very expensive-looking white blouse trimmed with lace. A small brown purse hung from her shoulder on a narrow strap. She wore a light blue skirt, long and full, shaped with crinolines I couldn't see but knew had to be there. Her bobby socks were spotless and her brown penny loafers shone in the sunlight.

She was at least four inches taller than I was.

"Are you a joker?" She spoke quietly, almost timidly.

At first I was stung by the fear that she was mocking me, but then I saw that she was sincere.

"Yeah." I grinned wryly. "Can't you tell?"

She missed the sarcasm. "I don't know where I am. I couldn't decide from looking at you. Is this Chinatown or Jokertown?"

"Both." Flattered that she was taking me seriously, I straightened to my full height and walked over to the gate. "This is the border. We're on the Chinatown side right here. My boss delivers seafood to Chinatown restaurants and grocery stores. But he hired me from the Jokertown side to load and unload for him."

She gazed down the block on the Jokertown side. "I wasn't sure . . . I got out of my cab on the Bowery and walked."

This was already the longest conversation I had ever had with a nat girl without being teased or ridiculed. "Can I help you find where you're going?"

She looked back at me through the chain link as though seeing me for the first time. "Oh." Her face tightened uncomfortably. "I've never spoken to a joker before."

"What's your name?" I was afraid that if I was too forward, she would turn and run or else maybe get mad and start calling me the nasty names I already knew so well from other nats.

"Uh . . . I'm Flo."

"I'm Chuck." I looked her over again. She didn't look like a Flo. Maybe a Florence. More like an Annette or a Mitzi.

"Pleased to meet you," she said primly, as if by rote.

I tried to think of more to say. "Do you like chess? Bobby Fischer won the US championship in January. He's only fifteen."

She was silent, still looking down the street.

"I'm sixteen," I added, lamely. "How old are you?"

"Fifteen." Her voice was distracted.

"I think it's great, having a teenager as chess champion."

"I bet Bobby Fischer is a secret ace." She turned back to me.

"You think so?" I had never thought about that before.

"All aces should be exposed," said Flo, sharply.

I had never considered that before, either. "I don't suppose it matters much. I think they do whatever they want."

"Do you live in Jokertown?"

"Yeah. My family lives right on the edge here." I hesitated. "We're Japanese Americans. We wouldn't be at home in Chinatown."

"How well do you know Jokertown?"

"Fine."

"I mean, really well?"

"Sure I do. I live here."

She nodded, looking up at the buildings.

"Where are you going?"

"Oh . . ." She shrugged.

"I get off soon. I could take you there." I was sweating heavily again, now from tension as much as from the heat.

"I don't know exactly where I'm going."

That sounded like a brush-off. Disappointed, I expected her to say goodbye. I looked at her pretty brown eyes, waiting.

"And now," the radio blared faintly, "here's a golden oldie from 1957! Here's Johnny Mathis!"

"Chances are, 'cause I wear a silly grin, the moment you come into view . . ."

Flo just stood there. It wasn't a brush-off, after all. I got the idea that maybe she wanted me to take the initiative.

The door from the warehouse office squeaked. Startled, I turned to see my driver, Peter Choy, coming out. He was in his mid-twenties and had the short, stocky build common to many of the Cantonese in Chinatown. His khaki driver's uniform was stained with sweat under the arms.

"All finished, Chuck?" Peter asked.

"Uh—almost." Belatedly, I turned to get the last crate of shrimp. I had left it too long and it was starting to smell.

"Say, Chuck, this one's about to go bad! What have you been—" Peter stopped suddenly, seeing Flo.

"Oh, pardon me." He winked at me and picked up the crate himself. "Hey, not bad, pal. You go on. I'll punch out for you."

"Thanks!" I grinned. "Thanks, Mr. Choy."

"G'wan, get outta here!" Peter carried the crate back inside.

"He's not a joker, is he?" Flo asked softly.

"No!" I shook my head, still grinning. "He's a great guy. And he's the only one who calls me Chuck."

"What does everyone else call you?"

I paused, regretting that I had brought up the subject. "Aw, nothing. Look—you want me to show you around?"

"Yes, please."

"Okay." I looked down at my sweat-darkened T-shirt and faded blue dungarees with the cuffs rolled up, both of which emphasized how chubby I was. "Sorry about the way I look."

She shrugged.

"Well . . . I'm getting awful hungry. Would you like to have dinner?" I opened the gate and stepped out.

She backed away, keeping her distance. "Um—in Jokertown?"

I knew of a little Chinese dive just up the street that I could afford. A girl dressed as she was might not like the atmosphere, but the only other choice within my budget was Biff's Burgers in the heart of Jokertown, where too many of my friends would be hanging around. I wanted to be alone with her.

"There's a Chinese place up the street, right on the border."

"Okay." Flo looked at my clothes pointedly. "Can you really take me out to dinner?"

"Aw, sure. Come on." I gestured and she came with me, walking well to one side. "I have money. I was planning to go to the hobby shop to look for some Slug Maligne baseball cards."

"Who?"

"Slug Maligne. He's the big, slimy joker who signed this spring as the Yankees' new backup catcher when Elston Howard got hurt. Somebody's got to spell Yogi. Slug's only got the one rookie card, but in Jokertown, it's real expensive already. A bunch of them would be a good investment."

"A joker? On the Yankees?" She grimaced.

"Aw, he'll do okay. Slug's not much on the base paths, but he can *really* block the plate."

"Oh."

I decided she wasn't a baseball fan.

The Twisted Dragon was only a narrow storefront, but I held the screen door open for her, watching her pretty face anxiously. I was afraid she would turn up her nose and leave. Instead, she stepped inside, clutching her little purse in front of her.

A couple of old, green ceiling fans creaked slowly over our heads. The hardwood floor had been worn clean of varnish years ago. None of the tables matched one another in shape or height, but they were covered with clean white tablecloths. The muffled sound of a TV came from the kitchen.

"Hi, Chop-Chop! How you?" The owner of the Twisted Dragon, a chubby little joker in a black suit that was too big, grinned broadly. His face was that of a Chinese dragon, large and scaled and whiskered. Inside his baggy suit, his body was twisted and angled weirdly. He spoke with a heavy Cantonese accent. "You want early dinner today, eh? You come this way."

I winced at the use of my street name and glanced at Flo. She said nothing. I gestured for her to follow.

The owner limped to a small table under a ceiling fan, with straight-backed, wobbly wooden chairs. I sat facing the door. Our host handed us food-stained menus and started to leave.

"How's business?" I asked quickly. I wanted to prove to Flo that I was really part of this neighborhood.

"Business good! Really good, Chop-Chop. Couple year, maybe I sell out. Or maybe move to bigger place, fix up real nice."

"That sounds good."

"Hokay, Chop-Chop. You decide, I send somebody back."

"I already know what I want," said Flo. She was holding her menu gingerly by the edges, as if it were a phonograph record.

"We'll order right away," I said. "What do you want?"

"Wonton soup and sweet and sour pork," said Flo.

"Make it for two," I said.

The guy nodded, taking our menus, and hurried away.

Flo was sitting rigidly in her chair. Her dark brown ponytail quivered slightly from side to side behind her, betraying her tension. Her eyes shifted around the nearly empty restaurant. "Are there other jokers here?"

"Uh—" I glanced around. "No, not yet. But it's early. The Twisted Dragon brings people from both sides of the street."

She nodded. Her face was covered with sweat. It wasn't *that* hot in here, especially under the fan.

"Do you like movies?" I asked, hoping to get the conversation going. "I want to see Marilyn Monroe in *Some Like It Hot*, but I'll have to sneak out so my mother doesn't get mad. I think Marilyn Monroe is beautiful." I waited for Flo to say something. When she didn't, I went on. "Saturday, I saw *I Was a Teenage Joker*, with Michael Landon. It was cool."

She shrugged, uninterested. "Is Jokertown . . . I mean, I know it's a neighborhood. But does it have *all* kinds of places?"

"Well . . . I guess so. What kind of places do you mean?"

She shook her head tightly and said nothing.

I watched her, puzzled. When a waitress thumped a heavy white porcelain teapot down on the table, I poured tea for Flo first. I was feeling protective.

"I'll help you, if you want," I said quietly.

"Suppose, um . . ." She looked down at the table for a moment. "Suppose someone wanted something that isn't normally available."

"Something illegal?"

She shrugged. "Can you really find *everything* in Jokertown?"

"Yeah. I think so." I waited, my heart thumping excitedly.

She was silent.

The screen door creaked. Flo didn't turn around, but I saw two jokers entering. One was a tall, slender man who had been divided down the middle by the wild card; the right side of his body was normal, but the left looked as though it had been made of candle wax, melted, and then solidified again. He walked with a slow, painful limp on his sagging, twisted leg and let his distorted arm swing freely. The other joker at least moved comfortably; he appeared to be normal, except for having the face of a teddy bear with a fixed, very happy smile.

The newcomers were seated across the narrow room. Flo glanced in their direction. Her eyes widened suddenly and she looked away, back down at our table.

"It's Jokertown," I said, puzzled by her reaction.

"It's so horrible," Flo whispered. "What that . . . alien . . . did. What he brought." The horror in her face was unmistakable.

I felt a familiar horror of my own, deep in my stomach, ruining my appetite. Maybe she was no different from other nats, after all. In the same moment, however, I finally understood something I had never realized before: She was *scared*.

Yet she was here—with me.

I decided to sit there and enjoy the sight of her beautiful face and figure as long as I could. When our dinner arrived, we ate in silence. Even some of my appetite came back.

When we had finished dinner, I carefully counted out the customary ten percent tip that Peter had told me always to leave. As I paid the check, Flo stared straight down at her shoes, avoiding the sight of all the jokers who had followed us inside for dinner. Then we stepped outside and I found that the heat had finally begun to ease a little.

"Well," I said uncertainly, looking up at her.

Flo glanced up and down the street in the shadows.

"Would you like me to walk you to the Bowery or something?"

She shook her head again and suddenly peered straight down into my eyes. "Can we talk privately somewhere?"

"Sure. We can just walk. Nobody here will bother us."

"No, I mean, where we can't possibly be overheard. Inside."

"Okay. Both my parents work second jobs to get by. They won't be home till after midnight. I'll take you home."

"Good." Her voice was breathy with anxiety.

The walk was okay. We passed Jube the Walrus on the way, pulling his cart full of newspapers on his regular rounds. He looked very surprised to see Flo, I figured because she was so pretty. Flo looked away, as though he weren't there.

My family lived in a modest two-bedroom apartment in a fairly small building. I closed the door and led her into the living room, where I switched on the lamps on each end table by the couch. The air was hot and stale, so I turned on the big standing fan in the corner, to sweep back and forth across the room. Then I opened the windows.

Flo paced nervously for a moment, looking around. Some framed pictures on the wall caught her eye, over the back of a pink canvas butterfly chair. "Is that your dad?"

I came as close as I dared and raised up on tiptoe to see over her shoulder. Her perfume was light and sweet. She was looking at a posed studio picture of my father in his Army uniform. A photograph of his whole platoon was next to it.

"Yeah, that's him."

"Is that the American Army?"

"Yeah. The 442nd Battalion."

"But they're all . . ." She trailed off.

"Nisei. Second-generation Japanese Americans. He fought in Italy, among other places. I was born while he was in the Army."

"Really? Where were you born?"

"In California."

"Where? San Francisco or Los Angeles?"

"Uh, no. A camp in Tule Lake."

"A what?" Flo turned to look down at me.

I backed away. "An internment camp for Japanese Americans."

Her brown eyes were puzzled. "What do you mean?"

"Well, it was a kind of prison camp. All the Japanese Americans on the West Coast were put in them."

"Even if your dad was in the Army?"

I shrugged uncomfortably. "Yeah."

She searched my face. I felt she was actually realizing for the first time that I was more than a joker.

My face grew hot.

"Want to sit down?" I gestured toward the wing-back couch.

Flo hesitated, then sat down on one end of the couch. I sat down on the far end, well away from her. I just waited.

Finally, looking down at her hands in her lap, she spoke almost in a whisper. "Do you know what an abortion is?"

"Yeah." I froze, staring at her.

"You do?" She glanced up in surprise, her ponytail swaying.

"Yeah, I've heard about them from guys on the street," I said softly. I could hardly believe this was what she wanted.

She spoke quickly. "Can I get one in Jokertown? Safely? And in absolute, total *secrecy*? And how much would it cost?" Her brown eyes were large now, watching me anxiously.

"I don't know," I said slowly. "But I can find out."

"Would you? Please?" Her voice was pleading.

"Sure." I got up and walked over to the phone sitting on the kitchen counter. A guy named Waffle was good for stuff like that. I dialed Biff's Burgers, but Waffle wasn't there yet. I hung up. "A friend of mine will call back."

"Okay."

I sat down on the couch again. I wasn't going to tell her what a jerk Waffle was. "He's twenty, and he knows about . . . stuff like this. We'll just have to wait."

"How long do you think it will be?"

"No way to tell, but he goes by Biff's every night. When do you have to be home?"

She shook her head, then looked away. "I have to find out."

"Your parents don't make you come home on time?"

"My mother's dead," she said, almost in a whisper. Then she smiled cynically. "My father is . . . very important. Always busy. He thinks I'm at a girlfriend's right now." She closed her eyes.

"Your father's important?" I looked at her stylish clothes again, especially the pearls. Those weren't kiddie beads.

"He works for the government. And he has powerful friends. So I *have* to keep this a secret. I can't even tell you who he is."

I was getting a little scared. "Look, you want to watch TV? I'm not sure what's on—maybe Dobie Gillis."

She didn't speak or even look up.

"You know, *The Many Loves of Dobie Gillis,* with Dobie and Maynard G. Krebs, the beatnik? Don't you like it?"

Tears seeped from under Flo's eyelids. She began to sob, fighting it quietly. Then she fumbled her purse open and pulled out some white tissues from a little plastic packet.

Before I even thought about it, I slid over to her on the couch. I guess if I understood anything deeper than baseball cards at that age, it was feeling scared and alone. When I slid one of my bright yellow arms across her rounded shoulders, under her ponytail, she leaned against me and really began to cry.

I put my other arm around her. Being shorter than she was, with short arms, made this awkward. She cried for what seemed like a long time, and I just sat there with my arms stretched almost around her, yellow against her white blouse.

Finally Flo took some deep breaths and used the tissues in her hand. Reluctantly, I withdrew the arm that was in front of her, but dared to keep the other over her shoulders. Then, with her tissues wadded in one hand, she turned toward me.

Her eyes were wet and red, her eye makeup running. She had put on more lipstick after dinner. It was bright red.

I had certainly never kissed a girl. With my immense front teeth, I wasn't even sure that I *could* kiss a girl, properly. I looked from her deep-brown eyes down to her perfect lips.

You know, I don't know where I got the guts, but I just did it. I kissed her. If she had jumped up and slapped me, I wouldn't have been surprised, but she didn't. She kissed me back.

It lasted a long time. I couldn't tell if my teeth were a problem. Then I forgot about them.

Tears were still welling from her eyes. She took one of my hands and slid it to the front of her blouse.

When I caressed her, she kissed me again.

This time she broke quickly and whispered in my ear, her breath hot. "Let's go to your room."

"But . . . I . . . don't have a, uh, you know. A rubber."

A tight smile altered her features for just a moment. "Chuck, I'm already pregnant, remember? Come on."

I got up, still clinging to her. I was certainly not going to argue very hard. Besides, it was her choice.

In my bedroom, we stepped over dirty socks and the wadded-up dungarees I had worn to work yesterday. I turned on the little fan my parents had given me.

Flo stopped by the bed and stepped out of her penny loafers. Then she began to unbutton her blouse. I sat down on the bed and switched on the little portable six-transistor radio on the nightstand under the lamp.

". . . *Never* knew *what I* missed *until I* kissed *ya . . .*" It was the Everly Brothers' new release, quick and bouncy.

The only light angled in from the hall. Standing half in the light, she let her skirt drop to a puddle around her feet and then unfastened her white crinolines. She unhooked her bra and tossed it aside, letting her large breasts swing free. Then she bent forward and slid her white underpants down. Only the pearls still glistened on her body.

I watched as she sat down next to me. Then I tugged my T-shirt up over my head, revealing my fat belly. I really wished I had washed up a little after we had come back here.

She was the one who knew what to do. Slowly, on the narrow single bed, a girl with a gorgeous face, large breasts, and slender, shapely legs made all my wildest adolescent fantasies come true.

"They ran so fast *that a* hound *couldn't catch 'em, down the Mississippi to the* Gulf o' Mexico . . ."

Johnny Horton was gleefully singing about the Battle of New Orleans on the little transistor radio. I opened my eyes and stared at a crack in the ceiling. "Oh . . . I must have dozed off."

Flo smiled at me. I wondered what she had thought of me. After all, I'd never done *that* before.

"I don't . . ." She was whispering. "I don't want you to think I—well, I don't always do this."

"I didn't think so," I said quietly.

Her face was close to mine. "My father hates the wild card. He taught me what it's done to people. He even . . . showed me."

"I don't have it so bad. Not when you look around Jokertown."

"My mom wasn't . . . like him. You sort of remind me . . . not your looks, but I mean . . . you're real decent."

"Thank you." For me, the idea that the people who had always despised jokers could have nice daughters was a new thought.

"Jokertown's . . . going to be destroyed," she said suddenly.

"Hmm?"

"Jokertown is going to be burned to the ground."

"What are you talking about?"

"I don't think I ever realized how horrible that would be."

I sat up. "Jokertown is going to burn?"

She shook her head tightly. "I said too much."

"You can't just say that and stop. Come on."

"No! I can't!" She flung herself out of bed, turning away. Then she started crying again.

I was amazed at her abrupt shift in mood. Talking about a fire scared me, though. I jumped up and turned her by the shoulders.

"What are you talking about?"

She shook her head, trying to move away.

I stayed in front of her. "You can't just say that and quit! I live here! *What about a fire?*"

She was sobbing and shaking her head. After a moment, though, she swallowed and looked up at me.

"All right! All right. Chuck, my father and some people he knows secretly made Jokertown, starting back in the late forties. They wanted it to be a magnet, where they could draw jokers together."

"What do you mean, 'made' it? Jokers just moved here 'cause it was cheap. Everybody knows that."

"That's right. Rich people bought the buildings here and provided the loans for businesses through their own banks. They did the same with places to live, setting up everything to be real cheap. Then, after drawing as many jokers here as possible, they're going to burn it all down."

"Aw, come on. Their own buildings?"

"The buildings are insured for lots of money. And if they have to, they'll take a loss in some cases. They can afford it."

It was starting to make sense.

"Even the fire chief is in on it. He'll make sure all the fire engines arrive too late, or never get there at all."

I truly felt like a kid. She was a year younger, but her manner was more mature, more sophisticated.

She came from the real world, outside Jokertown. Her father was wealthy and powerful. Even the way she spoke sounded older than her years.

"How do you know so much about it?"

"My father still thinks of me as a little kid . . . between my ears." She smiled bitterly. "He doesn't try to keep this stuff a secret from me; he's always taught me that people with the wild card are the greatest danger to American society ever. He's never thought of me as a security leak."

I was silent a moment. "When is Jokertown going to burn?"

"I don't know exactly. But I think the wiring of firebombs is going to start anytime."

"Look—can you tell me anything else? Any kind of a clue to what's going to happen?"

She paused. "The name Lansky. He mentioned it over the phone to someone late last night, after I got home. I remember he said it before, too, when he was talking about Jokertown."

"What about it?"

"That's all I really have." Her tone was apologetic.

I looked into her brown eyes.

"*I want to* walk *you* home," Fats Domino sang on the little radio. "*Please let me* walk *you* home . . ."

The phone rang. I hurried into the kitchen, stark naked.

"Hello?"

"Hiya, Chop-Chop; howsa boy?" Waffle's voice came through over Biff's sizzling grill and the roar of chatter behind him.

"Hi, Waffle. Look—you got to keep this a secret."

Flo came around the corner to listen. She had on her white underpants already. Now she was holding her bra, watching me.

I knew Waffle's information could always be bought, but I had no choice. "Where could a friend of mine get an abortion?"

"Damn! Way to go, Chop-Chop! Didn't know you had it in ya!" Waffle roared with laughter. "Haw! So, little Chop-Chop's got a girlfriend nobody knew about!"

I was glad Flo couldn't hear him. "Come on, Waffle."

Anyhow, Waffle came across. Since she was a nat, it would cost her three hundred for the doctor and two hundred for him. It would be done by a real doctor and we had to meet Waffle behind the Chaos Club in two nights at eight o'clock. I had to come with her. She okayed it on the spot.

I hung up. She liked the fact that this would be done by a real doctor. We had both heard about quacks in that business.

However, I told her to be down here by six o'clock. She couldn't risk getting slowed down in rush hour. If we were late, she might not get another chance. She agreed.

She had to go home now, of course. We got dressed quickly. Since she didn't want to flag down a cab in Jokertown, I agreed to walk her to the Bowery. Lots of nats came and went from the restaurants and bars there.

The night was cool and breezy. I walked with her in a glow of pride, aware that jokers were glancing at us in surprise as we passed. We stopped at the Bowery, where she hailed a cab.

"I won't go straight home," she said. "I'll go halfway home, get out, and take another cab from there. Just in case."

"Look," I said awkwardly, "can you come back tomorrow?"

"Tomorrow? You said the appointment is two nights away."

"Yeah. Just . . . well, if you want."

"Maybe, Chuck. Maybe. Tomorrow at the same time?"

"Yeah! Same place, same time—where I work."

"Maybe." As the cab swerved to the curb, she glanced quickly up and down the sidewalk before quickly kissing me on the mouth. Then she slipped inside the cab and slammed the door. It roared away again.

I gazed after the shrinking rear red lights of the cab, still only half-believing that this night had happened.

In the breezy summer night, I walked home in a dreamy state, seeing Flo's flushed face and bare breasts against the backdrop of streetlights and shadows. With the Everly Brothers singing in my head, I never once thought about Slug Maligne's baseball card.

". . . *Never* knew *what I* missed *until I* kissed *ya . . .*"

— — —

The next day was just as hot and humid as yesterday, but I didn't care. Whenever the Everly Brothers came on the radio, I turned the volume way up. I smiled a lot, remembering her.

Thoughts about a big Jokertown fire wouldn't leave me alone, though. Sometimes I looked around at the buildings near me and wondered which ones might go up. I had to talk to someone about my only clue.

When I punched out at the end of the day, I still hadn't seen Flo. I hung around on the sidewalk for half an hour or so, but I guess I knew after the first ten minutes that she wasn't coming. While I was disappointed, I wasn't devastated. I knew she'd be back tomorrow night. Besides, I had business. I finally took off for Biff's.

Inside Biff's, Connie Francis was on the jukebox: "Lip*stick on your col*lar . . . Told *a* tale *on* you—ooh . . ."

At this early hour, the place was nearly empty. Behind the counter, Biff was making hamburger patties. His face and body were those of a furry brown chipmunk standing up on his hind legs, in a T-shirt and a stained bib apron. He glanced up, bored.

"Hi, Biff." I got a Coke from him and headed to a round metal table in the rear. Two of the regular joker guys were back there.

The song ended. No other song came on. The place suddenly seemed as quiet as a tomb.

Cheetah and Troll were two guys I had always kind of known, but not well. They had been involved in petty theft and break-ins of nat-owned businesses. I had always been a little afraid of them. Now I knew they might be able to help and that I could trust them to keep quiet about it, too.

"Hi, guys."

"Hi." Cheetah looked me over cautiously. I had never just walked up to them before. Cheetah had the head and neck of a chimpanzee, except for the power of human speech. Above the waist, he had the short, hairy body and long arms of one, as well, inside a white T-shirt. Below the waist, he had human proportions and wore ordinary, dirty dungarees and tennis shoes.

Troll was nine feet tall and had green, warty skin. His crooked yellow teeth stuck out in every direction and his red eyes peered out from under a heavy brow ridge. He was muscular but still slender with youth. In his huge hand, with nails like sharp, black claws, a greenish bottle of Coke had almost disappeared. He sat on the floor, leaning back against the wall.

"Sit down, Chop-Chop," Troll rumbled.

I sat down next to Cheetah. "You guys ever hear the name Lansky before?"

Cheetah's eyes widened. Troll didn't react that I could see.

"Well, did ya?"

"Listen, keep your voice down about him," said Cheetah. "Meyer Lansky is one of the biggest racket guys ever."

"Yeah? What's he doing now? He must have something going."

"He's been seen around Jokertown lately. Word is, he came down personally in this big black Caddy to rent some warehouse space."

"Really? What's he keeping in it?"

"Chop-Chop, I wouldn't ask questions like that. He keeps his place guarded. You follow me?"

"Then where are these warehouses?"

"Chop-Chop! That kinda talk is dangerous."

"Why?" Troll asked, much more calmly.

"Well . . ." I felt I had to keep Flo out of my explanation, but the rest of it was joker business. "Look, I need some help. I might have to break into a place."

"What?" Cheetah's eyes widened in surprise. "Little Chop-Chop's turning into a juvenile delinquent? What's the deal?"

"I can't go into it, but it's big."

"Jokers shouldn't hurt each other," Troll said firmly.

"Not jokers," I whispered. "A place is gonna burn."

"What place?" Cheetah shoved his Coke bottle aside.

"I got to keep that quiet. But I *have* to find out what Lansky's doing in Jokertown."

"All right," said Troll. "He rented that redbrick warehouse where we used to throw rocks through the windows. And the one just down the street from it, too. Take your pick."

Cheetah laughed, showing his large chimp's teeth. "Half the windows in that red one are still busted out."

"Will you help me?"

"You just want to see what's inside?" Cheetah asked.

"If I find what I'm looking for, I want a sample."

"Like what?" Cheetah studied my face.

"I don't know, exactly." I turned to Troll. "You in?"

"If a place in Jokertown is going to burn, I'm in."

"Okay. After dark, at nine, right outside."

"We'll be there," said Cheetah.

I went home for dinner. Then I told my mother that I was going back to Biff's, which was true. I met Troll and Cheetah on time.

They simply fell into step with me in the darkness outside.

"You guys know more about this than I do," I said.

"Who says?" Troll demanded, in his low, rumbling growl. His belt buckle was higher than the top of my head.

Cheetah screeched with laughter. "Okay, Chop-Chop. We get the message. You just tag along."

We stopped in the shadows across the street from the red warehouse. Lights were on inside the front of the building. Pedestrians were still strolling nearby in the cool night air.

"This one or the one down the block?" Troll asked.

"Doesn't matter," I said.

Cheetah looked down at me. "This is your show."

"This one, I guess."

Cheetah led us down to the rear lot, with the loading dock. It was fenced and locked. None of the rear windows was lit.

Troll lifted Cheetah over the top rail of the eight-foot fence, then me. Last, he grasped the top of one of the steel fence posts and jumped. It bent slightly, but he was merely using it for leverage, not pulling with his full weight. At his height, the fence was just an annoyance.

Cheetah jogged quietly to the back of the building, craning his simian neck upward. He pointed with a long, hairy arm to a third-story window that was almost completely broken out. Troll moved under the window Cheetah had chosen. He held Cheetah around the waist and lifted him. Cheetah's long arms stretched up to the top of the second-story window, where his fingers found a hold lost in the shadows. Then Cheetah climbed upward out of his grasp to the open window and carefully moved through it, avoiding the bits of jagged glass still in the frame.

We waited in silence. Finally the rear door creaked open gently. Cheetah stuck his head out and gestured for us to follow him. "Just two guys down in the front," he whispered. "Playing cards. But they have guns."

I drew in a sharp breath. "Look, maybe—"

Troll gently shoved me forward. "Too late," he rumbled.

I followed Cheetah inside. At first the only light came from the streetlights behind us. Deeper inside, light came from the front of the warehouse, angling around tall stacks of wooden crates. I could hear the voices of the two men talking quietly to themselves, and then the rippling sound of cards being shuffled.

Troll, moving with a stealth that seemed impossible, went over one aisle between stacks of crates.

Cheetah slipped over to another aisle. I followed Cheetah, quivering with fear.

Near the end of the aisle, Cheetah turned and began climbing the stack of crates. I moved up close and simply watched. By now, I had no idea where Troll had gone.

"I'm sick of goddamned cards," said one of the men. "Three more lousy hours till we're off. You still got that flask on you?"

"Aw, come on. It's almost empty . . . hey, you hear somethin'?"

Suddenly Cheetah let out a shriek. I ran up to look around the corner. Cheetah was swinging on a rope that dangled from the ceiling on a block and tackle, toward the two men.

The two men were both in shirtsleeves, wearing shoulder holsters and narrow ties pulled loose. They had been sitting on crates, using a third one to hold their cards, an ashtray, and a couple of empty beer bottles. Now they looked up in shock, reaching for their guns. Jarring footsteps shook the floor as Troll ran toward them on his long, lumbering legs.

One man started to aim at Cheetah, then spun toward Troll.

"No! Not in here!" His companion screamed in terror and pushed his arm aside. "The whole joint'll go up!"

The first man hesitated, staring at Troll in astonishment. Then, ignoring his friend, he fired, apparently figuring he had nothing to lose. Two bullets ripped through Troll's shirt, careening off his hard, green skin.

The man fired again and again, backing away in horror. "Holy goddamned—"

Cheetah dropped onto his shoulders, still screeching insanely, and knocked his arm askew. As the man tumbled sideways from Cheetah's weight, Cheetah rolled and the gun skittered across the floor.

The man leapt for the gun, snatching it up in both hands.

Troll was still chasing the other man, who was on his feet and backpedaling as he continued to fire.

All the bullets ricocheted off Troll's skin, ripping up his clothes as they struck. Troll batted the gun out of his hand.

The first man was aiming for Cheetah.

I didn't realize I was running forward until I saw how close I was. Without thinking, I flung myself forward and collided with the man as he fired at Cheetah. The gun snapped twice in my ear as we rolled on the floor.

A much louder bang sounded high above us, but I couldn't turn to look yet. I knocked the gun away from the man, sliding it across the dirty floor. Then, before the man could recover, Troll stomped on his neck; it gave with a loud crunch.

The other man had escaped Troll, but was staring up over our heads someplace. A small fire had started in one of the crates up there. A stray bullet had hit something.

"It's gonna blow! The whole damn place!" the man screamed, looking around frantically, and tried to run past Troll.

Troll strode forward on his long legs. This time he slammed a fist the size of a volleyball into the side of the man's head. His neck snapped loudly and he collapsed to the floor.

"Never killed anybody before," Troll muttered, gazing down at the two dead bodies. "Hell, Cheetah. I didn't plan on that."

"Nobody tried to kill you before, did they?" Cheetah asked.

"Well . . . no." Troll grimaced and licked his crooked, yellow teeth. "Little .22 pistols. These racket guys like 'em."

"*Look* up there! He said it's gonna blow!" I pointed. "Come on, we gotta get outta here!"

"Aw, calm down, will you?" Cheetah demanded. "I thought you wanted to look inside one of these crates—"

A louder explosion came from high above us, by the fire. This time a couple of crates crashed to the floor. Two more explosions came from them when they hit, scattering more fire.

"Come on!" I turned and ran. Behind me, I finally heard Cheetah's quick footsteps and Troll's pounding ones. Before I reached the back door, a roaring explosion shook the entire building. I stumbled through the door and ran toward the fence.

By the time I reached it, they had caught up to me. Troll grabbed a steel fence post and simply pushed it flat, shoving the entire fence down and out of our way. On the other side, I turned to look back at the warehouse.

Another series of powerful explosions thundered through the building. Red-orange flames raged in most of the windows now. Crates crashed to the floor. Smoke was pouring out through the broken windows.

"We got to call the fire department!" Cheetah yelled.

"They might not come—that's part of the deal," I shouted. "You go ahead and call! Troll, we have to find help! Come on!"

More explosions shook the building. Part of the roof collapsed. Fire danced out of the open space high above us.

While Cheetah ran for a phone, Troll and I crossed the street to an apartment building. I started inside, but he didn't bother. He looked in a second-story window, where a couple of jokers were drinking beer and peering out to see what the noise had been. Troll shouted that it was a fire and to bring out the building's emergency firehose, fast.

I yelled for them to bring their neighbors. We would have to start a bucket brigade. Then Troll and I ran to the next apartment building, where we did the same.

Soon we had jokers of all shapes and sizes pouring out into the streets, running or limping or hopping or slithering. Some brought the hoses from their apartment buildings; others brought buckets from their closets or their places of business.

No one had a tool to use on the fire hydrants, but Troll was able to unscrew the protective nut with brute strength and hook up the hoses people brought out. He and some of the other strongest jokers held the hoses. I got people to line up in bucket brigades between the edge of the warehouse and some external spigots on the neighboring buildings.

Flo was right about the fire department, even with this accidental fire. They never showed up. The fire burned late into the night, and the explosions continued. None was big enough to level the building, though, and I figured out why. They weren't bombs in the sense of trying to destroy a building in one big bang. Instead, the stuff in the crates was intended to start fires that would spread afterward. All those small fires were pretty well lost in this great big one.

Actually, at first the bucket brigades didn't do much more than keep the fire from spreading on the ground. That was good, but nobody could get close enough to the building because of the heat and smoke to throw a bucket of water on it. Troll and the other big jokers holding the hoses made the real difference. With a couple of hoses on all three hydrants that were on streets by the warehouse, they kept up the spray.

It was long after midnight by the time the fire died down. Then the bucket brigades really moved in, but they were cautious because of the explosions. Finally the fire was under control and everybody cheered and ran around hugging everyone else. For that one night, all the jokers seemed to put their differences aside and work together to help their own part of town.

Most people started drifting away then. Troll and some of the others stayed until almost three in the morning to make sure the fire was out. Then he came up to me with this wet, heavy lump of metal in one hand and gave it to me. He also gave me a short piece of cord and a small lump of something that hadn't burned. I couldn't tell what any of it was, but I took it home with me. My mother had been too worried to be mad, but everything was okay when I told her I had been in the bucket brigade.

The next morning, I wrapped the unidentifiable stuff from the fire in a towel and took it to work. I stashed it on an empty warehouse shelf until lunchtime. Then, when Peter Choy sat down on a stool in front of the big freezer doors to open his lunch pail, I carried it over to him.

"Mr. Choy?"

"Hi, Chuck. You got your lunch wrapped up there?"

"Aw, heck, no. But, uh . . . look." I set it all down on the concrete floor and unwrapped it.

He laughed. "What is it?"

"I'm not sure. I got it from the fire last night."

"You were out there?" He leaned forward, looking closely. "I heard the explosions, but I went back to sleep."

"Mr. Choy, I'm afraid to go to the police. I don't think they'll listen to a joker—especially a kid like me. But somebody's got a whole bunch of these stashed away."

"More of them, Chuck?" His voice had suddenly grown serious.

"Yeah. Will you report it, if I tell you?"

"Tell you what. I'll go to the police with you."

"Aw, no. The fire chief is in on it. The cops might be, too."

He frowned thoughtfully. Then he closed his lunch pail and stood up. "I know where to go. No cops. Come on."

We hiked down to a little Chinatown dive on Mott Street.

By the time I had carried the load through the noonday heat that far, I was exhausted and soaked in sweat. For a change, my boss was quiet, instead of friendly and joking all the time.

Inside, Peter walked up to one of the booths. A skinny, chain-smoking man with his brown hair in a buzz cut sat hunched over, alone. Wearing a baggy black suit, he was poking through a bowl of pork noodles with a fork.

"Matt? I'm Peter Choy. We used to talk sometimes when I had lunch here regularly. On my old route."

"Sure, I remember." He tugged his tie a little looser and glanced at me. "So, you want to sit, or what?"

"I might have a story for you." Peter slid into the booth and gestured for me to join him.

"Chuck, Matt Rainey here is a Chinatown beat reporter for the *New York Mirror*. I want you to show him what you have."

I set the bundle on the table. Then I pulled the edge of the towel back just a little. Peter watched Matt's face.

"Say, I haven't seen a mess like that since Korea." Matt's narrow eyes widened.

"You can tell what it was?" Peter asked.

He tapped the big piece of metal with a fingernail. "Magnesium case for an incendiary bomb. It should have been filled with thermite, only this one didn't detonate. The case melted down from heat on the outside instead. Properly detonated, it could generate enough heat to turn steel machinery into a molten puddle. This other thing is a piece of detonating cord. Wrap that around a five-gallon gas can and *boom*. And the last thing . . . maybe part of a container for phosphorus trioxide, the stuff in hand grenades." He looked at me. "What of it, kid?"

"I have to be anonymous," I said. "You can't use my name or what I look like or anything."

Matt blew smoke out to one side and grinned cynically.

"You don't want your name in the paper? All that fame and glory?"

"You take it," I said.

"All right, then. Give."

"This was in the big Jokertown fire last night. Stuff like this helped start it. There's another whole warehouse full of these. And word on the street is, they belong to racket guys."

Peter turned and stared at me in amazement.

"Which guys? You got a name, kid, or just teenage gossip?"

"Lansky. He rented the warehouses."

Matt's eyebrows shot up. He puffed on his cigarette again and blew out more smoke. "That fire was real enough; I took a look this morning after I got the word. Where's the second warehouse?"

I told him.

"And you're giving me this tip free and clear? You won't come back later on, whining that I gypped you on this?"

"Aw, heck, no. I got to live around here."

Matt dropped the towel over the stuff. "Why not the cops?"

"He said the fire chief is in on it," said Peter. "Cops might be, too. And he's just a kid."

"*And* a joker. All right, I'll check it out. And I keep this. Now leave me alone, all right?"

I slid out of the booth, glad to get away from him. Peter thanked him. Out on the street again, though, even Peter let out a long breath of relief. Then we started to walk.

"In a sense, he's taking advantage of you," said Peter. "If that proves out, he'll get lots of credit that should go to you."

"It's okay with me," I said.

Tonight was the night. Before six o'clock, I started walking toward the Bowery on the route Flo had taken before, hoping to run into her on the way. I didn't see her. Starting to worry, I paced up and down the sidewalk, peering closely at every cab. Six o'clock passed. I paced more frantically.

When I saw Jube the Walrus down the block on his regular run, I ran after him. "Hey, Jube! Jube!"

"Evenin', Chop-Chop. Have you heard the one about—"

"Look, Jube, I'm in a hurry. That girl I was with yesterday—have you seen her?"

"No, Chop-Chop, I'm afraid not. You're expecting her, eh?"

"Yeah! And it's important—she wouldn't miss this!"

"No? Well, this isn't her part of town. I was surprised to see you with her. I never thought *she'd* come to Jokertown."

"You mean you know her?"

"Not personally, of course. From her picture in the paper."

"In the paper? Look—do you know who she is?"

"Whoa! Don't you?"

"Well—no. I just met her."

"Chop-Chop, she's Fleur van Renssaeler. Her daddy is Henry van Renssaeler, the congressman."

"He *is*? Uh—do you know where they live?"

Jube didn't know, but he was able to find out. I suppose it might have been in the society pages of an old paper or something. He told me to meet him back there on the corner in fifteen minutes, which I did. Henry van Renssaeler lived with his daughter and her two older brothers, Brandon and Henry, Jr., in a penthouse apartment. I never did find out why Jube bothered to help me. Looking back, I suppose he resented her father's attitude toward the wild card.

I wasn't going to go after Flo—Fleur—alone, though. First I hurried over to Biff's. Cheetah and Troll were hanging around there at that hour as usual. Tonight the place was full of other jokers, though, all talking about the fire. After last night, Cheetah and Troll were up for more adventure. Even back in those days, Troll had a sense of what you might call joker identity. When I got them aside, I told them I had to visit the home of a well-to-do nat girl and was real scared. They agreed to come along. So we headed uptown on the subway.

The apartment building was in just the kind of fancy area of New York you might have expected. In those days, you know, even rich people didn't have the kind of security you see nowadays. They didn't need it then.

We just walked inside and went over to the elevator. This young guy in a gray uniform was sitting there on a stool, reading a comic book. His eyes got real wide when he saw us, but he just took us up without a word.

I was nervous when I knocked on the penthouse door. The little peephole darkened as someone looked out. Then I heard a muffled gasp and footsteps and voices inside.

Finally the door was yanked open. This stiff, arrogant man in a suit and tie was glaring down at me.

He had to be Fleur's father, Henry van Renssaeler.

"Is Fleur here?" I sounded like a kid who wanted her to play.

"Get out of here!" He jerked his head toward the elevator door. "You filthy . . ." When he looked up and saw Troll behind me, his mouth just dropped open.

Behind him in the foyer, I could see a uniformed black maid and a couple of other servants staring at us. Then Henry swung the door to slam it in my face. Before it shut, though, Troll reached over my head and gripped the doorframe with one giant, warty hand. The door banged off his hand and bounced open again.

I felt another very large hand shove me forward, inside the apartment. Cheetah, laughing loudly, danced past me to a small table and ripped a telephone cord out of the wall. The servants huddled in a corner, where Cheetah held them by showing his teeth, waving his arms, and making his favorite chimp noises.

I turned. Troll ducked inside the doorway, slammed the door shut, and leaned down toward Henry, trapping him against the wall with a green arm as thick as my waist. Henry was sweating heavily, speechless.

"Where's Fleur?" I demanded.

Her father glanced down at me, but he didn't speak. I couldn't tell if he was being defiant or was just too scared. Anyhow, I turned around and yelled her name.

"Here!" Her voice was distant and muffled, but a knocking sound was much sharper.

I ran down a long carpeted hallway. "Fleur! It's Chuck!"

"I'm locked in! Over here!" She pounded on her door again.

I fumbled with the knob, but it required a key. "Troll!"

His footsteps pounded down the hall toward me.

"Look out, Fleur! Back up!" I stepped aside and Troll simply crashed into the door, smashing it down.

Fleur stood in the middle of the room, staring at Troll in horror.

"Come on!" I darted inside and grabbed her arm. "Have you got the money? For tonight?"

"No, I couldn't get to the bank." She snatched up her purse.

I dragged her out and pulled her down the hall.

Cheetah was still jumping around in front of the servants, but Henry had started toward us. He stopped, though, when he saw Troll coming back. Fleur looked away from him as I drew her past him toward the front door.

"Whore!" Henry yelled. "Filthy whore—*joker's* whore!"

We stopped at her bank in the neighborhood. She acted like she was in a trance, quivering and sweating but doing everything she had to do. Once she had the cash, we took Fleur back to Jokertown—on the subway, of course. I kept an eye on her wristwatch. We would just barely make her appointment.

Back in Jokertown, I thanked Cheetah and Troll. They took the hint and got lost. I led Fleur quickly up the sidewalk in the waning light. She clung to me, crying quietly.

"What happened? Did your father find out?"

Her voice was tight. "Not exactly. But he was real mad that I was out the other night—he checked up on me and found out that I wasn't at my girlfriend's, after all. When I started to leave yesterday, he locked me in."

"Now I've really done it—he saw you with jokers."

When we reached the rear of the club, Waffle was pacing restlessly by the back door. He looked like a human-shaped cookie cut-out of a waffle in both texture and color, and in his very flat shape. He wore a white T-shirt with the sleeves rolled up to his brown, waffled shoulders, and blue dungarees with the cuffs rolled up over white socks and dirty tennis shoes.

"Gimme the dough," said Waffle.

She handed me five one-hundred dollar bills. I held them out.

Waffle snatched them. "All right, follow me."

We followed him. He led us up a back alley and then opened a small unmarked door. He went inside first. This door opened on a narrow hallway. I shut it behind us.

Waffle opened an interior door. "They're here, Doc."

The elderly man who appeared was of Chinese descent, short and stocky like Peter Choy, with receding black hair and a deeply lined face. He wore a long white lab coat. His otherwise human face had a long duck beak. "I'm just Doc," he said calmly. "My nickname is Peking Doc. You don't need to tell me your name."

"Hi," said Fleur, in a whisper, as she stared at his beak.

Doc turned to me. "I'm sorry for the inconvenience, young man. Now, don't worry. I'll give your friend something to make her drowsy and everything will be fine. But it will be an hour before she wakes up and two hours before she's herself again. I'll have to ask you to remain in the next room." He pointed.

"All right," I said, turning to Fleur. "Uh—good luck."

"She'll be fine." Doc held open another door and gestured for Fleur to precede him.

She gave me a terrified glance and stiffly walked through it.

Waffle slipped past me and left by the back door. I went into the room Doc had pointed out. It was dark until I switched on a corner lamp. Then I picked up copies of *Reader's Digest* to look for the funny stuff.

Nearly an hour passed. Suddenly I wondered if Matt Rainey had accomplished anything today. I decided to find out, despite what Doc had said, and slipped outside, making sure that the door would not lock behind me. Then I ran to the nearest newsstand and snatched up a copy of the *New York Mirror*, tossing coins onto the counter. I hurried back to the clinic.

Doc was standing in the hall, glaring at me.

I swallowed, too scared to speak.

"Your friend will be fine," Doc said finally. "She has asked to see you, but she should not try to walk for another hour or so. I'll be in my office until then."

"Yeah, okay."

Doc showed me into a room where Fleur lay on an examination table under a sheet. Only a small lamp was on. Doc closed the door after me.

"How are you?" I whispered.

"It's over," she said quietly, blinking back tears.

"He said you'll be okay."

"Yeah."

"He said you still have to rest. I'll go back out—"

"Don't go. Please." Her voice cracked and she started to cry.

"All right." I sat down on a small wheeled stool.

She calmed down again. "What's that?"

"The final edition of today's *Mirror*." Unfolding it for the first time, I looked at the front page.

ARSON PLOT FOILED ran the headline in big, black letters. Under it, the byline added, "By Matt Rainey."

"He did it!" I started skimming the article. "He took what I found to the cops and they believed him! Yeah! And they hit the other warehouse early this morning—at dawn! Cool!"

"Really?" Her voice still came in a quiet whisper.

"And in time for the final edition—that's fast! Oops . . ."

"What is it?"

"Well . . . I'm sort of in here. He says he got some street directions from 'an alleged Jap joker.' " I winced at the phrase.

"My father's friends won't care about street directions."

"Wow—it says a mysterious black Cadillac turned a nearby corner and hit the brakes. It made an illegal U-turn and took off before the cops could get after 'em. I bet that was Lansky!"

I heard a loud knocking, actually a pounding, on the outside door. Doc's footsteps went from his office to the back door and the knob clicked as he unlocked it. I figured it was his next appointment. Then I heard scuffling out in the hall.

Fleur gasped and struggled to sit up. "What is it?"

I ran to the door. When I opened it, Doc was falling to the floor, holding his hands over his beak.

Henry van Renssaeler, his fists clenched, strode toward me, wild-eyed.

"Where is she? *Where is she*, you joker scum?"

"Hey—" I blocked his way, but he smacked me aside.

He marched past me into the examining room. "Goddamn filthy joker's whore!"

I rushed after him, but I didn't know what to do.

"Thought you could escape me? You can *never* get away from me!"

Fleur was staring at him, speechless.

"I overheard your little hero's question about going to the bank—and your answer! I sent one of the servants to catch up to you there and follow you. He tailed you here, then found a phone to report back to me at home. I was a little slow finding the place; I will not dirty myself asking jokers for directions. But you see, my darling daughter, you can't get away from me."

"You're too late!" Fleur spat back at him. "You're too late, *Daddy*. You can see what kind of place this is. You won't have another child—not through me, anyway!" She started sobbing.

I finally started getting the picture—the whole picture.

"Quiet! Quiet, you slut!" He started toward her.

"And he knows!" She pointed to me. "And now Doc has seen you—and the servant knows! *Everyone* will know, Daddy!" Fleur threw off the sheet and swung her legs over the side of the table. She jumped to the floor, but staggered dizzily.

Henry leapt to grab her.

I ran forward and hit his legs in a flying tackle. We both crashed to the floor. I grabbed one of his arms with both hands and tried to bite his wrist with my gigantic buck teeth.

Henry screamed and jerked himself away, falling again. I had hardly had a chance to nip him, but he was acting crazy. He scuttled away from me with a horrified look on his face.

Behind me, Fleur, who was stark naked, snatched up her clothes, purse, and shoes in a bundle. She darted behind me. I backed out, still snapping idiotically at Henry.

When we were out of the room, I slammed the door shut to delay him. Fleur was already jumping over Doc, who was lying in a daze watching us, as she headed for the door. Then I followed her out and pointed down the alley. I pulled her be-hind some old oil drums being used as trash cans.

While Fleur pulled on her clothes, I got down low and peered around the edge of an oil drum. Her father had stopped outside the door, looking around. He couldn't decide which way to go.

"You ready yet?" I whispered, glancing back over my shoul-der.

"Almost. Gotta get my shoes on," she whispered back.

Suddenly bright headlights swung toward us as a car turned from the street into the alley behind Doc's door. A long, shiny black Cadillac pulled to a stop. As one of the rear win-dows opened, Henry trotted toward it.

"It's Lansky," I whispered. "Or one of his lieutenants."

"Oh, no!" Fleur scrambled up next to me and looked.

As her father leaned down toward the open window, two loud shots snapped out, making the same sound as the guns in the warehouse last night. He crumpled to the ground.

The Cadillac backed quickly into the street, paused to re-verse gear, then smoothly glided out of sight.

I got up, still in shadow, and looked at Henry van Rens-saeler, US Congressman. He was lying motionless on his back, his face a bloody mess. I thought Fleur might be upset, but she walked toward him, looking at him.

"Is he dead?" she asked quietly.

"Yeah." I came up next to her.

She let out a long breath and sagged against me, crying qui-etly. When she spoke again, her voice was oddly strong. "They did it. All those self-righteous, stuffy, prim and proper know-it-alls, so perfect and good."

"They had Lansky arrange it again."

"Yeah. He was already scared. This morning he came into my room and yelled at me. I never saw him that scared before."

"His own friends killed him?"

"He didn't have friends, Chuck. Not real ones. He had business associates. I bet they arranged his death, 'cause he was in charge of their arson plot. The police might find a lead to him. Now he's a dead end."

"Yeah."

"Those people move fast."

"Like I said, Lansky or his guys must have been in that Cadillac when they saw the cops breaking into the warehouse. So they knew the secret was out. But how did they find him here?"

"That servant my father mentioned. He's probably in their pay to spy on him."

For the first time, though, one mystery finally fell into place: why the daughter of a rich, powerful man had come alone to Jokertown for an abortion instead of seeking out the illegal abortionists available to the wealthy. Jokertown was the one place where her father had no business associates or social contacts who might have gotten word back to him.

Maybe she had taken a measure of revenge on her father two nights ago by having sex with a joker. After all, I was just the kind of person her father hated most. She could not have planned on finding someone to wind up in bed with, but I remembered that she had not hesitated.

Now it made a twisted kind of sense. I felt a sinking feeling inside. As I had suspected in the beginning, having a nat girl from her background truly like me was just impossible.

"What about . . . us?" I asked her timidly.

"I have to go back and deal with my brothers now. We'll be inheriting stuff and dealing with lawyers and who knows what. I don't even know who my legal guardian will be."

"I meant, uh, you and me."

Fleur hurried around the body of her father, her ponytail

bouncing. I hurried after her in the breezy darkness. She was heading quickly for the street and didn't look sleepy now at all.

"Can't we talk?" I nearly had to jog to keep up with her.

She didn't say anything. In fact, she didn't even wait to reach the edge of Jokertown before trying to hail a cab. Suddenly her steps grew wobbly and she staggered to her right, dizzily. I grabbed her arm and steadied her. We stopped by the curb.

"I'll go straight home from here this time," she said quickly, still avoiding my eyes. She waved over my head and a cab suddenly swerved over to us.

"I, uh, I love you."

"Oh, Chuck." She finally turned her beautiful face toward me again. Tears came to her brown eyes as she looked at me. For one very long moment, she actually seemed to see me as a regular guy.

Maybe that was the only second in my entire life that I actually forgot what I looked like—just for a fleeting second.

Then Fleur broke the gaze. The cab had pulled up next to us. Without looking back, she yanked open the door and ducked inside the cab, slamming the door. The cab roared away up the street, taking her away forever.

". . . *Never* knew *what I* missed *until I* kissed *ya* . . ."

The Ashes of
Memory

2

"You never saw her again?" Hannah
asked.

Tanaka shrugged, shook his head, blinked. "A little different than the movie version, huh?" he said at last. "All the names were changed. They wrote me out, of course, leaving Rainey as the hero who uncovers it all. The Fleur character was older and she got involved with the reporter, not some ugly joker. And they hinted at the incest angle without ever saying it, but there wasn't any abortion. It was really weird for me, watching Marilyn Monroe. I always liked her, but this was spooky."

Hannah took a breath. "Why didn't Lansky ever try it again? If this group of people hated jokers so much, why'd they give up their grand plan?"

Another shrug. "I think the exposure in the paper scared them off. Rainey revealed the insurance scam, so that angle wouldn't work anymore; there wouldn't have been the financial payoff. That plus the murder."

"Maybe I should talk to Rainey."

"You'll need someone who does séances. He was killed a month later, found with a couple dozen bullet holes in a Jokertown gutter."

"Did the police ever charge Lansky with the murder?"

"You're kidding, right?" Tanaka sniffed. "They arrested two of his goons for it; they did a few years. Lansky was killed in the mid-sixties when he tried to muscle in on the Gambione family's holdings in Cuba."

"So everyone's dead. Doesn't leave me much."

"There's still a few around, but mostly that's right. Waffle never knew anything; besides, he's still just a street punk. Cheetah's not around anymore. Troll's over at the J-Town Clinic, he might talk with you, and Peter Choy, well, he owns *this* place now. If you want to check with him, he'll be in tomorrow."

Hannah shook her head. "Thanks for the information, but I don't think I'll need it." She reached for the recorder, stated the date and time again, and switched it off. She closed her notebook and put it back in her purse. She got to her feet. She hesitated—*C'mon, girl, you'd do it for anyone else after an interview*—then held out her hand to Tanaka. When he didn't move right away, she quickly brought the hand back. "Thanks for talking with me," she said. "I appreciate your time."

He stared at her from behind the glasses. "You think this has anything to do with the fire? I'm just curious," he added when she didn't answer. "After all, you came and asked me about the movie."

"I think there are a lot of sick people out there," Hannah replied. "One of them hated jokers enough to want to burn down a church when there were a lot of them inside. I don't need a conspiracy for that. There's nothing similar in Lansky's plot and what happened a couple days ago. The simplest solution is that we have a lone torch, probably a psychotic."

Tanaka blinked. His buckteeth gnawed at the flesh of his lower lip. "Nothing's ever simple in Jokertown," he said.

"You talked with him?"

The voice was eager and all too familiar and, once more, behind her. Hannah spun around on the sidewalk outside the Four Seas. Quasiman was looking at her expectantly, his head leaning against one shoulder.

Hannah moved quickly back from him, scowling. "Do you have to keep sneaking up on me like that?"

"I'm sorry, Hannah," Quasiman said. The hurt and apology in his voice made Hannah regret her irritation. She told herself it was only because the meeting with Tanaka had been such a waste of time. She wanted nothing but to get off the streets of Jokertown. By now, the lab should have had time to identify the accelerant. "Did you meet Chop-Chop?"

"Yes, I just talked with him."

"Then you know." Quasiman sounded relieved, as if he'd expected Chop-Chop's little tale to have convinced her of something.

"I know there are people who hate jokers, but I knew that before. About the fire, I don't know anything else."

"Chop-Chop wouldn't tell you?"

"As far as I know, he told me everything. I just don't see that it has anything to do with the fire at your church. I'm sorry."

"It all connects, Hannah. I've seen it; I just can't hold all the threads together in my head. I've been trying so hard."

"You keep saying that. If that's what you believe, that's fine, but you're on your own now. If you can see the future, then you should have seen yourself investigating this ancient link alone. If there's a connection, it's up to you to find it. I gave you my promised hour and now I'm done. Leave me alone to do my work."

"But I can't, Hannah," Quasiman answered, and his voice was nearly a wail. "I can't. My mind won't hang on to things. It's hard for me to concentrate. I'm not good at putting things together—too scattered." He reached toward her and she skittered backward, nearly colliding with an Asian woman walking past. A joker watching from the nearby bus stop cackled.

"Just stay away, damn it!"

"I need you," Quasiman persisted. "They need you, Hannah, all of the ones who died."

She remembered the bodies in the ruins of the church, the twisted, black shapes. *They all look the same once they're crisped.* Hannah stopped. "Quasiman, look at me. I'm one of those nats the jokers hate. I don't have joker friends; in fact, most of the people I know are wild card bigots. I've gone out of my way to avoid everything to do with the wild card since I came to New York. I'm really uncomfortable around people like you. I don't want you to touch me; I don't even want you near me."

"Father Squid said you have a kind face."

"Father Squid has a handful of slimy tentacles for a nose. What does he know about faces?"

"Hannah, there's a circus in town," Quasiman said. "You need to go there and talk to the Ringmistress. It's important."

Hannah gave an exasperated laugh. "What the—" She shook her head. "Where in the *world* did that come from? Now you want me to go to a circus? Look, you already sent me on one wild-goose chase."

"You have to go," Quasiman repeated. "You need to talk to the Ringmistress. I saw you there."

That caused Hannah's eyebrows to raise. "You *saw* me there?"

Hannah wasn't sure that Quasiman heard her, or was even listening. Both his legs vanished, causing a few Asian passersby on the sidewalk to gasp as Quasiman fell a few feet to the ground, where he sat looking like someone buried to his hips in the pavement. "Ask her about what happened in 1976," he said urgently. Before she could respond, Quasiman was gone entirely.

Ask her about *what happened in 1976 . . .*

Hannah cursed inside as she walked away from the Four Seas. She managed to hail one of the rare cabs here on the edge of Jokertown, and she sat in the back fuming as she looked out that window at the sights of Jokertown. "Stop!" she told the driver with a sudden impulse as they passed the corner of Hester Street and Bowery, where a newsstand stood with what appeared to be a walrus wearing a pork-pie hat and a florid Hawaiian shirt behind the counter. Hannah's cabdriver, at least, seemed only to be foreign, not a joker. He pulled the car over to the curb. "You stay here and keep the meter running," she told the driver. *I'd never find another cab around here, and I don't know what I'd do . . .* "I'll be right back."

She shivered despite the lingering September warmth, being exposed to Jokertown and a street crowded with those who had been affected by the virus. "Excuse me," Hannah told the walrus. "Would you have any information about a circus here in town? With a ringmistress?"

The walrus laughed, enveloping her in a scent that smelled oddly of buttered popcorn. "Ringmistress Zara," he said. "Sounds almost kinky, doesn't it?" The walrus picked up a paper from the stack on the counter and put it in front of her: *The Jokertown Cry*, Hannah saw emblazoned on the header. Jube's thick forefinger tapped the paper. "There's a full-page ad for the circus in there. That'll be fifty cents."

"Thanks," Hannah told him, rummaging in her purse. She found a dollar and put it on the counter. "Keep the change," she said, snatched up the paper, and walked quickly to the idling cab. "Hang on a minute," she told the driver as she got into the taxi. She opened *The Jokertown Cry*, flipping quickly through the pages. There it was: a gaudy full-page advertisement for *Ringmistress Zara's Wildest Show on Earth*, which was evidently set up at Ebbets Field in Crown Heights, Brooklyn. "Featuring Radha 'Elephant Girl' O'Reilly," the ad trumpeted amid cartoonish drawings of clowns, aerialists, and such, all nestled between the general circus hyperbolic claims.

Hannah sighed, rolling up the paper. *I don't know why I'm bothering. This is just going to be another dead end.* "Ebbets Field," she told the driver.

"There ain't no game today, lady," he answered. "The Dodgers are playing in Pittsburgh."

"Believe me, I know that. Take me to Ebbets Field, anyway."

The driver shrugged and pulled away from the curb.

Hannah could see the tents already erected in one of the Ebbets Field parking lots with several large RVs and trucks parked nearby. There were people already milling around the well-lit circus grounds, with the first evening show set to start in an hour; Hannah had the driver go around to where the circus RVs were parked. She paid the cabdriver and walked toward the RVs. One of the circus roustabouts, a joker with bulging Popeye arms and a head that was set on a stalk emerging from his bare stomach, came toward her as she approached.

"Sorry, lady," he said. "You buy your ticket at the main entrance over there." One of the arms above his head pointed. "This here's private."

Hannah flashed the man her credentials, holding them at waist level so he could see them. "I need to talk to Ringmistress Zara."

The man squinted myopically at the leather case and sniffed. "Let me get Pigtail," he said. "She's the one who says who can see the Ringmistress. You just stay where you are."

Pigtail, when she arrived, was a young joker woman with multicolored skin and a spike of hair and a gymnast's build. She introduced herself as Ringmistress Zara's "runner" and asked Hannah's business with her. "I'm not even sure the Ringmistress is here right now," she told Hannah.

"She'd better be," Hannah answered. She ostentatiously checked her watch. "The first show's in less than an hour."

Pigtail sighed at that. "Follow me," she said, and led Hannah through the maze of trucks to an RV that looked more like a sixteen-wheeler trailer, tall and wide with portable aluminum steps leading up to two open doors that ran from floor to roof of the vehicle. Inside, Hannah could see a seated woman in a red top hat and jodhpurs with a whip in her right hand. The woman had bright red skin. In another time, Hannah thought, she'd have been called demonic. Something looked off about the scale of Ringmistress Zara and the furniture inside.

"Wait here," Pigtail said. She walked into the RV and approached the Ringmistress. The problem with scale became obvious as Pigtail entered the space; she looked to be doll-sized against everything else. Pigtail spoke but Hannah couldn't hear what she said, though she saw Ringmistress Zara's gaze go to her.

"Did she say what it's about?" Hannah heard. Past Pigtail,

Hannah saw the woman rise, and her eyes widened with the sight. Ringmistress Zara had to be at least a dozen feet tall if not more. She gestured toward Hannah with a showy sweep of her hand.

Hannah walked into the massive RV behind Pigtail. She could see that there was another woman in the vehicle, her petite figure almost lost in one of the too-large chairs and attired in a showy dress. "Ringmistress Zara," Hannah said to the red woman. "I was hoping we could speak privately."

Zara ran her hand across the top hat, and Hannah realized it was actually part of her skull. "I don't speak privately unless I'm aware of the topic beforehand."

"My name is Hannah Davis. I'm working on the investigation into the fire at Our Lady of Perpetual Misery."

The other woman made an "aah" of sympathy at that, but the Ringmistress scowled. "You think *I* know something? Are you intending to try pinning that on one of my people? You can leave, Ms. Davis."

"Nothing like that at all. It was suggested to me that something that happened to you in the past might have some bearing on the case."

The woman in the chair rose and walked up next to the Ringmistress. "Maybe you should talk to her," she said. "I'll go."

She stepped past Hannah and Pigtail, who was still waiting and looking uncertain. As she started to descend the portable stairs, she turned to Hannah. "Good luck," she said.

"Pigtail?" Zara snapped.

"Yes, Ringmistress?"

"You may go with Radha. And see that Ms. Davis and I aren't interrupted." Then her demeanor changed. "Step right up," Zara said, her voice booming as she backed away from the entrance to allow Hannah inside.

The Wildest Show on Earth

Gwenda Bond

I might apologize for the resistance to talking, but circus folk in general like to run their business privately. We're part of the regular world—the one the people we show up to entertain belong to. But we're our own traveling closed society, too. There aren't many problems a circus can't outrun. That's usually part of why people join.

But that doesn't mean there aren't any. And our own rules, we treat those as inviolable.

So when one of my ace performers, insomniac Whitey, and a crew member came banging on my trailer door in the middle of the night while we were camped outside Bowling Green, Kentucky, in 1976, I knew either something important was up or I was about to fire someone. As ringmistress, my sleep fell into the category of sacred, my private space my sanctuary, then as now.

I answered the door with a growl meant to discourage future interruptions. "What?"

I cut an imposing figure—all the more when my precious shut-eye is disturbed. So you can imagine the gulp of the crewman at the sight of me towering over him in the door, whip arm curled up to my hip, regular hand rubbing over the giant top-hat-like red ridge atop my head. I might not've been in full costume, but my wild card means I wear my role as ringmaster always.

The crew guy said nothing, but Whitey wasn't so easily intimidated. "Some people you should meet, Zara," he said. He was petite and pale with the pinkish eyes and snowy hair of an albino. "Stowaways."

"How old?" Usually these were kids seeking refuge from smothering small towns or terrible home lives. Sometimes we took them on, sometimes they were too much trouble and I had to remind myself that I had a responsibility to my entire show now. I couldn't afford to make bad decisions and bring in trouble. Running a circus is a lot like being the head of a big, unruly family. My mentor, the legendary Ringmaster Patrick Bartley, who took me in as a young runaway, taught me that.

But I hadn't been in charge of my own show long at that point. This was our first tour—hard to believe now, but we were an upstart. We'd only been on the road for a few months, and the only reason we were drawing such big crowds was the growing fame of our finale performer, with us for a few months purely as a favor in memory of Patrick.

"These're not the usual type," Whitey said. "Left 'em with Dozer."

Dozer was night security—officially. A biker with a powerful engine for a torso that could power almost anything you hooked it up to. He reeked of gasoline and could put the hurt on anyone who gave him an excuse to launch himself at them. Whitey was his unofficial helper, for which he got a bonus. "Fine, I'll get dressed. Bring them to the office."

The office didn't live up to its name; it was just what we called the back half of the mess tent. But there was always a pot of coffee on in the kitchen trailer, and I needed it. Whitey had a Styrofoam cup and a tower of powdered creamer waiting at my usual spot when I arrived.

He'd also brought two women who weren't at all what I expected. Both were adults, though one was middle-aged and the other I'd put in her early twenties. They had tidy hair and wore nice clothes, blouses and skirts, and the older carried enough weight to let me know she'd had an easy time of it. The younger one had a hungry, haunted look about her. A wariness around her eyes that I found familiar.

"I'm Ringmistress Zara," I said, as polite as I could manage after a sip of stale coffee. "And who are you two?"

They exchanged a look, but neither spoke. They didn't flinch from my appearance, but from the way they fidgeted I could tell it didn't exactly make them comfortable.

I didn't have the patience to wait for them to get used to me. "Whitey, where'd you find these two?"

"They were under the bleachers in the Big Top. Sleeping." He was a nervous type and tapped his fingers against his leg. He hadn't bothered with a seat.

"Lucky the weather's not too cold for it," I said. "But I'm confused as to why two seemingly normal women who can afford to dress well enough"—I bent and glanced under the table, confirming what I suspected—"including shoes with barely any wear on them—are bunking without blankets under a circus tent. You two from around here?"

"Chicago," the younger woman said and then swallowed like she shouldn't have said a word.

"Long way from home," I said.

"Not far enough," she said. "Not yet."

"It's going to be okay." The older woman laid her hand over the younger woman's and patted it, then put hers back in her lap.

"What are you running from?" I paused. "Or, I suppose I should say, who?"

I didn't take them for a couple—not because of the age difference, but there was nothing to suggest that particular kind of intimacy between them. There was some connection between them, though. That much was obvious.

"Are you mother and daughter?" I tried.

"Not exactly," the older woman said.

"One of your cards turned?" I asked. Sometimes when it happened, running was the best option. Still.

"No," the younger woman blurted.

The older woman leaned forward slightly. "Can we trust you?"

What a question. "Well, we haven't kicked you out of here yet, though I'm not promising anything. Seems like you're not in a position to question trustworthiness yourself."

"That's fair." The older woman's lips compressed. She nodded. "I'm Miss Frost, and I'm not her mother, but—"

"But she's closer to me than my own mother ever has been." The younger woman put her elbows on the table. Her hair was the kind of white blond that usually comes from a bottle, but looked natural. Her features were delicate as a doll's. "I'm going by the name Miss Ash. It's . . . my husband."

So she was actually a Mrs. pretending to be a Miss, looking to run away from a Mr. At least this was familiar territory. Too familiar. "What about him?"

The two women looked at each other again. Miss Frost put her hand on top of Miss Ash's, reassuring. "He says he'll kill us both. We have no reason to doubt it."

A story getting more predictable all the time. Of all the circuses in all the world, why'd they have to waltz into mine? "You better back up a bit. Why does he want to kill you?"

"Do men need a reason?" Miss Frost countered.

Miss Ash slowly pushed up the sleeve of her blouse and the bruises there were quite clearly from the fingers of a grabbing hand. There was a rough red spot like a healed burn, too.

"I see," I said. "How determined do you think he is to find you? Does he have any idea where you went?"

"I don't think so," Miss Frost said, as Miss Ash covered the evidence of how she'd been hurt. "We covered our tracks better this time."

Ah. "So you've left him before?"

"We didn't go far enough that time. Didn't find a way to blend in somewhere he wouldn't come looking." Miss Ash recited the flaws in the previous plan flatly. "It was all I could do to . . ."

"He would happily have killed me then," Miss Frost said, a steel that I could admire in it. "She told him she'd go to the police. He agreed to let it go, as long as she stayed with him. He was quite clear about what would happen to both of us if she ran again. But . . . she couldn't stay there. Not anymore."

Miss Ash's shoulders caved in a bit, the effect to make her seem smaller. Harmless.

Their story was more than plausible, but something about it bothered me, even then. "How'd you get here? Bus?" That would make them easy to trace.

"That's what we tried last time." Miss Frost made it clear they hadn't made the same mistake. "I bought a car with cash, under a different—under this name."

Whitey poked his head in. "Why didn't you sleep in the car?"

"It seemed too risky," Miss Frost said, looking at me instead of him. "Just in case."

"How did you find out about us?" I asked. "When did we become part of the plan?"

"Yeah," Whitey said. "Did you say to yourselves, 'Let's run away and join the circus'?"

Miss Frost sniffed. "No, but when we saw the flyer posted at the rest area, it seemed . . . well, perfect. A place to hide. Who would pay attention to us with . . ." She waved her hand. Our poster highlighted our unusual cast.

"So then you'll be moving on tomorrow?" This was the real question. I'd happily wave goodbye to them. "We could give you some supplies for the road."

Whitey murmured surprise. We weren't in a position to be handing out charity, between our generator tab and our food bills. He knew better than to question me, though.

Miss Frost and Miss Ash gave each other a long look. "We need to stay on the road long enough for him to lose heart," Miss Frost said. "Then we can find somewhere to settle. We'll work for you, anything you need, for board and protection, until then."

I didn't answer right away. It was a bad idea. Trouble we didn't need. What were the odds two nicely dressed wife types had skills like scrubbing porta-johns and breaking down bleachers and brushing the ever-growing hair of our wolf-girl? Our first show was that night. It had taken two days to prepare and advertise in town. We'd be here for three more days, then on to the next town.

Chicago was a day's drive from here, not far. Letting them stay was risky.

Miss Ash absently put her opposite hand on the fabric of her right arm, over the marks she'd revealed to me. There was a resignation to the gesture.

"Fine," I said and shot Whitey a look at his snort of disbelief. "But my people come first. If you endanger any one of them, you're out of here."

Whitey chased after me when I got up and threaded back through the mobile homes and trucks with camper vans on the way to my trailer. We were still driving then—a caravan of campers and mobile homes and one large semi for the bulk equipment and those too large to travel any other way. Now we have our train caravan like Patrick's, but much nicer.

"What's got into you, Ringmistress? We can't afford two more mouths to feed," he said. "I doubt they know how to do anything."

"My decisions aren't up for discussion." I paused to make sure he understood.

"Of course."

"I don't imagine they'll be here long. Have them move their car to the back lot. Then get them set up in a roustie bunk, with some work garb. They can share." We'd see how they liked the accommodations they'd chosen. It would indicate a great deal about how much help the two of them might be. "And Whitey? Make sure none of the guys hassle them."

He tipped an imaginary cap and turned on his heel. "You got it, Ringmistress," he called over his shoulder.

Whitey wasn't wrong. The decision was an unusually soft-hearted one on my part. The Misses Frost and Ash caught me at just the right moment to elicit my sympathy. Bowling Green wasn't all *that* far from where I'd grown up down in horse country. I was already on edge, and my interrupted sleep hadn't been sound. There were too many old memories that seemed to fill the shadows in every corner, so close to what I'd used to call home.

When I was a little girl, I couldn't imagine being born any luckier. The front pages of the newspapers my daddy brought home and read with me on his lap were filled with stories of the Great Depression and its aftermath, but we were insulated from all that misery. My mother kept house and order with the help of a small coterie of staff, and my father indulged my tomboy nature. My name was Caroline, but he called me Caro.

I was a performer even then, spinning stories that no adult could have possibly believed. The neighborhood boys were all too susceptible. Once when I was eight I convinced Brady Montgomery, the next-door neighbor, that his sister's doll was haunted by the ghost of a murdered woman. I got them both to go through with an entire exorcism. I loudly read from the Bible and Brady made the sign of the cross on the doll's cloth face while his little sister clutched it to her chest. The culmination was setting the doll on fire in the backyard—a fire that unfortunately spread to the hydrangea behind it and led to quite a bit of excitement. After the flames were out, the Montgomery mama marched me back home. I thought Dad would bust a gut laughing once she left with his assurances that I was extremely sorry. My mother insisted I hang out more with the girls at church, and I promptly got in trouble for daring them to do unladylike things like jumping off tree swings in good dresses or playing poker.

But there's a time when you transition from little girl to just girl that changes how men look at you—even fathers. They no longer think unconventional women "cute" once they're closer to grown. We become problems instead.

I made myself a nuisance by beginning to notice things like how we only associated with certain well-off families, the ones my mother claimed had "good breeding," as if they were horses and didn't just own them. I complained about how I didn't particularly like these snobs. I'd much rather hang out with the staff or their kids. Speaking of which, as a teenager, I finally realized my parents were quietly racist. I can't explain why it took as long as it did, other than that I didn't understand how they could believe something so obviously wrong.

I made the mistake of assuming I could be loud about all these things without suffering the consequences. That maybe I'd change their minds.

I'm not sorry for that, or for anything that came later. But my sixteenth year turned into a nightmare I couldn't wake from. It began the day my father introduced me to a man named John Deaton. He had a broad jaw and wore a tailored suit and I didn't understand the significance of our meeting and chattered away to him about the news. That day was the first time my father ever hit me. Right after John left, he struck me with a backhanded smack across the face.

"A godly man is the only thing that can save you now," my father told me and he meant it. "Don't put him off the idea by pretending you understand politics." My mother pulled me aside and told me I should know how lucky I was to have them to look out for me and my future. She told me John Deaton would make me a fine husband. I hadn't put my father's plan together until that moment, my face stinging, swallowing my own blood.

I should've left town on the first train, but when you grow up indulged like I was, you somehow don't think the worst will ever happen to you. John Deaton, who I stood in front of and said "I do" to three months later while trembling with shock, was definitely the worst thing that ever happened to me. I'd thought protesting the marriage would make the preacher come to my aid. When he asked for anyone with objections to speak up, I did. I said I didn't want to be married, not to John or any man. The preacher married us anyway, disapproval for me all over his face. And I paid for my outburst that night. John made me wait for it, his anger coiling inside him like a snake for hours until he struck.

I'm ashamed to admit it now, but I caved under the pressure at first. It's easy to blame women who don't leave, or ask why they allow their husbands to treat them in such a way. No one ever seems to want to point the finger where it belongs: at the men. I quickly discovered John Deaton was more of a monster than I'd ever suspected. No one had taught me how to deal with monsters.

To everyone outside, John was pious, quick with a quote from the Bible, a man's man who was right with god. Inside our home, he did his best to *be* god, the smiting kind from the Old Testament.

John knew I hated it, though: serving him, washing and mending his clothes, being stuck inside and forced to do endless chores—and even more so accompanying him when we went out. He didn't just care if I played the part of dutiful wife. He wanted me to like it. He wanted to break me, which is something I've since discovered most monsters have in common.

And I suppose in a way he did.

My breaking point came in public. It was at a so-called Lunatic Ball at the state's big mental hospital. We'd think of this as absolute savagery now—which it was—something people would never actually do. But back then, it wasn't even that unusual. My parents had bought our tickets. John and my father were entering into business together. It was supposed to be a cozy, familiar affair, attending a fashionable charity party at an asylum together, where late in the evening there'd be the opportunity to dance with the patients.

Most of the families I'd grown up among were there, laughing and joking about how novel an experience this was while eating finger food. Wine and liquor flowed from the open bar at one edge of the ballroom. I could also see everyone's pleasure at my being quietly reduced to one word: wife.

"You should dance," John said, after some plainly overmedicated patients had been brought in for the enjoyment and jeering of the observers. "Come on, Caroline, let's find you a suitable partner."

My father laughed like it was funny. In horror, I let John tow me onto the floor and thrust me at a man quietly murmuring to himself. He'd been dressed in a straitjacket by the staff, which wouldn't make dancing easy for him.

"This one looks about your speed," John said.

I intended to swallow my anger. Gently, I put my hand over the man's waist and on one of his shoulders, and said, "Okay, it's okay." John's grin was wide as I tried to guide the patient away on the ballroom's dance floor.

I assumed I'd get through this, just like any of my daily humiliations. But then I heard what the man was saying to himself, "Don't want to be here, no, don't like this, don't want to be here," over and over and over. My rage woke from where it had been sleeping. And so did my disgust at what I'd let myself become.

I lightly squeezed the patient's shoulder and said, "I'll get you back to your room." I walked him over to one of the line of staff. "This man doesn't want to be here."

"Doesn't matter," the staffer said and frowned in confusion. "He can't hurt you, not with that on."

"No, but he doesn't want to be here. I want him to go back to his room." My voice was raised.

The music paused. John thundered toward me, my father and mother behind him. "What's going on, Caroline, my dear?" he demanded.

"What's going on is that this man is being forced to do something he doesn't want to do. I won't stand for it. Not anymore."

John was smart enough to take my meaning. He ordered me

back to the table, but I refused. I admit I lost my temper. I screamed. I ranted. I barely remember what I said. I probably scared the man I was trying to help.

Meanwhile, John got quieter the louder I became. He saw an opportunity and he seized it. My parents were right there to watch as he signed the emergency commitment papers for me. "Female hysteria" was the reason.

The funny thing was, after my initial intake, I had more freedom in that hospital than I ever did in John Deaton's house. Yes, many there were treated like inmates. And worse. But there was also a massive set of grounds and a farm where those deemed "mildly ill" could get assigned to work. So I waited, pocketing the medicine they gave me and flushing it. I bided my time, working in the gardens and out on the grounds, volunteering to read the newspapers in the common room out loud, and when I overheard some of the staff talking about a circus coming through town . . .

I'd always wanted to go, but Father had considered it a low-class entertainment. Even so, I knew it was one place you could always run off to.

So I did.

The ringmaster, Patrick, found me pitching in with clean-up after the show. "Come with me," he'd said. Now I realize some-one must have alerted him to my presence.

Going with him was a risk. I considered running. But Patrick had the kindest face of anyone I'd ever met or ever would. He could've been a movie star; he had the looks for it. But he loved the circus instead. He still wore his ringmaster's cos-tume: the classic equestrian look with more glitz. "I already know you're not afraid to work," he said outside the tent. "What's your name?"

The sky unfurled above us like a whole fresh set of stars I'd never seen before. "Zara," I said, and so Zara I became.

"Is anyone looking for you, Zara?" he asked, accepting my obviously made-up name without a blink.

"No. I'm just looking for a place I can be."

Patrick studied me, and then nodded. "We'll start with room and board. Salary negotiated based upon your observable skills, after I observe them." He winked, a kindly uncle who thought you were in on the joke.

That I might have lied to Patrick, that one time, still bothers me. I don't know if John Deaton searched for me, or if my father did. They never found me, not while Patrick was still around, anyway, and that was what mattered.

Before our first show in Bowling Green, I passed through the crowd of performers milling on the back side of the tent that night, our makeshift prep area. Bonnie in her shiny silver leotard bouncing on her toes, half of her face made up to match: a deuce whose minor talent played an essential role at the top of the first act. The aerialists stood serene and glittering, one with actual wings like an enormous pink bat who could hang by her toes for far longer than required by any tricks in their act. The joker clowns were clumped nearby in their classic black-and-white makeup, which would be embellished for different gags as the show went on, punching one another and laughing.

This never got old. It felt like walking through the staging area for a dream. For *my* dream.

Like most of the places we toured, Bowling Green was an overpopulated small town. Big enough to have a university, but not so large that people bothered to lock their doors at night back then. Small enough that a lot of people were suspicious of jokers and aces, including the local politicians— particularly given the Jokertown riots that had taken place earlier in the year and dominated the news. We'd paid through the nose for our permits.

Our routine was simple. We set up camp on the outskirts of our chosen cities or at their fairgrounds for a week and advertised as best we could to draw in spectators from around a given region for shows Wednesday through Saturday nights. I'd intentionally decided we'd visit places with relatively few wild cards, and not by accident.

My show had a purpose from the start, inspired by the fact we were launching in 1976, the bicentennial of the United States. Why not focus on more history? Ours. I believed that exposure to our performers—nonthreatening, gently and entertainingly telling the story of what it's like to be us, of what we'd been through—could help with acceptance and perhaps reach children who might someday have cards turn themselves. Lure them in with novelty, an up-close look at the freaks, and send them home with a rosier outlook on us poor unfortunate souls. A way to be loud on behalf of what I cared about, dressed up as harmless fun for the whole family.

Not to mention, there's also fewer kinds of live entertainment to compete with in most of these towns, which could charitably be called shit holes. No offense meant. We've already established that I was born in just such a shit hole myself.

The circus has its seedy side, which I love almost as much as when we turn the glitz and glamour on. I've already mentioned how many people who come to us have a deep mistrust of the police. That's more true now than in the old days, when most elite circus performers came from families with generations of history. The criminal element then was mainly among the crew and the candy butchers. Jokers and aces changed the makeup of the circus and required us to up our game.

Despite what you might guess, the training is—if anything—more intensive for performers these days. Everyone is expected to make the most of their talents. After all, people are paying for a spectacular spectacle, not just to gawk at aces and jokers. They can do that pulling up pictures from Jokertown or visiting it themselves. The crowds we drew then were mainly a credit to our headliner, but the entire show had come together nicely. I was proud of it. Of us.

Speaking of, our star performer was Radha. She approached me as I waited to make my entrance into the tent, small and lovely, brown skin covered in a sheen of glitter to match her spangled leotard. "Zara," she said, "heard we picked up some strays last night."

"We did," I said. I'd seen the Misses Frost and Ash in passing that day, hauling and scrubbing. Rumor had it the elder, Miss Frost, could sew and had been put to work mending costumes. While younger Miss Ash proved to be exceptional at oiling and checking the equipment we used in the big top. That my headliner knew they were here gave me pause, though. "Anything I should worry about?"

"No," Radha said. "I just wanted you to know that I noticed. Patrick would've done the same thing."

No higher praise. We exchanged nods as the music struck up inside.

At the swelling peak of the song, I entered the side entrance of the tent, pausing outside the ring to take in the audience. A good turnout. Lots of kids in tow. The people were in fine moods, smiling and shifting on the bleachers, ready for something different than the local movie theater could supply.

Time to turn on the magic. The band lowered to the faintest drumbeat of rhythm.

"Welcome to Ringmistress Zara's Wildest Show on Earth!"

My voice boomed out as I strode in from the wings, making a circle of the main ring before taking myself to the center for a flourish.

In my full regalia, shimmering makeup applied to accentuate my top hat ridge and my exoskeletal jodhpurs, a coat with tails in the classic style, and my bright red skin, I commanded the attention of everyone in the room. "We're delighted to have you all here tonight, for the *wildest* history lesson of all—ours!"

At my cue line and a lashing crack of my whip arm in the sawdust, Bonnie emerged from the wings, a giant flopping balloon in front of her, her silvered jaw the main part of her Dr. Tod costume. She pressed her lips to it as I interacted with the crowd and then quickly inflated it enough to carry her up, up and above the audience, her helium power and treading feet allowing her to float over their heads as the balloon grew and grew. Children cooed and pointed.

I told the story that went with the visual. "The year was 1946. We were all created by one great and terrible act: A dirigible piloted by Dr. Tod flying over Manhattan as Jetboy struggled to stop him from releasing his bomb. But, of course, he wasn't able to stop the release of the virus!"

Bonnie finished blowing up the balloon and then took her lips away to begin her descent. A winged aerialist dressed as Jetboy pursued her. They tumbled through the air in a fake dogfight. The balloon punctured and the two careened (safely) to the ground. Meanwhile, the confetti cannons fired and rained colorful paper down over the center ring, as the two of them disappeared out the side entrance. Our shape-shifters and costumed performers hid their exit as they emerged to dance and shimmy and caper, mimicking the transformations that had taken place. Radha did a series of handsprings and backflips, weaving between the others.

I could tell by the change of emotion in the room that everyone present rested in the palm of our collective hands. The atmosphere went electric, the audience already applauding. This would be a great night.

The show raced on in high gear. Our ace aerialists simulated Dr. Tachyon and his spaceship *Baby* arriving at the Air Force base—spinning through the air to land light as butterflies—and then careening back up to space in their big finish. Our joker clowns, with their makeup accentuating their bizarre features, mimicked the Exotics for Democracy, freeing nations as a continuing bit between acts. And on and on.

The crowd's delight was palpable. We breathed in their wonder and delight like air.

By the time Radha entered to close the show, still in her lithe, petite form, bounding across the ring doing acrobatics, the anticipation had built to its highest pitch. The rest of the performers were spectacular, but Radha O'Reilly's name put butts in the seats.

"And now, friends," I said, "because we are friends now, aren't we? We have one last wonder in store. She might even be called the eighth wonder of the world. Please welcome the famous Radha O'Reilly, joining us this evening all the way from India!" Radha stopped near me and executed a three-quarter turn to beam out at everyone.

"We must ask that those with heart devices leave the show at this point," I said and we waited in place. So far, no one had taken the cue. This woman being a danger would have seemed ridiculous to anyone who didn't understand her ace power.

"Thank you," I said. "And now I must ask that if you've chosen to remain, you stay in your seats, as you experience the wonder of what humanity is capable of now in one of its purest forms. Our tales this evening have been of the past. But now, let us look ahead to a future—where anything is possible."

I nodded to Radha.

Radha twisted in the way that managed to discreetly cover the shredding of her leotard. As she began to transform, the lights went completely out. Radha pulled energy into her to fuel her change. The crowd gasped. The backup generators kicked on after fifteen seconds.

The lights popped on at once, the spots playing over the magnificent Asiatic elephant marching around the center ring. More gasps and shouts and applause sounded.

Radha in her Elephant Girl form bent to one knee and I hefted myself onto her back. "What we might do in the future," I shouted, "when elephants can fly!"

Radha flapped her ears graceful as palm leaves and her massive body rose as if she was a bird and not one of the largest mammals on Earth. As if her weight meant nothing to gravity. I wore a grin of joy as we flew, diving and swooping over the applauding audience. I believed every word I'd said. I believed this was something akin to a miracle. This beautiful feat, that Radha could *do* this.

I didn't believe anyone could see it and hate us. What can I say? I was old enough to know better, but still young at heart.

Radha and I descended at last and the rest of the performers raced in quickly from the side entrance.

"Close your eyes, ladies and gentlemen, boys and girls," I said.

The lights went out again, all of us waiting while Radha's powers flared in a bright pulse as she changed back to her regular form. Muse Chan, leader of the clowns, handed me a robe, which I passed to Radha and she put on.

"Thank you and good night!" I boomed as the lights came back on, and we paraded around the ring one last time, accepting the adoration on offer.

A tired buzz washed through me as I took the last bow and exited stage left.

After the first night's show in any town, I always circulated through the crowd outside as they made their way home. Overheard reactions sometimes revealed suggestions for tweaks and improvements. And, of course, I could also make sure no one was planning anything that might put our circus family at risk. You'd be surprised how loud some people can get when they feel threatened by something they can't quite name or understand. Or control.

As I strolled through the crowd, smiling and waving at the kids, there were whispers, one to another. But I sensed it wasn't a reaction to me. A quiet sense of unease passed across everyone except the children, and even a few of them picked up on it, sobbing with overexcitement or a well-tuned emotional radar.

I had no idea what was causing the mood to shift, but it was palpable. I wasn't imagining it. I folded myself into a long shadow beside a ring toss tent and listened. I heard a vague "Oh, no" and "Well, what do they think caused it?" and "Really?"

I sought out Whitey, whose performance had been top-notch, as usual. "Find out why the townies are worried all of a sudden."

He gave me a lax salute.

Unsettled, I went back to my trailer to wait. I changed out of my costume, hanging it in a place of pride in the smallish closet, and put on a velvet dressing gown/smoking jacket our tailor had made for me. You can't exactly buy off the rack at nine feet tall.

A knock sounded at the door before long. "Come on in," I said, from my favorite chair—also a custom piece.

But it wasn't Whitey who appeared tentatively when it opened. Miss Frost poked her head in, then hesitated, as if now that I'd told her to come in, she realized she was intruding. She wore her crew garb. A pair of clean, but oddly-fitting pants, and a long-sleeved men's shirt. Her hair was tucked up inside a ball cap. It might not be what she was used to, but it would keep her safer than a more feminine outfit would.

"Miss Frost?" I rose to greet her. "Can I help you? Is anything wrong?"

She knit her hands together. "I just, well, I wanted to thank you. "

"Oh, so it's going well?" I knew that already, but I did the polite thing of pretending I hadn't checked up.

"I think so." She kept her head tilted demurely down. Gone was the more direct woman of last night. "It's a kindness. And I think . . . Miss . . . Ash, I think the work is taking her mind off things."

"Did you get to see the show?" I asked. "Like it?"

"Bits and pieces," she said.

"You should try to catch the whole thing." I had a feeling she needed the educational aspects as much as anyone.

She'd left the door open, barely coming inside, and Whitey appeared behind her now with one of the candy butchers. He gave me a significant look, then one at Miss Frost. She lingered, not taking his meaning.

"If that's all, you can head back to finish the cleanup detail," I said to her. "An extra set of hands is never amiss. Then get some rest. Tomorrow, we do it all again."

I felt an intense pleasure at the idea. Miss Frost only nodded and slipped out with another glance at Whitey.

"There's something about her smell," he said and his nose twitched. "It's not right." Whitey frequently said this kind of thing.

I didn't put much stock in it. He'd as much as admitted his senses were only that keen when expressing his ace. "I imagine she'd say the same about us," I said. "What'd you find out?"

"Sid?" Whitey said.

The candy butcher sold swirls of cotton candy and sweet sodas with his wife. They'd been with Patrick's circus before mine. I trusted them.

"Ringmistress," he said, "there was some talk, started up after intermission. Someone came late and there was news of a . . . death in town. Two deaths."

In a town this size, that would account for the change in mood as it spread after the show. I relaxed a little; it had nothing to do with us. "Were the people a big deal? Lots seemed upset."

"It was—and there was more, afterward. The cops think the couple was murdered," Sid said. "Mayor's nephew and his wife."

That explained even more. Murder couldn't be common here. "Do they know who did it? Jealous husband? Jealous wife?" I asked. "One of them cheating?"

Sid shook his head. "The cops found a silver canister—left open. The deaths looked like asphyxiation, like poison. They're sending it off to a university to do tests."

Now, that *was* odd.

"Maybe we should pack up," Whitey suggested. "Move on to the next stop early."

I understood why he suggested it. We were an unusual

variable here, one that would be too easy to point the finger at. But we had nothing to do with this. "It happened tonight?" I asked. "During the show?"

Sid nodded. "Sounded that way."

"No," I said. "We're not leaving. We had a great show, and we were all occupied during it." And if we left, it would make it look like we were guilty of something. "Just let our people know to stay out of town, okay?"

Whitey nodded.

Sid hesitated. "There was one other thing," he said. "No one can figure out why. No motive."

"It only just happened." But I should have trusted the unease in my gut. "We're only here for a couple more days." I tried to think of that as a comfort.

Whitey turned to leave and paused outside the door. He shot me a look over his shoulder, then said, "Miss Frost? Did you need something else?"

"No," she said, voice barely audible from my vantage. "I just thought I'd wait and walk back over with you. I'm not all that familiar on the grounds yet."

I frowned. The big top couldn't be missed. I didn't like any snoops except my own.

I stood in the doorway and watched the backs of all three of them disappear into the night.

Our version of Wild Cards Day in the circus is madcap fun, a hint of conflict, but then magic and transformation. The real thing was, of course, far more complicated and horrific. We don't so much as hint at the deaths of those who drew the Black Queen.

I'd been with Patrick's circus for several months by the point we set up in Jersey City, right outside New York City, in September 1946. "Stick with me, Zara, and you'll see the world," Patrick liked to say. And ultimately he turned out to be right, but for then New Jersey was the most exotic locale I'd visited. The very idea of being that close to New York thrilled me, but I was determined to keep my head down and work as hard as humanly possible.

So when several of our burlesque performers, who'd become de facto mother figures to me, and a few clowns set out for a day trip to go shopping and see the sights, I stayed behind.

We gathered bits and pieces of what was happening in New York from New Jersey media and stories and reactions from locals. And from the transformations and the dead.

Even outside the city, we had more than a few.

Patrick's expression grew grimmer by the hour. "What do we do, boss?" the crew kept asking. "Pack up, but we wait," Patrick said.

I was sent into town to buy extra ice for a train car we'd cleared for our dead. We would not be leaving them behind, but we would be leaving. We'd find a circus cemetery to lay them to rest in. Such locations dotted the country, little known but within the community.

But I'm getting ahead of myself. I carried panic like that bomb had gone off in my chest as I did what I was ordered. Patrick paced and packed, packed and paced.

Finally, just when I thought we might leave without them, those who would return that day straggled in. They had their arms looped around one another. They had the air of refugees from a great battle. There was Lucy, an Irish burlesque dancer with a sharp tongue, whose skin had turned a pale green and who vomited both gold and pyrite, unpredictably—about as fun as it sounds. She'd come to be known as Lucky Lucy. Tuck, our head clown, previously puckishly handsome, was now doubly so—Mirror Image, he'd come to be called, with a second identical head atop his neck. T2 as we called him, was the sarcastic to Tuck's—T1's—charming. Later, they did a bit where T1 sang arias and T2 made rude noises. And there was poor Vania, a dancer now covered in scales head to toe, who felt as if she'd become a monster in the excruciating, painful blink of an eye. Later, she'd shimmy and sway as the Dragon Lady. And then there were the four who didn't come back.

Patrick embraced Lucy and Tuck and the unchanged dancers and clown, one by one. He used the handkerchief he always kept on hand to dry Vania's tears, then pressed it into her hand. They all went to prepare for departure. Quiet. Tired. Trembling.

"Do we need to get the others?" I asked Patrick, quietly, once we were alone. "I can check morgues. I'm not afraid to go in."

I was desperately afraid.

We stood under a sky the gray of ash. Though we were learning more about what had happened, we still didn't know everything. But we knew that the world had altered forever. The others hadn't needed to explain what they'd gone through, beyond the fact they were the only survivors from the excursion party.

"No," Patrick said. "The bridges will be closed soon, if they aren't already. They would understand. We have to protect our own. We leave now, while we can. We get as far from this as possible."

We left as night fell, lucky to get the train going anywhere. There was an argument at the station, about whether rail travel had closed down already or not and if we should be allowed to depart.

I lurked behind Patrick as I watched him work his magic on the two men in the train office, just as surely as he did in the ring. Wheedling and storytelling and convincing until those men would have let us go anywhere.

As our lead car shook and started to move Patrick rubbed his cheek, raked a hand through his hair. It would turn out to be the only time we ever pulled up stakes and left before our shows were done. That's probably one reason I was so resistant to leaving early in '76.

"What's going to happen?" I asked Patrick. He had all the answers as far as I was concerned.

"I can't say," he said, which worried me. Until he added: "But the world will always need circuses."

Thursday evening's Bowling Green show went off with a few minor hitches the audience didn't even notice. Georgette, aka Couteau, French for *knife* in honor of her ability to toss any flaming knife, shoot any bow and arrow, and hit any target blindfolded or with her back to the crowd. She had a misfire of one of her trusty throwing blades saved by the fake blindfold of her partner in life and the act, Victoria. Victoria's special gift was reflexes that might or might not have been natural and steady nerves that definitely were. Still, the near-miss unsettled me. I asked her afterward, "You two arguing?"

"No," she assured me. "Something distracted me. Movement in the rigging." She shook her head.

That was in itself strange, but she shrugged it off and so I did, too. The audience had been slightly more subdued, so the mood shift happened in a different way than the night before. As they filtered out into the night, there were gasps and the frantic whispers of spreading gossip. A woman looked back at the tent, the glow of a security light bathing her, with what could only be described as fear.

Whitey appeared at my shoulder before I could seek him

out. I steered us away from the crowd. The rumble of conversation had that electric charge like before a storm. Like lightning could strike us at any moment.

"It happened again," he said.

Ah. "Tell me what you know."

We walked through the trailers on the back lot, doors open and music and the pops of bottles wafting out of them. The nighttime circus symphony, what would soon be filled with laughter. On cue, I heard the Chans' children giggle, no doubt getting a dramatic bedtime story. Their mother, Muse, was head clown and her face transformed at will, a comedy/tragedy mask in the flesh. She made it charming instead of terrifying—usually. Her husband's card turned at fifteen; so-called Zip or Zippy was frenetic, fast, and consumed about 10,000 calories a day. Luckily, his ability to demonstrate his speed on command in the ring was worth the expense. We waited in silent agreement until we'd passed their trailer.

"The same MO as the first," Whitey said, like he was some old-time detective. "Poison gas. A canister left behind. Results expected back on the first tomorrow. Cops are freaked out and . . . the gossip had a turn to it. Speculation."

"You don't say," I responded.

The *whoop whoop* of sirens sounded as a car crawled in the back entrance to the fairgrounds, lights flashing. They'd done us that solid at least, not pulling up in the middle of the departing crowd. Something told me the word would spread about this visit quickly, anyway.

"My least favorite kind of light show," Whitey said.

"Mine too. Tell everyone to stay inside. Get Dozer. I'll go roll out the red carpet."

The cruiser pulled up close to the back edge of where we were camped. Beyond there was a thick stand of trees. My trailer was one of the closest to the road, because I waited to park until last so I always led the caravan out. Tradition. Bonnie poked her head out of a trailer across the way and I shook my head. She disappeared inside.

I strode forward to meet the police car, refusing to squint in its lights. I put on my authority as surely as I did when I entered the ring.

The cops turned off the car and, for a moment, I wondered if I should've waited for Dozer. A glance over my shoulder told me that my people were watching, out of windows or leaving doors open. I'd meant for them to turn a blind eye. I'd have to tread even more carefully. The police weren't the only ones who could escalate this situation.

"Evening, Officers," I said, when they got out of the car. I thought the man who shut his door first might draw on me, despite the fact my normal hand was lifted in the universal language of "no threat here," palm up and open. My whip arm dangled at my side.

"You the one runs this freak show?" the other said.

So it was definitely going to be that kind of conversation.

"I have that honor." I paused. I couldn't see either of their faces well. I didn't want them in my space, but . . . "What can I help you with? We could meet in my trailer, if you like."

"No thanks. Tempted to put you in the back of the cruiser," said freak-show cop. "But you wouldn't fit."

"Why would you need to do that, anyway?" I regretted not being the kind of looker who could sell my next line. "What seems to be the trouble, Officer? Why are you here?"

I heard footsteps behind me. On the one hand, Dozer's presence might escalate things. On the other, it gave us a fighting chance if it did. Whitey would be hanging back somewhere nearby, and he would help, too.

"We've had some suspicious deaths occurring while you've been here in town." The first cop was the one who spoke.

"We heard the news about that poor couple." Time to let them know we wouldn't be pushovers. "From what I could tell, it happened during our performance. Are we in danger?"

The cops approached slowly. Seeing their faces, hard and suspicious, didn't make me feel better. "You think we're here because you're in danger?" the first said. "Can you believe this?"

Freak-show cop said, "Looking at her, I could believe anything."

"Now," Dozer said, uncovered torso gleaming in the moonlight, "there's no reason to be rude."

"You too," the first cop said. "Freak."

"Why are you here, then?" I said with as much calm as I could summon. I put a hand on Dozer's arm.

"Just seems like a coincidence," one of them said, "that you show up and all of a sudden we've got people being murdered. We wanted to let you know, officially, that if there's any more coincidences, we'll be back."

The air felt sour. "Noted," I said. "For the record, I'd like you to know that we have absolutely nothing to do with this. We're here to perform, that's all." I was just angry enough to keep going. "I can get you some free tickets, if you want."

Dozer snorted.

The cops turned and got back in their car and left.

"You think that's the end of it?" Dozer asked.

"Only if we're lucky. Make sure *no one* goes anywhere near town. Send one of the local advance guys we hired if we need something."

Dozer nodded and I began to calculate the math of pulling up stakes and cooling our heels for an extra weekend at our next jump. We'd lose two nights and one matinee's worth of receipts. Might be worth it.

– – –

But that didn't turn out to be an option. We got word the Nashville TV news ran a story on Friday morning saying that the test results had confirmed the canisters contained a VX nerve agent and the deaths were due to exposure. VX apparently required very little contact with to cause death; this had been applied directly to the victims' skin. They would have died within minutes. A stockpile of various chemical weapons, including VX, was maintained by the Army a few hours away in Richmond. The military spokesperson denied any were missing.

Oh, and the media also threw in that our circus was being entertained by local police as a possible "pool of suspects." It seemed every outlet in the area, print, TV, and radio, had picked the story up by noon. One shock jock speculated on air whether any of us had the power to make nerve agents with our breath "or something." No one seemed to care that we had zero reason to want random members of a community dead. All they were to us were potential audience members.

Journalists showed up to sniff around the big top, and Dozer had none-too-gently sent them on their way. A TV anchor did a stand-up from the road with it in the background, however. We couldn't stop that without appearing aggressive.

If we left now, we'd also look guilty and this would follow us. Our whole point was that people should be accepting and not fear us. It might ruin the entire season, which would mean ruining my ability to carry on Patrick's legacy. At least for the foreseeable future. So we had to stay.

We only had two more nights of shows. Tonight, then Saturday. Ticket sales, ironically enough, were up. The old saying there's no such thing as bad publicity isn't true. But at that moment it might as well have been.

I was outside feeling angry at the world when Miss Frost and Miss Ash drove up the road onto the back lot in their battered sedan. No one was supposed to leave the property. I'd repeated these orders at morning mess, and knew they'd been reinforced by Dozer and Whitey, too.

They parked in their usual spot and got out, wearing the same clothes they'd been in the night we discovered them.

"Where have you been?" I asked.

They would barely look at me. "We're sorry," Miss Ash said. "I just . . . I needed a break."

"From the people helping and hiding you?" I wasn't inclined to feel sympathetic.

"She's barely more than a girl," Miss Frost said, defensive. "She wanted a good meal. Is that a crime? We went to a diner. She had some steak and eggs. That's all."

The use of the word *crime* wasn't lost on me. Or the insult to our cooks. But I had no choice but to take her word for it. They'd been stealthy enough to slip off without anyone noticing.

"Hear anything interesting out there?" I asked. "You're welcome to hit the road now, if you think anyone here has done something wrong."

Miss Frost hesitated. It was Miss Ash who spoke up. "I didn't like hearing them accuse you. You've . . . you've all been nothing but kind."

"Then don't test that kindness again." I waited to see if Miss Frost had more to say, but she only nodded.

"Get changed. We'll need all hands on deck during the show tonight—just in case."

They at least had the sense not to ask in case of what.

The crowd's temperature that night was volatile. Half-cold, half-hot. We were professionals, and could pretend not to hear the jeers and comments every so often, the applause when it came more measured. But it made for an exhausting experience.

While the show went on, we were supposed to be in control of what they saw and felt about us. The police's lies and the public's bad assumptions had changed that. There was an air of being animals in a zoo. Which is why I looked especially forward to Whitey's act; it was the most appropriate of the entire evening.

"We remember all too well those dark days when Joseph McCarthy turned his sights to the persecution—the unwarranted persecution—" I added, especially for the listeners, and ignored a snort of derision from a man directly in front of me in the second row, "—of Wild Cards. He, in effect, decided to turn good people into rats and himself into, well, the rat-catcher."

Whitey strutted into the ring in a suit and tails in a way that never failed to make me smile. "The Rat-catcher, that's me," he said, softly, though his mic made sure it carried. "But I need some rats to pursue first . . ." He smiled and stroked his pointy chin as he scanned the crowd. He meant it as a threat to the audience. He hadn't taken the turn in opinion against us well.

Whitey didn't take much well. It endeared him to me.

I headed over to the side of the ring while he removed his coat and put it casually over a shoulder, strolling and doing his patter.

Miss Frost and Miss Ash were beneath the bleachers, watching from between the slats. Back in their roustie togs. Miss Ash gave me a nervous smile.

Finally, Whitey threw his arms out and his body exploded into the rats he took his name from. Hundreds—we boasted the number 1,000, but had never exactly counted—of milk-white rats circled the ring in a choreographed dance of leaping and running. They were obviously controlled, a bizarre chorus line. Whitey became the rats, but he still steered each one of them. I asked him to explain what it felt like once, being spread across so many consciousnesses, and he shrugged and said, "Can't. It's all me. I'm just multifaceted."

He could only pull it off once a day, max. And it was an amazing thing to watch, hundreds of snowy rats jumping through hoops the clowns brought out or evading their butterfly nets, while the clowns themselves made jokes about McCarthy, who had been no laughing, bumbling matter. I scanned the crowd to see how it was playing, and my eyes caught on that spot in the second row. Was this the same man who'd made the derisive snort?

My blood ran as cold as if McCarthy himself was after me with the net. I hadn't seen him in long years. I'd obviously changed much more than he would've. But I could swear that the man watching, stern-faced and disapproving, was none other than John Deaton. My husband still, legally.

"What's wrong, Ringmistress?" Miss Frost appeared at my side.

I shook my head. "Nothing, of course. Just a tough crowd tonight."

She made a sympathetic noise.

Under the lights, the rats headed toward center of the ring en masse, where they'd return to Whitey's pale human form once more. The rest of the clowns entered the ring dressed as the Four Aces and quickly concealed his now-naked form and pulled him from the ring, like McCarthy off the stage and into infamy and obscurity. He returned a moment later to wave a top hat, back in a second suit and tails. He waited for me to arrive beside him so he could bow and then go take off the "real rat suit" as he called it.

What else could I do? I did my job. I reentered the ring and talked about how we'd never repeat the evil of the McCarthy era because people are good and learned their lesson (to eye rolls) and tried not to notice that the man in the second row who might have been my husband had left.

It's not as if I had much hope of sleeping after that show and the man who looked like John made him a ghost haunting my thoughts. So I decided to pitch in on the watch and take a walk around the grounds.

There was no way the actual John Deaton could know about *me*, was there? If it had been him—which was unconfirmed—could his presence be simple coincidence? Could the news coverage have drawn him as a disapproving spectator? I was an entirely different person now. By name, by spirit, by vocation.

John Deaton would never want anyone to know he had ever been associated with me, the hideous female ringmaster joker. A woman so loud I didn't even use a mic to project in the tent. I could be certain of that much, at least, couldn't I? But then, if he did know . . . If he *was* here for me, the reason might be more sinister.

I didn't think John had it in him to challenge me. He'd loved being the bigger in a fight, the more physically powerful, and now he wouldn't be. I could defend myself, more than he knew. Did he have it in him to kill? Yes. I briefly thought about the murders. But I didn't see him as smart enough to pull off something like these VX attacks. What would the point be? If he was here for me, it was either for a divorce or as a threat. Or both.

His disappearance during the show meant it probably hadn't been him.

I took the big top fabric in my fist and pushed it aside to

enter. As soon as I entered the darkened tent I startled as I made out a hunched form, in a pale nightdress in the moonlight, messing around with the lightboard and sound booth. Then I got closer, and I recognized who it was.

"Miss Ash?"

She didn't jump or flinch, but she went still. I could see enough of her in the thin light from the booth to show me her shoulders moving up and down with a deep breath in, then out. She turned to face me. "Ringmistress," she breathed. "I'm sorry. I know I shouldn't be in here."

"You shouldn't," I agreed. "So why are you?"

"I couldn't sleep. Or, well, I was asleep, but then I had a dream . . ." She paused. "It was like he was here, watching me. I couldn't just stay still and I didn't want to wake up M—"

Her voice had escalated as she talked. "He's not here," I said. I could understand the racing of her thoughts. Or so I assumed. "I'll walk you back to bed."

"Thank you, Ringmistress," she said and hit a combination of buttons that darkened the board.

"What were you doing?" I asked. "It's nice that you're taking an interest."

I didn't want to spook her into not answering.

She wrung her hands together. "I think all the mechanical stuff is amazing," she said. "I just wanted to learn how it all works." She gave me a tentative smile and lifted her hands to separate them. "Boom! And confetti. I've never seen the like."

We crossed the grounds silently after that. It was quieter than normal, no one much up or about. There was a safety in staying inside and pretending nothing unusual was going on in this town. That nothing was a danger to us, as long as we kept our heads down, performed, and got out of here as soon as we finished our run.

When we approached the roustie bunks—a semi divided

up into sleeping quarters—it wasn't so peaceful. Someone else *was* awake. Miss Frost, her arms filled with contraband from the canteen car. A jug of water. A trash bag presumably filled with food. Who knew what else?

"Stealing from us?" I asked.

Miss Ash had frozen again, her go-to move when surprised, apparently.

Miss Frost blinked. "There, ah, there you are, dearie," she said to Miss Ash. "I was afraid he'd come. That he'd gotten you. I'm sorry, I just thought I would have to go after her and . . ."

"I understand," I said.

And I thought maybe I was beginning to. They were flouting orders. They'd left the premises. They knew how sympathetic I was. Had they brought John Deaton here? For a moment, I entertained the wild possibility he was the man Miss Ash was running from.

There was a simpler explanation, however.

I left them there with a "good night." When I returned to my own trailer, Whitey sat on the outside of it. "Boss," he said.

"I have a job for you," I told him.

My card turned three years after Wild Cards Day, when I was 20. I knew it was a possibility, obviously. We all did by then. But there wasn't a way to live your life assuming it would or wouldn't happen. So, for me, at least, I continued to assume I'd always be who I was and to help Patrick by doing whatever he needed to keep the circus going as it changed.

Changed, but still existed. He was right. People still needed the circus, and a whole lot of jokers and aces needed us, too. The circus life has always been a safe harbor for the misfits, the true outcasts, the ones who don't fit in anywhere but have something special to give despite that. Patrick was part boss, part showman, part therapist. And, for me, he was part father.

We were in Quebec for a show—the French, even French Canadians, love circuses more than anyone else on Earth—and had a packed house. As usual, I wore a funny echo of Patrick's costume, so I could run him objects during the show.

In this case, I darted out carrying the prop whip he'd circle in the air in his traditional glitzy equestrian ringmaster costume to release the ring to our actual, whipless Liberty horse act. It was led by a charming joker named Irina from Russia who was fourth-generation circus. When her card turned, it had left her with a mohawk of a mane and eyes positioned like a horse's that gave her an enhanced line of sight. Her animals would do anything for her, because she treated them as equals. It was like, in her they recognized part of themselves.

I suppose it was the same for me with Patrick.

In the ring, I passed him the whip, and then I bent double, wracked by sudden heat and sharp pain. And then . . . my card turned. With everyone watching.

I grew to the height I am now. I watched my skin deepen to this red. My head felt like it burst, producing its ridge, and my legs erupted with the exoskeletal protrusions. Last of all went my left arm. At first, when I saw it, I thought I was still holding Patrick's prop whip.

Patrick pretended it was part of the show. No one bought it, but he tried.

Then he gave his typical callout for Irina, and he put his arm underneath mine to help me up and out of the ring. The crowd applauded at the spectacle and then at the horses and their magnificent prancing entrance.

I towered over Patrick as we left the tent. "Focus on me," he said, sensing the moment I began to truly panic. What was I? What had happened to me?

I looked down into his kind, supportive, comforting face. "Good," he said. "Good."

"I want to see," I said.

I could talk, so that was something. I hadn't lost the power of speech. Some people did.

"I should think so," Patrick said. He led me past the gawp- ing mostly joker clowns, and toward a mirrored table where makeup touch-ups happened. The crowd of performers back- stage parted to let us by.

Patrick nudged me to face him before we were quite close enough to the mirror. "Are you ready to see?" he asked.

"I think so," I said.

He held my still-normal right hand and squeezed it as we turned together and moved closer. I looked into the mirror . . .

And what I saw there . . .

Yes, I was fairly unrecognizable to myself. The structure of my face was similar, but red, and everything else . . . When you put it all together, I saw what I'd become. The ridge, my top hat. My legs, their own jodhpurs. I'd never need a prop whip.

I was a ringmaster.

"I've been wondering who might take over when I'm gone," Patrick said then. "What do you think? Do you want to be ringmistress someday?"

"Yes," I breathed.

Patrick was something as important as any of his other roles to me, after that day. He was my mentor. He entrusted me with his life's work, with what he considered his mission. To enter- tain, yes, and also to protect our family at any cost.

He was not one to allow behavior that hurt others. Our cir- cus was to be a refuge, and all the more after the virus entered the world.

"Our protective instincts exist for a reason," he told me

once, not long before he died. "For whatever reason, a lot of our people present to predators as prey. Because they were once lonely or alone, it reads as vulnerability. Or they're treated like predators for their oddness, or pretend to be that, when they're anything but. As leaders, we don't have the luxury of turning off our skepticism about outsiders—or about new people of our own—not until we're sure of them."

I'd told him I was lucky he'd taken me in, then.

"My skepticism didn't present for you at all, Zara," he'd said. "You were born to be one of us. Otherwise I'd have left you where I found you."

Whitey had various tails—no pun intended—keeping an eye on the Misses Frost and Ash all day, but according to his regular reports back, no suspicious behavior had presented itself. They'd done their assignments like good worker bees.

As showtime neared and I got dressed in my trailer, I'd almost decided I was wrong that they were up to something. Despite what people often say, I'd never met any woman who would make false claims or pretend at abuse. The idea that I had now, and that I'd been taken in by it, turned my stomach.

I pulled the jacket of my costume on and checked in the mirror to make sure the sequin lapels were straight. The jacket's left side had a sequin-bordered arm hole at the shoulder designed to show off my whip arm. I traced the line of glitter down each cheekbone with my right index finger. Good enough.

We were going to be performing to a sold-out crowd. Members of the media had been caught trying to sneak around the back lot during the day. They were politely asked to leave and come back when the grounds were open to the public. There'd been no sign of John Deaton or the man who looked like him.

A restless tension circulated through me as I left my sanctuary and walked toward the Big Top. Whitey met me before I hit the crowd proper.

"You were right," he said, twitchy and wired as a junkie. "It's bad."

"Show me," I said.

We got a few curious glances as we passed through the milling performers out back of the big top. I put on a smile for them. "We're almost out of here," I said, loud enough they could all hear.

Radha and several others nodded in relieved approval.

"Not almost enough," Whitey muttered.

I quieted him with a glance. He'd take my meaning. No need to alarm anyone else, not yet. The tent was already filling. We had maybe fifteen minutes to spare before the start. A couple of the clowns were doing a bit down front to entertain while people came in, and Sid was strolling up and down the stands selling cotton candy from a passel hung around his neck.

"We gotta go up," Whitey said and nodded toward the rigging.

I hesitated. "Where are *they*?"

"Oh, Dozer took care of that. The so-called Misses will be waiting when you're ready to see them."

A small relief.

There were access points for the rigging at various places around the tent, mostly used by the aerialists and for the initial confetti release. That got set up before the performance and triggered from the sound and light board below, though we usually had a man up there in case something malfunctioned and it had to be triggered by hand.

That was the point Whitey steered me toward, a steel ladder positioned behind the back of the stands that would take us most of the way. The rest we climbed on the sturdy metal railings. No one below paid us any attention.

"What are we looking at?" I asked when we got close to the confetti cannons. There were three, with a few extra barrels so the confetti would disperse evenly across the crowd, all doubled so it could keep going as long as we wanted it to.

"Miss Frost volunteered to help load these," Whitey said. "Insisted she could do it on her own. They let her. I came back to double-check."

"And?"

Whitey slowly opened the back of one of the cannon barrels, which slid like a shelf. Usually it was filled with the tight-packed cartridges that released the colorful paper rain. Today, there was instead what looked to be several balloons made of a very thin layer of clear plastic enclosing an amber liquid.

"We can't be sure what it is without killing ourselves," Whitey said, "but I believe that's some kind of slickly produced plastic baggie full of VX. They planned to seal the exits."

That explained Miss Ash's interest in the board that controlled the confetti release the night before. The force of the ejection would burst the containers and release VX onto the performers and the crowd. Everyone came into the tent for the simulated virus release at the top of the show. They planned to kill us all.

And everyone would think *we* had done it.

I scrambled to come up with a plan. "Can we just skip the release?"

"Yes," he said. "But—"

I'd reached the same conclusion. "We can't—we can't leave it here during the show. We can't be sure they don't have some sort of fail-safe. Someone working with them. If anything went wrong . . ."

We both looked down at the tent full of people, half of them who probably considered us murderers already. They could never know we were about to save them.

"Here's what we're going to do," I said. "Get the generators ready. Radha will be changing early tonight."

The next fifteen minutes were a flurry of activity. Everyone obviously knew something was up when I started barking orders and telling people to do things they didn't normally— and particularly when the clowns were directed to get everyone sitting in the stands outside in front of the tent.

Backstage, I pulled Radha aside. "What's going on?" she asked.

"Those strays? Bad news," I said. "The worst news. I'll explain everything later. Right now, I need you to start the show. Fly around and keep them entertained out here for a bit while we get something that shouldn't be there down from the rigging." I considered. "Don't change back after you finish. We may need you to help with transport."

Those confetti cannons did get hefted up and down into the rigging, but it was a multistage process involving lots of rope and cursing. An Asiatic elephant would be faster.

The thing was, no one asked questions. Because they trusted me. They trusted one another. If we were doing this, there was a reason.

I deputized Muse Chan to perform my duties as ringmaster, because she had an outfit that was a play version of mine. She carried a red rubber whip with it and everything. I told her to announce we were giving them the "wildest show on Earth tonight," and no one would ever witness its like again.

I didn't add: *For good or bad.*

By the time I rushed back into the tent, it was clear of any civilians. Whitey and steel-nerved Victoria and a few longtime rousties were oh-so-gingerly moving the confetti cannons down with the ropes.

"Radha can carry them when she finishes," I said. "One at a time."

Which made me think who could go on next. We'd need to keep the people outside for a while longer.

I ran back out and flagged over the acrobats and the two aerialists who could fly under their own power. "You're on after Radha. Outside. I'll take over when we're ready to resume the normal order."

"Yes, Ringmistress," echoed back at me.

The outdoor lights went dark and then brightened and the crowd began to cheer. I looked up to see Radha as elephant gracefully looping through the night sky. There were oohs and ahhs. They might've hated us, suspected us, come to jeer, but no one could deny a once-in-a-lifetime sight like that.

"We're ready," Whitey said, when I got back inside. Sweat streaked his face.

The three cannons sat stacked in a row where they could be easily accessed by pulling up the back edge of the tent fabric.

"Thanks, everyone," I said. "Just a little longer now."

I went back outside to wait for Radha's landing. She set down a few feet from me a couple minutes later.

"Please, be careful," I told her. Her elephant eyes gazed at me and her big head nodded. "You're taking these back toward the forest. Dozer's preparing a deep hole. We bury them. We leave here alive and well. Please, be careful."

She lifted her trunk and patted my shoulder with it. A *there there* gesture of friendliness.

I led her over to the tent's edge and Whitey sprang into motion, clearing the way for her. She easily lifted the first of the heavy cannons with her trunk, both cautious and steady.

Whitey scrambled up her side and onto her back. "I'll show

you where to go," he said. Who knew if it was necessary, or if he'd just always wanted to ride on a flying elephant? I wouldn't blame him either way.

More applause sounded from around the front of the tent. I wiped my own brow with my right sleeve and watched Radha's stately progress toward the back lot until she finally lifted up to sail low—out of view of the crowd in front—toward the trees.

I nodded to those still assembled. "Good work, everyone," I said. "After we get through tonight, drinks are on me."

And then I drew my shoulders back and marched tall and proud around front and said, "Ladies and gentlemen, girls and boys, please allow me to escort you personally into the tent . . ."

The last thing I wanted to do was look at those two traitors and decide what to do with them. But that's not a choice you get to make, not when you're running the show. And it turned out to be easier than I expected. But I'm getting ahead of myself.

Whitey had asked Dozer to stash the two of them in Whitey's trailer, and posted a roustie who'd "never liked them" on watch. I'd never been inside Whitey's home on wheels before and had no idea what to expect when he led me there after the show. I dismissed the stagehand and told him to get some rest.

The inside of the trailer was sparsely decorated and immaculate. "Nice place," I said and attempted not to sound so surprised.

"Except for the new furniture," Whitey countered.

Miss Frost and Miss Ash—or whatever their real names were—sat on a spotless white vinyl couch, their hands tied behind their backs and their feet tied at the ankles. The ropes at their feet looked unforgivingly snug.

"Please," Miss Frost said, "you don't understand."

"He should've gagged them," Whitey said.

"Don't be hasty," I told Whitey. "I want my explanations. Let's hear what they have to say."

The rest of the show had been a bit off-kilter, but careened forward with a—well—wild energy that made it one of our most memorable. The crowd almost seemed to sense they'd dodged some sort of danger. The overall experience of the show would've made me think fondly of Bowling Green, but for everything else that happened.

"You deserve that," Miss Ash said. "You do. An explanation."

She exchanged a look with Miss Frost, who sighed. "We didn't choose you by accident. I used to . . . I worked for the CIA for a time. Doing background checks. I dug around and found your secrets."

My secrets. So there was a chance that had been John Deaton. "Whitey, would you mind giving us a moment in private?"

"Not at all, boss." He smiled at both of them.

After he'd gone, I narrowed my eyes. "You found my husband."

"Yes," Miss Frost admitted. "It was clear you'd be . . . sympathetic to Miss Ash from what happened to you."

"Why was he here, then? The other night?"

Miss Frost frowned. "We didn't contact him. That much I swear to you."

"Why the VX? Why any of that? Where did you get it?"

There was a hesitation and then Miss Ash spoke. "My husband is a bad man. He found us, and he told us what to do if we wanted to live this time."

There was a knock at the door and a man shoved his way in past Whitey. Barrel shoulders, cold eyes. Could I have stopped him? Maybe. Probably, even.

We could've called the police. We could've tried to get them to believe all this.

Miss Ash trembled. I knew who the man was before he said a word.

I stood. "You are never to cross our paths again. You got that?"

He didn't speak, but he let out a tight nod. Then he cut the ties at their ankles and the last thing I remember of the Misses Frost and Ash was the lack of apology for anything they'd done. I didn't feel bad about letting him take them.

I still don't. We never saw them again.

I lean back into my chaise in my train car. "And that's the story," I tell Hannah Davis, rapt across from me.

She asks a few more questions, perhaps buying all of it, perhaps not.

"He—they—would be the kind of people who could have committed that crime," I say. "Two women like that don't end up with enough VX to kill a town without powerful backers. I have to thank you for coming to talk. I'll be increasing our security. I'm sure Pigtail's waiting outside to help you out."

Hannah Davis nods, and thanks me back, and she leaves.

I sit and sip cold tea, and I reflect on what happened to them, in truth. I want to help catch the people behind the Our Lady of Perpetual Misery, but not enough to confess everything.

The two of them did admit to discovering my history and using it against me. They admitted to planting the VX, but they refused to give up who supplied it. Or why they'd done it in the first place.

And there had never been any husband arriving to fetch them, if there had even been a husband to begin with.

Was I supposed to just let them go? I had a duty.

Not many people know about my ace power, and I'm not ever planning to add another in any kind of law enforcement. So, when I took their lives, it was quicker and more painless than they deserved, but it was—oh, irony—with poison. My whip arm isn't just a whip. It also turns into a snake with fast, furious fangs.

I use my gift rarely. But if I ever see John Deaton in truth, he'd best not approach me. Not these days.

As for the bodies, well, Whitey is one of the people I trust most in the world. His rats are always hungry. We purposely skipped his act during that night's show, figuring the crowd weren't big McCarthy humor fans, anyway.

I took care of the Misses Frost and Ash, and he took care of the evidence. We kept our people safe, and we still do.

The Ashes of Memory

3

Hannah left Zara's RV, walking out into the light illuminating the circus grounds in the parking lot. She fought against the flow of the crowd coming toward Ebbets to see the circus, musing on what Zara had told her. It was a tragic tale, but it didn't seem to fit at all into the fire at Father Squid's church; in fact, unlike Chop-Chop's tale, there was no fire at all involved—and unless Dr. Sheets's autopsy of the victims found something entirely out of the expected, there was no horrible chemical agent involved in the deaths there.

Quasiman's two leads didn't fit. They didn't connect at all except they both involved attacks on jokers.

"Hannah?"

"Shit," Hannah muttered under her breath at the sound of the now-familiar voice. She turned to look to her right. Quasiman was standing there near the cotton candy booth. He hobbled over toward her, leaning heavily to his left as if that leg could barely support him.

"You spoke with the Ringmistress?" he asked.

"I did. And what happened to her had *nothing* to do with the fire at Father Squid's church. Nothing. And neither did Tanaka's story, for that matter. So if you don't mind, I don't need any more bad leads from you."

"But it's true," Quasiman persisted. "It's all connected. I've seen it. How can I convince you?"

"I'm afraid you can't."

The crowd around them had stopped moving. They stood in a rough circle around the duo, as if they thought that they might be part of the act they were about to see. Quasiman's left arm vanished, and the crowd applauded. "You see," someone said. "Part of the show."

Quasiman didn't seem to notice the missing arm. He gestured at her with his right hand. "If you *did* believe me, what would you do now?" he asked.

Hannah sighed, trying to ignore everyone around them. "I *don't* believe you."

"But if you did, Hannah, what would you do?"

Hannah sighed again, looking around to see if there was a break in the ring of people watching them through which she could flee. "I don't know. At least Tanaka's story was about a fire, so I might look up the guy he called Troll, probably, just to verify—"

Quasiman's face had lit up. He didn't give her a chance to finish. "Good!" he exclaimed. "The clinic's this way. Hurry." The hunchback waved a hand at her, then set off toward the Ebbets Field main entrance, limping badly. His pants flapped strangely around his right thigh, as if most of the muscles that should have been there weren't. *No wonder he's gimpy.* Quasiman never looked back to see if she was following.

"Quasiman!"

The joker didn't answer. Hannah stood, hands at her sides.

The crowd was still gathered around her, waiting to see what would happen next. There was a break in the onlookers where Quasiman had gone. "Go on, Hannah," one of them called out. "That joker can't walk far. Look at him."

"Damn it," she said. "This isn't fair."

But she followed, and so did several of their audience. "Quasiman!" He halted, looking back at her. *The least you can do is give the poor joker a ride to wherever he's going.* She waved down one of the taxis that had stopped to drop off people going to the circus. "Get in," she told Quasiman.

Their audience applauded again.

The connection didn't hit her until she saw the name engraved in stone over the doors of the clinic building: BLYTHE VAN RENSSAELER MEMORIAL CLINIC. Hannah remembered history classes and documentaries about the wild card, and now strange echoes of those were awakened. She was walking in a world where figures lived and walked who had only been names in books and newspaper articles: the alien Dr. Tachyon, whose people had brought the wild card virus to Earth; Tachyon's ill-fated love affair with Blythe, the wife of Henry van Renssaeler, which had ended during the HUAC hearings with Blythe's insanity, back in the fifties.

And now a joker named Chop-Chop had given her a tale about Blythe's daughter and Henry's plot to burn down Jokertown, and Ringmistress Zara had given her an equally odd tale of someone trying to poison a mass number of people to blame it on jokers. Tanaka was right about one thing. Nothing was simple here.

After leaving the taxi, Quasiman stopped at the walk leading to the building. "Hey!" Hannah called. The joker looked back at her but there was no recognition in his eyes. He scowled at her and started to walk back the way they'd come. Hannah stepped into the grass to avoid him. "Fuck," Hannah said. If she hadn't already been in front of the place, she would have left.

But she went in, flashed her Arson Bureau ID to the joker at the front desk, whose twin necks supported two identical and normal-looking heads. The nameplate on the desk proclaimed him to be *Better Than One*. Hannah suppressed a sigh and told him that she needed to speak to Troll.

"Just a moment," one head said. The other finished the sentence: "If you'll just take a seat over there . . ." He pointed to a row of plastic chairs against the wall, then picked up the telephone on his desk and spoke quietly into it with his left head.

Hannah gave the joker a tight-lipped smile, and sat down to wait, finding a corner seat and putting her briefcase on the chair next to her so no one would sit there. She tried to pretend that she didn't take any interest in the carnival freak show that continually walked past her.

"You're Agent Davis?"

Hannah was startled from her reverie. A centaur in a white lab coat was frowning at her. She didn't know why that startled her so much, as the clinic was awash in strangeness: a fish-faced joker with his head immersed in a globe of water was sitting across from her; a shape-shifting something that looked to be made of quicksilver had oozed from the clinic doors not two minutes earlier; the far corner of the room writhed with what looked to be a quartet of upright forearms, the hands of which were having an animated and soundless conversation with one another.

A human torso grafted onto a palomino pony's body shouldn't be so distracting. At least the centaur's upper body looked completely normal. In fact, that part of him was rather handsome. Hannah decided to concentrate on that. "Yes, I'm Agent Davis," she said.

"I'm Dr. Bradley Finn. The receptionist told me that you wanted to see Troll. This is his day off. But I want you to know—"

The centaur stopped. Looked down. One of the forearms was tugging at his rear left fetlock. Hannah could see little pseudopods at the bottom of the mobile limb. "Listen, Fingers, Dr. Cody will be with you in a few minutes, okay?" Dr. Finn said. The hand nodded like a hand puppet to Finn, then seemed to notice Hannah and waved. Feeling foolish, Hannah gave a quick wave back. Scuttling on the pseudopods, the arm went back to its companions.

The frown came back to Finn's face. "One of your people, a Peter Harris, was already in today asking about the fire victims that were brought here."

"You don't look pleased, Dr. Finn."

"That's because I'm not."

"I'm sorry, Doctor," Hannah said. "I'm sure your main concern is the well-being of your patients. But you have to understand that we need information if we're going to catch the arsonist. And that means we have to talk to the survivors, even at times when we'd rather not bother them. I know that's usually not easy for them after such a traumatic experience, and sometimes we're dealing with people in a lot of pain . . ."

Hannah stopped. Finn was holding up his hand. "Hold on," he said. "I think we have things a little backward. Why don't we go into my office?" He escorted Hannah through the clinic doors, his hooves clicking on the linoleum. They passed consultation rooms, most of them empty in the early morning. Another doctor, a woman with an eye patch, crossed from room to room down the hall in front of them, nodding to Finn. The doctor's office held a normal chair sitting before an abnormally high desk. Finn waved Hannah to the chair and moved behind the desk. She could see that the furniture was built for his convenience, so that he could work without having to bend down or sit. Hannah pulled the tape recorder from her purse, along with her notebook. She showed Finn the recorder. When he shrugged, she set it on the edge of the desk.

"I wouldn't have minded if your man Harris had actually wanted to interview people," Finn said without prelude, glancing once at the turning hubs of the cassette and then ignoring the machine. "I would have understood that. But all your Harris did was check to see who we'd signed in. That's what bothered me. I *asked* him if he wanted to talk to some of the victims, but he just laughed. He didn't *say* that he had better things to do with his time, but he sure as hell implied it. What he did say was that he was 'just following routine, that's all.' I asked him if he thought that maybe the death of a hundred or so jokers justified something more than just the routine. He told me, and I quote: 'Not from me, it doesn't.' I don't take well to bigotry, Ms. Davis, and your Harris is, frankly, a massive jerk."

Hannah could feel the heat of her cheeks. "Harris is working for me," she told the centaur. "I apologize, Dr. Finn. A fire like this isn't routine. Not to me. I assure you that I'll follow up on Harris's conduct. All the patients here were available for him?"

"The ones that lived were," Finn answered.

"I'm sorry, Doctor. I really am."

Finn looked slightly mollified. He nodded, fiddled with the stack of papers in his in-basket. "I hope so," he said. "Three of the people were brought in DOA; we lost two of the other dozen or so people during the night. Almost all the rest are in for a long and extremely painful reconstruction, if they can afford it. So are you going to talk to them?"

Hannah wondered if she hesitated a fraction of a second too long. "Yes. If you don't mind?"

"I'll take you in." Finn started out from behind the desk, then stopped. He cocked his head at her as a muscle twitched in his long, gold-silk flank. The long tail flicked once. "You asked about Troll," he said. "It's none of my business, but on Black Queen Night, Troll was here from the afternoon until the next morning. Any of us can verify that."

Hannah shook her head. "I—" she started, then let the air out of her lungs in a loud exhalation. "I think I can skip Troll. Someone thought he might know something about an old plot against jokers." She smiled to show that she gave the notion no credence, but Finn wasn't sharing the joke. "It's nothing," she said.

"Are you implying that this wasn't just random violence?" Finn was holding very still. Hannah could see the muscles tightening along his neck, and his tail was swishing back and forth like an angry cat's.

"No, I'm emphatically not saying that. In fact, in cases like this, it's very unlikely. One person can hate so intensely that they're driven to such violent ends, but *groups* . . . It's much rarer. Fortunately." Hannah smiled again. "I'd wager that most violence against the jokers stems from isolated incidents. It takes an unhealthy paranoia to see a plot behind every tree."

"A joker might think that's easy for a nat to say."

"Your nat might still believe it," she answered. This time he grinned back at her, a quick flash of teeth that disappeared as quickly as it had come.

"You're awfully naïve, Agent Davis."

"I prefer to think I'm optimistic."

"Right. I could tell you—" Finn stopped. Hannah didn't say anything. Every good investigator had to be part amateur psychologist, and she could see that something was inside him, pushing at the barriers. She waited, looking at him expectantly.

"I thought the same once, too. Since then, I've seen some of the nastiness and evil you don't seem to believe in." Finn shook his head. "I've *seen* it."

"Here?" Hannah asked quietly. A nudge.

"No, not here," he said. "Eight years ago, in Kenya. Funny, he tried to use fire, too . . ."

The Crooked Man

Melinda M. Snodgrass

No amount of money will make up for a
physiology that can't fit in the seats, or enter one of those
broom closets that pass for restrooms aboard your average
747. So there I was, making the long flight from Los Angeles to
New York, to Rome, to Nairobi on one of those big freight job-
bies designed to carry horses, cattle, other varieties of prize
livestock . . . and jokers.

The grooms, men truly without any kind of a country, had
the usual reaction to a palomino pony centaur, but when they
realized I had money to spare, and an addict's fever about
poker, they loosened up. I lost enough initially to get them
friendly, and the rest of the tedious journey passed in reasonable comfort and companionship. Actually, I'll let you in on a
little secret—flying freight beats the hell out of more traditional modes of travel. Plenty of room to walk around, and
when you get tired you bed down on the bales of hay and
straw.

In my case, Skully, an unprepossessing wisp of humanity
though he had a magician's gift with horses (maybe that's why

I liked him so well), broke open one of the bales of hay, and built me a centaur's nest.

As I folded my legs beneath me and went lurching in a groundward direction, he said in his thick Irish brogue, "Don't go eatin' all that hay now. We've got a lot of miles and hours to Africa."

I reached for my travel bag, and dug out a handful of Snickers, pears and grapes, an Edam cheese, crackers, a tin of sardines, and a ham sandwich prepared and lovingly wrapped by my sweet, indulgent momma, who would have packed the same gargantuan care package if I'd been flying first class on Delta airlines. My mother doesn't believe that anybody save herself can cook.

"Skully," I said, "I'm not a hay burner. Nor am I likely to go nuts and mount that attractive little thoroughbred mare, either, so relax and go to sleep."

He grinned rather sheepishly (after this many years I'm virtually as telepathic as Tachyon when it comes to people's weird-assed ideas about jokers—our manners, morals, and tastes. I was right; he *had* been contemplating my sex life), and settled back to squat on his heels.

"So why are you heading to the dark continent?" he asked.

"I'm a doctor, and a Peace Corps volunteer." (You can tell from the order in which I placed those two conditions which one most pleased me.) "I'm going to be working with the joker community outside of Nairobi."

"Won't real people let you work on them?" he asked. There wasn't any malice in the phrasing, just an honest curiosity, and that almost endearing lack of sensitivity that typifies most nats.

"Not real willingly," I said. "But that really isn't the reason. Jokers offer a fascinating range of physiological and epidemiological problems. That's candy to a doctor." I paused, wondering how to phrase this so I wouldn't sound like a sanctimonious asshole. I couldn't think of one so I shrugged and just said it. "And I am one hell of a lucky joker, so I feel like I ought to be giving a little back."

Skully shook his head. "Not me. If I had the brains and education I'd be making money . . ." His voice rose to accentuate the final word, then trailed away into sadness.

I smiled at him. "There's plenty of time for that."

"For you, Doc." He pulled the piece of hay from his mouth and tossed it away. He rose and followed it.

Again I felt that gulf—not because I was a joker, but because I carried around the curse (or blessing) of my family's wealth like a camel carries humps. I decided I couldn't solve the financial inequalities of the world right then, so arranging my tail across my flank (it gets cold in those planes), I pillowed my head on my arm and went to sleep.

Nairobi wasn't what I'd expected. Africa had always been this place of wonderful mystery for me: Tarzan movies (the good ones with Johnny Weissmuller, not Jack Braun); H. Rider Haggard; lost cities—all the usual WASP bullshit.

So, imagine my surprise and chagrin when I fetched up in this modern city with skyscrapers, traffic jams, people in business suits and tailored dresses. I shook my head over my own silliness, and grabbing my tote, suitcase, and medical bag, I approached a policeman, and asked directions to my hotel. He told me in elegantly accented English, and I started jogging away, only to be arrested by his soft, "Sir."

I slewed around, and stared back across my hindquarters at him. "Yes?"

"Kenya . . . is an Islamic nation . . . primarily."

"Yeah, so?" (And yeah, I was very stupid; what can I say?)

"According to the teachings of Islam, victims of the wild card are considered cursed of Allah."

It was great; I had found probably the only politically correct cop in all of Nairobi, but I could tell from the expression in his dark eyes that he thought the teachings were spot on the money.

"I appreciate the warning," I said. "But I really do need to reach my hotel. I'll keep my head down, and move fast." We nodded politely to each other, and I headed on my way.

In addition to traveling fast I can also travel light. Shirts, ties, and a couple of jackets, that's the entirety of my wardrobe. One nun at the parochial school I attended sent me home on the grounds I was indecent, insisting that Mom and Dad fit me out with a pair of trousers. I can still remember Dad's bellow—he said I'd look like a bad vaudeville act—and that was my last day in parochial school . . . thank God. (Sorry, I'm losing the thread here.)

This being Africa, it was warm, and the suitcase began to hang like an anvil off my right hand. I briefly regretted not phoning ahead and arranging for my version of a limo—a guy with a truck and horse trailer—but I'm not an animal, and resent being treated like one. I also have this weird recurring nightmare where they get me in one of those enclosed horse vans like the Brits use, and they trundle me away to the knackers. Not a nice dream.

As I trotted, I considered priorities. I needed to get to Kilango Cha Jaha, the village where many of Kenya's jokers were now squatting, and report to my superior, Dr. Etienne Faneuil. Now, while I'm a robust boy, and enjoy an aerobic workout as much as the next fellow, I didn't really want to travel around Nairobi and environs at the steady 4.2 miles an hour I can maintain when jogging, nor did I want to reduce travel time by running. The sight of a pony centaur galloping through city streets generally causes comment, and I'm always worried some asshole's going to decide it's round-up time and he's a cowboy.

So, the bottom line was I needed wheels: a custom jobbie, a van with handicapped controls on the steering wheel, a sliding side door, and the seats ripped out. Correction, all but one seat ripped out. I do occasionally have passengers, and pretty ladies don't like to sit on the floor, or stand like commuters on a subway.

I had been so deeply engrossed in my own ruminations that I didn't notice the cars that had fallen in behind me like a secret service escort. By the time I did notice, one had jumped the curb and angled across the sidewalk in front of me. Another was in the process of completing the trap to my rear.

I had a strong sensation their motives weren't friendly, so I let fly with both hind feet, and caught the opening car door just below the handle. One of my kicks generates a lot of power. I heard a yell and a curse in something that sounded suspiciously like unintelligible chatter from the driver of car number two as the door slammed back and caught his leg and hand as he tried to exit. That still left me with two assailants. And there was no doubt now that they were assailants. They were brandishing tire irons, and I sure as hell knew I didn't have a flat.

There was a high fence on my right, and beyond those walls I could see the tops of trees. I clumsily threw my suitcase at the two men in front of me. They easily dodged, and I felt a strong sense of ill use. This kind of thing always works in the movies my dad produces. My attempt at Rambo having failed, I opted for flight, and bolted across the hood of their Mazda. My hooves didn't do much for either the body work or the paint job. My agility seemed to surprise one guy. He just gaped as I went clattering past. His partner was less impressed. He swung the iron, and caught me high on the left shoulder. It hurt like a motherfucker, but I was down on the sidewalk again, with the width of a car between them and *me*.

Grimly clutching my tote and my medical bag, I galloped for the gate some fifty yards ahead, with the two guys running and shouting in pursuit. I heard a lot of *Allah*s and *Nur al Allah*s going past as I yanked open the latch and raced through. It was a park. Beautiful, pristine, peaceful. Later I found out I'd entered the Nairobi National Park. One hundred and ten kilometers of virgin wilderness almost completely within the confines of a major metropolitan center.

Wilderness . . . complete with wild animals.

Like lions.

It was not a good afternoon. I dislike being regarded as lunch almost as much as I resent being regarded as a monster. Let's just say I finally reached the peaceful shores of that paean to modern civilization—the Hilton Hotel.

My welcoming committee in Nairobi should have prepared me for the realities of Kilango Cha Jaha, but as I was waved through the gates by a pair of Kenyan military guards I couldn't help but wonder if the fences were to keep the jokers in as much to keep the fanatics out.

Kilango was your usual Third World shit hole, and as I drove I ruminated bitterly on the irony of the village's name— *Kilango Cha Jaha*, "Gate of Paradise." Yeah, right. There was a small river meandering through the mud-and-thatch huts, and a pall of cook smoke hung like a memory of a bad hangover across the entire village. Children, many of them completely normal, frolicked in the dusty streets, or paddled in the river. Somewhere a radio was blasting out Somali rock and roll.

I wondered at the lack of adult jokers. Were they all hiding shyly in their huts, venturing out only at night when darkness could disguise their deformities? Did they all have jobs (unlikely), and were at work? Jokers tend to fall into two categories: the ashamed, who keep so low a profile as to be almost invisible, and the flaunters, who delight in shocking the normal world that surrounds them.

I'm unusual (or at least I pride myself that I am) because I don't fall into either category. I just do my thing, and hope things don't get too uncomfortable in return. Still, I was bothered by the missing jokers.

Easing the van to a stop I called out in my halting Swahili to a nearby urchin. I must have picked one of the forty other ethnic groups that inhabit the country because I might as well have been speaking . . . well, Swahili, for all the good it did me. Fortunately, another child understood, ran up, and chinned himself on the van window. I repeated my request for directions to the health clinic.

"Sure, boss," he said. "Gimme a ride and I'll show you."

I nodded my assent, and he raced around, and clambered in the passenger side. From this position of moral and physical superiority he gazed down on his fellows. Now that he was closer I wasn't liking what I was seeing. His lymph nodes seemed enlarged, and there was a swelling in his joints.

"You sick, boss?" he asked after indicating the direction with an errant flip of the hand.

"No," I said.

"Yes, you are. You're a *mwenye kombo*."

My mind supplied the translation: "crooked person," i.e., joker. "That doesn't mean I'm sick," I explained patiently. "It just means I'm different." My guide seemed unconvinced. "I'm a doctor," I added. That got him, but it wasn't the reaction I'd hoped for. His eyes became suspicious slits, he stiffened, yanked open the van door, and hopped out. I jammed on the brakes, terrified he'd fall, and that my first act at Kilango would be squashing a hapless urchin.

Backing slowly away from the van he called out to me, "Just keep going that way, boss, you'll find it," and he was gone, vanishing in a twinkling of bare brown legs among the bare brown huts.

The clinic was what you'd expect from a public health facility in a joker village in the Third World. It was a squat, ugly cinder-block construction on the western outskirts of the village. Its position, huddled against the barbwire fence, seemed totally appropriate. It looked less like a place of healing than a soundproofed barracks where state enemies recant their sins. I parked, backed the length of the van until I could slide open the door, and jumped down. Medical bag firmly in hand, I pushed open the glass doors, ready to begin my first stint as a real live doctor.

The tiny lobby was filled with squalling babies and their tired mothers. In one small corner, a group of elderly jokers had carved out turf for themselves. There was one old guy with human faces covering his body. The sibilant whispers from all those mouths set an odd contrapuntal line to the soprano baby wails.

It's an odd quirk of the wild card virus, or maybe of the human psyche, that we end up with so many fuzzy animal jokers. I tease my mom occasionally that she shouldn't have had Dad take her to that rerelease of *Fantasia* just before my birth, but I realize that ultimately my condition was selected and molded by me.

The next largest joker variety are the warping of normal human physiology. Finally, we have the monsters from the id—shapes so grotesque and disturbing that you have no idea where the fuck they came from. This room was mostly sporting the fuzzy animal variety, which wasn't surprising given the cultural importance of animal spirits in African mythology.

There was a Clairol redhead, crisp in nurse's whites, behind the desk. She looked up at the sound of my hooves on the stained linoleum floor. Once I got a good look at her face, and mentally scraped away a couple of hundred pounds of makeup, I put her around fifty-five. She still had a pretty good body, but this was clearly one of those beautiful women who cannot accept the judgment of nature, years, and gravity.

"Yes?" she asked, and I was surprised to discover she was an American. I figured Faneuil would have a French staff. As a subspecies of humanity, the French take the cake for arrogance and xenophobia. Then I realized Faneuil had hired *me*, and my mental French-bashing went by the wayside.

"Doctor Bradley Finn," I hurried to say. "I'm the new Peace Corps . . ." There was something in her ironic smile that had the words dying in my throat.

"Ah, yes, we have been expecting you . . . since yesterday."

I felt like a ten-year-old caught playing hooky. I shuffled my feet, which is a lot of shufflin', and muttered my excuse about needing a car.

"Of course; you are an American."

The tone in which that was said made me want to start singing "The Star-Spangled Banner." I resisted the impulse because my singing voice sounds a lot like frogs fornicating.

"Uh, yeah, well, you might want to head home, get your passport punched, eat a cheeseburger, go to a ball game, remember what it's like." In response to my words, her face had gone red in that mottled way that only true redheads can achieve, which told me the color wasn't wishful thinking; it was just fond remembrance. "Now, could you tell Doctor Faneuil I'm here?" I added in my best Doctor Voice.

"I will inform Doctor," she replied in her best Great Man's Assistant voice. I was pleased at my acuity, but depressed by the prospect. Great Men's Assistants are always unmarried ladies who have devoted their lives to "doctor," and always referred to him without the buffering article. They are always a pain in the ass to any other doctor who happens around. "Doctor is presently with a patient," she concluded as if fearful I'd think he was out on the links.

"Yeah, I sorta figured. Well, could I wait in . . . Doctor's office? I'd like to get with a patient as soon as possible."

She didn't miss my hesitation before I said the word *doctor*. She gave me a look, and I had a feeling my smart mouth had just shoveled me out another hole, but she did lead me through the doors to the right of the desk, and down the hall lined with examination rooms. I concluded (correctly, as I later found out) that the doors to the left led to the small fifty-bed hospital.

As we walked I realized that what I'd taken for stains on the linoleum was actually dirt. It bugged me so I said, sharper than I should have, "Doesn't anybody know how to use a mop around here?"

"It is long rain season, we are understaffed, and Doctor thinks it best if we concentrate our energies on patient care."

"I didn't mean to imply that one of us health-care professionals should sully our hands with menial labor. I was thinking about some kid. Pay him a little each week. That sort of thing." Her flat, implacable stare was starting to get to me. I shut up.

"You have a lot to learn about Africa, Dr. Finn," she said as she opened the door to Faneuil's office and gestured me in.

She shut the door so fast and hard she almost caught my tail.

— — —

It took the French Schweitzer forty-five minutes to get around to me. By then I'd read all of his diplomas and citations three times, and perused the out-of-date medical journals twice, and decided I couldn't bear to look at pictures of him shaking hands with famous assholes again. Not that he didn't deserve all the kudos. His professional life had been an example of service and self-sacrifice spanning three continents. It was why I wanted to work with him. I'm just a typical American, and I hate to be kept waiting.

He wasn't what I'd expected even though I'd just finished looking at photos. He was much taller in person, an improbably long and lanky figure whose thin legs scissored along like a wading heron. A shaggy mop of gray-brown hair, a small, receding chin that combined with thin, almost transparent eyebrows to give his face a naked look. That made the jutting beak of a nose all the more incongruous on that unfinished face.

His smile, however, was warmth itself. A big relief after the popsicle out front. He strode across the room with that sharp, jerking walk, his hand aggressively outthrust.

"Dr. Finn, how pleased I am to meet you at last."

"And I you, sir." He had a good shake, and there was none of that almost imperceptible withdrawal that you get from most nats.

"You have met Margaret?" I correctly gleaned that he meant the nurse, and nodded. "Invaluable, but terrifying woman. She keeps me straightly in line," he concluded with a laugh.

My response was the epitome of tact and diplomacy. "I can see how she might," I said, and then added, "Well, I'm eager to get started." I let my voice trail away suggestively.

"You don't want to see your, how do you Americans put it, your digs first?"

"*Digs* is British, actually, but thanks, no. They'll still be there tonight, and I've got the whole afternoon ahead of me. I'd rather work, check out the clinic, get acquainted with our patients."

He laughed—a high whinnying sound. "Good, an 'eager beaver'—and that is an American idiom, yes?"

"Absolutely."

"We will put you to work."

"Good."

So I began my life at Kilango Cha Jaha. Southwest of Nairobi, our village was close enough to the city to obtain supplies with relative ease, but far enough away that the nats didn't have to look at us, and it was a real effort for Fundies to come out and raid the ghetto for fun.

My home was a traditionally shaped African hut, a *rondavel*. I bedded down on a mattress thrown on the dirt floor, surrounded by mosquito netting. Thatched roofs are eminently practical, but unfortunately they are also great homesteads for bugs of every kind, shape, and variety. And they grow them *big* in Africa. Mosquitoes the size of B-52s, bedbugs the size of bisons, roaches like touring limousines. I was especially tormented by critters with too many legs because I have a lot of hide, and it's naked to their assaults. I went through gallons of bug repellent, but I always managed to miss a place because it's tough to maneuver across the entire length of my back and hindquarters. I considered trying the rhino's approach—find a big mud hole, wallow, and cake myself—but I didn't think the AMA would approve.

Housing might lack even the simplest of amenities, poverty and disease were rampant, but God, did we have scenery! Our setting was magnificent; rising up almost directly from the western edge of Kilango were the Ngong Hills. *Hills* don't really do them justice; while the incline on the west was relatively gentle, when you reached the ridgetop you were gazing down several thousand feet into the Great Rift Valley. Slither and skitter down this escarpment to the floor of the valley, and you were in the Lolkisale Game Reserve.

It was there I met J.D. and Mosi. I had been mooching about the reserve when I came across the startling sight of a small herd of elephants calmly breaking down trees and masticating them. These were the first elephants I'd managed to find, and I quickly hid in the brush to watch. About a quarter of an hour later I was returned to my surroundings by a gun barrel being screwed into my left ear. I jumped, hollered, the elephants went pounding away, ears flying like sails and trunks upraised, and a disgusted voice with a pronounced Aussie accent said, "Well, I guess you aren't a poacher, but I'm damned if I know *what* you are."

I risked a glance, and observed a stocky man of indeterminate years, a bush hat crammed down over his thinning fair hair, and a face so seamed and lined with wrinkles and old scars that he looked as if he'd been tied to the tracks and toy trains had been run back and forth across his phiz for, oh, six or seven years.

Another man arose like a waking god from the brush off to my right. Well over six feet tall, he looked as if he'd been carved from a single block of obsidian.

"J.D.," said the God of the Night. "You are such an ignorant sod, I am sometimes ashamed to work with you." J.D.'s response to this was to seize his left buttock, and shake it at his partner.

Eventually introductions were made. The elegant Zulu with the Oxford accent was Mosi Jomo, and the Aussie J. D. Snopes. They escorted me back to Kilango, and stayed for dinner and a few hands of poker. As they were leaving, J.D. peered between my hind legs at my equipment, and said with a snort that I might want to stay out of Lolkisale. I didn't understand so he carefully explained that with *huevos* like mine I might get shot so my parts could delight the palates of Arab or Chinese gourmands, or be ground up and fed to some Japanese businessman to improve his potency. When I refused to curtail my rambles, Mosi mildly suggested that I might want to fly an American flag off my tail, and be very, very careful. I said I would, we parted, and I'd made my first friends in Kenya.

Thereafter it became a weekly ritual to gather at either my hut or the warden's house in Lolkisale for dinner and poker. I learned that Mosi played classical clarinet, and read Proust for fun. J.D. introduced me to Australian Rules Football, and proved to be a working man's philosopher. His comments on governments in general, and Third World governments in particular, I have shamelessly incorporated as my own. They also consistently beat the . . . er . . . pants off me in poker.

During those first months my admiration for Dr. Faneuil grew until I was like some kind of primitive worshipper at the altar of a loving and mournful god. I had never seen a man work so tirelessly to ease the passing of the dying. If I came in to make late rounds I would hear his deep voice murmuring in Swahili or Kikuyu, and never platitudes. His bedside manner left his patients feeling valued and respected: not jokers, not dying meat, but human beings. When the struggle for another breath ended, he would walk away to weep alone. I ached to comfort him, to help him, to ease his and their pain.

The only way I could think of was to stop the hemorrhage, and I didn't have a clue how to accomplish that. My first day I'd thought I'd be vaccinating happy babies, caring for minor injuries encountered in the fields, assisting Faneuil in surgery;

in short, being a healer. Instead I had joined him as a ticket taker for Erebus. Death reveled in Kilango, despite our best efforts.

I knew we were taking all possible precautions given the lack of funds, but I had done my residency at Cedars-Sinai hospital in Los Angeles, and I was used to practicing medicine with the best that money could buy. Medicine in the Third World is a whole other ball game. I'm convinced it was some doctor in Uganda, or Belize, or Cambodia who coined the phrase about necessity and mothers of invention.

The first time I vaccinated a child I was in worse shape than the screaming kid. See, nobody makes reusable needles anymore, and even if they did, no one knows how to use a whetstone and sharpen them. We use disposable needles that are sharper than sons a bitches—once. The second, third time, fourth time around, the patient feels like we're excavating with a pickax. It hurts, kids cry, and I get crazy. I also assumed I had solved the mystery of the resentful, suspicious urchin from my first day. I was wrong, and it just goes to show you that kids can be a hell of a lot smarter than so-called adults.

But we had to reuse needles because there wasn't money to keep us supplied in disposables. Don't misunderstand me, we weren't (or at least I wasn't) a bunch of quacks and incompetents preying on the hapless natives. We took all possible precautions to avoid contamination, but if it's a choice between reusing a sterilized needle and not getting a kid vaccinated against diphtheria—well, *you* try to make that choice.

Our procedure was elaborate. The used needles were first placed in a steel tray with tiny prongs over which we slid the base of the needle. The tray was then immersed in a bath of soap and scalding water. Next it went into a bath of hot water and Clorox, and finally into a special dip that had been concocted by Dr. Faneuil, which Margaret was quite brayingly insistent that we use. I thought it was probably overkill, but living saints have a tendency to be just full of funny quirks; you make allowances because they're living saints.

Anyway, three months into my tenure, I finally couldn't stand it anymore, so I hauled ass into Faneuil's office for the obligatory Young Whippersnapper Doctor to Older, Wiser Doctor talk. Faneuil was making notations in a file. When I entered he capped his fountain pen, closed the file, and folded his hands atop it as if protecting something precious.

"Sir, it's this needle situation . . . and the blood plasma situation, and the three in one vaccine—we're almost out, and half the kids in the village haven't received it. And can't the government get us a decent anesthesia unit? Sometimes I think it'd be safer to just hit 'em on the head with a brick bat. And our X-ray equipment . . ." I made a disgusted sound. "I'm surprised the nuclear regulatory commission hasn't waded in and declared us a nuclear power."

Faneuil bestowed a soft, kindly smile on me, but there was a waggish light in his pale eyes. "Bradley, as long as you're listing wants, how about a CAT scanner, or an MRI, or a dialysis machine? Money, Bradley, money. All those things cost money, and we haven't got any."

I licked my lips nervously, and plunged in. "Well, that's the thing, sir. My dad's a rich Hollywood producer. He's got a lot of friends who are other kinds of rich Hollywood parasites. They just love to get together over rubber chicken at some benefit dinner and raise the money. They do that real well. So, how about I get my dad to put together a planeload of goodies for us?"

"Sounds lovely, Bradley. You must coordinate it with the Kenyan government, the International Red Cross, and the World Health Organization."

"Why?" I blurted. "I mean, would I have to involve the UN if I wanted a box of chocolate and condoms for me?"

"Ah, but this isn't just for you, Bradley. Bureaucracies must fiddle; it's a law of nature."

"More like the jungle," I muttered, but I surrendered to the realities. "Okay."

I turned to leave, but was arrested before I exited by him saying, "Bradley, you have a good heart."

I felt myself blush. "Thank you, sir." Recovering, I added, "It's just the rest of me that's a little weird."

So, I had managed to impress Faneuil, and I was hangin' with J.D. and Mosi, but friends inside Kilango continued to elude me. There is enormous distrust of whites by Africans (understandable). Enormous distrust of hospitals and doctors by native people. (Also understandable. Hospitals are where you go to die.) The fact that I was a joker helped, but one out of three ain't so good. I decided the kids were where I needed to apply the wedge, and I proceeded in my usual shameless manner: I bribed 'em.

A call to Mom, and I soon had a supply of Frisbees, soccer balls, baseballs, bats and gloves, dolls, crayons and coloring books. Ironically these were a lot easier to obtain than my planeful of vaccines and needles. Dad was whacking through a jungle of red tape, but it was all taking a lot longer than I wanted. But you know Americans; if there's one thing we don't do well, it's wait.

Anyway, once I got the toys, I organized teams and started a Scout troop. I'd hoped Margaret Durand would handle the girls, but she gave me that "you must be kidding" smile, told me she was too busy (and implied I ought to be too busy), and declined. I combined the boys and the girls, and figured what the parent organization didn't know wouldn't hurt them. Faneuil laughingly called my kids the Ponytail Irregulars, which I admit bugged me a little, and made some crack about Americans and our unnatural appetite for sports. I got him back by referring to Frenchies and their unnatural appetite for snails.

You like to think that a group of people to which you belong—whether it be based on race, religion, nationality, profession, whatever—are good and decent people. That the flaws you see in Them, *we* never have. Unfortunately that isn't the case. Underneath it all we're human, and not too long out of the trees.

I had been invited up to Faneuil's for lunch, but I had a broken arm to set, and it was twenty past one before I folded my stethoscope into the pocket of my lab coat and checked my watch. When I saw the time, I put it in overdrive. My hooves rang hollowly on the hard-packed earth, and dust rose behind me as I galloped up the winding road toward the farmhouse that Faneuil called home.

Back in the 1920s the land that currently cradled Kilango had been a not-very-successful coffee plantation. All that now remained was a dilapidated irrigation system and the colonial owner's home. It was a low, rambling wood affair, with a screened veranda and a cupola on one corner. In my wilder moments I could picture the ghost of the imperialistic asshole who built the structure standing in that cupola, binoculars raised, watching the happy darkies toiling in the fields below.

Now it was happy jokers who were singin' and workin' in the sun.

As I ran I suddenly heard the shrill voices of children in the underbrush off to my left, and my stomach formed a tight, hard ball, for I know that hunting pack ululation. I had heard it enough when I was a kid. I hung a looie and followed the noise.

In a dusty depression eight children were flinging stones and beating with sticks a ninth child, who huddled inside this circle of torment. He had flung long, skinny arms across his head, and there were already a few smears of blood on the boy's dark skin. All eight of the tormentors were jokers, and five of them were in my Scout troop. It depressed the shit out of me that some of my kids were involved. I went flying through them like a bowling ball through nine pins, and they fell back before my furious onslaught.

The ringleader of this little gang of journeymen torturers was Dalila, an impossibly tall figure with a two-foot-long neck, and earlobes that brushed at her breasts. At fifteen she had scorned my overtures, and dismissed our activities as "childish." There was a lot of anger in this girl, and she viewed any kind of accommodation with nat society a sellout. She gestured at someone, then indicated me, and a child whose form was basically human came hissing and undulating across the dirt toward me. His body was twisted sharply into curves, and his legs were fused into a single limb, and when he opened his mouth I saw a single big tooth that looked suspiciously hollow to me. I reared, and brought my forefeet down near his head. He got the hint and withdrew.

The bleeding boy lifted his head to look at me, and I realized he wasn't a nat—he had eyes like a chameleon—and I had an explanation for the impromptu torture. Kenyans hate and fear chameleons.

I assumed my best daddy attitude, and daddy voice, and asked in my somewhat stilted Swahili, "Okay, now what's going on here?"

Tube Neck stepped forward, and indicated the shivering boy with a flick of a hand. "He's ugly—"

"Well, there aren't any of us who are going to win any beauty contests," I interrupted. "You're pretty damn funny looking, too, Dalila."

"He is evil," lisped Snake Boy. His palate had also been warped by the virus, and it was really hard to understand him.

"To have him here will bring bad luck on all of us," Dalila added piously, and I could have slapped her. She wasn't a superstitious rustic; she had been born in Mombasa. This was just a way to reassert control over her peers.

"There's death and evil everywhere—I'm looking at a little of it right now. Now listen up, you leave this kid alone, or I'll come by and stomp your intolerant and ugly joker asses into the ground." I turned to the kid on the ground, and held out a hand. "Come on, let's do lunch."

He scrambled to his feet, ducked his head in terror, and ran. I turned back to the kids. My five were shuffling uncomfortably. "I mean it, now," I said severely. "Any more of this shit, and all privileges are revoked." They looked confused. I put it in perspective by enunciating carefully. "No more baseball."

They ducked their heads, and slithered for the trees. I decided some lessons in tolerance were definitely in order, and I also decided I had to find the chameleon-eyed kid and get him into the Irregulars. I also needed to locate his folks and find out if he'd been immunized. He was obviously new to the village, and we didn't want anybody carrying in any diseases from outside.

His name was Daudi, which is Swahili for "Beloved One," and I think it showed a lot of class on the part of his parents to name him such, and keep him, and love him when most of their countrymen viewed him as evil and a monster.

The day after the attack I came calling. An older man was

perched precariously on a stepladder, thatching the roof of the hut. There was the sharp smell of newly hewn wood, and the walls were smooth with fresh mud wattling. Each week the flow of refugees out of Ethiopia, Uganda, and Tanzania swelled our numbers. Housing was at a premium so there was nothing strange about the family building their own hut. It was the placement that was strange—huddled against the barbwire and chain-link fence well away from the rest of the village. It depressed me that these people had come seeking a refuge, and as shitty as Kilango was treating them it was still obviously better than what they'd left. If it wasn't, they wouldn't have stayed.

I called out in as friendly and welcoming a voice as I could muster. It didn't seem to help. The man jerked around so fast that he almost pitched off the ladder. He relaxed when he saw me, but his dark eyes were still wary as he descended to the ground.

He stood before me, his eyes on the ground between us. I thrust out my hand. "Bradley Finn."

He hesitantly shook. "Our son told us . . . what you did." There was another long pause. "Thank you," he finally said.

I shrugged uncomfortably. "Hey, no problem. I wanted to come by, say welcome, tell you a little about the village— activities, services, that kind of thing. I'm a sort of Peace Corps Welcome Wagon."

He didn't get it, and I winced at my feeble attempt at humor.

He raised wise and knowing eyes to meet mine. "My name is Jonathan wa Phonda. You are welcome at our home, but I wish you would tell me what you really want."

I could feel myself blushing. "Okay, I was worried about your son. I wanted to invite him into the Scout troop—" He opened his mouth to interrupt, and I forestalled him with upraised palms. "Please. This village is about not having to hide.

I'll look out for him." (As I recall those pompous words all these years later, I could fucking cry.)

"I also need to make certain your family has been immunized. We're getting really crowded here, and we've got to be especially careful about infection."

Jonathan was back looking at the ground. "Doctors are not a thing I trust."

"I can understand that. Will you at least give me a chance?" I asked.

We were interrupted by a child's voice lifting in song. It was a beautiful boy soprano singing a hymn.

"My son," Jonathan said simply.

"Uh, wow," was my brilliant response.

"He sings for the comfort of his mother," Jonathan continued. The final notes seemed to waft away on the wind, and Jonathan suddenly indicated the door of the hut. "Won't you come in?"

"I'd love to, thanks."

I started forward, only to be arrested by him saying, "My wife . . . well, do not be too shocked. The disease . . . devours her."

I thought he was being poetical. No such luck. The woman who lay upon the cot was a lovely face with a misshapen torso. No legs. No arms. And the wild card had begun its inroads on her body. It's hard to describe what was happening to her. It was as if her blood had been replaced with acid, and it was slowly eating at her from the extremities in. The pain must have been indescribable, but she still managed to smile at me. The boy looked up in surprise at my entrance.

"My son, Daudi," Jonathan said with that father's pride that I hope to feel for my own son someday.

— — —

It took five months before Dad's rubber chicken act was cleared to fly. And my pop and I looked like we were communicating with Mars, from the size of his phone bills. And actually that's not true. We'd been cleared to fly three times before, but each time some new bureaucratic objection was raised.

One time it was a challenge to the registration and ownership of the plane. Somebody claimed it was South African, and it took two weeks to straighten that out. Then some moron got the idea we were pawning off outdated vaccine on the long-suffering natives of Africa, and Dad had to get affidavits from all the pharmaceutical companies. I forget the third crisis, but eventually all the bureaucratic drones were finished pissing in the soup, and a C-17 cargo plane was sitting on the tarmac at LAX slowly being loaded. I had wet dreams at night imagining all those cases and cases of lovely disposable needles that we could . . . well, dispose of.

In the village I continued to doctor, but I was fighting an uphill battle trying to get Daudi into the clinic for his vaccinations. He might have been only ten, but he was real mature for his age, and he kept asking me the unanswerable question: "If you can't save my mother why should I trust you?"

At first this was an ego thing. I was by God going to get this kid to trust me, and get him vaccinated so he would be protected. Then I grew to like him. Then to love him. He adored music, and his passion for new sounds led me into creating an ad hoc music appreciation course to satisfy his cravings. I initially tried rock and roll, the music I enjoy, but I think the wild card had affected Daudi's ears, making him hypersensitive. He couldn't take the decibels of rock, so I begged Mom for classical music tapes. Then for my old guitar and sheet music. And it wasn't all one way; by walking this small Kenyan boy through a history of music I found an appreciation for, and an understanding of, classical music that had eluded me as a youth.

It was my wont, once a month, to enjoy a weekend of liberty in a suite in one of Nairobi's best hotels.

One thing Africa taught me; I'm not cut out for sainthood. I'll work hard, I'll volunteer, I'll get down, and I'll get dirty, but God had seen fit to bless me with wealthy parents who loved me (despite my jokerdom), and I enjoyed—and continue to enjoy—the freedom and pleasures money can buy. I make no apologies.

This time I'd brought Daudi with me. He was going to experience his first opera, and I was going to suffer for the good of this kid's soul, and the improvement of his mind. I also sensed I was getting real close to the victory, and it made me glad that when Daudi finally did consent to be immunized I would be doing it with fresh and sharp needles. I wanted as little pain as possible for this child because it was clear that it was only a matter of days before his mother lost her battle with death.

Daudi was on the balcony, gazing in wonder at the city laid out beneath him, and I was preparing to wash the bod. This requires four rubber boots to keep from slipping in the shower, and I was just forcing a hoof into the last one when the phone rang. It was Dad.

"Hey, Pop!" I trilled.

"Don't sound so happy," came his gravelly voice across the thousands of miles.

I dropped back awkwardly onto my haunches. "It's my plane, isn't it?"

"Yes."

"It ain't flyin', is it?" I asked.

"No, and your old man is getting his ass audited by the IRS. Along with most of the people who donated money."

My tail flicked along my left side. I caught it, and began to nervously pull tangles from the silky white hairs. "I don't get it."

"They're claiming this is a bogus charity, and that we really intend to sell the supplies, launder the money in Europe, and quietly return a profit to our contributors. Until we can prove this is a paranoid fantasy, they've grounded the plane. Brad, they want to talk to you."

"I'm in Africa! What the fuck am I supposed to do? I'm doctoring. I've got patients . . ." Words failed me.

"I've tried to explain this to them."

"What are you going to do?" I asked miserably. I had heard the weariness in his voice, and I was afraid he was going to give up on it. This wasn't his problem. He had a new movie beginning production in three weeks, and he didn't need this kind of aggravation.

"I'm going to get that goddamn plane to Africa if I have to put it on a raft, put a rope in my teeth, and *tow* the son of a bitch!" I held the phone away from my ear. "Somebody with a lot of power doesn't want your plane to fly. Damned if I know why, and damned if I know who, but . . . well, you be careful, Bradley."

He never calls me Bradley unless he's really worried, and not much worries my dad. It was then I felt the first presentiment of danger. I shivered.

"Pop, I love you," I said. He grunted; overt emotionalism always embarrasses him, and I heard the nasal buzz of the dial tone.

I hung up the phone and stood staring blindly down at the carpet. Suddenly I felt small, warm hands sliding around my waist. I looked back over my shoulder. Daudi hugged me tighter. It's a wonderful thing with children. They never try to analyze, they just offer comfort in their simple, visceral way. I laughed and hooked a thumb over my shoulder.

"Hop aboard. I'll give you a ride." He smiled shyly and climbed on. I cantered once around the bedroom, took careful aim, gave a hitch of my hindquarters, and bucked him onto the bed. His giggles followed me into the shower.

Three days after our return to Kilango, his mother died. The next morning I found Daudi waiting for me on the steps of the clinic when I arrived for work. He didn't even cry when I administered the shots.

One night, late, as I lay on my mattress and read by the light of a kerosene lantern, I experienced a hideous epiphany. I was perusing the latest issue of *The Lancet* (*latest* being a relative term. It was actually several months out of date, but my professional mail was getting forwarded through my parents, and then to a P.O. box in Nairobi, and all of this took time. I also wasn't exactly overloaded with spare time to read) when I hit the article on the new antibody test for the HTLV-III virus—more commonly known as AIDS.

This was 1985, and Acquired Immune Deficiency Syndrome was not well understood. I was losing people to a whole host of gastrointestinal parasites, the most common opportunistic infections in our region, and about as unusual in Africa as fleas on dogs. So while I grieved and cursed, I initially didn't think too much about it.

Now this article had burst across the old brain pan, and I got a cold prickly feeling all along my scalp. Scrambling awkwardly to my feet, I dug like a frenzied dog in search of a prize bone through back issues of the review for anything I could find on AIDS. It wasn't much. The traditional medical establishment was leery about writing much about the "gay disease," and Rock Hudson hadn't collapsed yet in a hotel lobby in Paris and been forced to shed his square-jawed leading man image.

I read until 3 A.M. I then drove to Nairobi and called Dad. I wanted a lot of those antibody kits. I wanted them fast. And I sure as fuck wasn't going to tell the International Red Cross and WHO, so they could tell me how careful we all had to be.

No, my antibody kits would come in with a care package of Mom's chocolate chip, raisin oatmeal cookies, and the latest Ed McBain novel.

The final chemical solution washed across my tray of tiny, dainty beads. They turned a lovely purple. I stared at them and began to cry. Of the fifty people I had tested, all carried the HTLV-III antibody in their twisted bodies. And now the significance of all those patients dying from what the Africans had dubbed the "slimming disease" came clear. AIDS had invaded Kilango like the Germans entering Poland.

Our new deepwater well, all the vaccinations against diphtheria, and typhoid, measles, weren't going to make a damn bit of difference. Death had become a permanent resident in the village.

A part of me—the heedless, spoiled kid from Hollywood—didn't want to know the extent of the infection. The wiser part, the doctor, had to know so we could plot strategies to control the spread of the disease. I hadn't told Faneuil what I had done, what I was continuing to do. I figured I'd give him the bad news all in one dose. There were times when I cursed him and named him a fool. How could he not have seen the virological evidence before him? But I had missed it during the first five months of my tenure at Kilango.

But he's been here years!

Great men can have their little blind spots, my small excusatory voice whined.

Pretty fucking big blind spot!

Out of the 7,249 people living in Kilango, 5,056 were infected or displaying the symptoms of full-blown AIDS.

I went to Faneuil. He was at the house, resting during the worst heat of the day. I had sweat patches on my chest and flanks, partly from nerves, partly from the stultifying heat that seemed to run like warm syrup across the body.

He offered me a lemonade, saying, "Only mad dogs and Englishmen—" He broke off abruptly once he took a good look at my face. "Bradley, what is wrong? What is it? Are you ill?"

Suddenly I was in tears, my hands pressed hard against my face as if the pressure of my fingers could hold back this unmanly display. He got an arm around my shoulders, maneuvered me under the big ceiling fan, which was turning lazily. A few minutes, and the gulping sobs had been reduced to sniffles. Faneuil pressed a handkerchief into my hands.

"Here, Bradley child, here. Now, what is wrong?"

I told him. He sat very still, a wax effigy on the sofa, then his anger broke across me.

"How *dare* you! How dare you take this action without consulting me! I deny this test. I deny its validity. I have never heard of this test!"

Rage propelled him to his feet, and his long legs scissored as he paced the length of the room and back.

My first shock and chagrin was giving way to an anger every bit as white hot as his. It was Old Fart Doctor Syndrome. If they haven't heard of it, it's not worth shit, and of course they never hear of it because they stop studying.

"You're like fucking King Canute and the waves," I bellowed back. "You can rant and rail, and deny all you want, but they're still going to *die,* and a word from the mighty Faneuil isn't going to prevent it! You don't want to believe me . . . fine!

Try the CDC, the NIH, talk to some other Froggies. Montagnier at the Pasteur Institute, they isolated the goddamn virus! The test has been designed as a screening mechanism for world blood banks. I used it, maybe wrongly, as a diagnostic tool, but God, we had to know. We've got to do *something*."

He was trembling, his nostrils pinched tight as he said, "The first thing I am going to do is get you out of my hospital. Out of my village. You have no ethics."

"*Your* village? This is a joker village. And I'm a joker, and I think I have more fucking right to be here than you do. You contact the Peace Corps. I'll reveal what I've discovered here. You got lazy. You got complacent. That's bad, but it's not criminal. You ignore this, and it *will* be criminal."

He collapsed onto the sofa, and *he* began to cry. My anger cooled as if doused by the rain of his grief.

I felt sick . . . for his pain and guilt, for our dying patients. "I'm sorry, Etienne."

He lifted a tear-streaked face, shook his head, and waved a hand helplessly. "No, no, Bradley, you were right to shout. I was being a stubborn old fool. But the time for tears is past. Now we must act."

They were fine words, but they were just words. For those already infected or into full-blown AIDS, all we could do was ease their deaths and try to educate them to keep them from passing the disease to the few healthy members of our community.

The question that tormented me in those dark weeks was the *how*? How had the disease run with such ease through the community? Even assuming ten or twelve infected jokers arriving in the village, it could not have spread this comprehensively. Each night I continued my research.

Blood transfusion? Unlikely. We didn't do that much surgery at the clinic; we weren't equipped for it, and certainly for
no procedure that would require a large amount of blood. We
sure as hell didn't have a large gay population, and hetero-
sexual infection, while it is a growing phenomenon, was not as
easy as the media would like people to believe. No IV drug
users—

My thoughts tumbled to a halt like cars in an LA freeway
pileup. *But we sterilize our needles!* I told myself, laying aside
that worry. *We are careful.*

I tried to put it out of my mind. I quizzed Margaret again
and again about our sterilization techniques, and maybe it was
the hostile, shuttered look in her pale, pale eyes that finally led
me to add a new skill to my list of credits—breaking and entering. Maybe it was also the relaxed attitude that seemed to grip
the medical staff of Kilango. Having now realized that he had
a bunch of dying jokers, Faneuil didn't seem to care about preventing any further spread of the disease. I felt like a wild-
eyed, tangled-haired prophet crying to the heavens about
condoms and safe sex. And like most wild-eyed and tangled-
haired prophets, I was unsung in my own country.

Anyway, it was late one night. I was coming off rounds, but
instead of heading back to my hut I cruised across the lobby
and down the hall to Faneuil's office. It wasn't locked, which
surprised me at first (I'm a white boy from LA; we lock *everything*), and suddenly I felt very foolish. An unlocked door
wasn't very sinister. Still, I'd come this far, and vilified Faneuil's image in my own mind, so I entered.

Moving quickly, I flipped through the filing cabinets. Minutes went crawling past. In my own fevered imagination I had
been in the office for days. I kept having visions of myself
caught by Faneuil and Margaret, his eyes sad and hurt as I
tried to stammer out apologies. I almost quit, but there was

only one more drawer to go. I yanked it open. Began a cursory search. An icy-footed, long-legged insect seemed to go stalking down my spine. I collapsed back onto my hindquarters like a trick circus pony, and read quickly through the collection of articles in my hands.

They were all from the 1970s, and they dealt with things like needle transmission of infectious hepatitis. The number of viral particles necessary on a needle to cause serum transmission. Virus survivability rates at room temperatures.

There's a logical explanation for this, my mind yammered as it ran in circles around the confines of my skull. *We're sterilizing disposable needles. He's just worried and concerned. Making certain our system is as foolproof as man and science can make it.*

Because *if* we weren't, and *if* there was something unthinkable occurring, *I* . . . I thought of Daudi, and I couldn't finish the thought.

I replaced the articles and slipped out of the office.

Down the hallway to the storeroom where supplies were stored, linens washed, and needles sterilized. I had never paid much attention to the sterilization process—doctor's arrogance, that. After all, Margaret handled it. Now I was about to educate myself. I wanted to know the makeup of our final needle wash. If all was well I could release this paranoid fantasy about Faneuil.

It was hot in the storeroom. Through the south-facing window I could see a line of monsoon clouds billowing purple, black, and gray against the moonlit sky. Occasionally lightning shot jagged and orange from the belly of the clouds. A sharp gust of wind sent sand rattling against the dingy glass.

Alarmed by the sharp reports, the flies sleeping like fat black raisins on the ceiling let out a crescendo drone and stirred nervously. Flies are a constant in Africa. You stop noticing them after a while. I almost didn't notice this batch.

Instead I flipped on the light. Crossed to the solution. Awakened by the light, the flies came spiraling down, drawn by the scent of sweat and hide from my centaur body. One big motherfucker landed on my withers and bit down hard. Grunting in pain and annoyance I cranked my torso around and smashed the fucker. Blood squished against my palm. Disgusted, I turned back to look for a towel, and froze.

The flies were hovering over Doctor's special solution.

Sterilizing solutions all have one thing in common—they contain detergent. Flies don't like detergent. Whatever was in Doctor's Special Needle Dip, it wasn't detergent.

Suddenly paranoid, I closed the door to the storeroom behind me, and approached the tray. The needles looked like tiny deadly missiles as their points glittered beneath the surface of the fluid. I removed the tray and set it aside. I then used the tried-and-true doctor approach to anything unknown.

I dipped the tip of my little finger in the solution and tasted it.

It wasn't soap, or Clorox, or alcohol. It was dilute human serum. For a second the room took on the quality of a merry-go-round. I closed my eyes, and backed up so abruptly that I drove my ass into the far wall. It bruised the dock of my tail, and hurt like a motherfucker. The pain counteracted the faintness.

All the old spy movies of my youth rose up and clamored for attention. I knew I had to hide my presence in the room, and I knew I had to have a sample of the solution. I quickly filled and corked a pipette with the liquid. I was just returning the needles to the solution when I smelled smoke.

Terrified, I threw open the door, and slammed it immediately shut again at the sight of flames belching from Faneuil's office. Frantically I searched for escape. There was no way I was going to get my fat horse butt out that window. In my case it literally was out of the frying pan and into the fire.

Snatching up a towel from the linen cabinet, I wet it with tap water, then tied it across my face. I remembered clips from one of Dad's stirring firefighter dramas, so I stood to the side of the door as I opened it. Fire belched in as if shot by a small dragon. Once that initial billow passed I held my breath, and jumped through into the hall. My tail ignited as I vaulted over the fire, and boy did that serve as an incentive! If the ASPCA wouldn't get on you, I have a great way to encourage racehorses.

I turned right, and was running like a motherfucker for the lobby and the hospital. We had sixteen patients occupying beds in that ward, and I had to get them out. As I approached the lobby I could hear shrill cries of terror, and the racking coughs of people who are dying from smoke inhalation. The doorway leading to the hospital was a sheet of flame. I'm as brave as the next man, but I'm not suicidal. It was clear a second fire had been started in the ward, and if I tried to save them I would only succeed in joining them in death.

The fire was advancing from both fronts now, about to capture me in Hell's own pincer. The sounds of agony faded from the hospital. I turned and raced for the front doors.

They were locked.

Panic was hammering in my throat. Sixteen people had died because someone was trying to murder me. My knuckles were white as I gripped the push handle and rattled it impotently. But they had not considered one fact. I'm a joker with the body of a pony. Pit ponies in the mines in Britain can pull up to three times their own weight. I'm *strong*.

Whirling, I lined up my ass with the thick glass and let fly with both hind feet. The glass starred and cracked. One more kick, and glass formed a crystal waterfall. I had to jump the access bar. It was a little like threading a needle. I caught my hind feet and fell into an ungainly heap on the steps of the clinic.

As I lay there panting, and hurting (my burned tail hurt like hell), a bullet sprayed concrete dust into my face. I was on my feet and running in an instant.

I don't know how I thought of this in my terror and pain, but I found my hand going to the pocket of my lab coat, and the precious pipette of serum. Amazingly it was still intact. There was a mind-numbing crash of thunder from directly overhead, and the heavens opened up. Within seconds the dusty streets of Kilango had become rivers of sticky mud. I was slogging for my van. I had to get out. Get to Nairobi.

And do what? I wondered. In an instant a lifetime of loving support from friends and family had vanished. I was a joker and I distrusted all nats. I reached the van. Yanked open the side door, and clambered in. My hooves sounded like a chorus of castanets on the metal floor. Trembling, I pulled the keys from the ashtray, thrust them into the ignition, and turned.

Silence.

These assholes thought of everything. I was out of the van, and running for the steep incline of the Ngong Hills. The high-wire fence that surrounded Kilango looked intact, but there was a place where the kids had clipped out an opening, and then carefully folded the wire back into place to hide their sin. I had used it myself, and had kept the secret. There was the sharp report of a high-powered rifle being fired, and an angry supersonic bee ripped along my hip. I shrieked, bucked, and resumed running.

Where were those fucking guards? I wondered. Of course, there were only two of them, and they might be drugged or dead, or maybe just not give a shit because I was a joker, and someone had just declared open season.

My lungs were laboring, and my legs felt like four pillars of jelly by the time I reached the ridgeback.

I thought about heading north along the ridge toward Nairobi, then realized that my hunters had probably thought of that. Machakos, Konza, Kajiado—all were too distant for a tired centaur to reach.

I stared down into the shadow well of the Rift Valley. The game preserve was below. I'd take my chances among the flora and fauna of Africa. Hide out until the heat was off, make my way cautiously north, then climb back over the Ngong to Nairobi. I again reassured myself of the safety of my precious pipette.

I stood dithering on the edge of eternity—literally in my case—and wished for a flashlight. My pursuers threw some light on matters. If you've never seen a high-powered rifle fired at night, it is a sight designed to stand your hair on end. A tongue of flame several feet long gouts from the barrel of the rifle. Macho military types are always telling you how great this is because it pinpoints the bad guys for you. Well, that's swell if you're a macho military type and you also have a gun, but I was a terrified doctor who'd never fired a gun in his life, and I fucking *knew* where the bad guys were—they were chasing *me*!

I dove off the crest of the hill, and in a shower of pebbles and dirt began my skittering descent into the Great Rift Valley.

By ten o'clock I was a wreck. The sun looked like a polished bronze disk in the sky. Heat and dust hazed the horizon. I had no water. No sunscreen. No lip balm. My face and scalp were cooked, my lips blistering. The burned dock of my tail was agony, and without a tail I was tormented by flies.

Occasionally I had passed a watering hole, but the film-encrusted, muddy water looked awful. I'm also a doctor. I knew it was the little gollywogs swimming around in that ugly water that were going to tap dance in my bowels. But sooner or later I was going to have to drink, and then the real fun would start.

My grand plan about hiding wasn't working out so great. The Rift Valley is pretty sparse. Expanses of grassland are occasionally dotted with spreading, flat-topped trees that sprout like desiccated mushrooms. Despite the Long Rains season there was a lot of dust, and that was what kept me running.

My hunters were in vehicles, and the dust rose like a peacock's plume from the spinning wheels, pinpointing their location and warning me that despite my best hopes, they were not giving up. The pursuit continued.

I was nearing the end of my strength, so I sank down in the sparse shade of a Jacaranda tree, tried to regulate my breathing. I closed my eyes trying to relieve their burning, and wished for dark glasses. A Snickers bar. A Coke. A miracle.

Like a half-remembered song, I could now faintly hear the drone of the jeep engines. Wearily I unfolded my legs and lurched to my feet. I had to grab for support from a low-hanging branch as a wave of dizziness took me. The agonizing run continued.

Thankfully God looks out for fools, little children, the United States of America, and jokers. My miracle occurred. As I trotted through a stand of thorn trees, I struck gold. The grasslands on the other side were dotted with impala. I hesitated just under the branches of the final tree. Compared. Our hides were an almost perfect match. I gave an experimental sniff to my armpits. Very much a human scent. Rubbed a hand across my side. Sniffed again. Not human. Not animal. Something different—joker scent. Would the impala accept me?

Bending at the waist, I dropped my head as close to the ground as possible, attempting to present the profile of a grazing impala, and edged toward the herd. A big buck lifted his head, snorted, and shook those lyrate horns. The entire herd tensed for a moment. The buck and I regarded each other. With the highlight of white over his liquid brown eyes he had the quality of a lovely and frightened girl. I tried to appear non-threatening. It worked better on the impala than it's worked on most women I've tried to date. The buck snorted a final time and resumed grazing.

I slipped into the center of the herd, and cast about for any shed or broken horns. Yes, I know, it was a dumb idea, but I wasn't thinking too clearly at that point. Needless to say, I didn't find any.

The droning of jeep engines began to break up the quiet of the afternoon. The impala herd came to quivering alertness, and then I saw the inherent flaw in my plan. The hunters would come. Spook the impala. The impala would run. If I couldn't keep pace with them, Finn would die.

The great stampede began. Within minutes my lungs were close to bursting, each exhalation like fire across my throat. I was falling farther and farther back in the herd—back where the sick and the young were running.

I started to cry. Decided I wouldn't be shot in the back. I plunged to a halt, and whirled to face them.

There were two jeeps bouncing and jouncing across the veldt. In one a man stood upright, one foot balanced on the dashboard, the other in the seat, and his knee locked against the back of the car seat for support. There was a rifle at his shoulder. He called out something, and the jeep began to slow.

My skin was crawling, looking for cover. Tears and snot gouged slimy trails down my dust-encrusted face.

There was the earsplitting *crack* of gunfire. The shooter in the jeep flung away his rifle, his arms windmilled, and he collapsed backward off the jeep. I looked around wildly. It was a silly reaction, but I suddenly realized that I was patting myself all over my chest as if to ascertain I really *wasn't* shot.

My pursuers spun their jeeps in tight U-turns, and began to haul ass out of there. There were two more shots, and another guy in the first jeep and one in the second jerked from the impact. There was the gnashing and grinding of gears, the squeak from too old brakes, and a mud-and-dust-covered Mercedes truck pulled up next to me.

"He's not on the endangered list, Mosi, guess we should have let 'em shoot him," said J.D. "And now you've gone and killed that guy." J.D. shook his head piously, and tsked.

There was a flash of ivory in ebony as Mosi grinned at me, tossed up his rifle, and caught it by the barrel. He slid the rifle into the truck and then maneuvered himself back through the window. When he thrust his arm back out, he was holding a wad of Kleenex.

I blew my nose, wiped the moisture from my face. The Kleenex was mud-caked trash in my hands.

"How . . . how . . ." I stammered.

"One of our scout planes spotted the vehicles. We figured poachers, and came out to check," Mosi said.

It suddenly all struck me as hilarious, and I began to whoop with laughter. They were staring at me—J.D. with some consternation and Mosi with fatherly understanding.

"No, no poachers," I finally managed to gasp out. "'Cause somebody just declared open season on jokers."

— — —

The tie-up of this sordid little story took only a day. Mosi and J.D. got me back to Nairobi. The solution in the pipette proved to be AIDS-infected human serum. The posse saddled up and headed out to Kilango, only to find Faneuil and Margaret had already split.

Of the three gunmen who were shot, two were dead, and all the survivor could tell us was that he had been hired by Faneuil to torch the clinic and kill me.

Two men had been assigned to head the medical investigation: Pan Rudo, a doctor with the World Health Organization, and Phillip, Baron von Herzenhagen, of the Red Cross. Rudo was an elderly, elegant man with an almost terrifying brilliance. Herzenhagen was a fat, blond white guy who looked like a stuffed tomato after a few hours in the African sun. It was Herzenhagen who had the bad taste to ask me how I felt— after all, I'd been "administering vaccinations to the children of Kilango for months. Infecting them with AIDS. Inadvertently . . . of course." As if that little addendum made it all okay. He ended the interrogation with the solicitous suggestion that I might want to seek counseling, but the show of concern didn't fool me. He had wanted to make me feel bad. I eyed him, and said in a level voice, "I bet you wet the bed, set fires, and tortured animals when you were a kid." I then turned my back on him and walked out. I remember there was a little choke of sound from Rudo. Whether laughter or outrage, I never knew. As for Herzenhagen, I didn't see him again until he waltzed across my television screen as a special advisor to the vice president in charge of eradicating jokers on the Rox. It seemed a perfect role for him.

The Kenyan authorities and I searched through Faneuil's and Margaret's personal effects, seeking some explanation for the horror they had perpetrated. We found none. I really hadn't expected to.

The cops tried to see if I could shed any light on the motive. After all, this man was a *doctor*. All I could tell them is that doctors are people, too, with the same hates and fears and biases as the rest of our tribe. And unfortunately, the list of healers who had turned to murder is a long and honored one.

Faneuil had been a psychopathic bigot—end of story.

Still, it bothers me how he got out of Kenya. Out of Africa. He must have had help in high places. Which scares me, and sometimes keeps me awake at night. Memories of a young boy with a sweet voice also return to haunt me occasionally. In 1990 Jonathan wrote to tell me Daudi had died. And all I could think was that I'd killed him. It was Tachyon—or rather his example—who helped me get past it.

I looked at him, and remembered how guilt had nearly destroyed his life.

I have a lot of people left to heal. I'm not going to blow it on guilt. Yes, I have been an unwitting accomplice to Faneuil's murders, but my conscience is clean. I just wonder if the same can be said for Faneuil—wherever he hides?

Yes, I'm afraid it can. The world has said it's okay to hate us. Maybe next they'll say it's okay to kill us. Faneuil is just waiting for vindication. He's sleeping the sleep of the righteous.

The Ashes of Memory

4

Hannah threw the transcripts down on Malcolm's desk. "I want Harris fired, Malcolm. I want his ass out the door."

Her fury had been building all day, though Hannah wondered if her ire was because Harris hadn't done his job or because his failure had dumped the task on her. But if Dr. Finn's tale had not been enough, listening to the depositions of the fire victims under his care had fueled the inward anger.

Jokers or not, no one deserved what they'd gone through.

Harris missed being on the receiving end of Hannah's wrath: He was out when she returned to the office that morning, and the fury had gone to glowing embers under the work awaiting her. The initial lab report had been on her desk, confirming that traces of jet fuel had been found in the remnants of the basement plants; the materials in the delayed fuse were still being checked. Dr. Sheets's autopsy reports came in the late afternoon: nothing unusual there other than the bizarre variety of forms among the dead. CO levels in the blood and tissue samples indicated that most had died from smoke inhalation long before the flames reached them. There were, as Hannah expected, no traces of Ringmistress Zara's VX poison in any of them.

Hannah had requested a database check on convicted and suspected pyros in the city; the list was depressingly long. Aces like Jumping Jack Flash she discarded since there'd been nothing to suggest a wild card power had been involved in the fire. Those who were still incarcerated or already in jail, those who never torched occupied buildings, and those who had never indicated any wild card antipathy she moved to the bottom of the list. There were still a dozen names left in the priority category. She'd decided to take Arnold Simpson, another of the agents, and interrogate the first one: Kevin Ramblur, a street gang kid with the nickname of Flashfire who, it was suspected, had been responsible for snatching lone jokers from the street and setting them afire, when the floor clerk brought in Harris's transcripts.

"Pete said to give you these and that he'd talk with you later today," the clerk said. "He had a doctor's appointment."

Harris's report was a long litany of "not available for deposition" and sketchy logs. They were garbage; utterly useless even if she hadn't already known from Dr. Finn that all of them were outright lies. That had fanned the dull anger back into rage, and Hannah stalked down to Malcolm's office, rehearsing her first words.

"I'm not kidding, Malcolm. This is either incompetence, deliberate sabotaging of my case, or both."

Malcolm Coan, District Director of the Arson Bureau, New York State Department of Justice, had the eyes of a Great White, dark and frighteningly expressionless. The rest of his demeanor did nothing to dispel the illusion of a predator, nor did the fact that he insisted all his subordinates address him by his first name lend him any friendliness. Everything about the man was sharp and edged: the lines of his face; the carefully manicured nails; the fresh starch on his white shirt; the careful crease of his pants. He picked up the reports Hannah had thrown down on the empty expanse of his desk, shuffled them carefully so that the edges aligned, and then leafed through them without a word as Hannah paced in front of him, too agitated to sit down. Finally he placed the reports precisely in front of him and looked at her with those dead, unreadable eyes. He waited.

"All that's just trash," Hannah said finally. "Garbage. Harris says he went to the Jokertown Clinic but accomplished nothing. 'Not available.' Well, that's a bald-faced lie. I talked to the survivors of the fire myself yesterday evening and Dr. Finn was entirely cooperative."

"Are you in the habit of checking up on the work of your agents?" Coan asked. His voice was no different than the rest of him: cutting and thin. *Malcolm can make "good morning" sound like an obituary.* Hannah had heard that joke her first day on the job.

"No, sir," she answered. "I much prefer to believe that they'll give me their best effort. The fact that I caught this was entirely coincidental, but I did. Now I can't trust *any* of Harris's work, and I don't like his attitude, either. He obviously doesn't care."

"And you want me to terminate Mr. Harris."

"Malcolm, the regulations—"

"I know the regulations perfectly well, Ms. Davis." Coan smiled, but there was no amusement in the expression. "I also know Mr. Harris's work. In fact, I would have considered him for your position had I not been"—he paused before he finished—"persuaded otherwise. He has done excellent investigation for me in the past."

"With all due respect, not this time."

"Nonetheless . . ." Coan swiveled in his chair. The *Times* lay at right angles to the corner of his credenza. Coan plucked the front section from the stack and placed it on the desk so that Hannah could see it. "Today's edition," Coan said. "You will note that your fire has dropped entirely off the front page. You'll find no mention of it anywhere until page seven."

The anger inside Hannah suddenly went cold. "What are you telling me, Malcolm? That no one cares about jokers? I'd already figured that out."

"It means, Ms. Davis, that I have very little incentive to keep an already overburdened staff working overtime on your case. It means that since you dislike Mr. Harris's efforts so much, I can oblige you by taking him off this assignment. I can use him elsewhere."

"Take him off . . ." Words dissolved in her shock. "I'm already understaffed for something like this, Malcolm."

"I can't afford to lose good agents, Ms. Davis. I also can't afford to waste this much manpower"—he actually smiled at her with the word—"on this case. If you don't want Mr. Harris, that's not a problem."

"Malcolm—"

"And I need your preliminary findings report on my desk tomorrow morning at eight o'clock," he continued. "For the press, should they be interested."

"You're going to ignore what I've told you about Harris?"

"Give me a signed complaint and I'll make sure it goes in his personnel file along with my notes on this meeting and a formal reprimand. Will that be satisfactory, Ms. Davis?"

Hannah swallowed the remark she wanted to make. "Do I have a choice, Malcolm?"

"Frankly, Ms. Davis, no. You don't. This decision, at least, is mine."

Hannah nodded curtly. "Then I'll get started on that complaint," she said.

"Eight o'clock tomorrow for your report," Malcolm told Hannah's retreating back. "No later."

One of the lab techs was waiting for her in the corridor. She took a look at Hannah's expression, whistled softly, and handed Hannah a sheet of paper with exaggerated caution. "It couldn't have been too bad," she said. "Your head's still attached."

Hannah grimaced. "This going to make me feel better, Jo Ann?"

"I doubt it. We tracked down the fuse components that were identifiable. A pretty standard hobby store chip used with nine-volt batteries: That was your timer. The piece of small canister that you found had a few flecks of green paint on it. Suggest anything to you?"

"Oxygen," Hannah said, and Jo Ann nodded. "Anybody who works around oxygen knows that you can't let pure oxygen come into contact with petroleum products without combustion and probably a small explosion. So he made a timer to puncture the canister about the time the JP-4 was rising in the sink." A premonition ran cold fingers down Hannah's spine. "So who'd know about that reaction?"

"Anybody who works with oxy. Welders?" Jo Ann suggested. "Or someone in a hospital?"

Hannah nodded. She hated the thought that had just occurred to her. "Right. Thanks, Jo. This is great stuff. Excuse me, but I need to run a background check . . ."

— — —

Arnold Simpson was one of the agents Hannah liked. He acted no differently around her than anyone else. He didn't seem to have a problem with the idea of a woman in a position of authority. As he said once to her, after a staff meeting particularly thick with innuendos and unsubtle digs in Hannah's direction: *"Hey, I'm their showcase Black agent; you're the showcase woman. I know exactly what's going on. At least we ain't damn jokers."*

"This Ramblur guy doesn't exactly live on Park Avenue, does he?" Simpson flipped through the printouts Hannah had given him as she unlocked the staff Escort in the Bureau's parking garage. "Nice priors, too. Don't you just love our criminal justice system?" Simpson threw the file on the dash and swung his long legs around the passenger seat. "NYPD thinks he's the one been dousing the lone jokers and torching 'em, huh?"

"Yeah," Hannah said, sliding behind the wheel. "I talked with somebody named Ellis out at the J-Town precinct. Said they're pretty sure it was him. They just don't have enough to drag him in."

"You think maybe he's tired of doing things one corpse at a time?"

"We'll see." Hannah turned the key and put the car in gear. She started to pull out of the space.

She stood on the brakes, the tires screeching in protest. "Shit!"

Quasiman stood in front of the Escort, an inch from the bumper. Hannah didn't have any idea where the joker had been hiding, but there he was.

Simpson started to surge out of the car, but Hannah stopped him with a hand on his arm. "It's okay," she said. "I know this guy. Just give me a second, all right?" Hannah took a deep breath, trying to calm her racing heart, and got out.

"What the hell do you think you're doing?"

Quasiman actually smiled at her. It didn't help her temper. "You're Hannah." He seemed inordinately proud of the fact that he'd remembered her name.

"Yes, I'm Hannah. And you're in our way. Get the hell out of here before I call security."

"I saw something," Quasiman persisted. "I came right away so I wouldn't forget it all."

"More dreams? More crystal ball stuff about you seeing the future?"

A nod. "It's already half-gone, like a fog. That's why I had to come now. It's all leaving me so fast."

"Then you've wasted your time. Get it through your head— I'm not interested. You want me to solve the case, then let me get on with what I'm doing. Get out of our way."

Quasiman went berserk at that. He banged his fist against the hood, the sound echoing through the garage like a car crash. His fist came away leaving a dimpled crater in the metal. The joker shouted, nearly frothing in his effort to get the words out. "There was a doctor, Hannah! Fan . . . Fan . . . Fan-ool? And his nurse . . ."

"Go away!"

"They were in a jungle. Lots of green. Hot, very hot. And death that wasn't death." Quasiman was coming around the side of the car. Hannah jumped back in and slammed the door shut, hitting the locks. She was fairly sure that the joker could rip the door off if he wanted to, but he just continued his ranting from the other side of the glass. "You went to see someone called Rudo," Quasiman shouted, his voice muffled, his face smearing saliva across the glass. Hannah gunned the engine and he stumbled back. "You go to Rudo!" he screamed as she slammed the gearshift into DRIVE and careened away. "Green canisters, Hannah! There were green canisters!"

His voice trailed away as Hannah turned the corner onto the garage's exit ramp. The sound of Quasiman's voice seemed to echo far too long in her mind.

Green canisters . . . Fan-ool . . . "Damn it, how did he know I checked?" Hannah muttered.

"What?" Simpson asked. He was looking back over his shoulder.

"Nothing."

"So what the fuck was that?"

"A weirdo," Hannah said grimly. "Forget it. Let's go talk with Ramblur and the others on the list. When we get back, I think I might do something stupid."

Dr. Pan Rudo was as Hannah had pictured him from Dr. Finn's tale: thin, graying, elegant, and friendly in a mannered way. He looked to be somewhere in his mid-sixties, fine lines snagging his blue eyes and netting his mouth. He folded his hands on his desk and shrugged. Behind him, several stories down, the office window gave a view of the UN Plaza, crowded with people heading home after the workday. The walls of the office were lined with plaques and photos: Dr. Rudo with Albert Einstein; with the ageless Winston Churchill; with Marilyn Monroe; with every president from Carter to Bush. "I find myself at a loss, Ms. Davis. I can't imagine why you would be interested in poor, misguided Dr. Faneuil."

"I'm not exactly sure why, either, Dr. Rudo," Hannah admitted. "Let's say that I'm being a little over-thorough and maybe a bit paranoid."

Rudo smiled at her. "Ordinarily, I'd say that's an unusual

and attractive asset in your occupation. So how may I help you?"

Hannah gave Rudo a condensed version of what had led her to Dr. Finn. Rudo listened attentively, his hand steepled under his chin, nodding occasionally. When she had finished, he spread his hands wide in a gesture of sympathy. "I see why you might wonder," he told her. "I remember Kenya all too well. Dr. Faneuil was a terrible and tragic waste of incredible talent, and we all owe a debt of gratitude to Dr. Finn for exposing him."

"I ran a background check," Hannah said. "Dr. Faneuil began to work for the Red Cross and various other charitable health organizations in the early sixties. He went to Kenya in 1974, and fled in 1985 in the aftermath of the AIDS revelation. The records indicate he was known to be in Vietnam by 1986, and then . . . well, *nothing*. He disappears from all the records I could find."

"And you wonder if possibly he didn't return here with his vendetta against jokers still in mind?"

Hannah shrugged.

Rudo smiled. "Then I can set your mind at ease, Ms. Davis. I happen to know that Etienne Faneuil died in what is now called 'Free Vietnam' in 1988, when it was still the Socialist Republic. He is buried there, in a village called 'Xuan Loc,' about thirty-five miles east of Saigon, if I recall correctly."

"You're certain? The records I have don't indicate that."

Rudo laughed, gently. His graceful hands touched the Mont Blanc fountain pen lying alongside the leather desk pad, then returned to his lap as he sat back in his chair. "You're very persistent, Ms. Davis. But WHO has excellent sources all over the world, and I have both a very good memory and a certain vested interest in Dr. Faneuil, since I was peripherally involved in funding him in Kenya. Yes, I'm certain. I received the news of his death with mixed emotions, I must admit. In many ways, Etienne did much good in his time, as well as much evil."

"What about his nurse, Margaret Durand? She helped him with the genocide."

Rudo frowned. "I didn't know her well. I believe she followed Dr. Faneuil to Vietnam but I don't know what became of her. Just a moment . . ." He leaned forward again and touched a button on his phone system. "Dianne," he said, "before you go, make a note to call Aaron Cofield first thing tomorrow morning. Have him start checking for any information he might have on the present whereabouts of a Margaret Durand. She was Etienne Faneuil's nurse. Tell him that I'll give him a call with additional information later."

"Yes, Doctor," a voice answered, tinny through the small speaker. "Have a good evening."

"Thank you." Rudo touched the intercom button again and looked at Hannah. "There. I will send you the results. We probably have better international contacts, even into Free Vietnam despite all its recent uproar." Rudo sighed. "Remember, Ms. Davis, that Dr. Faneuil would be in his mid-seventies if he were still alive. I would imagine Margaret would be sixty or older. Does that fit your fire setter's profile?"

"Not really," Hannah admitted. "Dr. Rudo, thanks for your time. I'd appreciate your looking into Faneuil and Margaret Durand."

"You still think this might be something more than simple arson and murder?"

"I don't know, Dr. Rudo. I try not to have any opinion about it at all and just let the facts speak for themselves. Honestly, I don't think any of this will pan out, but I feel that I have to examine every possibility."

Rudo smiled again and stood, extending his hand. "That is best, certainly. If I can be of any more help to you . . ."

His handshake was firm and warm. "Thank you, Doctor. You've been more than helpful already. I have another appointment this evening, as a matter of fact—someone else who might know something about Durand."

"So you've been looking her up, also."

"Yes. Actually, her background is more interesting than Dr. Faneuil's."

"Fascinating. Then I'll simply wish you luck." He started to walk Hannah toward the door, then stopped. He cocked his head to one side slightly, as if appraising a painting or sculpture. "Forgive me for saying this, but as a psychologist, I notice things. Your accent tells me that you're not native to the city, and I suspect that you're not entirely happy here. If I can be of any help in that area . . ."

"Am I that transparent?" Hannah asked, genuinely shocked. She tried to laugh; it sounded utterly false.

Rudo chuckled with her. "No, Ms. Davis. I just pick up on these things. My offer's genuine. Sometimes a neutral ear . . ." He smiled again.

"I'll keep it in mind," Hannah told him. *The way work is going, the way my relationship with David has gone sour . . .* "Maybe," she said, not realizing until a second later that she'd spoken aloud.

"Please do. Trust yourself, Ms. Davis. You strike me as both dedicated and intelligent. I'm sure you will find your arsonist, and very soon."

"It was this picture, Mr. Dearborn. A rather famous picture, from what I'm told. When I saw her file, when I saw where she'd worked and what had happened there, I checked the Wolfe book out of the library. I also found out that you lived in New York now."

"*True Brothers.*" Dearborn gave her a lopsided grin. "Wolfe might be a fine writer, but he ain't a pilot, and no amount of poetic language can replace that. I never could read his book, but I remember the picture."

The retired Navy captain had an apartment in the Village, overlooking one of the little parks. He took the book from Hannah, studied the photo reproduced there through his bifocals. Dearborn looked almost skeletal. "Ahh, we were handsome then," he said, handing it back to her. His hand trembled with a palsy. *He's on medication,* the tenant downstairs had told her. *Really sick. Sometimes it makes him a little, well, rambling.* She'd tapped her head.

"We had hair," Dearborn said, chuckling. "Lots of it. We thought nothing could kill us. Nothing, ever. We were immortal."

He chuckled again, then leaned back on the couch. A television, the sound off but the picture still on, flickered in the corner of the room. All around, there were photos of Dearborn, standing alongside a series of aircraft. A half dollar was sitting on the coffee table. Dearborn picked it up and began flipping it. *Heads.* Flip. *Heads.* Flip. *Heads.* He noticed Hannah watching him and put the coin down again.

"Yes, that's Margaret Durand," Dearborn said. "Peggy, we called her. She was our flight nurse for the project. Thayer took the picture at Pancho's, in fact. He used my camera; I had an old Argus C3. Lot of those shots on the walls taken with it. In fact, I think it's still around here somewhere. *Life* bought the reprint rights from us afterward. Wolfe did, too." He licked dry, cracked lips. "Maybe except for Peg, I'm the only one left of the bunch, as I guess you've found out. The only one. Sometimes I think about that, and it scares me. I don't have much time left myself: colon cancer. Not too many people know or care what happened back then."

Hannah broke in as Dearborn's gaze drifted away. "I'm very sorry, Mr. Dearborn. Would you know where Margaret might be now?"

"Lord, no," Dearborn answered. "Afterward, we didn't really keep in touch. I think we were all ashamed. Too much mud got slung around and a lot of it stuck. Do you know about it? *Really* know about it?"

"No, sir. Not very much. Would you take a look at this other picture?" Hannah interrupted. "It's taken much later, around 1982."

Dearborn looked closely at the photograph, holding it up to the lamp alongside the couch. "Why, that's Peggy, too. Older and heavier, but I'd recognize that face and that smile anywhere. So she *did* get back into nursing. Where was this taken? Looks like Africa somewhere."

"Kenya," Hannah told him. "You're certain that's Margaret?"

Dearborn glanced at the photo again, then handed it back. "Positive." Dearborn frowned. "You said you were some kind of investigator. Is she in trouble again? Is she dead?"

"In trouble *again*?"

Dearborn sighed. A flash of pain seemed to run behind his eyes. His lips tightened and he groaned. "Mr. Dearborn?" Hannah asked. "Is there something I can get for you?"

"Pills," he said. "On the table in the kitchen. No," he said as Hannah started to get up. "Let me get them. It's one of the things I won't let myself do—I'm not going to give in to the pain and let someone take care of me. I take care of myself. Always have, always will." He moved off into the kitchen. Hannah could hear him running water, drinking.

"I'll be back in a minute," he said, and his footsteps moved away into another hidden room.

Hannah heard a door open and the sound of boxes being

moved. A few minutes later, Dearborn came out again with a cardboard carton. He set it down on the coffee table and looked at her. "No one really knows what happened," he told her. "No one. Not even Wolfe. I was never one to write things down, but Thayer was. His lawyer sent me this stuff after Thayer's car wreck. It was in the will that this went to any surviving member of the project. Poor guy: six months out of prison and he loses control on a curve. I never really looked at the notebooks; that wasn't a period in my life I particularly wanted to remember. But Thayer wrote it all down, the way he saw it, anyway. There's stuff about Peggy in there."

Dearborn pulled the box open. A yellowed newspaper clipping wafted out. Dearborn plucked it from the air and gave it to Hannah.

A Method of Reaching Extreme Altitudes

Michael Cassutt

(*From* Los Angeles Herald, *April 12, 1958*)

US TO TRY ROCKET FLIGHT BEFORE RUSSIANS?

ROSAMOND, CALIFORNIA. (*Herald* exclusive) The United States may undertake a manned rocket flight in the next few weeks in an attempt to beat the Russians into space, it was learned here today.

Officials at the Muroc Lake Test Site of the National Advisory Committee on Aeronautics referred this reporter to the USAF office here, which declined comment. NACA's Muroc Site is part of the larger, restricted access Tomlin Air Force Base.

Nevertheless, it is known that six Air Force and NACA test pilots are training for flights in a winged rocketplane known as the X-11A. Several of these pilots are reported to have taken part in as many as five unpowered free flights of the X-11A, in which the

Northrop-built vehicle glided to a landing on the dry lake bed at Tomlin.

The planned orbital flight would reportedly see the X-11A take off from Tomlin to rendezvous with a specially modified Boeing tanker at 30,000 feet. Following refueling, the X-11A would rocket into orbit on its own power, returning to Tomlin after making a single orbit of Earth.

The existence of the American orbital program, long rumored, comes three weeks after the announcement by the Soviet Union that it hopes to launch a manned spacecraft known as "North" on its own orbital mission sometime later this year . . .

(From the notebooks of Edgar Thayer)

In those days—which seem quite long ago, as I write, but were actually less than five years in the past—the Muroc Lake facility of the National Advisory Committee on Aeronautics wasn't on any maps.

This had less to do with security concerns (NACA was a civilian agency, anyway) than with the general lack of formality, or even public interest. Nevertheless, as I waited for the phone call in the ratty motel in Rosamond on the morning of April 12, I didn't need directions: I already knew where to find it.

I was fourteen years old and living in a small town in southern Minnesota when the wild card struck. Although we were not isolated—we had CBS radio coming through loud and clear on WCCO—we were not directly affected. For years I thought of the plague as less important than polio, which had crippled one of my classmates.

What fascinated me was the proof that there was life on other planets. I was already a sporadic reader of comic books—sporadic only because the vagaries of distribution didn't often bring them to St. Peter—and became a devotee of Heinlein's Tak World books. I discovered the first one, *Eclipse,* in the St. Peter High School library my junior year, and made such a fuss over it that my parents bought the next one, *Fire Down Below,* $2.45, for me the following Christmas.

They faithfully sent me each new one, all through my time at the University of Minnesota, and even during my first two years in the Air Force. I can remember eagerly unwrapping *The Sound of His Wings,* the 1955 volume—the last in the series, alas—while sitting in an office at Kirtland Air Force Base looking out on the very hangar where the Takisian ship *Baby* had been based before being moved to California.

So I was one of the few—very few—who still believed that humans might have a destiny in space. Who weren't ready to give up the dream just because someone had found us first.

My work in the Air Force was as an analyst with the foreign technology division. It consisted of taking captured German and stolen Soviet weapons—in my case, missiles—out to New Mexico and firing them off to learn how they worked. It was fascinating, and my experience in the infant field of launch operations got me assigned later to Cape Canaveral Air Force Station in Florida, where I worked on Pied Piper, our first satellite program.

That April morning in Rosamond I was twenty-eight years old, having left the service after completing my ROTC commitment. I had spent the intervening year at Aerojet in Pasadena, working on the rocket engine that would later be used in the X-11A. My background as a launch controller had come to NACA's attention, however, and I had been summoned to the high desert in great secrecy for an assignment of unlimited duration.

It was greatly upsetting to my wife, Deborah, who was left in the apartment in Pasadena, pregnant and caring for our five-year-old daughter.

For me, however, it was a dream come true.

They started early at Muroc in those days. The phone call from Dr. Rowe's office came before six . . . by seven I was at the administration building (*shack* would be a better word) thirty-two miles away, having passed through three successively picky Air Force checkpoints, while driving through the flat, trackless waste that was Tomlin.

(There had been a late spring rain that year, and the usually dry lake beds were covered with an inch-deep sheen. Rising over the Tehachapis, the sun and its reflection effectively blinded me: never the best of drivers, I could just as easily have driven off the road, rolled the car, and drowned in an inch of water.)

By nine I had been badged and cross-examined by a security officer named Battle, who had the air of a parochial school nun. Then I was taken into my first briefing.

It wasn't particularly dark in the conference room; the blinds had been drawn so that viewgraphs could be seen. But it took a moment for my eyes to adjust from the blinding brilliance of a desert morning.

Rowe was just discussing how some unexpected funding cuts were going to force stretchouts in the final testing phase . . . possibly delaying the first all-up launch of the X-11A by several weeks or more.

"Ah, shit, Doc," said a voice from the back. "Who needs the tests? We know it'll fly . . . let us fly it."

"That's easy for you to say, hotshot," a second guy said. "*You* won't be flying the first one." There was some general laughter.

Then Rowe noticed me.

"Here's the new arrival now," he said. "The most vital element in any program team . . . the *last* one to join. Ed Thayer." I shook some hands that belonged to vaguely familiar faces, then took an open chair between the two men who had been kidding each other.

To my right was the youngest pilot in the group, Mike Sampson, an Air Force captain. The file on him had been brief . . . first in his class at West Point, service as a fighter pilot in Germany, an engineering degree from Michigan. What was unusual is that he had also done graduate work in astronomy. Clearly he had his sights on a career in space, not just aviation.

The loudmouth who didn't care for the pace of the testing program was Al Dearborn, a naval aviator. Wearing a Hawaiian shirt and pants the color of a diseased liver, he looked more like the number two mechanic at a small-town filling station than someone who held the Distinguished Flying Cross. (He had shot down two MiGs in Korea.) One of my briefers had expressed amazement that Dearborn had gotten into the program at all, assuming his selection was a bone thrown to the Navy in exchange for minuscule financial support. In fact, Dearborn hadn't even finished in the top three when the Navy selection board made its choices, but two of the other finalists chose to stay in flight test at Patuxent River, while the third had managed to break his arm in a softball game.

Sitting across from me was Major Woody Enloe, USAF, blond and handsome in the manner of a teen movie star. Even sitting down, he seemed taller than the others. He was known as a pilot's pilot, the only one ever to have waxed Yeager in a dogfight.

Next to him was his reverse image, the dark, homely, clumsy Casey Guinan, a civilian pilot who had worked with Rowe since World War II. His file showed him to be a multiengine pilot and though the decision about who would fly the X-11A on its maiden voyage was still to be made, Guinan was sure to pilot the tanker instead.

I don't remember many details from the briefing. The first all-up attempt to get the X-11A into orbit was then still three weeks off. As Dr. Rowe pointed out, it had been three weeks off for six months now. There were ongoing concerns about the fuel lines—the X-11A had two engines, a jet *and* a rocket motor, which shared common tanks. So there was the obvious problem of pumping liquid oxygen from one aircraft to another at 30,000 feet. Which in turn made the X-11A itself a potential flying bomb.

Everyone knew the refueling concept was tricky . . . but the only other way to get a workable manned spacecraft—not just a tin can—into orbit was a multistage launch vehicle. The United States had the Convair Atlas ICBM, which had put Pied Piper into orbit. A multistage version of Atlas was years and millions of dollars away.

I did learn that my job would involve monitoring the two propellant systems. Fortunately I had helped design one of them—the rocket. So all I had to do in the next three weeks was become an expert on jet engines.

It never occurred to me that this was unreasonable, or impossible. There I was, sitting in a room with Wilson Rowe, who had been one of my idols, and the pilots who would be the first space travelers. I was *home*.

— — —

When the meeting broke up, Dr. Rowe called me over. He was then about fifty, slim, bald, with merry eyes hidden behind the engineer's thick eyeglasses. He had grown up with aviation . . . watching some of the first Army tests at Camp McCook in Dayton, Ohio, where he lived. (The story was that a Packard-Le Pere LUSAC 11, the earliest American fighter plane, had crash-landed in his family's backyard, thus ensuring that young Wilson would do nothing else in his life.) Getting into MIT, earning one of the first degrees offered in aeronautical engineering . . . working on America's first jets and rockets during World War II.

Those were the broad outlines of Rowe's career, but they said nothing about his ability to lead or inspire. During my brief career at Aerojet I had run into no less than four of his former associates . . . all of them spoke of him in awe as the man with the vision. The man who believed. The man who would cajole or seduce or threaten or bully to reach his goal.

The single biggest disappointment in his life was obvious to everyone . . . that he, himself, would never see the Earth as a sphere . . . never kick the dust of the surface of the Moon. You see, Rowe had paid his way through college as a barnstormer, flying his own specially modified Stearman in county fairs and settings even less formal all across America. It was his eyesight that forever kept him from becoming a professional pilot, a verdict he accepted gracefully, without complaint.

But even now, it was said, when the pressure got to be too much, he would sneak off to nearby El Mirage to go sailplaning.

"Mr. Thayer. I've been waiting for you."

At first I thought I had already done something wrong. "I came straight here from Security," I said.

He smiled, his eyes twinkling behind the thick lenses. "Not this morning. For weeks. Months."

Fumbling for my sunglasses, I followed him out of the briefing shack into the noonday sun. He never even blinked. I had a quick, nod-of-the-head tour. "Control center's over there . . . Aerojet office . . . Pratt & Whitney. Hangar Two." That hangar was practically a shrine to someone like me. The JB-1, the first American jet, had been towed here, complete with a dummy propeller on its nose to confuse Axis spies. (I had seen a replica of JB-1 at Jetboy's Tomb in New York, of course, during a Boy Scout trip there when I was thirteen.) This was also where Kelly Johnson's lovely XP-80 had flown, with the ill-fated Halford engine. "Oh, yes . . ." he said finally, as we approached another massive, never painted structure. "Hangar Three." We went inside.

It took me several seconds to realize that I was looking at the X-11A, vehicle number one. (Northrup, the prime contractor, was assembling birds two and three out in some town with the unlikely name of Pico Rivera.)

I had only seen a couple of rough sketches in *Aviation Week* . . . and they hadn't done it justice. They made the X-11A look like a slightly larger Bell X-1—a bullet with wings.

This was a winged beast more like an eagle. Or, to shift from the aero to the nautical, a manta ray. For one thing, it was twice the size of the X-1, fifty-five feet long, with a delta wing forty feet across at its widest. The tail, rising above the fraternal twin engines, reached eighteen feet.

It was the cockpit that reminded everyone of the X-1. It was so cramped that Enloe—never a noted humorist—was widely quoted as saying, "You don't climb in . . . you put it on." Because most of the X-11A's volume was taken up by engines and fuel tanks, there wasn't even room enough for the pilot to float around once reaching zero-G. Later models would be bigger, with better engines. There would *have* to be more room . . . if we were going to land X-11A or its children on the Moon.

"The world's first spaceship," I said, walking underneath it with its father.

"Is it? What's going on with the Russians?"

"My information is over a year old."

A tight smile. "That's not what I hear."

My background as an analyst was no secret to Rowe—to anyone. But who knew that I'd kept in touch with the Foreign Technology Division, more as a hobby than anything else? My wife, maybe. "All I have is raw data."

"That's okay. This isn't a quiz. I just want to know if von Braun and Korolev are going to beat me."

The fact that he knew those names told me he had access to whatever information there was. Von Braun had headed the Nazi V-2 rocket program and had been brought to the United States briefly after the war to build rockets for the US Army. After the wild card struck, the program was scrapped. Leaving his brain—or whatever was valuable in it—behind, von Braun returned to Germany, where he was scooped up by the Russians.

According to the stories—and they may have been just that: stories—he found a soul brother in a Russian engineer named Sergei Korolev.

Korolev was a lot like Rowe . . . a child of aviation who burned to go beyond it. He was flying gliders in his twenties and building rocket motors in his thirties. He had come close to being shot during the purges that destroyed the Soviet air force in 1938, wound up in a gold mine in the Arctic under a de facto sentence of death . . . only to be reprieved. He'd built Katyusha rockets for Stalin during the war, and then was put in charge of finding a use for all the captured German V-2s.

I would have given anything to be present when Korolev first met von Braun.

"They've adapted one of the German designs for a multi-stage booster—" I said.

"The A-10?"

"More or less. They call it the R-11."

"Interesting coincidence."

"It's a big brute—"

"You've seen it?"

Should I answer? I had seen Pied Piper photos, which were highly classified. But Rowe knew about Korolev and von Braun; surely he knew about our spy satellites. "Yes. It's twenty stories tall, maybe thirty feet across at the base, tapering like an artillery shell. I guess it puts out over a million pounds of thrust—"

He was shaking his head, out of pleasure or annoyance, I couldn't say. "And we have a tenth of that."

"And they will throw away nine-tenths of that rocket."

"The spacecraft itself . . . ?"

"A modified missile nosecone with a blunt bottom. One pilot."

He was thinking, almost certainly replaying endless debates over the very same issues, reaching the same conclusion. "We couldn't have done it. We built bombers, not intercontinental missiles." He smiled again. "But their way is faster."

"They haven't had a manned launch yet."

We were interrupted by a female voice. "Dr. Rowe?"

I turned. A woman in her early thirties wearing a white blouse and a beige skirt was walking toward us. She had copper-colored hair that was pulled back by a hairband and was wearing her sunglasses inside the darkened hangar. "They were looking for you over in administration," she said.

"Thanks, Peggy." He clapped me on the shoulder. "We'll

have plenty of time to talk later." As he went out: "By the way, Edgar Thayer, Margaret Durand. The rest is up to you."

Only when Rowe had walked off did she take off her glasses. I saw that her eyes were a blue so pale they looked transparent. Maybe it was the drab surroundings, maybe it was my personal situation. She was the most beautiful woman I had ever seen.

I had married a hometown girl for reasons that couldn't possibly have been any good. We both thought we were in love. We both wanted to get out of St. Peter.

Oddly enough, we hadn't been high school sweethearts: I had gone on three forced dates (to this day I can remember each excruciating moment) . . . two homecomings and one senior prom, each with a different partner. I knew Deborah, of course—I knew everyone in St. Peter High—and thought her quite pretty and nice. She even had a good sense of humor. But she had a steady boyfriend, one of the Borchert boys, from a farm family east of town, with whom she was constantly breaking up. Nevertheless, most high school couples in St. Peter had, like it or not, mated for life. It never occurred to me to ask Deborah out.

Not until I came home on my second summer vacation from St. Paul. I had left St. Peter a virgin; I had returned a veteran of half a dozen sexual encounters, some of which I hadn't had to buy. Romance was in the air. And Deb was in the middle of a surprisingly long breakup with Billy Borchert.

One thing led to another, as they say. When I went back to the University of Minnesota at the end of the summer, we were sort of engaged. When Deborah called three months later to tell me she was pregnant, we got married. And I, the panicked new father, worried about supporting a wife and child, joined

ROTC, committing myself to five years of service in the Air Force. (The way I looked at it, I was committing the Air Force to support me for five years.)

Deb joined me in St. Paul, where Caroline was born.

We had one good year, I think, that year when Caroline was in her crib. Living in married student housing only slightly better than a Selby and Dale tenement, we had no money for babysitters—when we did go out, even to see a movie like *She Wore a Yellow Ribbon*, it was a special occasion—but we were entertained by Caroline's antics. Deb made a stab at being the wife of an engineering student, helping me with my course work, reading some of the texts—I think she even thought about going to the U of M herself. But all she had really wanted was to save herself from becoming a farm wife. It was enough for her to have a child and be in the big city.

I don't know that I was ever in love with Deborah. I don't know that she was ever really in love with me. But, all in all, we had more good times than bad. Until the day I drove into Muroc.

"He likes you." Those were Margaret's first words to me. (I was never able to call her Peggy; that was one thing that separated me from the others.)

"Who?"

"Rowe."

"We just met."

"He knows all about you, or you wouldn't be here."

"That doesn't mean he likes me."

"He doesn't give tours of the X-11 to everyone he hires." She reached out and stroked the leading edge of the spacecraft, her red nails and pale fingers in stark contrast to the black titanium.

"You're keeping track."

"I keep my eyes open. Part of my job."

"Which is?"

"Flight nurse."

"I think I'm going to faint."

"Don't do it now." She walked past me, so close that I caught a wisp of her perfume. "I'm off-duty."

The big question around the office, I learned later that day, concerned the pilot who would be selected for the first X-11 launch. All four candidates had been given the same training and told they would all remain at some mental and physical peak.

In fact, the strain was driving them crazy. I got my first hint the next morning, when I went through suiting with Enloe and Guinan prior to a test flight. (Sampson and Dearborn had done theirs the day before I arrived.)

I later learned that it was Enloe who insisted on my presence: He had very firm ideas about who he wanted making decisions involving his life or death. He wanted to size me up.

I didn't know whether to admire Enloe, or write him off as some kind of obsessive freak. He made this run-through as realistic as possible, right down to paying forty cents for his low-residue breakfast from the officers' club. (I asked one of the chase pilots, a Major Meadows, why the program didn't pay for breakfast. He just stared at me and said, "Tradition." By which he meant, I realized, "superstition.")

The surgeon, Dr. Lawrence, had checked Enloe out prior to breakfast. So it was just Enloe, Guan, Meadows, and me. The moment the coffee had been cleared away, Enloe put on his long johns and flight helmet. (He had to pre-breathe for two hours, since the X-11A was pressurized with pure oxygen at five pounds per square inch, much less than sea level.)

While the suit techs periodically checked Enloe's helmet, I did the weather briefing and Meadows went over the flight conditions—ground track, call signs, abort points. Enloe absorbed it all without a trace of emotion. He was like an actor doing *Hamlet*, and it was impossible to tell whether for the fourth—or four hundredth—time.

Guinan was more of a mystery, eating a double breakfast while seemingly paying absolutely no attention to what was going on. He could have been some truck driver having ham and eggs between oil changes.

By now a second chase pilot, Captain Grissom, had joined us. He and Meadows donned regular flight suits, then helped Guinan with what looked like a brand-new one, right out of its paper bag. I didn't learn why until later.

Then it was into the pressure suit for Enloe: lacing the heavy boots, connecting the pressure hoses and electrical leads. "I want you to ride in the tank this morning."

"I'm supposed to be in flight control."

"They'll survive without you for one more day."

I wouldn't have dared to ask, but Enloe, as senior test pilot, had almost as much clout as Rowe himself. I stepped out the back door to use a phone, got through to Rowe and explained Enloe's request. Rowe's answer was brief: "Do as he says."

Outside the suiting room I saw two very strange sights:

First was Woody Enloe . . . all buttoned up in his orange pressure suit . . . bowing his head in prayer. Then lifting off the ground . . . hovering briefly . . . *flying*, one arm extended like Black Eagle, toward the flight line.

Enloe was an ace.

Second, in the hallway, just inside the door, was Casey Guinan . . . passionately kissing Margaret Durand. I almost ran into them. Guinan didn't even look at me. He merely patted

Margaret on the behind and went out. Margaret's glance met mine.

"*Everyone* likes *me*, Thayer."

Guinan's tank—I never heard the NACA-modified KC-135 called anything else—was already in flight . . . orbiting in a racetrack pattern, when Enloe took off, the stubby wings of the X-11A biting the desert air. I barely paid attention, so appalled was I at the tank's cockpit.

The controls had been specially modified so that there were almost no displays . . . just open panels. I could only think of them as wounds. Gone were the traditional pilot's chairs—gone, for that matter, was the co-pilot. In place was a couch, of sorts.

And squatting on that couch was what was left of Guinan . . . he had literally flowed into the controls. His head was pressed up to the windshield, one arm was wrapped around the control yoke, the other splayed across the throttles. Mercifully, I couldn't quite see what had happened to his lower torso and legs. His flight suit had exploded.

Guinan was an ace, too.

I tried to put it out of my mind, concentrating instead on listening to Jack Ridley, the navigator sitting next to me. He noticed my alarm. "Don't worry, Ed. I've got backup controls, if anything happens to Casey. But he actually gets into the hydraulics. Told me once he could feel the breeze on the wings."

"But he's an ace! Is that even legal?"

Ridley just smiled.

We weren't able to observe the climb out to altitude. My imagination might have failed me where Guinan was concerned, but one thing I could imagine was the shattering roar of the 11A's Pratt & Whitney . . . a big brute designed only for one thing: thrust. To hell with fuel efficiency.

Enloe took the 11A off runway 22 and headed straight toward Death Valley. He would circle back and intercept us at 31,000 feet, in the heart of the Tomlin Test Range. I glanced through some of Ridley's charts and noticed that the rendezvous would take place while we were almost directly over the concrete hangar where the Takisian ship *Baby* was entombed.

I was plugged in throughout our takeoff and Enloe's, noting the sequence of test events on my knee pad. As rendezvous approached, Ridley indicated I was to go to the boom station in the rear of the tanker.

I had expected the tank to be cramped with extra insulating equipment—it wasn't just carrying room temperature jet fuel, as designed, but a liquid oxygen slurry that had to be kept at minus 400 degrees.

In fact, there were tons more equipment, in addition to special pumps and a bigger boom. But there was still room to move around: Guinan's tank only had to refuel one relatively small spacecraft, not a dozen jet fighters.

Flopping onto the observer's couch, one of three at the boom station, I tried to keep out of the way as Sergeant Vidrine, the boomer—who must have been a joker, since he had three arms—dumped a few pounds of LOX and kerosene through the twin nozzles, clearing them as the 11A crawled up behind us. Then the boomer and Enloe began talking.

My briefing had told me that this was to be a full-load refueling, with Enloe dropping away to fire the 11A's rocket motor for twenty seconds . . . enough to test the system and, incidentally, to propel him higher than any human had ever flown.

Enloe and the X-11A approached . . . the boom was toggled into place . . . the fuel dumped in less than four minutes. Vidrine said, "You're full with regular and super."

"Roger. Disconnect."

The exhilaration I had felt upon Enloe's invitation had worn off—a casualty, I first thought, of clear air turbulence, the smell of JP-4 jet fuel, and the sight of Guinan. Or worrying that I was surrounded by wild card freaks.

Then I realized what the problem was: No one seemed to be having any *fun*. Enloe said little, confining himself to cryptic callouts of altitude, fuel, speed. Dearborn, the communicator for the flight, was surprisingly terse. Only Vidrine and the chase pilots—who were making a bet involving beers at Pancho's place—added a human touch. It certainly had none of the rakish charm of the heroes of the Tak World novels, who were always bickering and stabbing one another in the back. I could have been listening to a couple of guys tearing down an engine block for a '49 Chevy.

The X-11A dropped several hundred feet behind us while the tanker rolled to the right. Dearborn counted down. At zero a tongue of flame shot out of the 11A. It was out of sight before I realized it.

Only then did I remember where I was . . . six miles over the California desert, refueling the world's first real spaceship. It went so far beyond the amazing that we had to invent new ways of describing—and appreciating—the experience.

There was a dicey moment during Enloe's altitude run . . . some pogo effect in one of the rocket's pumps. He had to shut down at seventeen seconds and wasn't able to crack the 100,000 foot barrier.

"Next time we'll go all the way," he said. I didn't hear a trace of disappointment in his voice.

The X-11A was on the ground before we were, though Enloe would be tied up in debrief through lunch. That was where Rowe and the rest of the team would be, so I was eager to join them.

But Margaret was waiting for me as I walked away from the tank. "What did you think?" she asked brightly.

"I think we're just about ready to go."

"I mean Casey." She raised an eyebrow. Only then did I realize she was inviting me to picture the two of them in bed.

"I've got work to do." I started walking away.

"I know. Rowe sent me to pick you up." She opened the car door for me. When I hesitated, she said: "Get in. Don't be such a baby."

She was amazing. I told her, "I'm not used to talking about things like this."

"Sex? Or aces?"

"Neither."

"You'll learn."

We drove in silence for a minute. "Rowe wanted me to give you a message."

"I'm listening."

"He says that unless there are any further technical problems, we'll attempt a launch on May 7th."

"That's great."

"He also says the Soviets announced today that they will try to put a man into orbit tomorrow morning."

(*From* Los Angeles Herald, *April 14, 1958*)

RUSSIAN ROCKET FIZZLES!
Red Spaceman Lucky to Be Alive!

Moscow (AP). The first attempt to put a man into space ended prematurely today with a huge rocket explosion, according to TASS, the official Soviet news agency. The pilot, Konstantin Feoktistov, was lifted to safety inside his vehicle, which was equipped with its own parachute.

The accident took place at the Soviet rocket research center at Kapustin Yar, on the Volga River just east of Stalingrad. Previous unmanned Soviet rockets, some of them carrying orbital satellites, have been launched from this site since 1947, under the direction of space scientists Sergei Korolev and Wernher von Braun.

According to TASS, Feoktistov, a 32-year-old engineer said to be a protégé of Korolev, boarded the bell-shaped *Sever* spacecraft atop its giant R-11 rocket at seven-thirty local time. He wore a special protective spacesuit for the mission, which was to see him orbit Earth three times.

Liftoff of the R-11, said to stand twelve stories tall and weigh over a million pounds, took place shortly after nine. The R-11's twenty-four first stage engines ignited, lifting *Sever* (which means "North") into the sky.

But at an altitude of 9,000 feet, as the rocket was passing through the area of maximum dynamic pressure, there was an explosion. Automatic devices aboard *Sever* ignited an escape rocket mounted forward of Feoktistov's cabin, pulling it free of the fireball.

Sever then descended by parachute into the swamp five miles east of the launch site, as debris from the exploding rocket rained down around it. Reached by rescuers within minutes, Feoktistov was reported to be injured, but not seriously. He is rumored to be convalescing at a resort on the Black Sea.

> TASS quoted von Braun as comparing the failure
> to those of the World War II V-2 . . .

(From the notebooks of Edgar Thayer)

We got the news of the Soviet failure at Muroc the same way everybody else did . . . from the radio. For everyone's convenience they had moved me from the motel in Rosamond to the Tomlin visiting officers' quarters—logically enough, seeing as how I would only be around for a month—which left me twenty miles closer to the action. Which on that particular night was at Pancho's Happy Bottom Riding Club, just west of the base.

I had spent the rest of the test day in debriefing and can't remember who suggested that we have a Soviet Watch at the bar. It might have been Al Dearborn, who, it was said, had run up such a tab that Pancho herself had had to make him a part owner in the joint. I do remember asking if Dr. Rowe would join us, only to be told that Rowe probably didn't know where Pancho's was.

Anyway, we were there early, before six, ostensibly for steaks: Dearborn, Sampson, Grissom, Meadows, Ridley, a brace of test engineers, and me. Enloe and Guinan showed up soon after. It was the single wildest evening I have ever spent, though it began innocently enough, just beers with Dearborn.

Midway through the third Budweiser, I got the nerve to ask him how he managed to handle the pressure . . . not knowing who was going to make the first flight.

"Listen, buddy, I *do* know."

"Don't keep me in suspense."

"You're looking at him." He saw my amused disbelief. "Look, I'll prove it to you. Give me a quarter." I produced a half dollar. He took it and flipped it. "Call it."

"Heads."

Heads it was. In fact, Dearborn got it right fourteen times in a row. "Pure luck," I said.

He winked. "Bingo. That's me: Mr. Lucky. Fall in shit, come up smelling like roses. It might not be pretty, but it got me where I am today. Another beer?"

Through the haze of my growing intoxication, I realized that Dearborn, too, was an ace. I didn't know whether to be shocked, or just amused. In those days, to use a term from another circumstance, aces were largely in the closet. Yet, just like people in those other circumstances, they were everywhere you looked . . . if you looked closely.

At Muroc, however, it seemed that no one cared. Or that none of the aces cared if anyone cared. As if the rules had been suspended.

(I just wondered what Sampson's wild card talent was.)

True to his reputation, five minutes later Dearborn caused some local talent to materialize, two blondes and a brunette, who made themselves right at home on various laps. One of them had brought a camera, an Argus, I recall, and they were posing for photos with the famous pilot.

By seven I was so drunk I was necking with blonde number one on the pool table, to the raucous cheers of Sampson and Meadows. Even Enloe cracked what I hoped was an approving smile.

I was still à deux with the blonde when I realized that Margaret had come in. She gave me a wink as she squeezed past us, murmuring, "Pretty fast work for an engineer," and took a place at the bar between Guinan and Meadows. Soon Enloe and Dearborn had joined them.

Everyone seemed to be having a good time, particularly the three 11A pilots. At some point Meadows called over to Mike Sampson, and with some reluctance he joined the group. Meadows had picked up the camera and was trying to take a snap of the pilots with Margaret. He was too drunk to make it work. Equally drunk, I disengaged myself from my blonde and rolled off the pool table long enough to point out that he wasn't advancing the film. Without a word he just handed the camera to me, so I took the photo . . . Margaret in the middle, Enloe and Dearborn to her right, Guinan and Sampson to her left.

I'm not sure exactly what happened after that. Sampson's voice suddenly got very loud: "If I wouldn't *fly* in formation with him, I sure as hell wouldn't get close enough to *fuck* him." Followed by Margaret: "Shut up, Mike." Guinan added: "If she wanted to be with you, buddy, she'd still be with you."

Sampson leered. "I never heard any complaints."

Margaret shot back, "You were too busy watching yourself perform."

The next thing I remember is Sampson tapping my blonde on the shoulder. "Let's go, baby." Her lipstick smeared, the blonde straightened like she was on a string. She actually followed him out.

Now, a juicy scene like that would have silenced any ordinary bar, but the general din and jukebox wail never diminished. I'm not sure anybody but me actually heard the three-way lovefest.

I staggered to the bar, where Pancho thoughtfully had a cup of coffee waiting for me. Then Enloe summoned Guinan over to the table where he was sitting with Grissom and Meadows, leaving me alone with Margaret.

"Well, go ahead," she said. "Say it."

"Say what?"

"Call me a tramp, or whatever it is boys from Minnesota say. You're just radiating disapproval."

"I think it's the beer. Honest."

She stabbed out her cigarette and swung around on her stool. "They're awfully fun," she said, nodding toward what had become the pilots-only table. "A bunch of eighteen-year-olds with their first hot rods." She turned back to me. "How old are you, Thayer?"

"Twenty-eight."

"That means you're still fourteen. In boy years."

"Boy years?"

"Like dog years. A boy's real age is only half his chronological age. Believe me, I've done all the research." She took out another cigarette. "There are girl years, too."

"I can't wait."

"They're a little trickier. The conversion factor is one-point-five. When I was thirteen—"

"You were actually twenty."

"Of course, that's only good up to twenty-one. Then the conversion factor begins to diminish until you're twenty-nine when you're twenty-nine."

"And twenty-nine when you're thirty-three."

"My. A college graduate." There was that smile again. She looked over at the table in the corner, where Enloe, Guinan, and the others had their heads together. "Do you suppose Casey's ever going to come back?"

I glanced at the clock. "He's probably waiting for the 8 P.M. news."

"You're probably right. Damn you and that stupid Russian rocket. I hope it blows up."

"It might do just that." My head was clearing.

Then Dr. Rowe walked in.

He was dressed as he always dressed, except for the fact

that his tie had been slightly loosened. For the first time, there was relative quiet in Pancho's. Rowe seemed amused. "Anybody know what happened with the Russians?"

"Pancho, what's the matter with you! Turn the damn radio on!" Dearborn shouted from the table.

Rowe stepped up to the bar and ordered a beer. As he waited, he glanced at Margaret and me.

"Margaret. Ed, what do you think?"

"I don't think they've had enough test flights."

He got his beer and stared into it for a moment. "I hope you're right." He looked up. "And I hate myself for it."

Three minutes to eight. Rowe went to a table—alone. Margaret slid off the stool and took my arm.

"Let's go," she whispered.

"Don't you want to know?"

"No."

We found her car. She slid behind the wheel and I got in beside her. Then we just sat in silence.

Finally I said, "What was the big rush?"

"I just wanted to get out of there." She pulled up her knees, dropping her shoes. Through the car window came a hot breeze that rippled her hair and blouse.

Suddenly I pulled her toward me. After a moment, she pushed me away. "Something wrong?"

She smiled, and unbuttoned her blouse. "I've just decided we're perfect for each other."

(A handwritten note)

*I can still remember each time we made love . . .
each move within each time. On the couch in her
office one Friday when everyone had gone. (Sliding*

my hand under her skirt to her moist center. We
didn't even take our clothes off.) In the car outside a
motel in Rosamond, where Deb and the kids had
come to visit me. (Her head in my lap . . . hair caught
in the steering wheel . . . stains on my jacket.) The
motel in Lancaster on a hot afternoon. (The shades
drawn against the heat if not the light, her riding me,
drowning me in her breasts . . .)
Pathetic. But this is what happened.

(From the notebooks of Edgar Thayer)

The news of the Soviet failure encouraged all of us. We started receiving visitors . . . a couple of generals from the Western Development Division, which supervised the missile program and who, until that week, had believed the idea of space travel to be so much cream cheese, and from Aeronautical Systems, who were running around trying to take credit for Rowe's project, which they had been forced to fund.

A Senator Kennedy showed up, too.

Since I was spending twelve hours a day in flight control, I was oblivious to most of this. We were debugging our data processing network while at the same time the engineers in Hangar Three were putting together and tearing down the LOX pump that had caused the pogo. There were orbital operations to be rehearsed and worldwide communications to integrate.

Oh, yes: on April 20, after Sampson and Dearborn flew another test, Rowe announced that Enloe and Guinan would make the first all-up flight. Major Wilbert Wood Enloe would become the first man in space.

I saw Dearborn moments after the announcement. He was

still shaking his head, like a man who'd been in a bad fight. Sampson didn't react at all. I concluded that he hadn't expected to get the first flight.

Enloe began to fly daily landing approaches in an F-104 that had been modified to handle like the X-11A.

I didn't see Guinan at all in those several days between the incident at Pancho's and the announcement. When I chanced to meet him at the commissary on the 21st he acted as if nothing whatever was the matter. "No hard feelings?" I said.

"Like I told Mikey, if she wanted to be with me, she'd still be with me." He was piling enough food on his plate for three men. "Enjoy it while it lasts, buddy boy. Because one of these days, she'll pull the same thing on you."

I hated Guinan for saying that, though I already suspected it was true. Margaret had told me—*confessed* is not the word; she might as well have been discussing a change in the weather—that she had slept with three of the four pilots so far.

Dearborn, Mr. Lucky, had been first. "He made a pass at me five minutes after we'd been introduced. I mean, I was putting a cuff on him—to check his blood pressure—and just like that he had his hand on my thigh." (I had my hand on her thigh.)

"You were powerless to resist," I said. "After all, he *is* an ace."

"I'd like to think that was it. I just took his hand away. He couldn't believe it for a moment. Then the next thing I knew I was locking the door and, well . . . you know." She blushed.

"Show me." And she shifted so her head slid down my stomach.

Sampson had been second. "Dearborn told him about me, then told me he had told Sampson, just to get his reaction. You know, Mike had been sitting in the office outside . . ."

Except for that drunken night at Pancho's, I would have sworn Sampson was a straight arrow. It was hard to picture him lusting after Margaret, and I said as much. "That was the whole idea. He's not married, he doesn't have a girlfriend. No one could even remember *seeing* him with a woman. I think the guys thought he was some kind of freak."

"Who knows what aces think of one another."

"Anyway, I noticed he was hanging around the medical office one day for no particular reason. I pretty much teased him into asking me out to dinner.

"It was very sweet. He insisted on picking me up—and he drives some beat-up little foreign car, a Renault, I think. Nothing like any pilot I've ever known—and taking me all the way to Lancaster to some romantic, out of the way little Italian place."

"The *only* romantic, out of the way little Italian place in Lancaster."

"That must be true, because who do you think we saw the moment we sat down? Wilson Rowe."

"With Mrs. Rowe?"

"Not unless he's married to a twenty-year-old."

"His daughter."

She laughed. "I don't think so."

I raised myself on one arm, momentarily shocked out of the mood . . . which was well into the realm of the ridiculous. Here I was, ensconced in the bedroom of a woman not my wife . . . daring to be disappointed by the idea of Rowe having an affair.

Then, in the time it took for Margaret to place her hand on my chest, forcing me onto my back, I relaxed, embracing it all. We were isolated, working impossible hours in reduced circumstances on what was supposed to be this magnificent adventure. The fact that Margaret had been intimate with the other aces, except for Enloe, made me feel I was part of a select club. After all, the normal rules of behavior no longer applied.

"Sampson," I said, moving my mouth from one breast to the other. A cool wind had come up.

Margaret's nipples were hard as pebbles.

"Let's just say he . . . surrendered."

"He's an ace, too, isn't he?"

"Mikey is . . . intense. I mean, he went on for hours." She laughed. "No wonder he doesn't screw very often. He'd kill someone."

"I must be a hell of a disappointment . . ."

"Not quite. It kind of scared me." We rolled over so that I was above her. "So it was only natural that I would turn to Casey." She laughed at some private joke, then whispered in my ear. "I was bad."

"I'm listening."

"I was like a dog. I just wanted to fuck him, then get rid of him." She laughed again. "Just like a man."

"I'm hurt."

"You don't feel hurt."

I was inside her now. "All these aces . . ."

"I never overlap. When I find a new one, the old one is history."

I lost my ability to speak.

We had simulations the weekend of the 30th, so even if I had wanted to drive all the way down to Pasadena, I couldn't have. This left me with some free time to spend with Margaret, but, unfortunately, she was pulling the late shift at the clinic.

About ten o'clock on Saturday night I was dozing on the couch in my room at the BOQ, too tired to function, too lazy to go to bed. *Have Gun, Will Travel* was on the TV.

There was a knock at the door. Margaret, still in her nurse's uniform. "Come with me," she said. It never occurred to me to do anything else.

She was unusually silent—tired, I thought—as we pulled out of the base on our way to Pancho's. But we went right at the gate instead of left. I said, "If this is a kidnapping, I insist that you have your way with me . . ."

"All right."

"Where are we going?"

"It's a surprise."

Moments later we drove through the NACA facility without stopping. I was disappointed. "I was sort of hoping you were going to sneak me into the 11A cockpit."

"This is even better."

It was still a bit of a drive . . . out to the Mohave Highway, then east again, finally turning south onto Rich Road. Then, at Leuhman Ridge, she pulled off on a dirt road trail.

"Isn't this the restricted area?" I asked as she got out.

"Yes." She left the door open, the headlights on, and the radio playing loudly, some hillbilly music out of Bakersfield.

In front of us stood a concrete bunker. Between our car and the bunker was a chain-link fence with a padlocked gate. "I hope we're not supposed to climb."

She produced a pair of keys. "Now, that shows initiative," I said.

Moments later we were opening the steel door to *Baby*'s tomb.

The surroundings were unimpressive. This was nothing more than a concrete-and-steel bunker, the kind originally used to store explosives. A row of bare lightbulbs provided the illumination.

There, in the middle, sat *Baby*.

I was surprised at how small it was, probably half the size of the X-11A. And where the spaceplane was sleek and winged,

Baby looked like a seashell. Its skin was rough to the touch, like that of a shark. I ran my hands over it . . . almost unable to believe that it had traveled here from another world, another star system.

"Like what you see?"

"Yes," I said. "Thank you." Only then did I turn and look at Margaret. She had slipped out of her uniform and stood there naked and, even in that ghastly light, golden. She glided up to me and brushed her lips against mine.

"You have nothing on," I said.

"Don't be silly," she said, unzipping my pants. "You forgot about the radio . . ."

We made love right there on *Baby*.

It was, I suppose, final proof that I was no longer the boy who lived the Tak World novels.

On the morning of May 6—launch minus one day—I arrived at the control center as usual at seven. Margaret had again had late duty at the medical office, so I had spent the night at the BOQ, the better to make my ritual early morning call to Deb and the children. (The more enmeshed I got with Margaret, the more faithful I was about calling. Strangely, I was looking forward to seeing them in as little as a week's time.)

A delta-winged F-106 from the Tomlin test force roared overhead on takeoff, and I stopped to watch it climb into the sun. My ears were still ringing when I heard a man say, "Beautiful."

George Battle stood behind me. In his mirrored sunglasses he looked like a demented Teddy Roosevelt. "Don't you love the smell of JP-4 in the morning? I'd have given anything to be a pilot. Eyes."

"Aviation's loss."

Battle, from my brief encounter with him, was clearly one of those people who pride themselves on having a sense of humor—and don't. "In three days this place'll be swarming with reporters. Bastards."

"I haven't noticed a lot of them so far."

He gave a tight smile. "Thank you."

"Well, this will be the first manned space flight in history. People will be interested."

"I encourage people to be interested in the rocketry and such. My worry is that some of these reporters will cover the human angle." I didn't know what he meant, so he prompted: "What do you really know about Margaret Durand?" he said, straining to keep things casual.

"I know all I need to know," I said. "Since you've obviously been spying on us—"

"I'm in charge of security around here—"

"—maybe you should just tell me what exactly—"

"It isn't as though either of you've been a model of discretion."

Both of us stopped. We realized we were shouting. "Look," I said, "I realize it looks bad—"

"How it looks isn't the point—"

"But we're all under a lot of strain—"

"Oh, *that* excuse!"

We were talking over each other again. This time Battle took the lead and I tried to restrain myself.

"Her background checks out fine. Medical school in Texas, ten years as Navy nurse until hired by the Committee. Never married. Churchgoer." He added the last item with a certain relish. "It's perfect. Too perfect, maybe. I'm just warning you— all of you—that once your rocket goes up"—he was oblivious to the double entendre—"your lives are going to change. You're going to be under a microscope. And you'd better be ready. Dr. Rowe." Battle made the transition from warning to greeting so smoothly I was late in catching it.

Rowe was just getting out of his car. "Good morning, George. Don't arrest Thayer until after tomorrow. I need him until then."

Battle, still oblivious, cleared his throat. "We were just talking about the weather."

"A personal conversation? Well, don't let it happen again." Then Rowe gestured toward me. "Ed, come here a second." Dismissed, Battle slunk away. Rowe opened the trunk of his car and pulled out what looked like a magazine wrapped in plastic. "Recognize it?"

Inside the plastic was a gray pamphlet published by the Smithsonian Institution and dated December 1919. I didn't need to open it to know what it contained. "Goddard's paper on multistage rocketry and flights to the Moon."

"'A Method of Reaching Extreme Altitudes.' The very paper ridiculed as 'absurd' by *The New York Times*." He handled it as if it were a priceless artifact. Which it was, to the two of us. Then, a bit too casually, I thought, he tossed it to me. "I want you to put this in Woody's personal pack."

"For the flight?"

"It should get into space, don't you think? After all that was said about it."

Rowe walked over to the fence and leaned on it. From our vantage point we had a clear view into Hangar Three. The tech crew was hard at work preparing the X-11A for its big day.

"Battle says everything changes tomorrow."

"Everything changes every day."

"You don't think the world will be different once Enloe lands?"

He had a distant look in his eye. "I suppose." He stepped back from the fence. "Maybe I'm just looking at the end of an era and not liking it much. Because it's my era. When rockets were toys for bright children and crazy adults."

"It has to grow up sometime. If we're ever going to get to the Moon. Have cities on Mars."

"I know." He smiled sadly. "I just wish it didn't have to hurt so much." He clapped me on the shoulder and nodded at the package in my hand. "Don't forget."

I had a few moments before the seven-thirty briefing, so I decided to drop by the suiting room. I found Major Meadows there giving a tour to some ten-year-old boy. "I told you not to touch the helmet!"

The kid just rolled his eyes. "This looks like airplane stuff. Where's the spaceman things?"

"These are the spaceman things," Meadows explained patiently. "My son, Mark," he said, by way of introduction and apology.

"Pleased to meet you, Mark."

He ignored me.

"Come on, Mark. I'll drop you at school."

I held the door for the two of them.

It's funny, when I think back. If I hadn't held the door, I wouldn't have seen Margaret come into the building with Enloe.

They were laughing. I knew that laugh.

Margaret leaned close and said something to Enloe. Her secret voice.

They were holding hands. My hands.

I ducked back into the suiting room. I was too stunned to do anything but find Enloe's personal pack, open it, and gently place Rowe's gift inside it.

Then I stood there for what seemed like a long time.

Eventually I heard voices. Enloe and Guinan on their way to the briefing. My briefing. I knew I should leave. Right now. Any moment. Finally I forced myself out the door.

The next morning, May 7, 1958, dawned beautifully bright in the high desert. I was up at four, unable to sleep later, and at the control center by five-thirty. As was everyone else. It was like Christmas morning: something grand was going to happen.

I stopped by Hangar Three, where Sampson, in white overalls, was setting up the cockpit.

Guinan's tank had already rolled out to the flight line. He was in the cockpit. Ridley and Sergeant Vidrine waved as they walked toward the tank.

I spotted Enloe on his way to breakfast with Grissom, Dearborn, and Meadows. He gave me a double thumbs-up. All I wanted to do was make the final suit check, and get to my console.

Going into the suiting room, I ran right into Margaret.

She seemed startled, almost pale. "Ed!"

"Sleep well?" I said. I couldn't hide my emotions any better than she could.

She sighed as her color returned. "You knew it was going to happen eventually—"

"Eventually. Not this fast."

"It pretty much *had* to be this fast, Ed." She looked at me with defiance. I never wanted her more than at that moment.

"Well," I said. "I suppose I should take one last look—"

I tried to brush past her, but she blocked me. I put my arms around her and pressed her against the wall. She wiggled away, smoothing her hair back. "Not out here."

We literally fell into an equipment closet. It was dark, crowded, with barely enough room for one person. Which is what we were, briefly. It was a fast, almost brutal collision of raised skirt, cold belt buckle, and torn panties.

For a moment we held each other, panting. "What about your rules against overlapping?"

"I changed them."

Once back in the light we both realized we were late. Maybe that was the reason we ran from each other.

As I plugged into the console next to Dearborn, I nodded to Rowe at his station in the back. Lost in thought, he didn't see me. Which didn't bother me in the least.

"Glad you could make room for us in your busy schedule," Dearborn said.

"Had to answer a call of nature." If he only knew.

"Curtain's going up," Dearborn said. He keyed the intercom. "Tank, this is flight. Comm check."

Moments later, Guinan's tank was airborne.

We had film cameras mounted in the KC-135 and at two places in the 11A cockpit. I mention this because we weren't able to see anything . . . we had to rely on the audio comm lines and telemetry. As did the rest of the world: NBC had managed to convince NACA and the Defense Department to allow it to broadcast the attempt live. (The Soviet failure made our image-conscious policy makers eager to show them up publicly.)

As the 11A approached the tank from behind and below, we heard Enloe, Guinan, and the boom operator speaking from the script, which had by then been through a dozen in-flight rehearsals.

Suddenly we heard Grissom, in the lead chase plane, holler, "Watch it!"

At the same time Meadows, the other chase pilot, called, "Midair!"

"Abort." (According to the tapes, that was me, though I don't remember saying it.)

The next thirty seconds were confused. Guinan said he was rolling left. Grissom told him he had lost part of his tail and right wing. Guinan's broken reply: "Can't hold."

I literally punched Dearborn on the shoulder. "Where's Enloe!" Forgetting that all along Dearborn had been calling, "11A, this is flight. 11A, this is flight."

At the same time I was hearing from every console at once. The one that registered was propulsion—the engineer monitoring the X-11A's rocket. "We're at redline."

"Woody, shut it down!" I didn't wait for Dearborn to make the call.

No response. No response. Finally, Meadows's voice. "Dust on the lake. Ten miles north of Boron."

Dust on the lake? That's when I realized that it was all over. One of the aircraft had crashed. But which one?

Then I heard Grissom's voice. "Tank's down, too. Five miles from Boron."

Rescue crews were already on their way, but it was too late. The X-11A had suddenly pitched up as the boom was being inserted. This would have been inconvenient, but not disastrous, except that the two craft were physically connected. The 11A actually pivoted around the boom, slamming into the tail of Guinan's tank, rolling across the bigger plane and shearing off the right wingtip.

Guinan might have been able to save the tanker with damage to the tail or the missing wingtip, but not both. He was helpless to stop the beast—laden with fuel—from rolling over and plunging to the earth.

Even so, he managed to retain some kind of control: the

KC-135 was almost level when it hit . . . in the proper attitude for landing. But it broke apart and exploded, leaving a blackened smear four hundred feet long across the desert. The only recognizable structure was the crew cabin with the bodies of Guinan and Ridley. (It was later determined that Vidrine, the boom operator, had been decapitated in the initial collision.)

Both of the men in the cockpit had suffered "severe thoracic trauma," in the bland words of the investigating board. There was one curious bit of damage to Guinan that could not be explained by the impact:

He had lost his right hand.

Enloe's death was more chilling. The cabin films, one frame a second, show him in control and in position up through the beginning of fueling. Suddenly—in the space of one frame—his hands fly off the controls, as if he is reacting to an explosion of sorts in his lap. (The board later concluded it was due to a failure in the oxygen hose attached to the belly of his suit. It literally blew apart.)

At that delicate moment, the lack of a steady hand—and the sudden, reflexive push on the pedals—is enough to throw the 11A into its fatal pivot.

Even though he is in his flight harness, Enloe is flung toward the camera by the collision with the tail of the tank. The cabin remains intact. The light changes, shifting from sun to shadow to sun, as the 11A rolls across the tank, clipping the wing.

The canopy shatters. Enloe, in his pressure suit and helmet, seems unhurt, though one of the straps of his harness comes loose. Sun, shadow, sun, shadow. Faster and faster, until the rate of rotation exceeds the frame speed.

The last two frames show a mountainside reflected in the faceplate of Enloe's helmet.

(From the Special Committee Investigating the X-11A Disaster, Maj. Gen. John B. Medaris, Chairman)

MEDARIS: Mr. Thayer, the 11A did not contain an ejection seat.

THAYER: No, sir.

MEDARIS: Why not?

THAYER: Because of Major Enloe's wild card abilities. He was literally capable of flight.

MEDARIS: But he did not fly away from the 11A.

THAYER: No, sir.

MEDARIS: Why not?

THAYER: I don't know. The medical telemetry shows that he was conscious until impact, or shortly before.

MEDARIS: Was he impeded in any way? Could he have gotten out?

THAYER: Film from the chase plane shows that the 11A cabin was relatively intact until impact, and that one or both of his harness straps were loose.

MEDARIS: He should have been able to fall out and fly. Is that what you're saying?

THAYER: That's one possibility, yes, sir.

If he wanted to!

(From the notebooks of Edgar Thayer)

Three days after the accident we held a memorial service out on the flight line. The Navy hymn. The missing man formation. Margaret was there, in sunglasses, somber, serene, and distant. I stood next to Rowe. He and I had been in the hands of the investigating board since the hour of the accident. I hadn't slept more than a total of four hours. At that point, I didn't think I'd ever sleep again.

When it was over, I caught up with Margaret, who was hurrying toward her car. "Don't run away from me, goddammit!"

"All right, Ed." She turned toward me, waiting. "What do you want?"

"I'm in trouble."

"I heard. Why you?"

"They think they've found the cause of the accident. It was in Enloe's life support system, which I was supposed to check."

"But didn't?"

"No."

She shook her head. It might have been sympathy. "What's going to happen?"

"I'm going to be in a lot of trouble."

"With the program . . ."

"Oh, it's finished. They'll investigate for two years and realize there's nothing wrong with concept. But there's no more money. Especially since the Russians are grounded, too."

"I'm sorry, Ed. I mean, I'm sorry for you. This was your dream." Then she said something that didn't shock me until much later. "What the hell, Ed: They were aces. It wasn't as though human beings were the ones going into space."

"I never cared about that. I worked for Dr. Rowe."

She started to laugh. "Yes, Dr. Rowe. When you get a chance, ask him why he hired you."

"What the hell is that supposed to mean?"

"Talk to Rowe. He's got all the answers."

Without a kiss, without another word, she got in her car and drove off.

I found Rowe cleaning out his office. An air policeman stood guard outside.

"I had an interesting conversation with Margaret Durand."

Rowe smiled for the first time in days. "Oh, yes, Peggy Durand. I'm going to miss her."

"She told me to ask you why you hired me. She seemed to think it was important."

The smile stayed on his face, but his eyes closed. He sank into his chair. "You know, a few years ago I began to have dreams. Visions of the future. Winged spaceships taking off from runways and flying into orbit. Space tugs landing on the surface of the Moon." He swiveled his chair to look out at the desert. "Even things like aces and jokers being treated with respect."

"None of that seems very likely now."

He turned back to me. "Oh, that's the hell of it, Ed. I also dreamed that I would try to make this happen. That I would build the first winged spaceship . . . but that it would fail. Fail horribly. And all because of some young Judas named . . ." He stopped himself. "Never mind."

He said this nonsense with such conviction that I began to get chills. "Well," I said, playing along for the moment, "why didn't you do anything about it? You brought me in here . . . you threw me together with Peggy . . ."

"You can't change things, Ed. That's what hurts the most. I thought I could. I hedged my bets." He laughed bitterly. "I even put my most prized possession on that ship, *hoping* . . . It didn't make a damn bit of difference."

"What am I supposed to say? That I'm sorry?"

"It wasn't up to you." He was trying to make me understand. "It *will* happen, you know. The good part of the vision, those winged spaceships. I can still see them. But Enloe and Guinan had to die first."

There was a knock at the door. George Battle was there to take us away.

It wasn't until days later, sitting in confinement in Los Angeles, awaiting transfer to Washington, that I realized Rowe had made quite a confession to me. He, too, was an ace . . . with the power of foresight.

Actually, given the nature of the power, I should say he was a joker.

Did he take comfort in knowing that eleven years after the X-11A disaster SpaceCom would be formed? That in thirteen years a whole squadron of Hornets would be flying into orbit—Hornets whose design was based on the X-11A? I hope so. He was a good man caught, like all of us, in the world created by the wild card.

He was the real victim.

(*From* The Albuquerque Journal,
January 28, 1967)

X-11A DESIGNER DIES

LANGLEY, VIRGINIA (AP). Wilson Rowe, the engineer who designed and ˚oversaw the ill-fated X-11A rocket plane program, has died here of cancer at the age of 62. He had been living in seclusion for the past several years following charges of sabotage that were lodged against him and his team.

(From The True Brothers *by Tom Wolfe, 1979)*

Yeager quit testing rocket planes in 1954 and returned to operational flying in Korea. Four years later he was back in the United States, commanding a squadron of F-100s at George Air Force Base, fifty miles away from Tomlin, when the X-11A blew up.

It caused a colossal panic, with newspapermen and congressmen leading a pack that bayed through the woods about wild card treachery and communist sabotage. This was the End of Everything.

The first soul to be dragged off the sled was the 11A's intense young flight director, Edgar Thayer, who was actually sentenced to prison for "gross negligence." He served ten years in the Federal lockup in Lompoc, California, only to die in a car crash as soon as he got out.

Thayer's mysteriously timely death led to the revival of a few wild theories, however. It had been rumored, *The True Brothers* said, that *someone else* had screwed up Woody Enloe's equipment.

Tomlin flight operations weren't like some goddamn Hitler bunker . . . lots of people went in and out of there that day. Sure, Thayer should have checked . . . but *who cut the hose in the first place?*

None of the Brothers could ever understand why nobody but Thayer and Rowe got called to testify. What about Battle, the head of security? He was a weaselly son of a bitch. What about Margaret Durand, the flight nurse? She was every True Brother's choice for Space Age Mata Hari, but she just vanished! Disappeared into the mist!

Yeager, of course, wasn't about to turn himself into some kind of bounty hunter. He spent a few weeks with the panel investigating the accident, came to his own conclusions, then went off to the Sierras in search of golden trout.

At the party the night the first Hornet took off, however, it was Yeager who raised a toast to the True Brothers who should have made it, Woody Enloe and Casey Guinan . . .

The Ashes of Memory

5

"May I copy these?" Hannah asked. **"If** you don't mind . . ."

Dearborn was staring out of the window at the light-speckled night landscape of the city. She could see the reflection of his drawn face in the glass. "They were good men, and they all died. So young . . ." The sadness in his face and voice brought sympathetic tears to her own eyes. Hannah blinked them away.

Dearborn sighed and turned back toward Hannah. "I guess maybe I was the lucky one, after all," he said, and his laugh was bitter and short.

"Mr. Dearborn—" Hannah began.

"Take the papers," he told her. "Keep them, publish them, burn them. I don't really care. I don't really care at all anymore."

- - -

"I can't believe that you're falling for this garbage."

David was standing with hands on hips alongside Hannah's desk in their apartment. Blue light from her Macintosh's monitor made his face seem almost spectral.

Hannah saved the file and looked up at him. "David, I know it's far-fetched. I don't like it, either, but it all hangs together in a bizarre way: the old arson plot of Lansky, the circus attempt at a mass poisoning, van Renssaeler, Faneuil infecting all those jokers in Kenya, the fire there, Durand being part of the X-11A disaster, jet fuel. It all hangs strangely together."

"I thought you had a list of pyros," David interrupted. "Instead you're chasing shadows."

Hannah glared at him. "Don't be condescending. I have checked out the list. Simpson and I interrogated a few of them this afternoon."

"And?"

"And we have a good suspect. Ramblur, the one they call 'Flashfire.' "

"Then bring him in. Sweat him until he cracks. Case closed, and you're the hero."

"Right. What if the hunchback's right and the torch is just someone else's tool? The person who ordered those poor people murdered walks and the torch hangs. I don't want that, David. I want the bastard that said, 'Burn the church.' " Hannah switched off the computer.

"Nothing you've got would convince *anyone* that the church fire was anything more than a lone psychotic's act, Hannah. Thinking it's more is stupid."

"Stupid?" The harshness of the word made her sit back. She took a slow breath, staring at his unrepentant eyes, hoping that his gaze would soften, that he'd realize how he was hurting her. *You don't have to believe me. Just talk with me like my lover instead of some almighty deity.* "David, even you have to admit that some of the links are suspicious. The use of an oxygen canister in the trigger, that's something someone in the medical profession would know. Jet fuel, too—Durand would have known how flammable that is. Maybe Quasiman's right. The priest said he catches glimpses of the future. Maybe this *is* part of something bigger."

"Oh, just fucking great! Now you're listening to the Psychic Hunchback's conspiracy theory. Supermarket tabloid stuff. Hannah, Hannah . . ." Words seemed to fail him; his head shaking, he exhaled like a steam kettle and grimaced. "You're acting like a paranoid idiot."

Hannah laughed at the verbal attack, unbelievingly. "And you're acting like an insensitive bigot. I just want to be sure. If I could get the information I need from Saigon . . ."

"*Saigon?* This is insane, Hannah. They're jokers." David spoke as he might to a slow child. "For Chrissake. *There's no goddamn plot.* Someone hated the fucking freaks enough to set the place on fire; that's not too hard to believe. It's a local fire, a local problem. Now you're gluing on a globe-spanning conspiracy fantasy."

"So now I'm fantasizing?"

"What evidence do you have, Hannah? Where's your proof?"

"Damn it, David, there isn't any proof. You know that. It's just a feeling I have."

"Right. Fucking woman's intuition, huh?"

"Shut up, David. Just shut the hell up!" Hannah stood up, the chair clattering backward to the floor. She waved her hand at him. "If you don't want to listen, fine. Then leave me alone. Get the hell out of here."

David laughed at her, braying in her face. "Who the hell's apartment is this? Hannah, listen to me. Do your goddamn job and drop this nonsense. I had a hell of a time convincing Malcolm and the others to get you this job, but I did. Don't throw away everything I've given you."

"I didn't want you to give it to me, David. I told you that from the beginning. I was willing to find my own job, my own place."

"But you sure as hell took the offer, didn't you? You sure came panting after me when I called."

"You arrogant son of a bitch!" Hannah picked up the brass paperweight that sat on the desk. David just looked at her. Hannah breathed heavily, staring at David, amazed at the revulsion she felt for him. It was as if she'd found a rip in a favorite teddy bear, and looked to see maggots writhing in the stuffing.

She set the paperweight down, then the tears came in gasping sobs.

"Hannah," David said. She could feel the warmth of his body alongside her. "Hey, I'm sorry. I really am." His hand brushed her arm, and she felt his lips brush the back of her neck. "Just forget everything I said. I didn't mean any of it."

But you did mean it, David, and I can't forget. I won't ever forget. Hannah wanted to tell him that, but she didn't.

DAVIS: Mr. Ramblur, do you understand the rights that I've just read to you?

RAMBLUR: Yeah. (pause) I've heard 'em before. If I want my damn shark of a lawyer here, I can call him. So what? I don't need him. I ain't done nothin'.

SIMPSON: Then you'll be happy to answer a few questions for us.

RAMBLUR: I'm fucking ecstatic. If I were any happier I'd come in my pants.

DAVIS: Would you mind if we went inside?

RAMBLUR: If you were alone, I'd say that'd be lovely,

blondie. But since you have your bodyguard here with you, yeah I'd mind.

SIMPSON: (unintelligible)

RAMBLUR: Yeah? Well, ask your questions and get the hell out of here. I'm missing *As Takis Turns*. (He laughs) Just remember I'm talking with you on my own time. When I say I'm done, I'm done.

DAVIS: Where were you on the night of September 16th, Mr. Ramblur?

RAMBLUR: Out. Celebrating Black Queen Night.

SIMPSON: With someone or by yourself?

RAMBLUR: With friends. You want alibis? I can give you a dozen people who'll say they saw me.

DAVIS: Would any of your friends be jokers or aces?

RAMBLUR: (laughs) Not a fucking chance, lady. I don't have garbage for friends.

DAVIS: Do you burn your garbage or just throw it out on the street?

RAMBLUR: (laughs) You're a pretty fucking clever bitch, ain't you? Bet you're real popular back at the office with a mouth like that. Well, let me tell you something. (pause) I ain't gonna cry over that church burning. I ain't sorry at all it happened. Fire is clean. Fire purifies. And there ain't no place that needs purifying more'n Jokertown.

"Hannah?"

The voice caused Hannah to drop the transcript. Quasiman was standing in her cubicle. He seemed to have all his body parts today, at least the ones she could see. "Damn," she muttered. "You are just about the sneakiest SOB . . ." To cover her embarrassment, she straightened a few of the papers on her desk. Quasiman took a step toward her. Hannah scooted her chair back until it hit the wall.

The hunchback noticed, and the open hurt in his twisted face brought red-faced guilt to Hannah's, but she didn't move back. "I remember you," he said. "I know that doesn't sound like much, but you don't understand how difficult . . ." Quasiman sighed. "I made Father Squid write everything down. I make him read it all back to me every night, just so some of it stays. I keep saying your name, trying to keep your face in my mind. I even pray."

"Stop," Hannah said. "Just stop. I don't want to hear any of this. You need to leave."

"I just wanted to know," Quasiman said, "if you've found out anything?"

Yes, I've found out that I'm not in love with the man I moved here for. I've found out that I don't really like him or what he believes in. How's that for a revelation? "Nothing I can tell you," she said. "I'm working on it, okay? Now let's get you out of here before Security throws a fit. You don't have a pass."

"Will you find out soon?" Quasiman persisted. "I'm worried, Hannah. I can't keep holding things together much longer. What I've seen . . ." A look of pain crossed his face.

Hannah sighed. "I'm sorry."

"But you believe me. You do." The earnestness in the hunchback's voice was almost painful. "You're still looking."

Hannah shook her head. "I'll admit that I'm disgusted and surprised by some of what I've learned. I won't say that I'm convinced there's anything to your conspiracy. I'm willing to go a little further, okay? It's just that following up isn't easy. You need to be patient, Qua—" She stopped. "You wouldn't happen to have a regular name, would you? I feel really dumb calling someone 'Quasiman.'"

The joker shrugged. With his distorted back, it was an ugly

gesture. "If I have, I've forgotten it. And whoever I was before, I'm not exactly that person anymore, am I?"

"I'm sorry," Hannah said. The words seemed wholly inadequate. Quasiman nodded and shrugged again. "All right," Hannah continued. "Just so you know, just so I can get you out of here, let me tell you why I'm stymied. I'd like to get some information from what used to be Vietnam. The trouble is, I'm not getting any cooperation. We've opened tentative diplomatic relations with Free Vietnam in the last month, but the Feds have been no help. The UN's stonewalling, sending me from department to department. I've talked to Dr. Rudo at WHO, who said he'd see what he could do, but I haven't heard from him yet. There's actually a Free Nam delegation in town trying to get emergency funding from the UN; I've sent messages to them but I'm getting no answers there, either. I haven't got the pull to get through the buffers to a decision-maker. If I can get to someone there before they leave . . ."

A slow smile had come over Quasiman's face during Hannah's explanation. He was positively grinning at her. "What?" she asked.

"Mark Meadows," he said.

"Who?"

Quasiman just grinned. "Right at the moment, we jokers have good relations with Free Nam."

"Agent Davis?"

Hannah rose from her seat in the anteroom of the Free Vietnam suite in the Washington Omni. The man standing at the entrance to the room could have been thirty-five or fifty-five. He was Caucasian, not Vietnamese; in excellent physical shape, not much taller than Hannah, but muscular. His face had a weather-beaten quality, as if he'd spent much of his time outdoors, and the aquiline nose had been broken, bending just slightly to the right over a gray walrus mustache. His hair was crew cut, the light brown brush sprinkled generously with more gray. Hannah liked his eyes best of all: they were a pale, almost colorless blue, striking in the tanned face. "Minister Belew? Thank you for seeing me."

"Minister-Without-Portfolio," Belew corrected. "I haven't the foggiest idea what that means, but it sounds official. You have some identification?" He made the request like someone used to such precautions. Hannah handed him the leather case. He looked over the photo more carefully than most, glancing back at her once and running his thumb over the state seal to make sure it was raised and embossed. "Department of Justice, eh? State, not Federal. You have a nice drive down from New York?"

He handed the case back to her and pulled a chair over so they faced each other over a small lacquer table. Hannah saw him look at the tape recorder she'd placed on the table alongside her purse. "Do you mind?" she asked.

"Yes. But since Mark's asked me to cooperate with you . . ." He shrugged. "Can I call you 'Hannah,' by the way? And I'm a lot more comfortable being J. Robert than 'Minister.' I'm from the military; this diplomacy business is still foreign to me. The first thing you need to know is that I'm only a small fish in our group. Ambassador Ngu makes all the decisions, he and President Moonchild back in Saigon."

Hannah had the feeling that Belew was being deliberately casual. She also decided that it didn't matter as long as he was willing to talk. "I understand. Still, I appreciate you seeing me on short notice." Hannah turned on the recorder and noted the date and time. Before she could ask the first question, however, Belew spoke again. "I guess you know Father Squid called Mark Meadows in Saigon yesterday. Mark spoke to

President Moonchild, and who has instructed me to make arrangements for you to fly to Vietnam and perform any investigations you need to make there, *if—*" Belew paused for a long breath, "I think it's necessary. I understand you believe the Jokertown fire was more than just simple arson."

"It's something I'm checking out."

"Just who is it that you're investigating in Vietnam?"

"A Dr. Etienne Faneuil. Also a nurse with him: Margaret Durand."

Belew frowned, but his eyes never left their appraisal of her face. Hannah had the odd feeling that the man was almost flirting with her. There was nothing overt, but the undertone was there in his intense scrutiny, nonetheless. Hannah had been hit upon enough to know the signs: Belew was interested, if in a distant way.

"I don't know either of them," Belew said. "May I ask you why someone half the world away is connected with a fire in New York?"

"It's possible that several people were involved, that's all. It may be that this was a hate crime against jokers."

Belew smiled. He had a dangerous smile, one that Hannah unwillingly found attractive. The man definitely had charm. "That's hardly surprising."

"It is if it's been going on for years. It is if this is just the latest in a long line of incidents caused by one particular group of people."

Something moved behind Belew's eyes. Suddenly he was distant, no longer so intent on Hannah. He'd put himself on guard.

"What?" Hannah asked quickly, trying to get past that reserve before he realized that he'd thrown up the barrier. "I just reminded you of something."

Belew gave a short chuckle. "All of us jokers and aces have seen things like that, Hannah."

Hannah sat back hard against her chair. "You're . . . ?"

"An ace," he finished for her, and laughed. "J. Robert Belew. Also known as 'the Mechanic.' If I'd known it would impress you that much, I'd've mentioned it before."

Hannah ignored the warmth of her cheeks. *Damn it, quit acting like a schoolgirl. He's trying to deflect you from something.* "Minister . . ."

"J. Robert." A beat. "Without-Portfolio."

She ignored that. "Why'd you react when I said this might be just the latest incident?"

"Mind if I ask you something?" Belew looked away for a moment, then back. "I've done a lot of interviewing myself and I know you're supposed to stay in charge of the questioning and all. I promise to be a good boy and let you do your job afterward, but I'm curious about one thing."

His smile forced her to smile in return. "All right," she said. "Since you promise."

And with that, Belew's smile vanished like a conjurer's rabbit. He leaned forward toward her. "Just why's a nat concerned about this? Pardon my blatant sexism, but why's an attractive young woman getting involved with a bunch of ugly, nasty jokers?"

"It's my job."

Belew shook his head. "I'm sorry, but that won't wash. Your job is to find an arsonist, nothing more. My bet is that you're catching a lot of flack for going about it this way. No, don't answer, I can see that I'm right about that. So I have to ask myself why you're doing this. Maybe you want fame; maybe this is how you're going to climb the ladder, get yourself a promotion."

"No," Hannah answered.

"Then why?"

"Because someone killed far more people than I like to think about. Murdered them. And from what I've seen so far, it's possible that the person who set the fire was no more than a match in the hands of someone else. I don't have much interest in a burnt match, Minister. I want the hand that dropped it."

Belew didn't say anything for several seconds. Hannah let him wait, patient. The tape recorder hummed on the table. Finally Belew leaned back in his chair, regarding her with caution. "Mine's a long story and a dozen years old. It doesn't have anything to do with fires. It's also one I won't tell at all unless I know that it's also a story that you need to know. I won't tell it unless I know it's going to lead to something." His gaze was a challenge. "How am I going to know?"

Hannah stared back at him. "I'm the only one who can answer that question. And I can't be sure I need to know your story until I've heard it. You either trust me or you don't. It comes down to that. But you obviously think that there's something to what I'm investigating, or you wouldn't have asked all your questions in the first place." She gave him a short-lived smile.

Belew snorted. "Fair enough. Tell me this, Hannah: when you've got all your facts, what are you going to do with them?"

"Whatever I need to do," she answered. "And whatever I can."

Belew continued to hold the stare for several seconds. Finally, he looked away and laughed. "At least you don't make promises you don't intend to keep. That's more than I can say for most of the people I've worked for. All right," he continued, and something in his posture softened. "My story starts with a call from the Oval Office . . . ."

A Wind from Khorasan

The Narrative of J. Robert Belew

Victor Milan

President Carter's head was sticking out of one of those terrible polyester sweaters of his like a turtle's. He looked at me with his sad Eleanor Roosevelt eyes and said, "I want you to lead a mission to rescue the hostages in Tehran."

It was April 16, 1980. The sunshine of a pleasant spring morning spilled in through the French windows of the Oval Office. The roses were in bloom.

I sucked on my moustache. For one of very few times in my life, I had nothing to say.

"It has been decided," said National Security Advisor Zbigniew Brzezinski, looking as always like a shaved chow dog, "to employ a picked force of aces."

"It's my understanding, sir," I said carefully, "that Delta Force has been preparing a rescue mission for several months."

"How did you know about that?" barked the fourth man in the room. He was a little guy, about my own height, but weedier. He had a mustache even bigger than mine, if not quite as splendid, and a balding head shaped like a doorknob. He was no one I expected to see here, and no one I was happy to. "That's supposed to be classified."

"Mr. Battle," I said, "I'm in the business. I specialized in high-risk operations when I served in Special Forces, and, as you no doubt know, have continued doing so on a contract basis ever since. As a matter of fact, I was hoping to be included in the mission." I thought about it a moment. "If not exactly on these terms."

"You are perfectly correct, Major Belew," the president said. "Zbig and Mr. Battle have proposed an alteration to the plan that had been decided upon. I know that this is kind of an eleventh-hour thing, but I believe in my heart that it's worth doing."

"Major Belew," Battle said, pushing his head forward with his eyes shining like anthracite, "you're an ace." He said it breathlessly, as if it were a revelation. Since it wasn't to me, I just stood there and waited.

I still didn't know what he was doing there. I had passing familiarity with his dossier; he'd been a hanger-around the fringes of black ops for years. He'd done a hitch in the Army way back around the time I joined, back in the fifties, but he had managed to avoid getting into combat. After the Army he got his law degree and joined the FBI. He didn't stick with the Bureau long. He wandered into a succession of official and semiofficial government and political jobs—sort of like Cyrus Vance, Carter's secretary of state, but at a lower level.

One would not expect him to be doing any jobs for Carter. Battle had been a Nixon man. He got himself into some rather warm water over a certain third-rate burglary back in the early seventies, and dropped out of sight for a while.

When I didn't respond, he went on. "It's been decided that the rescue mission presents a perfect opportunity for aces to show how much they contribute to this great country of ours.

They—you—haven't been in such a good odor since the '76 riots."

"One of the major complications to this operation," Brzezinski said in his ponderous Eastern European accent, "has been the number of operators required. The current profile calls for one hundred thirty-two men. A force that size creates logistic nightmares."

"Makes it a bit hard to be discreet, too," I said.

"Prezisely."

The president stood gazing out the window with his hands clasped behind his back. "We reckon using aces will enable us to do the job with far fewer people," he said. "With the help of the Justice Department, we have assembled a team of six. You will make seven, if you agree to go."

I felt the skin of my cheeks get hot. The president turned back to the room.

"Also, there seems to be an ugly tide of bigotry rising in this country, against those touched by the wild card. This could be an opportunity to reverse that tide before it gathers momentum."

He looked me in the eye. "What do you say, Major? Will you lead an all-ace rescue team?"

It was approximately the craziest idea I'd ever heard in my life. Seven aces against a country full of well-armed religious fanatics, jumping in at the last minute on top of a mission that had been under careful construction for upward of five months. And aces from *Justice*, for the good Lord's sake! It was like playing Russian roulette with an autoloading pistol.

There was only one thing to do. I snapped to attention and saluted.

"Mr. President," I said, "I'm your man."

— — —

The sun was already up and hot, eight days later, when our three Sea Stallion helicopters touched down in an abandoned salt-mining district near Garmsar, fifty miles southeast of Tehran. That meant we were already behind schedule. With luck that wouldn't signify, since we had nothing to do but keep out of sight—and keep from suffering sunstroke—until dark.

"Thanks for the ride, guys," said Jay Ackroyd, dropping to the rock-hard yellow ground. The jarhead crewmen squinted at him, suspecting he was being sarcastic. He was, to be sure, but he gave them a big grin and a wave. "It's been real."

They scowled and turned back to the work of unloading our gear. "Real reminiscent of a root canal," he said, turning away. "Write if you guys find work you're more suited to, hear?"

We had flown overnight in a C-130 Hercules from the former Soviet airbase at Wadi Kena in Egypt to a point in the desert two hundred miles southeast of Tehran and ninety miles from the nearest settlement. Desert One was more name than it deserved. A hundred men from Delta Force would hold it while we went in. Our support would be coordinated from there.

The flight from Desert One, mostly in the dark, hugging broken, tortuous terrain, had not been easy by anyone's standards. Notwithstanding that, I was frankly not impressed. I've been on a lot of heliborne missions, in the Nam and later. The jarheads only got us there by the skin of their teeth.

"Who picked these bozos for a secret mission, anyway?" Ackroyd demanded of me. "I wouldn't let 'em walk my dog, if I had one. Join the Army and see the Navy, not to mention the Marines."

I gave him a qualified grin. I was also somewhat concerned about the patchwork nature of our supporting elements. It was as if every branch of service wanted to get its oar in, and some of the personnel weren't adequately prepared for this kind of job. The Marine pilots had been so nervous that even our operators right off Civilian Street noticed.

Ackroyd didn't miss much, in all fact. Have to give him that. He was an ace private investigator.

Well, he was an ace, and he was a PI. He was in his thirties, brown and brown, an inch or two taller than me. The sort of man you could never pick out of a crowd, a considerable asset in his line of work.

He seemed fit enough, physically.

He was our ace in the hole, if you'll forgive the pun. The big reason we could dispense with 111 of the 118-man strike team Delta planned to take to Tehran. Since there was no way they could hope to keep the whole operation quiet, there had to be enough guns on the line to provide security; and it would take a lot of warm bodies to escort fifty hostages across Roosevelt Street to the Amjadiyeh soccer stadium, where the choppers would pick them up.

Ackroyd changed all that. He just pointed his finger at you, and *pop!* you were somewhere else. No muss, no fuss, no noise to alert Student Militants that their hostages were being freed. He was perfect.

Except he could not seem to take the situation seriously. At least, he declined to take me seriously.

My *amour propre* is usually not too delicate, but I was hoping that, at the narrow passage, he wouldn't take time to toss off a quick one-liner every time I gave an order. He had what today would be described as "an attitude."

There was a commotion from the Sea Stallion's open side door. A small man with dark hair cropped close to his round head in a military 'do was engaged in a jostling derby with one of the Marines.

"Hey," I said sharply, "what's going on here?"

The jarhead stepped back away with an insincere smile. "I was just giving the sergeant here a hand."

Sergeant First Class Paul Chung, US Special Forces, thrust his chest out like a banty cock and glared at him. "I can take care of myself!" he snapped, dusting himself off where the jarhead had touched him. For all his Asian appearance, his accent was pure Philly.

He stepped straight out of the chopper and floated to the ground, arms folded across his chest.

He was the only serving military man we had—I did my twenty and got out in the mid-seventies, myself. He was second-generation Chinese American, but he looked Central Asian. It gave us something to play on, since Iran has a sizable Turkmen minority up in the northeast.

Informally he was known as "Dive Bomb." He could adjust the weight of any or all parts of his body at will, sort of like Hiram Worchester. He could add mass to a punch, or he could make himself featherlight and drift on wind currents. We figured to use him for recon, or if we needed someone to get over the ten-foot wall that surrounded the compound or onto a roof.

I watched him tightly as he grounded and walked away. He had an attitude, too, what you usually call your Small Man Syndrome—not everyone handles it as gracefully as I, though then again, I'm more middle-sized. I'd been *hoping* he was too professional—or too smart—to start a dustup with our ride out of here.

The Marine in the doorway muttered something about "ragheads" and turned away. When the sun had come up, Chung had gotten on his knees and bowed toward Mecca to pray; though American-born, he was a practicing Muslim. The Marines got quite a kick out of that. I decided he might not need a chewing-out, after all.

Amy Mears appeared in the door, blond, frail, and ethereal as a Maxfield Parrish nymph. A good enough–looking kid with short black hair and eyes of startling green materialized beside the chopper.

"Here, honey," he said. "Allow me."

She nodded. He grabbed her by the waist, plucking her neatly from the suddenly helpful hands of the crew, and swung her down. He offered her his forearm.

"I never knew you were such a gentleman," she murmured.

"Yeah," the kid said. "I got class coming out the ass, baby."

Her smile slipped. She gently liberated her arm.

That was Billy Ray. A kid he truly was, too; he was all of twenty years old, still a student at Michigan University. He had been on his way to NFL stardom as a running back until he busted his leg in three places in the first quarter of the Rose Bowl. People began to suspect there was something unusual about him when he tried to get back into the game before half-time. A blood test for xenovirus Takis-A ended his hopes of an athletic career; he had jumped at the offer from Justice to get in on a secret mission.

He was security for our team. He was a hand-to-hand combat expert, stronger than a nat, quicker, and a great deal meaner. There was anger in those green eyes, lots of it. If he could direct that anger against the enemy, he could be a lethal—and silent—asset.

Ackroyd materialized at Mears's elbow, guided her away from Billy Ray with a greater degree of deftness than one expects from window-peepers, at least outside of detective fiction. Ray's eyes tracked them like green laser beams.

I watched him tightly. If he *couldn't* control his rage, he'd blow the lid off the mission. There had not been time enough for me to decide which was most likely. Roll the bones, roll the bones . . .

The choppers lifted with a whine and headed for their own hideout. The team had rattled around inside one of the big RH-53s; two of them would be enough to lift off team and hostages both, if something should happen to Mr. Ackroyd, which God forbid. The third was along as backup.

Choppers are unreliable beasts.

We were truly out in the boondocks, and unlikely to attract more trouble than we could handle. Just in case, I issued disguises and weapons and turned a deaf ear to grumbling. We took shelter from the lethal sun in a fossilized shack with busted-out windows that let the hot Persian wind blow right through to our bones.

I was hoping my team would get some sleep during the day. Naturally, that was optimistic. Everybody was keyed up to the extent they barely fit inside their skin. They didn't have the soldier's knack for snatching sleep where you can find it, or a soldier's gut appreciation of why that's needful.

Harvey Melmoth volunteered to take first watch. I went out to pick him a nice spot on a little hardpacked sand hill where he could keep watch on the surrounding desolation.

"I don't need *that*," he said in a whisper; he couldn't talk any louder than that. He pushed away the Kalashnikov AKM I was trying to hand him. A fold of his red-and-white-checked kaffiyeh fell in front of his mouth, further muffling his words. "I won't take life."

He was a little balding guy dwarfed by his baggy Western-castoff Third World battle dress. He had a prissy little mouth and blue eyes swimming behind round spectacles thick as armor plate. He looked as if a walk back into the stacks would tax him; an obstacle course would drop him dead in his tracks.

And yet here he was, key component in the hairiest commando mission since the West Germans took down the hijacked airliner at Mogadishu.

His ace name was the Librarian. His power was to project a zone of absolute silence for a radius of about five meters. He would be crucial in enabling us to gain entry to the Embassy, neutralize any guards we encountered, and get to the widely scattered hostages without alerting our enemy.

"Think of it as a prop," I said, pressing the rifle on him. "The point is, if people see you holding that thing, they're liable to reckon we're too mean to mess with. If we don't have to fight, it's less likely that anyone gets hurt. Us *or* them."

He showed me a timid little chipmunk smile beneath his moustache. "I'm not worried, Major. Adventure fiction is bad fiction. We're having an adventure. Surely I can't die in a bad novel?"

"Uh-*huh*," I said. "Make sure to lend your guardian Muse"— he nodded brightly—"a hand by keeping your eyes open."

He reached inside the baggy tunic he wore. "Is it all right if I read?" he asked, pulling out a paperback copy of *Jude the Obscure*.

"Later," I said and walked back to the shack.

"I'm not afraid," Chung was saying when I returned. "Whatever happens, I can handle it."

"I like to see confidence," I said, "but a man who feels no fear is either stupid or psychotic. We're in danger every minute we're on the ground here, and I don't want anyone to forget it. Fear is our friend; it's Evolution's way of keeping us on our toes."

Ray was sitting on the table, kicking the heels of his cowboy boots against the dusty plank floor. "What's to be afraid of? Nobody ever died from pain."

I gave him a hard look. "Say that after you've done time in the basements of Evin Prison with SAVAMA beating on the soles of your feet with a steel cable."

He jutted his jaw. Ackroyd made a contemptuous sound.

"The Mechanic versus Kid Wolverine! The fight of the century!" He gave a sideways look to Damsel.

"What do you think, kid? If the macho bullshit gets any deeper in here, we could always stand on the table to try to keep an airway open."

Lady Black had turned her cape reflective side out. She looked entirely cool. Her laugh sounded the same.

"You've got your own swagger, Popinjay," she said. He scowled at the nickname. "They've got their tough talk, you've got your smart mouth. It's all insecurity talking."

Ackroyd glowered and found something fascinating in the white-bright landscape outside. He did not savor the taste of his own medicine.

Joann Jefferson—Lady Black, so-called for obvious reasons—was a Justice Department operative, a cool, tall woman in her mid to late twenties. Her skin was black, but nowhere near as black as her form-fitting suit, or the flip side of the cape she had pulled about her clear to the eyes. The garments seemed to suck in light like a black hole.

Her power was to draw energy into herself. She would be useful for turning out the lights at need—during our wonder week of training at Delta's Camp Smokey in North Carolina, she had shown that she could blow out a generator in seconds flat. Since she could also drain electrochemical energy from a human body, she could render a sentry quickly and quietly unconscious—or dead, an alternative she abhorred.

She gave me a quick glance above the dazzling folds of the cape. I looked hurriedly away. The old Adam was staring; she was no beauty, I suppose, but she was a handsome woman, and her poise and quick dry wit made her thoroughly attractive.

Besides, Lady Black could not control her energy drain. The suit was insulated, the cape energy absorbent on one side and reflective on the other, to modulate intake/output. However warm her blood might run, her embrace would be mortal cold.

Of course, bouncing away from her my eyes struck Mears. She was gazing at Paul Chung and smiling.

Her Justice Department employers had codenamed her *Damsel*. She had curly blond locks hanging in enormous blue Walter Keane waif eyes. In a purely physical way she was far prettier than Lady Black. Just the same she was less to my taste; she was what you might call vapid.

Her talent was to make nats into temporary aces. When he was running over the team's dossiers with me, Battle indicated that the Powers That Were hoped she might be able to really boost the power of an individual who already happened to be an ace; a human blast of nitrous oxide, as it were. When I asked him whether that had actually been tried, he dodged behind the ever-handy National Security / Need-to-Know barricade, like a rodeo clown giving the slip to a Brahma bull. I took it that meant "no."

You should realize how common that kind of thing is in the military, and shadow ops in particular. You would think when lives and great causes are at stake, everything would be run in a bright, clean, efficient manner. Well, that's McDonald's, not special missions. When we were prepping for the raid on the Son Tay POW camp in 1970—which was a smashing success, by the way, except Intelligence neglected to tell us the NVA had moved all the prisoners out a few weeks before—one of the squaddies made up patches that showed a mushroom and a pair of cartoon eyes against a black background, and sported the legend "Kept in the Dark—Fed Only Horseshit."

I was not particularly encouraged when Mears took me aside in the Camp Smokey rec hall. "I don't think they quite understand my power," she said plaintively.

"What do you mean?" I asked.

She bit her lip, looked around the room. Chung was refusing to concede another hopeless game of ping-pong to Billy Ray, who wasn't even using a paddle. Ackroyd was offering color commentary to Joann, who paid him no mind.

"I can't just turn my power on and off," Mears said. "I have to really care about a guy. There has to be *chemistry*."

When I accepted command of the mission, I accepted it on the government's terms, a decision I was to repent at leisure. They picked the team for me; I had no input. I was not allowed to drop Mears. I could have offered to resign, or held my breath until I turned blue; Battle, with Zbig Man backing him, had made it abundantly clear one would do as much good as the other.

Understand, please: I'm a professional warrior; I'm also, unfashionable as it was then, a patriot. When my country tells me to saddle up and go, I saddle up and go. But I don't believe in the Tooth Fairy, the Easter Bunny, or the infallibility of the top brass.

Back in our cozy Persian hideaway, Chung was failing to notice Damsel giving him the dewy eye. He was in a funk because all his conversational gambits seemed to fall flat. I could only hope he would wake up and see which way the reaction arrow pointed—and that Damsel wouldn't panic if we came to daggers-drawn with the happy lads of Pasdaran.

Well, this was surely an interesting crew, from a sociopsychological standpoint: take a bunch of civilians who happen to have been gifted with extraordinary powers courtesy of an alien virus, put them under intense stress in a situation they were in no way equipped to handle, and just watch those social dynamics fly.

. . . As I said: bizarre. You can see the outlines of a real workable mission, here. You can also see seams you could sail the

Nimitz through. There was something here I could not put my finger on.

I checked my watch. Nine hours to sunset. I hoped nobody's personality would disintegrate before the enemy even got a shot at us.

The sun had dropped almost to the distant blue ripple that was the mountains near the holy city of Qom when Ackroyd, on watch, came racing down the hill waving his arms and shouting, "We've got company!"

"Fine," I said, stepping from the shed. In my hand I had my sidearm, a Tokagypt 9mm, based on the old Browning 1908 by way of the Soviet Tokarev. It was a trophy from an earlier adventure a little farther west, and a nice touch, I thought: just the thing an officer of the Nur al-Allah's Palestinian auxiliaries would tote. "Now get back to your post and keep an eye on them."

It was a pair of vehicles, a battered Chevy truck and a dapper little tan Volkswagen Thing that looked as if it ought to have a *Panzerarmee Afrika* palm tree stenciled on its side. "Take up firing positions," I ordered, "and get ready to rock and roll."

"Why?" Ackroyd demanded. "They're what we were briefed to expect."

"Because I said so," I said, "and because if we take one little thing for granted, we will all end up dead, and not as soon as we'd like to be."

The two vehicles stopped in swirls of white dust in front of the shack. A lanky form unfolded from behind the VW's wheel and removed Ray-Ban shades from the front of a large round head topped by a Panama hat.

"What's this?" he said, gesturing to the Kalashnikov barrels poking out the shack's windows. "Perches for birds?"

"My operators," I said, "getting a crash course in life behind enemy lines. How on God's green earth did they get you into Tehran, Casaday?"

Okay. Casaday grinned without apparent sincerity. He was old-line CIA; I had rubbed up against him a few times in Vietnam, and occasionally since. He was the sort of shadow operative who didn't put much stock in notions like sincerity.

"That spooky ace bastard Wegener, from GSG-9," he said, "arranged to slip me in as a member of a Krauthead TV crew."

"The people pointing guns at you are all ace bastards, Casaday," I pointed out. "Hearts and minds. Do you speak German?"

He laughed. "Fuck no. But then, neither do many of these sand niggers."

"Don't get cocky; a lot of Iranians've worked as *Gastarbeiter* in Germany. Who's your friend?"

The pickup driver had dismounted and leaned his back to the door. He looked like a local, with a dark hawk's face and curly black hair. He wore Levi's and a white T-shirt that molded itself revealingly to his iron-pumped pecs, but he had that spoiled rich-boy look to him. I can recognize it right off; I have a touch of it myself.

"Name's Daravayush," Casaday said, lifting the hat and taking a handkerchief from a pocket of his white linen suit and mopping the line of his blond hair. It was getting thin, I was pleased to note. I was forty-five, ten years older than he was, and mine wasn't. "He's your trusty guide and native bearer. Used to be one of the Shah's bodyguards."

I raised a brow. I had encountered little rich Iranian boys who thought they were tough before. But Pasdaran—the Iranian Revolutionary Guard—and SAVAMA, Khomeini's secret police, were hunting former members of the Shah's entourage with fanatical zeal. What they did when they caught them was unpleasant even by the standards of Third World atrocities. To run the risks he was by staying in-country, our interpreter had to have some unlooked-for depths.

"You been in touch with Desert One?" Casaday asked.

I nodded. You might have read about the hijinks at the base camp, since they weren't classified, as our part was: how Delta blew up a gasoline tank truck and captured a busload of Iranian peasants. But you have to understand, what happened there had no effect on us—until later.

"Well, you're getting your two AC-130 gunships flying top cover tonight, as promised. The Iranians have those two Phantoms ready to scramble at Mehrabad, and that armored division still has elements at the Ordnance Depot near the Embassy."

I nodded. This was all known and factored in. Our mission planners estimated that the armored vehicles at the Abbas Abad depot would take a minimum ninety minutes to reach the Embassy after the alert was raised, even though it was just a few blocks away. I concurred, knowing something about how regular soldiers conduct their affairs—and not just in the Third World, either. Still, it was reassuring to know the Night Shadows would be up there with their Gatling guns and 105-mm howitzers, in case the tanks or the Phantoms tried to wade in.

Casaday climbed back into his jeep. "I can't say it hasn't been real," he said, and drove away.

I gestured the boys and girls out of cover. "Let's get ready to roll, people. We have a diplomatic reception to attend in just a few hours. We don't want to be late."

"Who's this?" Billy Ray said, pointing to the pickup driver.

"Our guide. Name's Daravayush."

"*Gesundheit*," said Jay, with an eye on the Damsel, of course.

Daravayush grinned. "You can call me Darius," he said in excellent English. "It's the Western form of the name."

"Are you an ace?" Damsel asked, eyeing his biceps.

"No. I was told that you would make me one."

She got a little vee between her brows. I took it he did not light her Bunsen. Well, they could hash it out themselves. I got busy getting my grumbling troops in motion loading our traps in the truck.

The neighborhood Komiteh was trying to do its Ayatollah proud. They had a clapped-out little Paykan sedan pulled across the street, and fires going in oil drums either side of it— for dramatic effect, no doubt, but also for warmth; Tehran is high desert, nestled right up against the Elburz Mountains. It gets *cold* at night in April.

"What do I do, boss?" Darius asked out the Chevy's open window. He had an edge of nerves to his voice.

"Drive right up," I said. "I'll handle it."

Tehran had that dark, hunkered-down look of a city in a war zone. According to our intelligence, that was mainly because the zanies had purged the people who knew how to run the power grid, but occasionally you heard a pop or a little rainsquall ripple of gunfire, off in the distance. Periodically you got the boom of something bigger, bouncing around along the boxy modern buildings and blue mosque domes.

We'd gotten into central Tehran by freeway, getting waved through a couple of Pasdaran checkpoints without a pause. Now we were working our way down on the Embassy from the north. The Embassy itself was in a fairly nonresidential district, but unfortunately we had to pass through a few neighborhoods on the way. That meant exposing ourselves to the mercies of officious Soviet-style block committees.

Or exposing them to ours; that was the kind of role we'd picked to play.

As the truck's brakes squealed us to a stop, I gave my crew the once-over. Chung was wound tight as a bull fiddle, just vibrating. Damsel sat right up next to him, her highly Western hair and face obscured by the folds of a kaffiyeh, her highly female figure muffled by bulky paramilitary drag.

During the day she'd been showing more and more attention to the sergeant, which had caused Billy and Ackroyd to throw out their chests and strut around her even more.

Right now Ackroyd was flexing the forefinger of his right hand as if to warm it up. His "gun," he called it; it was the crutch he needed to make his projecting-teleport trick work. His real gun was propped against the side of the truck, getting its furniture all banged up. He had no interest in firearms, claiming that his ace gave him all the firepower he needed. I had not managed to pound into his head that the piece was necessary to sustain our appearance.

He wasn't a stupid man, Jay wasn't. Not by any means. He just didn't see anything past his preconceptions. I wouldn't think that would be a big help as an investigator, but military analysis types are the same way. Go figure.

I couldn't see Ray's mouth for his headdress, but his eyes smiled at me, mean and green. He cracked his knuckles. I gave him a little nod. *Yeah, boy, we might need to see how much of a Wolverine you are.*

The Librarian was hastily tucking his copy of Hardy under his fanny. He still had that idiot composure. No worries about him breaking here, anyway.

Lady Black was in the front seat with Darius, huddled

under a black chador head-covering that went quite naturally with the rest of her getup; she looked like every other woman in Iran who didn't want to get her face slashed by the fundamentalists. The veil was a major help. There was *no way* we could explain wandering the streets of Tehran with a black woman. She must have been sweltering, but she didn't complain once the whole trip.

I jumped out of the pickup bed, ostentatiously readjusted the Tokagypt in my belt, and swaggered forward with my finest terrorist bravado. Which was fine indeed, since by that time in my long, bad life I was a pretty experienced terrorist.

There were a half dozen of them in their baggy Western-castoff style clothes, a couple of wizened old codgers, couple middle-aged men with important bellies, an adolescent with a cocked eye and an eight-year-old with a mock Kalashnikov carved out of wood. A cheap portable radio was scratching out Vivaldi, of all things. The *allegro non molto* from Concerto Number Four, "Winter," from *The Four Seasons*. Western classical music was the only music the mullahs would let the government radio play.

One of the middle-agers drew his gut up into himself and said, "You must show papers."

"'Papers'?" I repeated in atrociously accented Farsi—which, fortuitously, was the only kind of Farsi I spoke. "*Papers? What kind of nonsense is this? Papers?* We are strugglers in your Revolution, you mutes who cannot speak the language of the Prophet!"

He blinked at me. I got right in front of him—today we'd call it *in his face.* "Speaking of papers, you pustulent dog, can you read your *Q'ran* in the True Tongue?"

His fleshy lips worked. He swallowed visibly. *Gotcha.* Pious Muslims are supposed to be able to read the Book in Arabic. Persians are notoriously lax about this.

"You *filth!*" I screamed, not omitting to give him a spray of spittle. "Just as I suspected! You are not Muslims at all! You're filthy Jew spies! I wouldn't be surprised if you were jokers, too! Pull up your shirt, so that we may gaze upon the abomination of your deformities!"

He actually started to do that. Then he stopped himself. "Please, *jenabe agha,* honored lord, we are good Muslims, we did not realize—"

"Then get out of our path, you pigs, you twisted menstrual rags!"

The teenybopper popped the clutch trying to get the Paykan out of our way and knocked over one of the oil drums. Flaming junk went everywhere, igniting the hem of one old codger's robe. He started hopping around and squalling. I was rather hoping to see him go up, but the others knocked him to the ground and were beating out the flames when we pulled around the corner and out of sight.

"'Abomination of your deformities'?" Darius said out the driver's window. "Your command of our language is truly . . . formidable, Major."

I grinned at him and got my head cloth back in front of my face. Tanned as I was, I was still a little pale to pass for an Arab indefinitely.

"That's all it took?" Ackroyd said. "You just *yelled* at them? Jesus, we never had to bother with all this ace-commando crap. We could have just sent half a dozen New York cabbies. They'd knock this town on its keister."

"That's why we're going in disguised as Palestinians," I said.

"But the Palestinians observe the Treaty of Jerusalem," the Librarian whispered. "What are we doing here with all these guns?"

"The Palestinian *government* observes the Treaty," I said, "mostly."

"Lot of the Palestinians don't much care for that, Harvey," Billy Ray said. "They still wanna push Israel into the sea. So they turn into evil, wicked, mean, and nasty terrorists."

I nodded. Ray was not just a humming bundle of muscle and fury, after all. "We're radicals, terrorists, here as allies of the Nur, who's a great buddy to the Ayatollah. We're an arrogant lot of bullies; we have a modus vivendi with Pasdaran. Anybody else who gets in our way, we shoot—and the Palos *will* do that."

"You mean you treated those boys back there with grandmotherly kindness?" Chung asked, black eyes glittering. He was the only one of us not wearing a kaffiyeh.

I nodded. He gave a too-shrill yip of laughter.

Damsel huddled closer to him. "I'm scared," she said.

Ackroyd caught Billy Ray's eye. He rolled his. Ray gave him a tight grin and a tighter nod. I was glad my facecloth hid my own expression.

Chung glanced back. "I wonder what they made of me."

"Probably took you for a local. That was the plan, anyway. You and Darius are the only ones who'll pass."

He worried his lower lip with his teeth. "I hope they don't think I'm Kirghiz. I *hate* it when people think I'm Kirghiz. Back in my unit, they called me 'the Flying Kirghiz.' I *hate* that."

"Paul," I said, "you're *supposed* to be Kirghiz. Or Turkmen, which is almost the same thing. They got both flavors in northwest Iran, along with Kypchak and Kazakh and Uzbek."

"Oh my," added Ackroyd.

"What damn difference does it make?" Ray growled.

"I'm *Yunnan*," Chung said, in a pleading key.

"What does that have to do with the price of pussy in Pakistan?" Ray asked.

"A lot," Chung said. "We're not Kirghiz."

"Paul, nobody knows what Kirghiz are," I said.

"A nomadic people of the Tienshan and Pamir highlands of Central Asia," Harvey whispered, "belonging to the Northwestern Group of Turkic-speakers. They were the last Turkish rulers of Mongolia, being driven out in AD 924. In the thirteenth century Jenghiz Khan forced them from the Yenisei steppe to their current habitat."

"Okay, so *almost nobody* knows what Kirghiz are."

"Paul, old buddy," Ray said with a nasty smile, "lighten up. Yum-yum or Curb-jizz, you're all towelheads to me."

Chung's round brown face went pale. I could see the muscles knotting under his skin, feel the rage beating off him.

"Ray," I said quietly, "put a sock in it."

He showed me a defiant glower. I matched him, keeping my face emotionless. After a moment, he looked away.

Darius thumped his free fist on the top of the cab for attention. I craned forward to talk to him, glad for the interruption.

"Do you speak Arabic, Major?" he asked.

"No."

"What happens if we encounter real Palestinians?"

"Drive the other way," I said, "fast."

Crouching to peer over the five-foot parapet of the apartment roof, we watched the woman, so muffled by her chador she resembled an ambulatory black sack, walk down Roosevelt Avenue with a bunch of oranges in a net bag. The two walking guards, their German G3 rifles slung over the backs of their woolly-pully sweaters, spared her a single surly glance through the darkness and kept pounding their beat. The four boys flanking the gate never even looked her way.

"Jesus," Billy Ray said under his breath. "Doesn't she know there's a revolution on?"

"Life goes on, son," I said. "I've seen it before, a thousand times. No matter how tough things get—and the Tehranis have it pretty easy here, as far as emergency situations go—life goes on. Even if artillery is dropping a few blocks away, people still go to the store and cheat on their wives and goof off at their jobs. Kids still play."

"Gee, you make it sound so *attractive*," Ackroyd said. "Almost like having a real life."

"Only Americans think having things easy is a necessary condition of life," I said. "For most people it's a goal, not a sine qua non."

Billy Ray showed teeth to the Damsel. "Don't you love it when he talks dirty?"

She moved over so her flank was touching Chung, rested her arm on his hunched shoulder. He gave her a strained, slightly furtive look and concentrated back on the street.

Our building lay across the street from the northern part of the Embassy compound. In happier times it had been an upper-middle-class apartment. Even though life does go on, the occupancy rate had dropped precipitously since the street filled up with armed zealots. If they got to raising a fuss in the middle of the night, you didn't want to lean out the window and yell at them to shut up. I felt reasonably safe from chance detection up here.

Darius duckwalked over and grabbed the Damsel by the arm. "Hey," he said. "You're supposed to make me an ace. It was in the deal. Let's get to it, huh, baby?"

"What are you talking about?" She tried to pull away. "You're hurting me."

"Where do we do it?" he asked. "Right here on the roof? I've always wanted to be an ace. I also always loved little blond girlies like you—"

About that time Ray caught him by the upper arm and

threw him across the roof. About twenty feet. He landed hard, rolled over, picked himself up, groaning to his knees.

"All right, buddy," Billy Ray said. "If we can't get along, let's get it on."

Darius came up with a Browning Hi-Power in his hand. Ray moved like a mongoose, crossing the intervening space in three lightning steps and kicking the pistol away before the Iranian could squeeze the trigger. The Browning went skittering across the gravel with a sound that turned my bowels to ice water.

"Harvey," I said. The Librarian was quick on the uptake, I'll give him that. He dropped his Hardy and scrabbled to my side.

The roof became quiet. *Very* quiet. Ray had grabbed Darius by the front of his T-shirt and dragged him to his feet, preparatory to punching his face in. Darius was digging in a back pocket of his jeans, no doubt for a knife. When he produced it, Ray would pull his arms and legs off and shower him down on the Pasdaran like confetti, I hadn't any doubt.

I grabbed up an AKM, racked the bolt, and fired a burst into the roof at their feet.

It didn't make the slightest sound. A bomb going off would have made no more, though the rolling overpressure would've kicked up quite a fuss once it got beyond the limits of the Librarian's hush-field. The bullets gouged into the asphalt at the combatants' feet and stung their legs with gravel. *That* got their attention.

I pulled a finger across my throat. The gesture signified both *cut* in the directorial sense and what I would literally do to their gullets if they kept this nonsense up. Billy Ray released Darius, and the two stepped away from each other. I gestured for them to take up positions well apart from each other, then touched Harvey on the arm and smiled at him.

Sound came back. It was very strange, like having a switch thrown: suddenly the city sounds were there again, the distant traffic noise, the faint yammer of an argument from the building next door, a gunshot, blessedly far away.

"Ray, get on the horn to Angel Station. It's time to check in." Since he was strongest, our Wolverine got to carry the AN/ PRC 77, which was a heavy beast. Using the radio was a touch on the risky side, with the Abbas Abad garrison less than a mile to the west. But we needed to communicate, and word was that the people who could operate—or at least *maintain*— the Shah's radio-direction finding equipment were high on the list of purgees.

I put the Kalashnikov back on safety and returned to my own spot by the parapet. My mood was black.

I had had to use a weapon to keep discipline. That's the worst possible command procedure. It was a lick on me.

The primary mission of Special Forces, and their despair, is taking indigenous forces and trying to turn them into soldiers. Or at least credible guerrillas. Indiges are notoriously unstable and exasperating to deal with—that's i-n-d-i-g-e-s, by the way. Most of my Special Forces brethren leave out the *e*, which would make the *g* hard. Most of my Special Forces brethren are slightly on the illiterate side, I fear.

We, all of us in what you civilians call the Green Berets, have a special secret fear. It's that we might someday be called upon to whip Americans into fighting trim, and they'd be just as aggravating as indiges from the ceiling-fan country of your choice. And guess what? I had five Americans, well educated, intelligent, reasonably well socialized, and aces into the bargain. Guess what? They were acting just like indiges.

Darius was looking at Damsel as if to burn her clothes off with those hot black eyes. She was shrinking up against Paul Chung.

The warmth of her nicely rounded little body at last pene-
trated his paranoid insecurity. He put an arm around her.

I moved over to Darius. "What *is* your problem?"

He spat in the gravel near my feet. I let it go by. "When I was
recruited by your government, I was told I could become an
ace. It's why I agreed. I want it." He flicked his eyes toward
Damsel. "I want her."

"I don't know anything about that. I wasn't party to any
such agreement. If you have a grievance, take it up with the
person you cut the deal with. Meanwhile, keep your hands off
my people."

He laughed. It wasn't a pleasant sound. "She'd have come
around quickly enough, if I had met her when I was with
Sazman-e Amniyat Va Ettelaat-e Keshvar," he said. "She would
have had no choice, you know? But I think she would have
come to like it." He shrugged. "Or not. She's just a woman.
Who cares what she enjoys?"

Since shooting him through the head would reflect poorly
both on my wit and my command abilities, not to mention giving our position away, I moved away. I made sure not to hurry.

Ackroyd caught my eye, flipped his head off to one side,
obviously signaling for a private chat. I nodded and walked to
meet him beside the elevator housing.

"Just what the hell is going on here?" he demanded in a
fierce whisper.

"Isn't it a little late in the day to be asking that question?
There are fifty Americans held hostage in the Embassy, we're
here on a commando raid to rescue them—"

"Get serious," he hissed. I forbore from pointing out the
irony to him. "Don't you think there's something a little funny
here?"

"Eight of us versus four and a half million heavily armed
fanatics? My sides are splitting as we speak."

He made an irritated wave of his hands. "No, look. I mean, look at *us*. What do you see? A handful of deuces. Second-string aces."

"There are some pretty potent powers here," I said.

"Give me a fucking break. Where's Howler? Where's Golden Boy? Where's Cyclone, for Christ's sake? You'd think he'd eat this up with a spoon, he's such a headline hound."

[I should set the record straight here for the first time. I've heard a lot about how Cyclone was involved in the Embassy raid. Matter of fact, I read it in the Xavier Desmond book about the WHO world tour—the UN, not the rock band—that came out after his death.

The late Vernon Henry Carlysle took no part in the mission, at any level. I was surprised to discover he was not involved. This was just the kind of high-profile stunt that usually drew him like a fly to honey.

It may have been a command decision by old Vernon, as in, "If I'm not in command, my decision is no." Or maybe he was just smarter than I am. Or maybe the people who set the thing up had reason not to want to use him. But he wasn't in it.]

"Maybe they were busy," I said in as neutral a voice as I could manage. If a commander has his doubts, he's an irresponsible fool to share them with those under his command.

"That's crap," Ackroyd said. "I know 'military intelligence' is a contradiction in terms, but not even you buy that. We've been set up like bowling pins."

"No." My head seemed to be shaking of its own volition. "The mission has some problems. It may turn into a total SNAFU. But that's the nature of events, not conspiracy." I showed him the teeth underneath my moustache. "What you said about oxymorons isn't exactly untrue."

I saw no conviction in his eyes. "We're talking about our

country, here," I reminded him. "Our own people. *Americans.* They're not going to set us up for a fall."

"What about Watergate?" Ackroyd demanded, volume rising. "What about the McCarthy hearings?"

But then Billy Ray was waving to me and holding up the radio's handset. It might be that I wasn't ungrateful for the interruption.

"Got 'em," Ray said. If he resented the means I'd used to break up the fight, he didn't show it. I can say this for the kid, he did not seem the grudge-holding type. If you made him mad, he either busted your head right off, or he put it behind him.

I nodded thanks, walked over to take the mic. "Angel Station, this is Stud Six, over." *Stud*—as in seven-card—was our unit code name. *Six* is military-speak for the man in charge.

"Jack of Hearts, we have a problem, over."

"*Knave* of Hearts," I corrected. "What's your problem, over?"

"Angel Two is down. Repeat, Angel Two down."

That meant one of the Sikorskies at Angel Station—the chopper hide-site, a few miles north of the vacation spot where we'd spent the day—was sick and not expected to get better. It was no big deal. That's why we brought three; in a pinch, we and the hostages could all cram into one and take off again. Conceivably.

I rang off. Joann Jefferson was looking at me again. I went and sat down beside her.

She was flushed and breathing rapidly. She had not shown nerves before; I hoped she wasn't getting near any major fracture points.

"Knave of Hearts," she said. "I still can't get over that. Not ace or king."

"Using aces for code names would be giving a little too much away. Besides—I know what I am."

She laughed. She had a good laugh—hearty, though she had presence of mind to keep it way down.

"And I'm the Queen of Spades."

I shrugged. "You picked it."

"I know what I am, too." She nodded to Damsel, who was talking in a low voice to Chung. "So why aren't you chasing after little girl lost, there? I'm pretty sure you're the type who likes girls."

"K'ung-fu Tzu tells us that gentlemen never compete. She has ample suitors, anyway, I think."

She gave me an arched eyebrow. I grinned. I do that, too, when I am, shall we say, extremely skeptical.

"You don't like blondes?"

"I have very Catholic tastes, which isn't altogether surprising in a High Church boy like myself. But I'm also a professional. I have this iron-bound rule about sex with subordinates: I don't do it. Not, I hasten to add, that I'm often tempted by those under my command. I like girls, and prefer women, but that's the extent of it."

I tugged the end of my moustache. "Maybe my tastes aren't quite so Catholic, after all. Still, I find women infinitely variable, and infinitely diverting."

She laughed again—giggled, more. "You are more full of bullshit than any white person I ever met," she said. "I like you. You're funny. And you treat me like a person. You don't expect me to make the coffee, and you don't go . . . bending over backward or anything."

"Ms. Jefferson, I am a male chauvinist pig in good standing. I don't let that interfere with my job, either. What you are to me now is precisely what the others are: an operator, to use the jargon of this milieu. One, I'll add, who's given me considerably less trouble than certain others."

She bit her lip. "After this is over—I mean, if we survive—" She looked away then. "Never mind. I'm sorry I opened my mouth. I don't have much experience at this."

"Practice never hurt anybody." I undid the Velcro cover and checked my watch. "We still have a few minutes before H-Hour."

She shook her head. "It's stupid, anyway," she said, and it was her turn to be little girl lost. "I can't *touch* anybody, you understand? If I do, I kill them. I can't *help* it. I can have friends, if anybody wants to be friends with a black freak like me. I can't—"

I reached a fingertip and touched her briefly on the cheek. She jumped. My whole finger went numb.

"When you have the luxury to think about anything but the mission," I said, "consider the ramifications of my special gift. One can do wonders with prosthetics."

She frowned, slightly, which made her look almost intolerably cute. I decided I wasn't missing anything in passing Damsel by. "Right now, it's time to go back to playing soldier. Listen up, everybody."

They clustered round, Darius hanging slightly back. "It's almost time to move, people. So bring it on home: Tell me what you're going to do."

Ackroyd pointed a finger. "The guy in the watchtower goes bye-bye the second we hit the street."

"We walk up to the walking guards and I greet them as a pious *Turkmen* comrade," Chung said.

"I make everything quiet," Harvey whispered.

"I black one out," Joann said, "both if I can."

"If not, I pop him," Ackroyd said.

"Or I take him," Ray added with a flash of teeth.

"Or I just shoot him," I said. "We'll play it by ear. Same drill with the boys at the gate."

"Right," Chung said. "Then I get light and kite up for a peek over the wall—"

"While I make the gate open. Slick as a whistle, we're inside."

"We go straight," Ray said, "for the Chancellery." It was the biggest structure, and the closest to the main gate. Most of the hostages were being held inside. Since many of its doors were hardened, it had been expected to be the toughest target for Delta, since they'd have to use explosive entry. For us it was a breeze.

"Then we proceed clockwise," the Librarian said, "very methodically."

There were only six buildings, out of a total of fourteen, that were feasible to house hostages, not to mention captors. That simplified things.

Ackroyd cast a glance over the wall at the thickly wooded compound. "I can't get over how big it is."

"That's what twenty-seven acres looks like, city boy," Ray said. "Why the surprise? We been through a full-scale mockup twenty-five times, back at Smokey."

Ackroyd shrugged. I understood him. No matter how exact a model is, it can never really prepare you for the reality. If only more of our mission planners could grasp that little fact . . .

From overhead came a welcome noise: the faint baritone hum of a Night Shadow's four engines. Our Archangels had arrived to watch over us.

I raised my eyes to the sky. A few clouds, mostly stars. "'Lighten our darkness, we beseech thee, O Lord; and by thy great mercy defend us from all perils and dangers of this night,'" I said.

"Zero hour, people. Time to move as if we have a purpose."

We were so high on adrenaline when we hit the ground floor of the apartment where we'd been lying-up that we were damned near flying. We all had weapons in hand, even though it was questionable whether a week's hurried training made any of our civilians a greater threat to the bad guys than to themselves. But what the hey? With luck we wouldn't need to shoot anybody. We were aces, and even if none of us was exactly Golden Boy or the Great and Powerful Turtle, we were hardcore.

We were *on*. Felt we were ten feet tall and covered with hair. Felt *immortal*.

You know what always happens when you get to feeling that way. Whom the gods would destroy, they first make cocky.

Damsel stopped at the foot of the echoing cement stairs. She made Chung halt, too, by grabbing his arm. She went up on tiptoe—she was that tiny, that she had to stretch for Chung—and kissed him on the cheek.

"You're the one," she breathed. "You're my Hero."

Darius sneered. Blocked right behind the clinch, Billy Ray said, "Give me a flicking *break*."

But something happened to Paul Chung in that moment. I saw it in his eyes. He seemed to, well, *expand*. What it actually amounted to, I couldn't imagine.

"Let's get a grip here, people," Ackroyd muttered. "'We got guns, they got guns, all God's children got guns.'"

"He's right," I said, tapping Chung on the shoulder. Was it my adrenaline-fueled imagination, or did I feel a kind of electric tingle? "We're in a war zone now. Move out as I taught you, by pairs, rolling over watch to the front doors, then out into the street and across."

Chung and Mears hunkered down inside the stairwell, covering with their AKs. Thirty feet away, across the lobby, the night was black and empty beyond the glass doors. Taking Darius with me, I dodged quickly out and to the left. We pressed up against the wall to our side of the long-dormant elevator bank.

I waved the next pair forward. Ray and Jefferson ran across a debris-littered floor to take up position on the far wall.

Ackroyd and the Librarian advanced to the door. They and Mears and Chung were supposed to flank the entrance while Darius and I hit the street. If the Pasdaran guards thought there was anything unusual about a *fedayeen* patrol emerging from a mostly deserted apartment building—and in Tehran, there really wasn't—they would be too circumspect to say so. They were scared spitless of us, too. A reputation for craziness is a wonderful thing.

But it doesn't make you bulletproof.

In spite of everything we'd drilled in, little Harvey walked bolt upright, as though he was heading back to roust some boisterous teens from the stacks. As he reached the front of the foyer a guy in a sweater popped right out on the sidewalk in front of him, screamed something with *Allah* in it, and cut loose with an Uzi from the hip.

The glass blew in around us like a crystal razor snowstorm. Harvey's right leg snapped out from under him. He pitched onto his face.

Ackroyd pointed a finger. The gunman vanished.

I raised my AKM. The doorway filled up with bodies and bearded screaming faces. I held down the trigger and gave them something to scream about. They fell back from the door.

The echoes of gunfire seemed to keep on rebounding off the foyer wall as the Iranians fell back to regroup. I scuttled to Harvey, bent over him. I rolled him onto his back. His face was pale, his pants leg wet with blood. The blood wasn't just blasting out, though. That meant the femoral hadn't been hit, which meant he was not going to bleed to death in the next thirty seconds or anything. Which meant the best immediate action was—

"Ackroyd!" I yelled. "Pop him out!"

The detective pointed. Harvey vanished, gone to the medevac tent back at Desert One.

"Jesus!" Ackroyd said. "Which way do we go now? Up the stairs?"

"We don't want to get trapped on the roof," I said. "Out the back—into the alley."

Darius hit the back door first and stopped dead. Locked. "Out of my way, diaper head," Billy Ray growled. He walked into the door and right on through without slowing.

The night air was cool and full of the sounds of angry voices. There was a mob out on Roosevelt, between us and the Embassy, howling for infidel blood. It must have assembled in the time it took us to get down the stairs.

Real coincidental, wasn't it?

No time to think about that now. The mob had nerved itself to risk the fate of their writhing, moaning brethren blocking the front entrance and swarmed in, trampling them in their lust to catch us. I gave them another whole magazine through the foyer to reveal to them the error of their ways.

"Come on," I said. "Next building. We need to get some space between us and them."

Another heavy steel door faced our alley from the next brick building—they take security seriously in these ceiling fan countries. Not seriously enough to keep Billy Ray out when he was this motivated, though. As we crowded into the darkness of a short hallway filled with musty storeroom smells, we heard the baying of the pack flood into the alley at our backs.

There was an interval of running, hearts drumming, as we crashed through doors, dashed up short flights of stairs and down alleys. And then we had space to try to force some stinking alley air back into our lungs while Billy unlimbered the radio.

Damsel was crying. Chung had his arm around her. He was standing tall, taller than his inches.

"What happened?" Ackroyd demanded. He grabbed the front of my blouse. *"What the fuck happened?"*

"Calm down," I said. "Something went wrong."

"Something? We're blown. Harvey may be dead. All you can call that is *something?"*

"I call it war. He's a casualty. We need to work on not joining him. And he's not going to die—they'll patch him up at Desert One."

"Right."

Ray handed me the microphone. "Archangel One, Archangel One, this is Stud Six. Archangel One, we need the Sword of the Lord in one hell of a hurry."

"Stud Six, this is Archangel One," a voice came crackling back. "You're going to have to wait for it. Maximum sorry, over."

"Angel One, what the hell are you talking about? Roosevelt Avenue is full of angry mob. We've got one man down. We need the streets swept. Over."

"Stud Six, I say again: You're gonna have to wait, over."

"Archangel, *we have no time."*

"Orders, Stud Six. They had an accident back at Desert One. Chopper crashed into a C-130. Be advised we can take no action without clearing it through the man upstairs."

For some reason I was very particularly struck by the fact that our line to the president ran through Battle and Brzezinski. I had little time to ponder the thought, because just then a vehicle cruised past the end of the alley. A light-colored Volkswagen Thing. At the wheel sat a tall man in a Panama hat and tropical suit.

He turned his big head to stare at me. He still wore his sunglasses, like a traffic cop. He drove on.

A moment later the pack came swarming around the corner. I dropped the microphone and grabbed for my AKM.

"You were right!" I yelled to Ackroyd. "We're screwed, blued, and tattooed."

Not many of the charging Iranians had guns—just a mob, not the Guard yet, thank God. But they had clubs and fists and stones and—yes—swords. And numbers, of course. We can't forget those.

I had too many of my own people between me and the mob to fire effectively. I switched the selector to single shot and poised, waiting for a shot.

Chance put Ray and Ackroyd at the front. The detective reacted more coolly than I imagined he could. He just started aiming that finger and picking off the rushing rioters, *pop-pop-pop*. Every time he pointed, one vanished.

Unfortunately, he didn't have a full-auto teleport. They swarmed us.

That was where young Billy came into his own. He caught by the face the first man to reach him.

Bones crunched, blood flowed. Billy hurled him back against his buddies.

The youthful Wolverine became a whirling dervish of fists and feet. He stove in skulls against the brick walls, ripped limbs from sockets, popped out eyes. He rammed his hand into a big bearded man's chest, pulled his heart out, and showed it to him. Ackroyd, who'd fallen back, overwhelmed, turned away and puked.

Someone swung a length of pipe overhand at Billy's head. He threw up an arm to block. His ulna cracked with a sound like a gunshot.

He grabbed the pipe-wielder by the loose front of his shirt and head-butted him. When he let the Iranian go, the man's eyes were rolled up as if to stare at the deep dent in his own head.

I stepped forward past the indisposed Ackroyd, jammed my Kalashnikov into the gut of the next man up, blew him down. Then I hosed the alley.

The survivors of Ray's fury turned and fled. As they departed the alley, their better-armed and smarter—or luckier—comrades leaned around the wall and began to rip fire at us.

Billy Ray said, "Fuck," and stepped back. Blood started from his shoulder where a round had taken him.

"I can handle this," Chung said.

"Paul, they're too far away to punch," I called over my shoulder. I was busting caps desperately now, not concerned with hitting anything, just trying to get the bad guys to pull their heads back.

"I've gone beyond that now," he said. "*She's* made me a new man."

"Paul, what are you talking about?" Lady Black asked.

"Watch." And he raised a few inches off the ground, and took off down the alley like an F-4 on afterburner.

Now, keep in mind, he *couldn't do this*. It would be like me suddenly discovering that I could deadlift a tank, or shoot fire from my fingertips. He'd had his ace for years; all he could do was get lighter than air and float, or glide slowly down. He had no powered flight.

You couldn't tell that to him. He hit the gunmen as if he'd been fired from a cannon and knocked them flying in all directions. Then he began to swoop back and forth, driving back the mob like a flying hammer.

Damsel held clasped hands before her face. "My *Hero*," she breathed.

Billy looked at me. *What the fuck?* he mouthed.

I shrugged. The Librarian was the one with all the answers, and he was gone.

Lady Black was at Ray's side. "You're hurt," she said.

He had a bullet through one shoulder and a bad break in the other arm, and I noticed he'd taken a good shot to the face with a rock or some such, which had pushed his right cheekbone in pretty well. He shrugged her off. "I'm fine," he said, and the words were only slightly distorted.

There was no rear door in the next building, and I could hear voices inside the one we'd last vacated.

"We need to get moving down the alley," I said. "Paul! Paul, come on!"

I don't know if he heard me. He was swooping back and forth, enjoying a power he'd never known, having the time of his life.

I saw him fly back into view at the head of the alley. He paused a moment, hanging in midair, to flash us a V-for-victory.

From out of sight down the street a heavy machine gun hammered. Paul Chung came apart in midair like a melon dropped from a skyscraper.

"*Paul!*" Damsel shrieked. She started to throw herself toward the place where the bloody bits of her Hero were raining from the sky. Ackroyd caught her arm.

"Come on," he said, "let's get out of here!"

We ran. Into the alley stormed the mob, heartened by the arrival of heavy support. Shots cracked.

One caught Amy Mears in the calf. She screamed and went down. Her wrist came out of Ackroyd's grip.

The crowd flowed over her like surf.

Ackroyd started popping frantically, dancing, trying to get a line of sight to her. The mob formed a writhing impenetrable wall between them. I caught a glimpse of Damsel as her head rag came free, revealing her unmistakably Western and feminine mass of curls. The crowd howled in outrage mixed with lust. There's nothing like old-time puritanical religion to give a mob the taste for rape.

"Help me! Oh, God, help me!" Amy screamed, as her clothes were wrenched away. The mob closed in between us, forcing the rest of us back like incoming tide.

Billy Ray waded back into the crowd. Somebody hit him in the chest with a fire axe. He rocked back, busted the hardwood handle with a hammer-fist blow, then plucked the sharp stub from the wielder's hands and jabbed it through his belly.

For the moment the mob had lost interest in chasing us, but they hadn't forgotten us. Guns flashed. Billy Ray grunted again as more bullets hit him.

I grabbed Ackroyd by the arm. "In the name of God, come on! There's nothing we can do!"

"They'll rape her!"

"They'll do worse to us if they catch us. Run, you idiot."

He flailed at me with his arms. I slapped his face. Then I took my own advice. He followed, weeping.

Lady Black was helping support Ray. The pain and sheer structural damage were taking a toll. Another man would've been dead long since. He was still on his feet, if barely.

Yeah, he had his ace, which gave him strength and endurance and the power to regenerate damage—if that system hadn't been overloaded by what was done to him. What kept him going now had nothing to do with the wild card. It was guts.

Lady Black had them, too. If I'd been her, and seen what

was happening to my fellow female up the alley, I'd have taken off in huge bounds like a gazelle.

Oh, yes, we were a gutty bunch. Even Ackroyd, who'd stood his ground as long as any man ever did in the face of odds like that. The problem was those odds. Comes a point when they beat guts, every time.

The pack was holding itself up in the narrow alley, fighting like hyenas over the spoils. Rape was gone from even their reptile brains by now—I hope. I saw one wave something white and slim above his head, brandishing it like a trophy. Damsel's right leg, I think it was . . .

Around the building, out onto the street. And after all we'd survived and sacrificed, we weren't home free: Here came a fresh bunch around the next corner back from the alley, waving swords and clubs and cheering as if Tehran had just won the World Series.

Lady Black and Billy had fallen inevitably behind. Ackroyd and I looked at each other. In his eyes was raw hatred, but also raw determination. We turned and faced the mob, prepared to go down fighting.

Bearded faces opened in triumph. Clawed hands reached for Joann and Billy. Jay was popping the bastards, and I was running through magazines as fast as my piece would cycle.

It was all for nothing.

Lady Black let go of Billy and stepped to the side. She reached to the front of her baggy blouse, tore it open. Then she grabbed the neck of her protective black suit and pulled it down to her navel, baring her chest.

The sheer unexpectedness of it made the crowd falter briefly a few steps from her. Possibly they were admiring the prizes they were about to lay hands on.

White light exploded from Joann's face and chest. My vision went away for a moment.

When it returned, I could just make out a street filled with writing bodies. As I blinked away great bright balloons of afterimage I saw that many had their faces burned and fingers seared away. Others lay still, blackened to motionless mummies.

Joann stood there with a faraway look in her eyes. "It's been building for a long time," she said. "Building and building."

I grabbed the hanging front of her suit and pulled it up. She nodded, absently, and started pulling it back into place. The pursuit was off our tails. For the moment. We turned and made what speed we could.

"Archangel One, Archangel One, do you have an answer yet, over?"

With a little room to move, we had found a three-story building with pointed-arch doors and windows and climbed up to the roof. Since our pursuers didn't know where we were, the risks of staying at street level outweighed the risk of being trapped up here.

Down in the streets they still hunted us. They'd broken into packs now, a few in vehicles, most on foot.

Joann bent over Billy Ray, who lay on his back with his head propped on the radio pack. The unit miraculously still worked. Jay Ackroyd sat with his head between his knees and just breathed. He had thrown away his kaffiyeh. His hair was in serious disarray.

"Stud Six, I'm afraid the word is negative, over."

"Negative on what? Fire support or pickup? Over."

A pause. Atmospherics crackled. I wanted to squeeze an answer from the microphone with my fingers.

"Stud Six, that's negative on both." Archangel One had the decency to be weeping openly. "We got the word. We're pulling out; Angels One and Three are already gone. It's over, man. Over."

I didn't think he was handing the conversational ball back to me. Nonetheless I grabbed it: "On whose orders?"

"This came all the way from the top." And in the sudden thunderous silence I barely heard him say, "Good luck, Stud Six. Archangel One—out."

"They're leaving us," Ackroyd panted. "The fuckers are pulling out and *leaving* us."

"That about sums it up," I said, throwing down the mic. No point in handling it gently anymore.

He raised his head and looked at me and gave me a shaky smile. "Well, I guess I drew the short straw, didn't I?"

"How do you mean?"

"I pop you all back to Desert One," he said. "Then I guess I get to go play Twenty Questions with the Revolutionary Guard."

"No."

He stared at me. "Hey, do you think I'm a fucking moron, you tin-plated hero?" he flared. "I can't pop myself. Or are you such a stupid fucking military jock you didn't realize that?"

"I realize it," I said. "But you aren't popping me anywhere."

"What the fuck are you talking about?"

"I'm talking about, I'm not leaving you behind. I've lost three people already. I'm not losing more without a fight."

"You left Damsel quick enough."

"She was *gone*, Jay." I was surprised how quiet my voice was. I just didn't have the energy to get emotional. "There was nothing we could do for her without getting the rest of us killed. It was a command decision. I made it. I have to live with it."

"I know all about that," Joann said. She had torn her chador into strips and bandaged Ray as best she could with it. Now she moistened a fragment from a canteen and dripped water between the boy's bloody lips. He was breathing with a sound like the A train. I didn't think it was too good a sign.

"How did you do that back there, by the way?" I asked.

"All that energy I store up," she said, color draining from that handsome face, "it has to go *somewhere*."

She shook her head. "I'm going to see them every time I shut my eyes the whole rest of my life," she said, "those faceless men—"

I squeezed her shoulder. "It goes away after a while," I said. "Or at least, you don't get the dreams so often." She looked up into my eyes.

"I know, child," I said quietly.

I turned away.

"Where's Darius?" she asked suddenly. "I haven't seen him since, since—"

"Since they nailed Harvey, back at the apartment," Ackroyd said. "Motherfucker ditched us."

I nodded. "I never did like cops much," I said, "especially secret ones."

Ackroyd frowned. "You mean—he wasn't just a bodyguard, was he?"

"No."

"He was SAVAK. A torturer."

"One of the worst, I suspect."

"When did you know?"

"Not for sure till he told me, up on the roof. But I suspected it the minute I laid eyes on him."

"You son of a bitch," Jay said. "You'd jump in bed with the fucking Devil himself, wouldn't you?"

"If it helped me accomplish my mission." I held up a hand. "Save the denunciations, Ackroyd. It's time to use your magic finger. Billy first."

"Hey—" the kid said, trying to rise. He had come back around at some point. "You can't—get rid of me. I won't go—"

Joann pressed him down with her fingertips. "You have no choice, Billy," Ackroyd said.

I hunkered beside the boy. "If you live, son—and I'm afraid you will, as tough as you are—you're going to need an ace name."

"What's the matter with . . . Wolverine?"

"Your alma mater might sue. No, I have the name for you. I name thee Carnifex."

"What's—that mean?"

"Latin for 'Executioner.'"

He smiled and gave me the circled thumb-and-forefinger OK sign. And vanished.

Ackroyd pointed his gun at Lady Black. "Ready, Ms. Jefferson?"

"Just a moment." She stepped up, briefly held his face in both gloved hands. Then she did the same to me. I hugged her. I had to keep my head well back—she was taller than I. But I hugged her hard, and she hugged me back.

She stepped backward and was gone.

I jumped, caught Ackroyd by the wrist, shoved his hand and pointing finger skyward.

"Try that again," I said, "and I'll break both your trigger fingers. Got that?"

A moment, and he nodded. I let him go, but kept a wary eye upon him.

"I didn't send them to Desert One," he said.

I froze in the act of stooping to gather the Kalashnikov magazines I'd made Lady Black and Billy carry, and relieved them of before Ackroyd popped them out. "We've been given the royal shaft," he said. "I don't trust anybody right now, least of all the military. I sure as hell wasn't sending them back to Desert One."

— — —

A moment. I nodded. "Smart move. Where'd they go?"

"The scoreboard in Yankee Stadium." He shrugged. "It's kind of a catch-all target for me."

I laughed. "You must be seriously suspicious, if you'd trust them to Steinbrenner instead of our own people. I wonder if the Yankees are playing at home tonight?"

I held out Joann's Kalashnikov. "Take this."

"No way. I don't have a clue how to use it." An ugly smile twisted his lips. "The recoil would probably throw my aim off so I'd shoot you."

"We don't want that, now, do we?" I drew my Tokagypt, reversed it, offered that.

"No." He held his extended forefinger up. "This is all the gun I need."

"If we get in the middle of it, you and I might not be able to take everybody out, me shooting and you popping," I explained, choking down my impatience. "You have to know that by now, after what happened in the alley. We need to make them put their heads down. Pointing your finger at them just won't cut it."

"All right." He snatched the pistol away.

I let him lead off down the stairs, not my favorite tactical move, but I still didn't trust him behind me with the fickle finger of fate.

Halfway down the block a pickup truck with cracked and faded blue paint was parked. I smiled, tapped Ackroyd's shoulder, headed us toward it. "Pray it has fuel," I said.

"What, did you happen to bring a key?" I shook my head. "I suppose you're going to hotwire it, then?"

"Better. Got a penknife?"

He stuck the Tokagypt down the front of his pants and dug

into a pocket. I winced. I wanted to remind him where the expression *going off half-cocked* came from, but this was no time to start teaching him to handle firearms with respect.

He looked past me then, and his eyes got wide. He grabbed the Tokagypt out of his waistband and aimed it at a doorway behind me. He had somehow gotten the safety off; the pistol barked as it came online.

I fell against the door of the truck, momentarily half-blinded and deafened. I smelled burning hair—mine—singed by the muzzle flash.

Panic sent a spasm into Ackroyd's finger. He pumped the trigger, spraying bullets wildly all over the front of the building until the last round went and the slide locked back.

I grabbed the gun out of his hands. "Jesus *Christ*, you idiot, what the hell do you think you're doing?"

He pointed. "Someone in that door. Pointing a gun at you. I—*oh, dear God*, no!"

He raced past me to the door, knelt down. When I came up with him, AKM at the ready, he was sobbing convulsively and stroking the cheek of the person he'd shot.

A boy of about eight, lying sprawled in the doorway. Curly dark hair, black eyes wide open to stars they'd never see again. One of those toy wooden Kalashnikovs lay on the steps beside him.

I took Ackroyd by the shoulder and pulled him away. He sat down on the curb by the truck, dropped his face to his hands, and bawled like a baby.

I laid my left forefinger on the curb and chopped the tip off with Ackroyd's knife. Blood spurted. I held the stump up.

"Our keys," I said.

Ackroyd stared horror-struck between his fingers. "Oh, God, you're sick, you're really sick."

I pressed the stump over the lock, felt my soul flow, become one with *mechanism*. I opened the lock unto us, then pulled my finger away. It came free with a soft sucking sound.

I slid my AKM in, climbed in after it. I shut my door, leaned across to open the passenger door. "Get in," I said, putting command into my voice.

Dully, Ackroyd rose and walked around the truck. As he slid in and shut the door I pressed my severed finger against the ignition. The truck coughed once and started.

"Quarter tank," I said—I felt it, the way you have a rough idea how hungry you are. "Slovenly drivers here. Don't keep topped off."

"It was the gun," Ackroyd said in a voice of lead. "If I didn't have the gun, he wouldn't be dead."

"Yes, he would. He looked like he was holding down on us. I would have dropped him myself. I told you, I'm taking you out of here." I exerted my will, and the engine coughed once and started.

We picked up an honor guard a quarter mile from the airport. A Nissan pickup, filled with authentic heroic Palestinian freedom fighters. Somebody must have passed the word; it was oh-dark thirty, and there were no streetlights, so they could not have gotten a good enough look at us to see our faces were paler than the Tehrani norm. But they passed us going the other way, whipped a U, and came on, blasting over the top of the cab with their trusty Klashin.

I put the pedal to the metal. The rear window blew in and sprinkled us with sugared glass. Ackroyd ducked.

"Can't you make the driver disappear?" I asked.

He gave me a hate stare. Then he raised his head, cautiously, poked his finger up over the bottom of the now-empty window.

I was splitting my attention between screeching down the narrow street at eighty miles an hour and the wing mirror. I saw the Nissan lurch to the side and hit a parked Paykan. *Fedayeen* went rolling out like apples from a vendor's cart.

"Bull's-eye!" I cheered. "Well done."

He grinned and bobbed his head. Then he realized those bodies sprawled all over the street there were not dummies or stuntmen. Some of them would be getting up again slowly, if ever. He turned his face forward and buried it in his hands.

"More company," I said, a few seconds later, looking in the rearview.

"You want me to murder them, too?"

I shook my head. "Too many. If one gets too close, I may call on you. But save it."

"I don't believe I'm here," he said. "Why did they do this to us? Why would they set us up like this?"

"So we could take a fall on behalf of the wild card. We fail. Maybe the hostages back there die. Who's to blame? Aces, of course. President Jimmy, too, I guess—he's too soft on us wild cards to suit some tastes."

"And you went along with it," Ackroyd said.

I felt my cheeks begin to burn. "Yeah," I said, "yeah, that's right. I *like* the thought of dying. I like the thought of people under my command getting tortured and killed. I like being in charge of the biggest balls-up since the Mayaguez raid—"

No, I told myself, *you don't have the luxury to snap now. You're good at handing out tough talk; it's time to shut up and soldier, soldier.*

And count your losses later. I made my jaw clamp. It was much tougher than making the truck go where I wanted.

"I'm sorry," Ackroyd said. "That was cheap."

"Yeah. So please shut up for a while."

There was some more wild driving, bullets cracking past our ears—they don't whistle, they go faster than sound for the most part, make little sonic booms—and then Ackroyd said, "There's a chain-link fence up ahead."

"Mehrabad International Airport," I said.

"Uh—don't you think you should slow down?"

"No," I said, "because then I couldn't do—"

I hit the fence. Metal broke with squeals of protest, and dragged sharp claws back along the truck like fingernails on a blackboard.

"—this."

"*Jesus Keerist!*" Ackroyd yelped. "You're out of your fucking mind!"

"If you don't quit saying that, you'll give me a complex."

He turned in his seat. "I don't know what kind of jackass scheme you have in mind, but it isn't working. They're still on our tail."

"No worries." I was heading toward a point I remembered from studying the aerial recon photos.

"Look up ahead."

There they were, as advertised: the dark broken-nosed shapes of a pair of American-made F-4s.

"What are those?"

"Your tax dollars at work. Gifts to our noble ally, the Shah of Iran."

"What are you planning to do," he asked, "ram them and go out in a blaze of glory?"

There were a pair of men in flight suits standing by the nearer Phantom, performing a preflight check.

Or trying to. One of them was scratching his head under his helmet. The other was kicking the tires. Pilots hadn't fared so well under the new regime, either; these guys probably knew a lot more about Khomeini's book *The Explication of Problems* than they did about the flight manual on this baby.

The one scratching his head saw us. He tapped his buddy

on the arm. He gave off bending to peer into the wheel well and turned to stare at us.

I steered right for Fric and Frac. They fled.

There were ground crew with their little carts fussing with the plane. Hoping some of them still had a clue as to what they were doing, I stopped the truck, stepped out, and fired my Kalashnikov in the air.

They joined their pilots in bunny impressions.

We'd extended our lead over the pursuit, but they were closing fast. I drew my Kabar sheath knife and laid my left hand on the tarmac.

"What the hell are you doing now?" Ackroyd demanded.

"Don't look," I said, and cut off my hand. It was not a neat process.

It hurt like the Devil, I have to tell you. Maybe I'm sick as that *illegitimatus* Battle, with that dumb stubbing-the-cigar-on-his-own-arm trick of his—I was surprised he didn't whip that out on poor President Jimmy.

"Climb aboard," I said, and started up the hook-on ladder into the pilot's seat. I only have so long before the blood loss starts to get to me.

Ackroyd had watched the whole thing—why should he start to listen to me now? He managed to pull himself off his knees despite the dry heaves and scurried up into the back seat. Following my example, he jettisoned the ladder.

I pressed my stump to the console. Any-old-where would do. "Ahh—" Nothing like the feel of *fusion* with a fine piece of machinery.

"Poor girl," I said. "They've treated you badly. But you'll pull through for us, won't you?"

I could feel Ackroyd's eyes boring through the headrest into my skull. "Don't we need flight suits?" he demanded.

"I'll try not to do anything radical enough to black us out."

I felt for the twin engines, revved them, felt their power surge. It's why pilots are such an arrogant lot—there's nothing like the feeling of the unbridled *power* a jet fighter imparts. And they only get it at one remove, poor sods. I got it *all*.

A horrible light dawned on Ackroyd. "Do you know how to *fly* this thing?" he demanded.

"No."

He started to clamber out. "I just remembered," he said, "I have an appointment to get my nails done. Pulled out by the roots, that is."

I dropped my canopy on him, trapping him. "Calm yourself, my boy," I said—I was starting to feel giddy now, I don't mind telling you. "This baby knows how to fly *herself*."

Outside, our pursuers drew up alongside in their vehicles, apparently afraid to open fire on one of the Ayatollah's personal warplanes. What they did didn't matter. I showed them our tail, and flame, and we rose into the sky and freedom.

The Shiites have a prophecy, that the Antichrist will appear in the desert of Khorasan, to lead an army of 144,000 Jews in battle against the faithful at Armageddon. Desert One lay smack in the middle of Khorasan.

I wonder if Battle knew that all along. Probably not.

Later they said it was Cy Vance who talked Carter into puppying, after the crash at Desert One. The loss of life shook him, and his bowels turned to water at the thought of what the world would say if he turned a Night Shadow's mini guns on a crowd of civilians in the streets of Tehran.

Well, all that's true enough—at the crunch, Jimmy Earl didn't have the sand to carry through. But it wasn't just Vance working on him. It was Brzezinski. And Battle, back at Desert

One, spinning long-distance tales of how the mission was a wash and it was time to cut his losses.

I told them over and over at debriefing how I'd seen Casaday there, leading the mob. They said over and over that I was mistaken. That it wasn't Casaday, couldn't have been. Then they told me that he had been trying to pull the mob off our trail.

Eventually I was told—officially—to drop the matter. I'm a good soldier, and even I have to sleep sometime. I dropped it—openly.

You wonder how I got the idea there was some kind of high-level conspiracy against wild cards—what brought me clear around the world and back to Vietnam. Do you have an idea now?

That's the story you wanted, but it's not all the story. Here's how our adventure differed from the bad fiction poor old Harvey thought couldn't hurt him: Our escapade had *consequences*. It left marks on the souls of those who survived. It always does.

Billy Ray survived, of course. He even kept the name I gave him. I'm flattered. We just shipped him back from here; he was a prisoner of war, of sorts. Working for that devil, our old friend Battle.

Casaday was here, too, but he got away. Which was good, because I would have killed him on sight, and Mark would disapprove of that. And I respect Meadows. It's not many hippie peace-freak wimps who conquer their own country from the communists.

Lady Black—well, once she wasn't my subordinate anymore I was free to follow certain leads she'd given me. She's a lovely child. We've continued to keep in touch. In more ways than one. I'll spare you the details, but I will say that metal isn't the only kind of substance my spirit will enter into—and some of the other ones conduct energy *very slowly*.

As I told her, I do wonderful things with prosthetics.

Ackroyd never crossed my path again. We're both happier that way. I guess he still blames guns for killing that kid. A real shame his moral courage doesn't match his physical. If he faced up to what he did—instead of blaming objects—I wager he'd sleep better.

By the way: Harvey Melmoth. The Librarian. He died, you know. Exsanguination resulting from an insult to the *arteria femoris*, the report read.

Bullshit. I told you, that bullet never hit his femoral artery. I've seen enough of those wounds to *know*. Jay Ackroyd was right all along, you see. They sent us to Tehran to die.

It was a conspiracy. It's still going on; what you're investigating is part of it, too. It was following up strands of that conspiracy that led me to Mark and back to Nam. It's big, and it means to finish the wild cards for good.

One last thing, before you turn that tape recorder off: President Carter took personal responsibility for the failure of the rescue mission, and ordered the records sealed in an effort to protect aces from the storm of recrimination. That was big of him; too bad it didn't work. Aces were blamed, anyway, even if the public didn't know which ones were involved.

But he was wrong again. The responsibility was mine, and mine alone. I lost three good men and women—I don't count Darius, and I hope they pulled him apart much more slowly than they did Amy.

The rest of my team was permanently scarred, one physically, all mentally.

Their blood is on my hands. I grieve them every day. The responsibility is mine.

So ends the narrative of J. Robert Belew, USSF, retired.

The Ashes of Memory

6

"Hannah, don't sit down! Let's *move!*"

"At least let me drink my coffee; traffic was hell coming from Washington. What's up, Arnold?"

"The call just came in from NYPD. You know that creep Ramblur we talked to the other day? Flashfire? He blew himself up."

"Jesus."

They arrived to chaos. Ramblur had lived in the basement of his apartment building. A hole had been blown in the corner of the foundation, and half the windows in the building were gone. Black streaks showed where fire had gushed from the apartment, but there looked to be little actual fire damage. Hannah and Simpson, both now in slicks and helmets, walked over the thick snarl of firehoses and into the water-dripping stairwell. Chief Reiger greeted them at the door.

"Well, Miss Davis! Arnold, how are those kids of yours?

Come to see what's left of Flashfire? Come on in, but I warn you, it ain't a pretty sight."

The chief was right about that, Hannah decided immediately. Ramblur had evidently been at a workbench set along the wall. Most of the damage to the room seemed to be from the initial explosion—there'd been a small fire, but the force of the blast had snuffed out most of the flames. There were shards of glass everywhere and a few unbroken containers of variously colored powders and granules; Hannah opened the screw-top lid to one of them and sniffed. She sifted a little of the powder inside onto her palm. "Calcium hypochlorite," she said. "This guy had a regular chemist's shop here. Better tell your people to be careful, Chief, and you'd better keep the tenants out. If he has lithium or potassium around, all you have to do is get them wet and we'll have a real beauty of an explosion and fire here again. Where is he, by the way?"

Reiger snorted and pointed across the room. Hannah looked, then gasped involuntarily. Ramblur was unrecognizable. The entire front of the body was a charred mess. The right arm was missing; so was part of the torso on that side. The corpse was in two parts lying close together, severed just below the rib cage; bone poked whitely from the black-and-red tangle. He'd been flung across the room so viciously that the plasterboard above him was cracked and dented from where he'd hit. The entire mess still steamed. "Bet he didn't even have a chance to say 'Oops!' " Reiger said. Swallowing once, Hannah went over and looked more closely at the remains. She crouched down in front of Ramblur, studying the skeletal, charcoal-black face. The jaw hung open as if in eternal surprise.

"You'd think a pyro with his background and this kind of stockpile would have known what he was doing," she said.

"Maybe he flunked chemistry 101," Reiger said. "Or maybe something slipped."

"Maybe."

Simpson had gone into the bedroom of the apartment. Now he called out, "Hey, Hannah, better take a look over here."

"On my way." She rose, walked across the room, then stopped at the door.

Simpson was holding an iron bar in one hand—a piece of steel rebar exactly like those that had held the doors at the Church of Jesus Christ, Joker. At his feet were two canisters the size of small fire extinguishers. Both of them were a bright, telltale green. There were several gallon-and-a-half drums near the bed. Hannah already knew what they would find in them: jet fuel.

"Congratulations, Ms. Davis," Chief Reiger said, peering into the bedroom behind Hannah. "Looks like you've caught your torch."

The pool clerk congratulated her like everyone else in the department as he came into her cubicle. Hannah gave him the same tight-lipped smile she'd given the others. "Thanks, Ned. Listen, I have a meeting with Malcolm at three, and I need these tapes and transcripts copied before then. Think you can do it?"

"Sure. Plenty of time. Bet you get a commendation."

"We'll see," Hannah said. "The earlier you can get that done . . ."

Ned had them back to her at two. Hannah put the copies in a box, sealed it, and walked it down to the mailing department. Then she went and finished typing her report for Malcolm.

The director glanced through the report, riffling the pages without reading, then set it down in front of him. He folded his hands over it and looked up at her. He gave her his best imitation of a smile. "Very good work, Ms. Davis. I'll be drafting a letter for your personnel file with my recommendation that you be considered for promotion."

"Malcolm," Hannah started, then exhaled. "I don't want to close this case. I want to keep working on it."

"Whatever for?" Malcolm blinked. Hannah realized that it was the first time she'd ever seen him do that. "All the evidence is here, Ms. Davis. In fact, it's rare that we have such a clear-cut case against a person."

"That's exactly what bothers me, Malcolm. I'm not saying that Ramblur didn't set the fire. He probably did. I already had the paperwork in motion to get a search warrant for his apartment. But it seems awfully convenient that he managed to blow himself to kingdom come just before we moved."

"And what angle do you wish to pursue in this?"

Hannah hesitated. "I want to go to Saigon and see what I can find on Dr. Faneuil and his nurse. I have the Free Vietnam government's permission to go there, and they're willing to pay my way . . ."

Hannah stopped. Malcolm sat behind his desk like a blue-suited statue, his eyes cold. "Let me get this straight," he said, and there was no mistaking the sarcasm in his voice. "We have an airtight case against the arsonist. We have found not only his history of arson and his prejudice against jokers, but also the very materials that were used in the fire: the rebar, the oxygen canisters, and the jet fuel. Yet you want to pursue a far-fetched conspiracy theory—one that not only takes you out of the city, out of the state, but across the entire Pacific Ocean to a country that half the civilized world has yet to recognize as legal. No, Ms. Davis. Absolutely and emphatically, no. Please do yourself a very large favor and accept the rewards your hard work on this case will undoubtedly garner."

"Malcolm, you have to trust me in this. After all, it's not costing us anything but my time. Not even the plane fare. All I'm asking for is another week or so. If I have to, let me take an unpaid leave. I just want to be sure."

"Ms. Davis, which is more likely: that a deranged pyromaniac with a grudge against jokers would burn down the church, or that the fire was a deliberate part of some decades-old conspiracy?"

"I know what it sounds like . . ."

"Do you? Do you really? Ms. Davis, I am aware that you have gone to the World Health Organization, that you contacted the UN, that you spoke with Free Vietnam's delegation in Washington. I'm telling you now—enough. You *will* drop this investigation."

"Or?"

His expression didn't change. "I should think that someone with your obviously creative imagination would be able to figure that out," he said.

Hannah stood. "I don't need to," she told him. "I quit."

She threw her identification and pass down on his desk.

David came in while she was packing. He stood in the doorway of their—his, she reminded herself—bedroom and watched her throwing clothes into her suitcases. "Malcolm Coan called me at the office," he said. "I thought I might find you here, but I really didn't think you'd be this crazy, Hannah. What is it with you? Can't you stand success? You enjoy wrecking everything anyone's done for you?"

Hannah didn't answer him. She continued to fold her blouses, to cram pantyhose into the corners of the suitcase. "So this is it?" David said. "You've walked out on your job, now you're walking out on me, too?"

"Yes," she said. "Very observant of you, David. Go to the head of your class."

"Where are you going?"

"To some friends."

"I didn't think you had any friends here. I thought they were all *my* friends." David suddenly laughed, bitterly. "Oh, I get it. Joker friends. Twisted freak friends. Infected friends. Is he good in bed, Hannah? Did the wild card give him two dicks, or maybe a prehensile tongue?"

Hannah slammed the suitcases shut, clicked the locks closed savagely. "You're sick, David. Listen to yourself." She swung the suitcases from the bed and started to push past him.

He blocked the door with his hand.

"Move, David," Hannah said. "Please. I don't hate you; this just isn't working out, and I need to do this. Don't destroy my good memories of you with something we'll both regret."

David glared at her. Hannah thought that he might actually strike, but at last his hand dropped from the doorjamb and she moved past him into the living room. He stayed where he was, staring at her as she moved to the door to the apartment and opened it.

"The jokers aren't worth this," he called after her. "Nothing touched by that damn virus is worth it."

She shut the door. Quietly.

And she wondered.

"Father Squid? Quasiman?"

Hannah knocked again on the door of the apartment a few blocks from the ruins of the church—the address Father Squid had given them when he left the hospital. She heard footsteps beyond the door. A chain rattled, and the door opened to reveal the priest standing there. Quasiman was standing in the middle of the shabby living room behind him, looking like a misshapen statue. Hannah backed up a step. "Ms. Davis?" He looked at the suitcases.

"I'm in the process of moving. I also need to talk with you. You're going to get a package in a day or two."

"Why don't you come in, Ms. Davis?" Father Squid said.

"Hannah," she replied. "Please. Father, I think I've just done something very crazy and very stupid."

"That hardly makes you unique," Father Squid said and smiled under the forest of tentacles. He opened the door fully and stepped back. "Come on in. You'll be welcome, for as long as you need."

Father Squid and Quasiman saw Hannah off at Tomlin International two days later. Ambassador Ngu hadn't seemed to care that Hannah was no longer official; the paperwork and tickets arrived at Father Squid's apartment on schedule from the Free Nam delegation. Hannah's passport was still valid from a trip to Paris the summer before, and Belew had promised that all the necessary entry papers would be waiting at Saigon International.

The flight was an interminable nineteen hours: New York to Dallas/Ft. Worth, Dallas to San Francisco, San Francisco to Honolulu, Honolulu to Tokyo, Tokyo to Saigon. Hannah arrived exhausted, desperately weary of planes and airline food, and bedraggled. The passengers on the flight in had been largely jokers of various descriptions, heading for this new Promised Land of joker freedom. Hannah, as a nat, had been the one out of place, and the jokers had made that abundantly clear to her. She'd been glad to escape the stares, the whispered comments, and the rudeness.

She told herself that she'd simply experienced what they went through every day. The rationalization didn't ease the hurt.

The tropical heat and humidity hit Hannah almost immediately, sucking the air from her lungs and causing her cotton blouse and bra to stick to her skin. Palm trees swayed in the hot wind; in the distant haze, the airport buildings shimmered. Inside the air-conditioned but still sweltering terminal, Hannah queued with everyone else for customs. A man approached her as she stood there. He was white, and looked normal enough until she noticed the tiger-like tail protruding from the rear of his jeans and the incisors that showed as he smiled. "Hannah Davis?"

She nodded, unsure.

"Name's Croyd Crenson."

The name was somewhat familiar to her, though she didn't know why he was here, since all the stories she'd heard about Crenson placed him in New York. "You're the one they call The Sleeper? Every time you wake up, you look different and have different, uh, *abilities*?"

Croyd grinned. "That's me. Mark Meadows sent me to meet you." He held out his hand and she saw that the tips of his fingers were thick and rounded. The tips of retractable claws gleamed. She took the proffered hand tentatively, and the man grinned. "They're great for peeling oranges," he said. "And other things, too."

Hannah took her hand away quickly. Croyd continued to grin. His tail lashed and curled around her ankle. It tugged gently. "Come on," he said. "We'll get you past here and collect your luggage."

The tail tugged again, much higher up the leg this time, past the hem of her long skirt. "Aahh, pantyhose," he said as Hannah angrily brushed away the tail. "Nobody wears real stockings anymore." Croyd chuckled. "The tail's great for other things, too," he said. When she didn't answer, he shrugged. "Come on."

He escorted her past the line, had a brief conversation in halting Vietnamese with the official at the gates, showed him a sheaf of official-looking papers, which the man stamped dutifully, then they were waved on. The luggage turntables were close by, but as they approached, Hannah and Croyd both stopped.

"Quasiman?"

The hunchback turned. Hannah's suitcases sat alongside him.

"Hey, Hannah," the joker said, smiling apologetically. "I remember you, but I've forgotten where I am. Awfully hot here, isn't it? I knew where I was, a second ago . . ."

"Saigon," Hannah told him. "In what used to be Vietnam."

"Oh." Quasiman accepted that placidly. She might as well have said Manhattan.

"How," Hannah asked, "do you keep doing that? Showing up where I am?"

Quasiman shrugged, but one shoulder refused to lift, suddenly hanging limp as if all the muscles had been cut. "I just think about a place, and I'm there. Didn't you know that? I thought I had told you, but I get confused with what I've done and what I'm going to do."

Hannah gaped, wondering how in the world she could have been so stupid. All those times he'd snuck past or just showed up . . . "Great. You teleport. What else haven't you told me?"

Quasiman grinned.

At least Croyd seemed to accept Quasiman's presence with equanimity. "Quas with you?"

"He seems to be. You know him?"

"Yeah. I know him and the priest both. He don't exactly need a passport to get by customs. Seems more coherent than normal for him; you must be a good influence. Come on—I got a car waiting in front." At the car, a ten-year-old Renault whose trunk barely held Hannah's suitcases, Quasiman climbed in back. Croyd opened the passenger-side front door for Hannah. "You can sit up front with me," he said. "You definitely got the best seat in the house." His tail lashed the ground. His gaze was not on her eyes.

Hannah got in the rear with Quasiman and curled in the corner.

The short drive into the city gave Hannah some small feel for the land. The area around Saigon was flat and heavily farmed. Rice paddies shimmered in the sun in precise green rectangles. Workers in conical straw hats labored in the fields, the pants rolled up to their knees as they moved through the standing water. Carts piled recklessly with furniture or produce or simply packed with families moved ponderously on the side of the road, pulled by oxen and urged on by children wielding long bamboo sticks.

Then, almost without warning, they were in the city itself: crowded, loud, and dirty. Even with the windows up and the air conditioner's fan roaring, she could hear the sounds of street merchants hawking their wares and the constant blaring of horns in the streets packed with a combination of cars, bicycles, and carts. The city seemed over-full and very foreign, and she saw no Caucasian faces at all. Whenever they stopped, people stared at their car, pointing and talking. Hannah, already uncomfortable sitting with Quasiman in the back, found herself pressing hard against the corner. Quasiman seemed to have fallen asleep with his eyes open. He swayed back and forth with the car's motion as if he were a test dummy. Hannah had to keep pushing him away from her every time they turned left.

They came out of the warren of small streets and made the turn onto the boulevard leading to the Presidential Palace. The line of cars in front of them pulled out slowly into the traffic. As Croyd turned the wheel to follow them, a rusting green Corolla rushed out from the curb, wheeled around them, and stopped in the middle of the intersection, directly in front of them. More horns blared, Croyd's among them, as the occupants of the car got out and began running.

"Go!" Quasiman awakened suddenly, shouting at Croyd and hammering on the back of the seat. His fists put permanent dents in the headrest. "Get past them!"

Hannah knew that if she'd been driving, she'd have hesitated. She would have turned back to Quasiman to see what in the world the hunchback was shouting about.

She would have been too late.

Not Croyd. He stamped his foot on the accelerator, downshifted, and yanked the wheel right. The car hit the curb, slalomed across grass in the little park on the corner as pedestrians scattered out of their way. They went over the curb again, the suspension bottoming out with a screech, then fishtailed back onto the boulevard. "What . . . ?" Croyd yelled back at Quasiman.

His question got no further. A sinister, low *kah-RHUMMPP!* behind them lifted the rear of the car sideways. They landed hard, throwing Hannah against the side, with Quasiman on top of her. The car stalled.

Hannah found that she was looking back through the rear windshield. In the intersection, the car that had cut them off was a blazing inferno. She could see bodies in a street littered with broken glass and sheet metal. She felt schizophrenic. Part of her was busily deciphering the mess: *thermite fuse, cheap electronic timer, make sure the tank's about half full so you have plenty of room for fumes. You'd need ten, fifteen seconds to get clear . . .*

The other part of her wanted to scream.

"Jesus," Croyd muttered. He started the car again and jammed it into gear. They lurched away from the scene. "Car bomb. I'm getting you folks to the palace, fast. Hang on." Leaning on the horn, Croyd rushed them away.

Hannah looked at Quasiman. He was frowning. "You're hurt," he said, and reached for her forehead.

She let the stubby, wide fingers touch her, let him brush her hair back from the cut. "Just a scratch," he said, and the relief in his voice was open and gentle. "You'll be okay, Hannah."

"Thanks," she told him. The word seemed so inadequate.

And then the shakes hit her.

"That's, like, an incredible bummer. Wow. I mean, I'm just totally wiped out by this. I am really, really sorry. I feel, like, personally responsible, y'know. I'm just glad you had Quasiman along with you."

Mark Meadows didn't exactly fit Hannah's mental image of a prime minister, or for that matter, of a Federal fugitive from justice or a biochemist genius who could become any of several aces, including the legendary Radical, just by ingesting concoctions of psychoactive drugs he'd created.

To Hannah, Mark looked entirely . . . innocuous, passive, and powerless. Father Squid had explained to Hannah how, with the help of some of Mark's ace "friends"—brought into existence by those psychoactive drugs—Mark had reclaimed his daughter Sprout from the so-called care of the State of New

York after losing the custody battle in court. Hannah had a difficult time picturing the man angry.

At first impression, she would have called him—like some of her parents' friends—an "old hippie." He was tall and thin, his thinning hair shoulder-length and pulled back in a ponytail. A scraggly goatee hung like Spanish moss from his chin. And his clothing . . . the only word Hannah had for it was *bright:* loose Vietnamese pants cut from a garish paisley cloth, a strident blue-and-orange-striped tunic, and a green silk scarf. He wore open-toed leather sandals. He looked out across the lawn of the Presidential Palace to where a smudge of distant smoke still burned beyond the walls, shaking his head.

"Some heavy shit has gone down out there over the years," he said. "There's still lots of bad karma floating around. But we're putting things together again. Weird political shit like this still happens every once in a while, like a flashback on a bad trip. You shouldn't have had to see it, but the violence is there, part of the total scene. It's getting rarer and rarer, though."

Mark turned back to the room. He smiled at Hannah. The man had what could only be described as a radiant smile, Hannah decided. Almost beatific, like the picture of the saints she remembered from parochial school. Hannah touched the gauze bandage on her forehead, grimacing slightly as she probed the throbbing lump there. An unbidden shiver ran through her. "Prime Minister—"

He waved a hand at the title. "Call me Mark, Ms. Davis. I don't really do anything here. This is Moonchild's place, hers and the people's. White folks like us are just guests."

"Then I'm Hannah," she replied. "That bomb. I have to think it was meant for . . ." Hannah swallowed. She couldn't finish the thought.

Mark had. "I know," he said sadly. "But you gotta believe that it also wasn't meant to be, y'know. Fate had a hand in things and made sure you were safe." Mark patted her on the shoulder, like a brother might. "My friend Moonchild'll make sure that you stay that way, too. Nothing else will happen to you while you're here. I promise. Moonchild's going to make Free Vietnam a Land of Peace. Man, so much evil has come from here, I figure that the cosmic balance has got to be restored. When a place has been this fucked up for so long, imagine what it's going to be like when it turns around. When that happens, this will be like a paradise."

He was so earnest that Hannah could only smile back at him. He seemed to be one of those people who had an eternal innocence in their souls; despite all that life had dealt Meadows, he'd kept that.

"So why don't you tell me about everything that's going down?" he said.

"I'm not sure where to start, but I'll try." For the next half hour, Hannah gave Meadows a synopsis of what she had learned. He was a good listener, interrupting only to ask a few questions or to clarify something, otherwise nodding sympathetically and shaking his head.

"Far out," he said afterward. "It's like a downer, y'know, all that energy wasted on hating. Fucked up, just totally fucked up." He gave a deep, ponderous sigh. "I can help you, sure. I'll arrange for you to go anywhere and do anything you need to do here. You can go to Xuan Loc yourself and dig around— you know what you're looking for, and that's as safe a place as any. You want to find out about this Faneuil dude, no problem; I'll ask Ai Quoc's staff. He's the interior secretary and he'll look up all the records we have on Faneuil. I know Pan at WHO; he's a good guy. I'll give him a call and prod him."

"I'd appreciate it."

"Hey, here's your guardian angel now," Mark said. Quasi-man had entered the room, hand in hand with a lovely, light-haired child, a girl on the verge of womanhood. "I want you to meet my daughter, Sprout."

"How did Faneuil die?" Hannah asked.

Ngo Dinh Yie, one of the elders of the village, pursed his lips and nodded as Croyd translated, then closed his eyes as if remembering. "He was old," Ngo said. "His heart burst. That is what the nurse told us."

"Margaret Durand?"

"Yes. She was with my son, Bui, who also lived in the doctor's house, and said that they had found him dead in his bed. He had died in his sleep, peacefully."

"Did you see the body?"

The old man frowned, pressing his lips together again. Ngo's face looked like a crumpled brown paper sack. "No. The nurse, she and Bui took care of the body, wrapping it in a sheet and putting it in the coffin the village woodcarver brought for them." Ngo shook his head. "Western customs. Wasteful."

"Then how did you know it was Faneuil?"

Ngo looked at her as if she were crazy. "I saw his hand, outside the sheet. The doctor always wore a ring, a big gold one with a blue stone and little diamonds set around it. I saw his hand, the doctor's hand, and I saw the ring. We buried the doctor that evening. There." The elder pointed to the field where a green mound swelled just before the jungle claimed the land. "Everyone grieved. Everyone loved the doctor. I would do anything he asked me to do. Anything."

"I'm sure you would," Hannah answered. She nodded to

Croyd, and he dismissed Ngo. Hannah stopped the tape recorder and leaned back against the rough wooden railing of the pub.

Ngo's story matched everyone else's. Three days of interviews and searching the few existing records had yielded nothing more. The recent war had destroyed most of the paper trail pertaining to Faneuil. The conflict had swept over Xuan Loc also, inflicting heavy casualties on the inhabitants. The survivors spoke almost universally with affection for the doctor. Faneuil had set up a small clinic in the village, offering medical care for the surrounding area. Hannah could find nothing overtly malicious in Faneuil's care of the people, but then there weren't a great number of jokers in the area, either. On the surface, Faneuil had been a benign and beneficent presence in the jungle, healing as best he could with extremely limited funding and supplies.

Everyone told her that Faneuil had died of a heart attack, even though no one she spoke with had actually seen the body. The two who had—Ngo Dinh Yie's son, Bui, and Durand—vanished within a week of the doctor's burial. Supposedly they had gone to Saigon, but Meadows's people had found no trace of them there. And that seemed to be where the trail ended.

The best thing that could be said for their time here was that it had allowed her to begin to deal with the paralyzing fear that had come in the wake of the bomb attack. The first night, in the palace, Hannah couldn't sleep. She relived the explosion in her nightmares, and sometimes she was one of the broken bodies strewn on the street. The constant fear was only now beginning to recede. She didn't think she would ever like Saigon now, no matter how well Moonchild, Mark, and his friends succeeded in their vision of a Land of Peace.

In a way, Hannah found it amusing. For years she'd been

prowling through the aftermath of fires and explosions, reveling in the messy work of finding the cause. She'd learned to look at the victims as just pieces of the puzzle. She'd felt sorry for them, yes, but she'd never really given much thought to the pain and terror they'd felt. She'd never really put herself in their place and imagined what they must have experienced, how it affected them. The fires, the explosions—they'd never reached out for her.

Now she knew. She wondered if she'd ever be able to see a fire the old way again.

She wasn't looking at *anything* the old way anymore.

"Might as well go inside," Hannah said to Croyd. "Too hot out here."

The one-room building had been Xuan Loc's bar, evidently of Vietnam War vintage, built in a quasi-American style with an old wooden bar running the width. Quasiman was sitting at one of the tables, staring into space. He'd been that way for an hour, and Hannah was beginning to wonder if he'd come back. Croyd went behind the bar and pulled a bottle of beer from the Styrofoam cooler. Croyd had brought cooler, ice, and what seemed to Hannah to be an inordinate supply of beer from Saigon. The ice was long gone, but Croyd didn't seem to mind. "Want one?" Hannah shook her head. Croyd extended a claw from his forefinger and pried off the cap. "Real useful," he said. He went to sit with Hannah and the vacant-eyed Quasiman. Croyd prodded Quasiman's shoulder with a finger. There was no reaction from the joker. "Nobody home," Croyd said, then looked at Hannah. "What's next? You want me to round up some more of the locals?"

"I guess," Hannah said.

"You're not getting what you want, huh?"

"No. Just dead ends and more dead ends. No one actually saw Faneuil dead, but everyone's sure he is. Everyone loved him. He's a frigging saint." Hannah sighed. "I'm not surprised that Dr. Rudo couldn't find out anything, either."

Croyd didn't say anything. He was looking at her strangely. He took a long, slow swallow of the beer and set the bottle down again with an undisguised belch. Hannah could feel his tail brushing her feet under the table. "Rudo?" Croyd said. "Dr. *Pan* Rudo?"

"Yes," Hannah said. "He's one of the directors of WHO."

"And he's been *helping* you with this?"

"Yes, among others," she said again. "Why?"

Croyd sniffed. He took another pull at the bottle. The tail swished around her knees, poking tentatively between them. "Damn it, Croyd—"

"Sorry. Pan Rudo, huh? He sent you here? He knew Faneuil?"

Hannah didn't answer. "You know Dr. Rudo?"

"Knew him," Croyd said. "A long while back." He let the tips of his claws rap sharply against the glass bottle. "But I won't ever forget him . . ."

The Long Sleep

Roger Zelazny

"Tell me about Pan Rudo," Hannah said.

"Now I'm talking early fifties," Croyd answered. "That may be too far back for whatever you're after."

She shook her head.

"I want to hear about it," she told him.

He clapped his hands together abruptly, squashing a darting moth.

"Okay," he said. "I was around twenty years old at the time. But I'd been infected with the wild card virus when I was going on fourteen—so I'd had plenty of experience with it. Too much, it seemed. It still depressed me a lot in those days. I got to thinking about it, and I decided that since I couldn't change the condition maybe I could change my attitude toward it somehow, come to better terms with it. I read a lot of pop psychology books—about making friends with yourself and getting well adjusted and all that—but they didn't do me any good. So one morning I saw a piece about this guy in the *Times*. He was chairing a local conference. Kind of interesting. Neuropsychiatrist. He'd actually known Freud, studied with him for a while. Then he was at the Jungian Institute in Switzerland for a time. Got back to physiology then. He was involved with a group doing *dauerschlaf* research while he was in Zurich. Ever hear of it?"

"Can't say that I have," she said.

He took a swallow of beer, moving his left foot to crush a pawing beetle.

"The theory behind *dauerschlaf* is that the body and the mind heal themselves better and faster while a person's asleep than when he's awake," he said. "They were experimenting with the treatment of drug withdrawal, psychological disorders, TB, and other stuff by putting people to sleep for long periods of time, using hypnosis and drugs. They'd induce artificial comas to promote healing. He wasn't into that much when I met him, but I'd learned of it earlier, because of my condition—and the connection intrigued me. I checked him out in the phone book, called, got his secretary, made an appointment. He had a cancellation for later that week, and she gave me that one."

Croyd took a quick swallow.

"It was a rainy Thursday afternoon in March of 1951, then, that I first met Pan Rudo—"

"Do you recall the date as well?" Hannah asked.

"Afraid not."

"How is it that you recall the year, the month, and the day of the week so readily?"

"I count days after I wake up," he replied, "to keep track of how far along I am in my waking cycle. It gives me an idea of how much rationality I have left, so I can make plans for things I want to get done. When the days dwindle down to a precious few I avoid my friends and try to get off somewhere by myself so nobody gets hurt. Now, I woke up on Sunday, I came across the article two days later, I got the appointment for two days after that. That makes it a Thursday. And I tend to remember months when things happen, because my picture of a year is kind of a jagged thing based on seasons. This was spring and rainy—March."

He took a drink of beer. He swatted another moth.

"Damn bugs!" he muttered. "Can't stand bugs."

"And the year?" she said. "How can you be sure it was 1951?"

"Because it was in the fall of the following year, 1952, that they tested the hydrogen bomb in the Pacific."

"Oh," she said, brow furrowing slightly. "Sure. Go ahead."

"So I went to see him the year before the hydrogen bomb got tested," he continued. "They were working on it then, you know. They'd decided to go ahead on it back in '48."

"Yes, I know," she said.

"A mathematician named Stan Ulam cracked the equations for Teller. Speaking of mathematicians, did you know that Tom Lehrer was a Manhattan Project mathematician? He wrote some great songs—"

"What happened when you got to Dr. Rudo's office?"

"Right," he responded. "Like I said, it was raining, and this trench coat I had on was dripping wet when I came into his reception area, and there was a pretty oriental rug on the floor. Looked as if it had silk in it, even. The receptionist hurried around her desk to help me, saying she'd hang my coat in their restroom rather than have it on a brass coat tree near the door, which looked as if it held her own coat as well as the doctor's.

"I reached out and caught hold of all the water on the coat and the rug with my mind, and I removed it. I wasn't sure what to do with it then, so I held it in between places. You know what I'm talking about? You hear about aces and jokers who can teleport things—I've had the power a number of times myself—making things disappear in one place and reappear in another without seeming to pass through intervening space. But did you ever wonder where something is when it's in between places? I think about things like that a lot. Now, I wasn't sure of my range yet—though it seemed I could send smaller objects farther off than larger ones—and I wasn't sure how much water I'd just picked up, so I couldn't say for certain that I could send it all outside his sixth-floor window and let it fall down onto Park. I had been experimenting this time, though, with hiding things in between places—at first just to see whether it could be done—and I learned that it could. I'd learned that I could make things disappear in one place and not appear in another for a while—though I felt a kind of pressure in my mind and body while I was doing it. So I just held my water and smiled.

" 'No need,' I told her. 'See? It's okay.'

"She stared at the thing as if it were alive, even running a hand over it, to make sure. Then she hung it on the tree.

" 'Won't you have a seat for a moment, Mr. Crenson?' she said. 'I'll let Dr. Rudo know you're here.'

"She moved toward the intercom on her desk, and I was about to ask her where that restroom was—so I could get rid of my water—when an inner door opened and Dr. Rudo came into the reception area. He was a six-footer, blond and blue-eyed, who put on a professional smile and extended his hand as he came up to me.

" 'Mr. Crenson,' he said. 'It is good to meet you. I am Pan Rudo. Won't you come into my office?' His voice was rich and resonant, his teeth very white.

" 'Thanks,' I said.

"He held the door for me and I entered the next room. It was brighter than I'd thought it might be, with a few pastoral watercolors bearing his signature and architectural etchings signed by others on the walls, another oriental rug on the floor, lots of reds and blues in it. A large aquarium occupied a table to the left of the door, bright fish darting and drifting within it, a chain of bubbles along a rear corner.

"'Have a seat,' he told me, his speech slightly accented—German, and maybe something else—and he gestured toward a big, comfortable-looking leather chair facing his desk.

"I took the chair. He moved around the desk and seated himself. He smiled again, picking up a pencil and rolling it between his hands.

"'Everybody who comes here has problems,' he began, maintaining eye contact.

"I nodded.

"'I'm no exception, I guess,' I told him. 'It's hard to know how to begin, though.'

"'There are certain broad categories most people's problems fall into,' he said. 'Family, the people you work with . . .'

"'No problems there,' I said. The pressure of holding the water was bothering me, and I looked around for a suitable container into which I might deposit it. A metal wastebasket would have been fine, but I couldn't see one anywhere about.

"'Money? Sex?' he suggested.

"'No, I've got plenty of money, and I get laid pretty regular,' I said, wondering whether I could move it beyond his window and let it go. Only, it was even farther away than the one in the reception area.

"I shifted in the chair and checked out the other side of the room.

"'Mr. Crenson, is something bothering you—I mean something physical—right now?' he asked.

"'Yeah,' I admitted, 'I'm having trouble holding my water.'

"'There is a restroom outside,' he said, beginning to rise. 'I'll show you—'

"'Not that way. I mean, like this water is sort of—in my head, I guess.'

"He froze. He stared at me.

"'I'm afraid I don't understand exactly what you mean,' he said then. 'Water—in your head?'

"I grinned.

"'Well, yes and no,' I said. 'I was speaking sort of—figuratively. I mean, there's this water from my coat and I'm holding it with my mind and it's getting to be sort of a strain. So I should put it somewhere. Maybe I *will* just take it to that restroom and dump it there, if you'll show me—'

"'Mr. Crenson, do you know what a defense mechanism is?' he asked.

"'Sure, I've been doing my homework. It's something you do or say or think to keep from doing or saying or thinking something else you really want to but for some reason are afraid to. Oh, you think that's what this is. No, it's real water, and I'm carrying it and can make it be anywhere I want it to be inside of about a ten-foot radius from where I am right now—I think.'

"He smiled.

"'Then why don't you deposit it in the fish tank?' he said. 'And we can get on with our conversation.'

"'That's not a bad idea,' I said. 'It's pretty full, though.'

"'That's all right,' he said.

"So I moved the water into the tank. Immediately, the thing overflowed. Dr. Rudo's eyes widened as he watched the water run down the sides and spill onto the floor. Then he gave me a strange look and reached out and worked his intercom.

"'Mrs. Weiler, would you come in here a moment?' he said. 'And bring a mop and a pail? We've had a small accident. Thank you.'

"Then he lowered himself back into his chair and studied me for several seconds.

"'Perhaps you should begin by telling me how you did what you just did,' he said.

"'It's kind of long and involved,' I said. 'On the other hand, it's also the cause of the problem I came to see you about.'

"'Take your time,' he told me.

"'It was back in September of '46,' I began, 'the day Jetboy died . . .'

"Mrs. Weiler came in a couple of minutes later and was about to mop the wet area. I beat her to it and transported it all from the floor into the bucket. She stepped back and stared after the splash occurred.

"'Just take it away,' Dr. Rudo told her. 'Then phone everyone who has an appointment this afternoon. Cancel all of them.

"'Go ahead, Mr. Crenson, the whole story, please,' he said then, after she'd left.

"So I told him what it was like, and the thing that made my case different from all the others—how I fear sleeping more than anything else, and the things I do to postpone it. He questioned me at great length about the sleeping; and that was the first time I can remember hearing the word *dauerschlaf*. He seemed taken by my case and its parallels to an experimental European therapy technique he'd apparently once had something to do with. Also, as it turned out, he had heard of my case; and from the way he quoted medical journals, it seemed he'd read every important paper published on the wild card virus.

"I talked all afternoon. I told him about my family and old Bentley and the second-story work I used to do. I told him about my transformations, about my friends, about some of the scrapes I'd been involved in. I found myself starting to like the guy. I'd never really talked that way to anybody before. He seemed fascinated by the jokers and aces, by the different manifestations of the wild card virus I'd seen. Got me to talking about them at some length, shaking his head at my descriptions of some of the worst joker cases I've known. Even got into a long philosophical discussion with me as to what I thought it might be doing to the whole human race. I told him that not too many nats dated jokers, if it was the genetic angle he was thinking about, but he just kept shaking his head and said that wasn't the point, that their existing at all was like a cancer on human life in general, that you had to think of it sociologically as well as biologically. I allowed as he could have a point, but that it seemed one of those 'So what?' points. The situation was already in place, and the real questions involved what you were going to do about it. He agreed with me then, saying that he hoped it would be soon.

"Most of all, he seemed fascinated by my long sleeps—my *dauerschlafen*—and the way they pulled me apart and put me back together again. He questioned me about them at great length—how I felt going into them, coming out of them, whether I remembered anything that happened during them, whether I had any dreams while they were in progress. Then he told me about *dauerschlaf* as a form of therapy, of how his earlier work in Europe had involved the production of prolonged comas in non–wild card patients, by means of drugs and hypnosis, to capitalize on the remarkable recuperative abilities of the body and mind during sleep. He'd apparently gotten some very positive results with this, which was one of the reasons he found my case intriguing. The parallel struck him so forcibly, he said, that he would want to pursue the matter for that reason alone, even if he couldn't do more than adjust my feelings otherwise. But he felt that it could also be the means for doing even more for me."

Croyd finished his beer, fetched a second bottle, and opened it.

"Mr. Crenson," Hannah Davis stated, and he met her eyes, "your tail seems to have developed wandering hands."

"Sorry," he said. "Sometimes it has a mind of its own."

The tiger-striped appendage emerged from beneath the table to lash behind him. Croyd took a drink.

"So the man represented himself as being able to cure your wild card condition?" she said.

"No," Croyd replied. "He never said that he could cure it. What he proposed later was something different—a rather ingenious-sounding way of stabilizing it in a fashion that I'd no longer need to fear going to sleep."

"Of course he was a fraud," she said. "He took your money and he got your hopes up and then he couldn't deliver. Right?"

"Wrong," Croyd said. "He knew what he was talking about, and he was able to deliver. That wasn't the problem."

"Wait a minute," she said. "It would have made world headlines if someone had found a way to mitigate wild card effects. Tachyon would've picked up on it and been distributing it on street corners. If it worked, how come no one ever heard about it?"

Croyd raised his hand, and his tail.

"Bear with me. If it were simpler, I'd be done talking," he said. "Excuse me."

He was gone. A man-sized form flashed past the bar at the corner of her seeing. She heard a door open and close. When she looked toward the sound, there was no one in sight. A moment later, however, a shadow flashed by and Croyd was seated before her again, sipping his beer.

"Rapid metabolism," he explained.

"Pan Rudo," he continued then, as if there had been no interruption, "seemed quite taken with my story. I talked all afternoon, and he took pages and pages of notes. Every now and then he'd ask me a question. Later, Mrs. Weiler knocked on the door and told him it was quitting time and asked whether he wanted her to lock the office door when she left. He said no, he'd do it in a few minutes. Then he offered to take me to dinner and I took him up on it.

"We went out then and had a few steaks—he was surprised at my metabolism, too—and we continued to talk through dinner. Afterward, we went to his apartment—a very nice pad—and talked some more, until fairly late. He'd learned my story by then, and a lot of other things I don't usually talk about, too."

"What do you mean?" she asked.

"Well," Croyd said, "then, and in the days that followed, he told me about some of the more popular psychological theories. He'd even known the people who'd developed them. He'd studied with Freud for a while, and later at the Jungian Institute in Switzerland at the same time he was doing *dauerschlaf* research there. He told me about Freud's ideas on infantile sexuality, stages of development, sublimation, about ids and egos and superegos. And about Adler's drive to power and Rank's birth trauma. He talked about Jung's personality types and his theory of individuation. He said he felt that they all had something to them, some more for some people than others, or at different times in a person's life. He said that he was more interested in the final forms that these things took, in the emotional constructions they led to for a person's dealing with life. He felt that life is a compromise between what you want and what you get, and that there's always fear involved in the transaction—and it doesn't matter which of all the classical sources it springs from, it's just something that's always there. He said that we tell ourselves lies in order to deal with it—lies about the world, lies about ourselves. He had this idea, actually, from the playwright Ibsen, who called the big one—the big phony construct about yourself and the world—a 'life lie.' Rudo felt that everybody has one of these, and that it was just a matter of the degree of its falseness that made the difference between psychosis and neurosis. He told me that his whole approach to problems that weren't organic involved finding out a person's life lie and manipulating it so the patient can come to better terms with reality. Not to get rid of it. He said that some kind of life lie is necessary. Break it or tamper too deeply and you damage the personality, maybe drive the person completely nuts. He looked on therapy as a means of economizing the lie for better accommodation to the world."

Croyd paused for a drink.

"It sounds very manipulative," Hannah said, "and it seems as if it puts the therapist in a kind of godlike position. You help this guy find the key to your personality, then he goes in, looks around, and decides what to throw away, what to keep, what to remodel."

"Yeah, I guess it does," Croyd said, "when you put it that way."

"Granting that this approach is effective, it looks as if even a well-meaning adjustment might sometimes cause some damage—not even considering the possibility of willful abuse. Is that what he did to you? Mess with your self-image and your worldview?"

"Not exactly," Croyd said. "Not intentionally or directly. He explained that he did want to explore my life lie because he had to know my fears, because they would relate directly to what he had in mind for stabilizing my condition at a level I'd find emotionally satisfying."

"You did pick up the jargon, didn't you?"

"Well, I was reading a lot in the area the whole time he was working with me. I guess everyone does that."

He took another drink of beer.

"Are you stalling now?" she said. "Because you don't want to talk about those fears? If they're not essential to the story you can leave them out, you know."

"I guess I am," he acknowledged. "But I'd probably better mention them, for the sake of completeness. I don't know how much you know about me . . ."

"Mark Meadows told me a few things about you. But there were a lot of gaps. You sleep a lot. You lie low a lot—"

He shook his head.

"Not that kind of stuff," he said. "See, I'd thought of seeing a shrink for some time before I actually did. I guess I read a lot more in the area than I really let on—not just self-help books—some fairly heavy-duty stuff. There were two reasons for this. One is that I know what it feels like to be nuts—really out of your mind. I do it to myself regularly with amphetamines, because I'm afraid to go to sleep. And I usually wind up pushing it too far, and I can remember some of the crazy things and some of the terrible things I did when my thinking and my feelings were all screwed up. So I know what psychosis feels like, and I fear that almost as much as I do sleeping."

He laughed.

"'Almost,'" he said. "Because they're really tied up together. Rudo showed me that, and I guess I owe him for the insight, if nothing else."

"I don't understand," she said, after he'd risen and stood staring out at a sudden rainfall for at least half a minute.

"My mother went crazy," he said then, "after the wild card business. Most likely, I was a big part of it. I don't know. Maybe it would have happened anyway. Maybe there was a schizoid gene involved. I loved her, and I saw her change. She spent her last years in asylums, died in one. I thought about it a lot in those days, wondering whether I might wind up that way, too. I was afraid of that kind of change. Then every time I took drugs to postpone sleeping I *did* go bonkers. I'm sure I know what she felt like, some of the things she went through . . ."

"Wouldn't it have been better just to sleep, then?" Hannah asked. "After all, it was going to happen, anyway."

Croyd turned and he was smiling.

"That's the same thing Rudo asked me," he said, and he walked slowly back to the table.

"I didn't know the answer then," he continued, "but he helped me to find it. It's a part of my life lie."

He seated himself and folded his hands before him. "The way I came to see it, sleep for me represents a big unknown change. In a way, it's like death, and all of my normal death-fears are attached to it. But there's more to it than that. Rudo made me look into it deeply and I saw that my fear of insanity is also there. I always know that I'll be changed, and at some primitive level of my mind I fear that I'll wake up psychotic, like her, and it'll never go away. I saw her change too much."

He laughed then.

"Ironic," he said, "the way we make these stories we're always telling ourselves work. In a way, I drive myself crazy regularly to keep from going crazy. That's one of my places of irrationality. Everybody's got them."

"I'd think that once a therapist discovered that, his first order of business would be to try to get rid of it."

Croyd nodded.

"Rudo told me that that's what most of them would try to do. But he had the feeling it was the thing keeping me sane in the long run."

She shook her head.

"You've lost me," she said.

"Understandable. This part doesn't apply to nats. It has only to do with manifestations of the wild card virus. Rudo, as I said, had read all of the literature on the virus. He'd been impressed by certain conjectures based on anecdotal evidence, since there was no way of running controlled studies on them, due to the psychosomatic component to the virus's manifestation. Like, there was once a kid—we called him Kid Dinosaur— who'd loved dinosaur books. He came up with the ability to turn himself into kid-sized replicas of different dinosaurs. And there's Hits Mack, a panhandler I know who can go up to any vending machine, hit it once, and have it deliver him anything he wants from its display. That's all. It's the simplest wild card ability I know. Takes care of his meals and allows him to devote a hundred percent of his panhandling income to booze. He once told me that something like that had been a daydream of his for years. Lives on Twinkies and Fritos and stale chocolate bars. Happy man.

"Anyway," he went on, "Rudo felt that the anecdotal evidence was persuasive, and that there was a way to test it now. Me. He proposed inducing *dauerschlaf* in me by means of drugs and hypnosis that worked with the fears behind my life lie and caused me to change in an agreed-upon fashion. If it worked, it would show that there was a psychosomatic component. It wouldn't be of help to any joker or ace in the world but me, though, and it could only be used to help me because of the periodic nature of my condition.

"So we set out to prove it, if we could. If the results were positive, he'd explained, then I could decide on the sort of body I wanted to live in for the rest of my life and whatever power I wanted to accompany it, and he'd induce it. He'd do it again for several times after that, to reinforce it, along with suggestions that it would always turn out that way, and I'd be set as a well-adjusted ace."

Croyd finished his beer, went back for another, stamping out a line of passing ants along the way.

"Is that where he crossed you up?" she asked.

"Nope, we tried it and it worked," he said. "He was right. So were the other people who'd made guesses along these lines. I told him I wanted to come out looking like Humphrey Bogart in *Casablanca*—I'd always liked that movie—and when I woke up I was a dead ringer for Bogie."

"Really? And what about a wild card ability? Was he able to do something with that, also?"

Croyd smiled.

"Yes," he said. "It was just a small ability, but for some reason it stuck. Maybe because it was so small it didn't take up much space wherever these things are managed. It followed me through any number of changes. Haven't used it in years, though. Wait a minute."

He raised his beer can, took a slow drink, stared off into the distance.

"Play it, Sam," he said in a strangely altered voice. Then, "Play it!"

The tape recorder clicked to a halt. Then the PLAY button was depressed. The sounds of a piano playing "As Time Goes By" emerged from the small speaker.

She stared for several moments at the machine, then reached over and turned it off. Immediately, she set it on RECORD again.

"How—How do you manage it if there's no tape recorder around?"

"Almost anything that can be induced to vibrate in the audible range will do," he said. "I don't know how. Maybe it's even a smaller ability than Hits Mack's."

"So you woke up looking like Rick, and you could provide your own soundtrack whenever you wanted."

"Yes."

"What happened next?"

"He gave me a couple of weeks to enjoy it. Wanted to observe me and be sure there were no undesirable side effects. I went out and got stopped on the streets and approached in restaurants for autographs. Rudo wrote up his notes. He did send me to some friends for a full physical at that time, too. I still had an abnormally high metabolism and my usual insomnia."

"I wonder whether those notes still exist, somewhere?" she said.

Croyd shrugged.

"Don't know," he said. "Wouldn't matter, anyway. I wouldn't want anyone to mess with the process that way again."

"What happened?"

"We saw each other regularly during the next couple of weeks. I went over ideas of what I wanted to look like and what I wanted to be able to do. I didn't want to stay the way I was. It was fun the first few days, but after a while it wears kind of thin, looking like someone famous. I wanted to be sort of average in height and build, sandy-haired, not bad looking but not real handsome. And I decided on a kind of telepathic persuasive ability I once had. You get in less trouble if you can talk your way out of things. And it could come in handy if I ever wanted to be a salesman. Rudo in the meantime said that he was studying medical literature, looking for anything else that might be useful in my case, to help nail down the change good and tight, to make it permanent. Once, when we were having lunch together, I remember him saying, 'Croyd, for all of that, you know you'll still be a caricature of humanity. I just wish it were within my power to wipe out everything that demon bug did to you—wipe out all of the others, too, for that matter—and leave the human race as clean as it was before.'

"'I appreciate everything you're doing, Doc,' I said. 'Seems like you've been devoting almost every waking minute to my case these past few weeks.'

"'I think it's the most important case I've ever had,' he replied.

"'Any new developments on the technical end of things?'

"'Yes, I think there might be a way to reinforce the change by using certain levels of radiation on your nervous system,' he said.

"'Radiation? I thought we were going the purely psychological route through *dauerschlaf.*'

"'This is some very new stuff,' he said. 'I'm still looking into it.'

"'You're the doctor,' I said. 'Keep me posted.'

"He picked up the tab again. Like always. And he wasn't even charging me for his therapy. Said he looked at it as a service to humanity. Gee, I liked the man."

"Mr. Crenson," she said. "The tail."

"Call me Croyd," he said.

"Croyd, I mean it. I don't care if it is a unique experience. This is business."

"Sorry," he said, tail flicking out behind him. "What are you doing tonight? This is a kind of dull place and—"

"I want to hear the rest of the story, Croyd. All this psychological talk's got me thinking maybe this is your way of avoiding it."

"Maybe you're right," he said. "I hadn't thought of that, but you may have a point. Sure. Okay. On with it.

"The days passed and I was really feeling good. I knew I wouldn't be dropping any speed this time around because I wasn't afraid to sleep. I'd seen my life lie—with sleep, madness, and death all twisted together—and I saw that I could face it, that the problem would be gone once the condition was stabilized. And Rudo was going to fix that good, once he'd worked out how this radiation therapy would apply, on top of the *dauerschlaf*.

"One day he asked me to lunch and we took a walk in Central Park afterward. As we were strolling, with him looking at the landscape as if he wished he were settled somewhere painting it, he said to me, 'Croyd, how much longer have you got?'

"'What do you mean?' I asked.

"'It's time for you to sleep again,' he said.

"'It's hard to tell for sure till I start getting the feeling,' I said. 'But based on past experience I've got at least a week.'

"'I wonder about inducing it beforehand,' he mused, 'to swing it.'

"'Swing what?' I asked.

"'First, let me ask you another question,' he said. 'You told me that you'd studied with an old second-story man named Bentley, and that you were engaged in that sort of business yourself.'

"'That's right.'

"'Just how good are you at that sort of thing?'

"'Not bad,' I said.

"'You still know how to go about it?'

"'I'm not out of practice, if that's what you mean.'

"'What if it were a place particularly security-conscious, well guarded?'

"I shrugged.

"'Couldn't really tell you till I cased it,' I said. 'Sometimes, you know, I'd come up with a wild card talent that really helped in these things.'

" 'Now, that's a thought . . .'

" 'What's the angle, Doc? What're you leading up to?'

" 'I've worked out what you need, Croyd, for the radiation part of the therapy. Unfortunately, the necessary materials are not available to civilians.'

" 'Who's got them?'

" 'Los Alamos Laboratories.'

" 'If they're medically useful you'd think they'd let some of the stuff loose, for humanitarian—'

" 'They wouldn't be useful for anyone but yourself. I had to adjust all of the equations to take your wild metabolism into account.'

" 'I see,' I said. 'And you're wondering whether I might be able to pry some of the stuff loose? Helping myself to help myself, so to speak?'

" 'In a word, yes.'

" 'That might be managed,' I said. 'How soon could I get a look at the premises?'

" 'There's the rub,' he said. 'I don't know how it can be done.'

" 'What do you mean?'

" 'The whole city is closed. There are checkpoints. If you're not authorized personnel you can't get by. It's a government installation. Top secret atomic research.'

" 'Oh. You mean it's not just the Lab, but the whole damn city's off-limits?'

" 'That's right.'

" 'This sounds a little trickier than breaking into an apartment or a store and cracking a safe, Doc. Are you sure we can't get this stuff someplace else?'

" 'Positive.'

" 'Shit!' I said. 'I don't know . . .'

" 'There are two possibilities, Croyd,' he said. 'You just re-

minded me of one of them. Now, neither one might be sufficient in itself to get the job done, but together—Together they
might be sufficient.'

"'Better let me in on it.'

"'I've an—associate,' he said, 'who might be able to help.
He has connections at the Lab, I'm pretty certain.

"'But he would have to be very circumspect.'

"'What does that mean?'

"'He could get you into the city without arousing suspicion. He could probably get you a look at the outside of the
place—perhaps even a map of the inside.'

"'Sounds like a good start,' I said.

"'I'm going to be speaking with him as soon as I can reach
him, and I'll find out more about the setup there. In the meantime, I'd like for you to be thinking of something. If we were to
induce another change before we get there, what wild card talent might serve you best for the initial scouting? Bear in mind
that we should be able to run another change after that, to provide you with whatever would then feel most suitable for the
job itself.'

"'All right,' I said. 'You'll call me then?'

"'Yes.'

"I had some unrelated business to take care of at the time, so
I went off and spent a couple of days settling it. Then one evening I got a call from Rudo asking me whether I could come
over to his place.

"I told him yes, and caught a cab.

"'Croyd,' he said, 'I have learned things about this atomic
city in New Mexico. You must have a pass with a photo on it to
gain entrance. Such visitors' passes can be obtained in Santa Fe
if you know someone in Los Alamos who notifies them that
you are coming to see him, and then meets you at the Los Alamos gate.'

"'We know such a person?' I asked.

"'Yes, we have a man on their security staff who'll take care of it,' he said. 'That is, my friend has a friend who will manage things in this regard. It used to be under military security, but now the Atomic Energy Commission is providing the guards—and, as fortune would have it, there is a man in such a position who will be glad to do me this favor. This will get us into the town, and we will be staying at Fuller Lodge, which is where visitors are put up.'

"'That does make it sound a little easier,' I said. 'Will your friend be able to get us to the place where I'll have to do the job?'

"'I got the impression that he could point it out to you, but that actually getting you inside would be too risky for him.'

"I nodded.

"'I guess that's where the right wild card power will come in handy.'

"'I wonder,' he said. 'Getting in may not be the biggest problem. Getting out of town with it might be.'

"'You said we could do the *dauerschlaf* business twice on this job?' I asked him.

"'Why not?' he said. 'What have you in mind?'

"'I come out looking bland,' I said, 'and equipped with a power that can get me a closer look at the premises. We visit the city and I case the place. Then I decide what's needed for the job and you induce it. I do the business, we take the goods to some nice, safe spot, and you give me the final treatment—radiation and all—and I can spend the rest of my life in a relatively normal fashion. And if there's ever anything you need, I'll take care of it for you.'

"He smiled.

"'Your stabilization will be reward enough,' he said, moving to the bar and fetching us Cognacs in balloon snifters. 'I think this is going to prove an educational experience for both of us.'

"'I'll drink to that,' I said, taking a big sniff.

"We touched glasses lightly.

"'Confusion to our enemies,' he said.

"So we worked out my physical appearance for the job, and I detailed the power I thought I'd need. Then Rudo set about inducing the *dauerschlaf* that would provide it. We decided to travel across country by train to Lamy, New Mexico, where the travel agent would arrange for us to be met at the station by a pickup truck for the luggage. This was because I was to be a part of the luggage. It was decided that it would expedite matters for me to continue my *dauerschlaf* in a well-padded packing case. The agent also made us reservations at a place called La Fonda, in Santa Fe.

"And so I have no memories to speak of concerning the train trip. I went to sleep in Rudo's apartment and woke up in a packing case in a hotel room in Santa Fe. It's no fun being luggage. I woke in a pretzeled condition, with a little light leaking in around the upper edges of my confinement. The lid was still nailed tightly in place—as we'd agreed, to prevent any curious hotel maid from thinking the good doctor'd included a corpse as part of his travel gear. I listened for a while—a thing we'd also agreed upon—but heard no voices. Then I rapped on the nearest side of the case, to get his attention if he was present. There was no response. Since I could detect no motion, chances were I wasn't in transit. And the light seemed an indication I was no longer in a boxcar. So I assumed I was either on a railroad platform, in the hotel lobby awaiting transport to a room, or in the room itself, with Rudo having gone out somewhere. It seemed too quiet for a platform or a lobby, though. So . . .

"Twisting myself into a more congenial position, I extended

my arms upward, felt the lid, and began to push. There followed a squealing of nails as it rose, and more light came to me. The lid came free on my right, then above my feet and head, finally falling aside to the left, nails bending, the wood making small splintering sounds.

"One deep breath then, and I rose to my feet, still unsteady. I was nude, since shape changing tends to ruin garments. But my suitcase held a variety of clothing, purchased with my target physique in mind; and even as I rose I saw that piece of luggage, across the room on a rack.

"I stepped out of the case and made my way into the bathroom, where I showered. The mirror showed me a dark-haired, dark-eyed man as I shaved; about five foot eight, and of medium build. I finished putting myself in order and went back into the room, where I opened my suitcase and hunted out suitable garments.

"After I'd dressed I departed the room and found my way downstairs and into a Spanish-style lobby. From there, I saw a bar with tables at which people were eating. Which was what I was looking for—food. I was, as always on awakening, ravenous. But I stepped outside for a few moments first. There was a lot of adobe around me and what looked like a small park off to my left. There was a cathedral off to the right. I could investigate them later. The sun, which I'd come out to check, stood a little past mid-heaven. Since I didn't know which way was east or west, it could be a little before noon or a little after. Either way, lunchtime, with half a day ahead of me.

"I went back inside and made my way into the bar. I found myself a table and read the menu. A number of items, such as enchiladas, were unfamiliar to me. So I just decided to order everything on the menu and work my way through. I'd also stopped at a newsstand I'd noticed off the lobby and picked up copies of all the papers they had, as is my wont upon awakening, to find out what had happened in the world while I slept.

"I had a succession of interesting things wrapped in tortillas, to the accompaniment of refried beans and rice, and was sitting there reading and waiting for the desserts to start arriving when Rudo came in, clad in a white suit and natty sport shirt, camera over his shoulder. I was puzzled not at all as he strode on by me to order a Ramos Gin Fizz at the bar. You get used to being ignored by friends and acquaintances when you change your appearance every time you sleep.

"I caught his attention when he turned to sweep the room with his gaze. I raised my hand and nodded.

"'Ah! The eminent Dr. Rudo,' I said, faking a slight German accent.

"His eyes widened, then narrowed. He rose from his stool immediately and approached me, brow furrowed, drink still in his hand.

"'I don't believe I recall . . .' he began.

"I rose and extended my hand.

"'Meyerhoff,' I said, since I sometimes like to put people on. 'Carl Meyerhoff. We met before the war. Was it Vienna or Zurich? You were doing work with that long sleep business. Fascinating stuff. You had your little problems, I recall. I trust everything is going satisfactorily for you these days?'

"Quickly, he looked over both shoulders as I seated myself again. How long could I keep this going? I wondered. Several minutes would be great. So long as he didn't switch to another language . . .

"He drew out the chair across from me and seated himself quickly.

"'Meyerhoff . . .' he said then. 'I am trying to remember . . . You are a medical man?'

"'Surgeon,' I replied, figuring that was far enough away

from psychiatry that he wouldn't trip me up with some comment involving his specialty. 'I got out when things got bad,' I added cryptically.

"He nodded.

"'I was fortunate in that respect, also,' he said. 'So, you are practicing here in the southwest?'

"'California,' I said. 'I'm returning from a medical conference now. Just stopped here to do a little sightseeing. Yourself?'

"'I am practicing in New York,' he said. 'This is a holiday for me, also. Striking landscapes here for painting, and the light is so pure. We met at a conference—or some hospital perhaps?'

"I nodded.

"'I heard you speak once on this *dauerschlaf* therapy. I believe there was a small party that evening. We spoke for a time of some of the troubles . . .' I let it trail off, open to interpretation as to troubles with the therapy, with friends, associates, family, European politics. His reactions had me curious now, and I wanted to see what he'd say. And if he got very evasive that would be interesting, too.

"He sighed.

"'They looked at things differently in those days,' he said, 'where I came from. And the early work, of course, had to be experimental.'

"'Of course,' I said.

"'When did you leave?'

"'In 1944,' I replied. 'Spent some time in Argentina. Came here later under the Project Paper Clip dispensation.'

"He raised his drink and took a swallow.

"'Yes, I've heard of it,' he said. 'Governments can be gracious—when they want something.'

"He laughed. I joined him.

" 'Fortunately, there was no need for me to employ such a route,' he went on. 'Some of the past died with the bombings and the records they destroyed, as I understand it.'

"He took another drink.

" 'You are staying here at the hotel?' he asked.

" 'Yes.'

" 'We should have dinner together. Would you care to meet in the lobby—say, seven o'clock?'

" 'That would be pleasant,' I replied.

"He began to rise, just as the waitress arrived with four desserts and my check. I picked up the check and glanced at it.

" 'May I sign for this?' I asked her.

" 'Sure,' she answered. 'Be sure to put down your room number.'

" 'That would be 208,' I said, accepting the pen she offered me.

"Rudo froze, looking back, studying my face.

" 'Croyd . . . ?' he said.

"I smiled.

"His face went through an amazing variety of changes, finally settling into a scowl. Then he seated himself and leaned forward.

" 'That—was—not—funny,' he told me. 'I—do—not—appreciate—such—monkeyshining.'

" 'When you get a chance like this every time you wake up, you might as well play it for a few laughs,' I said.

" 'I am not amused.'

" 'Sorry,' I said, as I attacked the flan. 'Just wanted to brighten our day.'

"He succeeded in convincing me that he had no sense of humor. But after a few minutes he was mollified, watching me eat desserts.

" 'I have located the office where we must obtain visitors'

passes,' he finally said, 'for our trip to Los Alamos. It is nearby. Our names should be on the list of expected visitors. Photographs will be required. We should stop by this afternoon and take care of that.'

" 'Yes,' I said. 'How'd they get on the list?'

" 'Our man in Los Alamos sent down word that we were coming to visit him.'

" 'Handy,' I said. 'How long have we been in town?'

" 'Here? This is our fifth day. I included instructions when I induced the *dauerschlaf* that you sleep for as short a time as possible. You were out for several days in my apartment and several more in transit.'

"I nodded as I gestured at the stack of newspapers.

" 'I'd noticed the date,' I said. 'How far is it to Los Alamos?'

" 'It is about thirty-five or forty miles north of here,' he replied, 'in the mountains. I've obtained a car.'

"We strolled outside after lunch, and he steered me to the left. The area that had struck me as parklike proved to be the Plaza. We passed around it in a clockwise fashion, stopping to study the work displayed on blankets by Indian craftsmen under the *portal* of the Palace of the Governors. Lots of silver and turquoise and some pretty pots. I bought a *bola* Rudo didn't like and wore it.

"He led me then to a one-story building nearby, where we entered through a small doorway. We came into a little suite of rooms where a woman sat at a desk.

" 'Hello,' he said. 'I am Ivan Karamazov and this is Croyd Crenson. We were told to come here to pick up our visitors' passes for Los Alamos.'

" 'Let me check the list,' she said, and she opened a drawer and withdrew a clipboard holding a stack of papers. She hummed as she checked through these. Then, 'Yes,' she said, 'I have you here.'

"She passed us some forms to fill out and told us we'd need to have our pictures taken after that. She told us the passes would be ready later in the day, or we could pick them up in the morning, since we'd said we'd be driving up the next day. We thanked her and departed.

"We walked around for a couple of hours after that, then went for a drive. Rugged, bright country. Lots of little pine trees. Big mountains. Small town. Quiet. I kind of liked the place. Wouldn't have minded spending a few weeks there.

"When it got dark we returned to the hotel and ate a big, leisurely meal, with several bottles of wine. In the dining room this time. We went back to the room afterward and talked a while longer. Then Rudo stifled a few yawns, said something about the altitude, and decided to go to bed. I went out and spent the night walking, about the town and into the country. There's something about walking at night, when things are slow and quiet, that I've always enjoyed.

"And this place was very quiet, and very dark, once I got out from town. Sitting on a hillside later and listening to the insects and looking at the stars, I realized that I was really happy. I didn't have to do drugs anymore, I wasn't afraid of sleeping and waking up in God knows what shape, and pretty soon I'd be able to pass for normal. I felt like I wanted to sing or something, but I didn't. I just sat there and watched the night and listened to it and felt good.

"In the morning I walked back and paced the streets again and watched the town wake up. The first place I saw that opened I went in and had breakfast. Then I went back to the hotel and waited for Rudo to wake up. When he had, and had gotten himself into shape, we went downstairs and ate. We took our time over coffee, and I had a few more snacks, while we waited for the office to open for our visitors' passes.

"After we picked up the papers, we headed for the car.

Rudo drove, taking us over to the Taos Highway and following it northward, in the direction of the Espanola Valley. Somewhere along the way we passed a big rock off to the left, shaped like a camel. The sun was very bright, and there were mountains to the left of us and mountains to the right. After a long while, Rudo found us a road that went off to the left, switching its way back and forth upward among orange cliffs. We went higher and higher, and there was no guard rail. The views became spectacular, the drop frightening. There were more pine trees, and big boulders, and orange buttes. At least Rudo seemed a careful driver.

"After a long while, things leveled off and we continued on a level plane. A little later, we saw a military gate in a barbwire fence blocking the road, tanks parked on either side of it. We slowed and came to a halt before it. One of the guards approached us, and we presented him with our passes.

"He checked to be sure that we matched the photos. When he was satisfied, he opened the gate and had us drive through and park. Then he placed a phone call and told us that our party would be down to meet us shortly.

"We waited, and about ten minutes later a car came down the road. It pulled up near us and parked. Its driver got out and came around to greet Rudo, calling him 'Karamazov' as they shook hands. He was a tall, pale, blond fellow. Named Scott Swensen. He clapped me on the shoulder when we were introduced, and he suggested that I ride with him and Rudo follow us in our car to the Lodge.

"As we drove into the town, we passed a small airport to the right. Scott gestured to the left about then and said, 'Look over there.'

"I did, and across a canyon, on a mesa, I saw a collection of green wooden shacks enclosed by a barbwire fence. There were several armed guards at the fence's gate. Ahead, I could see where the canyon ended and one could reach the place on level land.

"'Unimpressive bit of local architecture,' Scott said, 'eh?'

"I shrugged.

"'Whatever gets the job done, I guess,' I replied.

"'Right,' he answered. 'Exactly right. What you are looking at there is the DP Site.'

"'Please translate,' I said.

"'Stands for *deuterium* and *plutonium*,' he answered. 'They use the one to derive the other. They do it in there. It's the plutonium you're interested in, I understand. Hard to come by.'

"'What's it look like?' I asked. 'Big bars? Chunks of coal?'

"'Naw,' he said, chuckling. 'They can only process it in minuscule quantities—a few drops in the bottom of a vial. You could pick up one of those little gray containers and stick it in your pocket—almost.'

"'You make it sound easy,' I said.

"He laughed.

"'I understand you're strong as all shit,' he said, 'the kind of guy who might be able to tear his way through that barbwire fence, overpower the guards, kick his way into the storage building, and help himself to a couple of plutonium containers.'

"'Funny, I was just thinking about that.'

"'Wouldn't work,' he said. 'You might be able to do all of that, but you'd never get away with it. You'd be stopped at the gate if you went that way. And the part of this town that doesn't have a fence abuts a wilderness. They've got mounted patrols back there with dogs. But say you got past, either way. You'd still be a hell of a distance from anything that could take you far enough away, fast enough. A massive manhunt would be mobilized very quickly. But this time it wouldn't just be a few guards.

" 'There'd be aerial surveillance as well as ground-level parties. You'd be up against squads and squads of trained men with heavy firepower. Even if you won a skirmish or two, you'd never make it. You probably would make headlines all over the world, though.'

" 'I understand that they take this stuff seriously,' I said. 'But I won't be overpowering anybody, and I won't be leaving here with anything I didn't come in with.'

" 'You've found a better way to go about it?'

" 'I intend to.'

" 'Well, I'm Security, and I don't see one.'

" 'Just get me to the Lodge. I'll take care of the rest.'

" 'And leave in the morning without it and figure a way to come back for it later?'

" 'More or less.'

"He laughed again and clapped me on the shoulder.

" 'You know, I admire that,' he said, 'and I'm real curious what you'll work out to try.'

"For all I knew, Swensen could be playing a game with Rudo, having conned him into bringing in an ace burglar to test the Security apparatus. I'd no idea how deep their relationship might run. And even if he was on our side, the fewer people who know your business the better. Suddenly, I wondered what the repercussions on aces and jokers might be if I were to mess it up and get caught. It occurred to me suddenly that it could be major.

"I laughed and clapped him on the shoulder.

" 'You'll find out afterward,' I said.

"We arrived at Fuller Lodge a little later. Rudo pulled into the parking space beside us.

" 'I'll go inside with you,' Scott said, 'see you checked in.'

" 'Thanks,' I told him, and we got out of the cars. 'You going to join us for lunch?' I asked then.

"'I've already eaten,' he replied, 'and I've got to get back to work. Tell you what. I'll come by around six-thirty and have dinner with you.'

"'Sounds good to me,' I said, and Rudo nodded.

"We began walking toward the Lodge.

"'Are there any restrictions if I just want to take a walk?' I asked.

"'No,' he answered, 'and you've got passes giving you a right to be here. Walk around. Go anywhere you want. If you get too near something that's off-limits, someone will just tell you. Oh, and don't take any pictures.'

"'Didn't even bring a camera,' I said. 'But tell me, how would the people at an off-limits place know that I wasn't supposed to be there?'

"'You need an access badge to enter secure facilities,' he said. 'If I were to get you one, it would be too easy to trace back to me. Sorry. My hands have to stay clean. I can't afford to leave any tracks on this matter.'

"'No problem,' I told him.

"We entered, got checked in, and he bade us good afternoon. We went to our room then and washed up. Afterward, we headed for the dining room for our late lunch.

"On the dining room wall, to the side of the archway, was a framed newspaper clipping with a photo. Curious, I wandered over and read it after I'd ordered.

"The photo was of a man, a scientist, named Klaus Fuchs, who had once worked here. The story, which I remembered from the previous year, told how Fuchs had given key hydrogen bomb secrets to a Soviet agent—'in the interest of world peace,' as Fuchs had put it—the actual communication of this information having taken place on the Castillo Street Bridge in Santa Fe, over which I'd passed the previous night when walking out Canyon Road way. I remembered the story as I read it.

At the bottom of the piece, in red ballpoint, was written, *Security Is Everybody's Business,* and it was signed by Scott Swensen. I tried to figure how observation of that injunction could have stopped Mr. Fuchs, but I failed. Could I get this sort of press, I wondered, and be hung here?

"After a comprehensive lunch I stretched and told Rudo, 'I think I'll take a walk now.'

" 'I'll join you,' he said.

" 'You don't really want to,' I said, exerting my new power for the first time. 'What you really want is to take a nap, since you've gotten so sleepy.'

"Immediately, he began to yawn.

" 'You're right,' he said. 'I am tired. What I really want is to go back to the room and stretch out and go to sleep.'

" 'Do it, then,' I told him. 'Do it now.'

"He got to his feet. 'Have a good walk,' he said, and he departed the dining room.

"After I'd settled up, I stepped outside and sniffed the air. A great day for walking. I headed back down Jemez Road in the direction from which we had come.

"When I came to the place where the shoulder of land continued out past the end of the canyon and led to the gate of the DP Site, I took that route. As I approached the gate two armed guards approached it from the other side.

" 'Hey, buddy,' one of them called out. 'This place is off-limits unless you're authorized personnel.'

" 'I *am* authorized personnel,' I told him. 'I'm a general— three stars. You can see them now. You can also see my badge and my pass. I'm here to make a special inspection; you want to open the gate for me so I can do that.'

" 'Just a minute, sir,' the nearer one said. 'Sorry I didn't recognize you. That bright sunlight at your back . . .'

"He hurried to unlock the gate.

"As I entered, he said, 'The sign-in sheet's in the first building, sir.'

"'Take me there.'

"I followed him inside and glanced at the form he placed on a desk before me. For a moment, I was tempted to sign Swensen's name. But I didn't want to get the man in trouble just to be cute. I touched the pen to the form and handed it back to the guard.

"'There, I signed it,' I told him. 'You saw me do it.'

"'Yes, sir,' he replied. 'Thank you. What is it you would like to inspect, sir?'

"'The plutonium storage place,' I said. 'Take me there.'

"'Right this way, sir.'

"He opened the door for me, followed me outside, and led me to another, similar-looking green shack.

"Two other guards passed near, casting curious glances our way. They must have assumed everything was in order since I was escorted, and they continued past us. I called them over, though.

"'This is a special inspection,' I told them. 'We need you to accompany us into the plutonium sector.'

"They followed me into the building, where the first guard led me back to a rack that held a number of small gray containers. He stopped before it and looked at it.

"'That's the stuff?' I asked him.

"'Yes, sir,' he replied.

"I studied them long and hard—size, texture, shape. Finally, I reached out and hefted one, held it a moment, replaced it. I wiped it carefully with my handkerchief then and nodded.

"'Everything is in order,' I announced. 'Let's go back outside.'

"We departed the building and I halted to study it and its position in relation to the other buildings.

"'Good,' I stated. 'The inspection is finished. You men are doing a fine job. I am going to sign out now and then I am going to leave.'

"I returned to the first building, where I repeated my sign-in procedure. Then I had all of them accompany me to the gate.

"'This inspection was so secret,' I told them, 'that you are going to forget it occurred. As soon as that gate closes behind me I will begin walking. As soon as I am out of sight you will forget that you ever saw me. This inspection will not have happened. Open the gate.'

"They swung it wide before me and I stepped through and headed back to the Lodge. I picked up some magazines, went back to the room, and read them while Rudo slept.

"At a little after six, I roused him and suggested he get ready for dinner. He did that, and Swensen proved punctual. We had an enjoyable meal, Swensen having a collection of jokes I hadn't heard, which kept me chuckling through dessert.

"Over coffee, he said, 'I guess you'll be about your business soon. Good luck.'

"'It is finished,' I said. 'I know what I need to know now. Thanks.'

"He stared at me. 'How could you have?' he asked.

"'It was easier than you might think. We'll be leaving in the morning.'

"He shook his head.

"'I'm not sure whether to believe you,' he said.

"I smiled.

"'It doesn't matter,' I said. 'Doesn't matter at all.'

"We departed the following morning, making it back to La Fonda in time for lunch. I'd explained to Rudo that I had to know the appearance and physical location of something in order to teleport it, and that I had succeeded in zeroing in on the plutonium in this fashion. Now the only thing that I needed was the ability to teleport. Not to the minimal extent I'd possessed it that day I'd walked into his office holding my water, but a bit more heavy-duty and longer-range—a thing I had had experience with in the past. Rudo seemed confident this could be achieved with another bout of *dauerschlaf*. After all, he had a perfect batting average—with Bogie, and this time around with my appearance and the hypnotic persuasive ability. So I told him to make me a teleporter, and he said, 'No problem,' and we repaired to our room after dinner.

"Only one thing seemed slightly strange that afternoon. When Rudo opened a drawer to get out his medical kit with the *dauerschlaf* drugs, I caught a glimpse of a large photo lying beside it. I would have sworn it was a picture of Klaus Fuchs.

"And so I stretched out on the bed, as he directed, and he administered the first of the drugs. As the world began to swim away, I realized that I was happy. Rudo began speaking to me softly. His voice was a distant thing . . .

"This one was different. There was the long dark time I always know. But it seemed that at some point I awoke briefly, did something, and went back to sleep again, visions of the gray containers dancing momentarily behind my eyes.

"When the real awakening occurred it was more than a little traumatic. Someone had hold of my shoulder and was shaking me, shouting at me.

"'Wake up, you bastard! You're under arrest!' a large, uniformed individual was calling, as I tried to focus my eyes.

"I groaned, then, 'Awright! Awright!' I said. 'What's going on?'

"I was dragged to my feet, supported there, still trying to throw off the effects of my long sleep. I saw another cop then—much shorter, mustached—over by the dresser. He was holding one of the gray containers from the DP Site. Another still rested on the dresser.

"'. . . The stuff is even labeled as property of the Lab,' he was saying.

"'Get dressed, Fuchs—or is it Crenson?' the larger one said. 'That the name you're using this time? And if you so much as breathe a suspicious breath, I might get very nervous.' He patted his sidearm.

"'I'll hold my breath,' I said, patting my pants as I donned them, to be sure the wallet was still there, if Rudo hadn't run off with the money. I'd had a lot in it, and I wanted it near.

"'Why are you arresting me?' I asked.

"'If you don't know that, you're stupider than you look,' the big one answered.

"'Tell me anyhow,' I said. 'Okay? Who said I did whatever I'm supposed to have done?'

"He shrugged.

"'We had a telephone tip that you were here. He didn't give his name. We're just going to hold you for the Feds. They'll be up from Albuquerque in the morning to pick you up.'

"It was dark outside the window. I could hear a car passing on the street below. They let me put on my socks and shoes before they handcuffed me. I tried to figure what might have happened. All I could see was that Rudo had set me up. He'd kept his hypnotic control—maybe by means of posthypnotic suggestion—when I'd come out of *dauerschlaf*. Then he'd told me to teleport the plutonium containers here, as he knew I'd planned, and I'd done it. Then he'd put me back to sleep, leaving the evidence in plain sight, had cleared out, had made that phone call. The only thing I couldn't see in it was, why? But if I needed any evidence of such intent—or of his twisted sense of humor—I got it as the cops hustled me out. I caught a glimpse of myself in the dresser's mirror as I passed by. I was a dead ringer for the man in the photograph, Klaus Fuchs. Security is everybody's business . . .

"They drove me over, though the station was only two blocks away. There, I surrendered my wallet, which they said they'd keep safe for me. I was able to determine on handing it over that my money was still in it. I hoped it would stay there. I was conducted back to a cell then and locked up. I might have made a break on the way over, or even there in the station before they locked me up. But I was still disorganized, and I wanted a little time to think.

"So all I did was watch which key it was on his chain that my jailer used to lock my cell. As he turned away, I already had hold of it with my mind. I teleported it into my right hand and put it in my pocket. I went and sat down on my bunk. I'd been in better jails and I'd been in worse. At least I knew where this one was located in relationship to everything else in the area, from my walk the other night. There was no point in escaping unless you knew where you were going and what you were going to do.

"After perhaps twenty minutes I had decided what to do. So I got up, unlocked the door, stepped out, and closed it behind me. I passed a small room from within which I heard sounds of typing. No need to look for trouble. I continued on.

"There were two cops up front. One was drinking coffee and the other was talking to someone on the telephone. I backed up beyond the doorframe and waited for the sound of the phone being cradled. The safe wherein they'd stowed my wallet was an old one, of a sort Bentley'd taught me to open in the dark.

"I moved in quickly when I heard the telephone drop into place. It took one calculated punch each to render the cops unconscious. Then I propped them in their chairs to look as if they were dozing. The safe was old and crotchety and started taking longer than I'd thought it would. I didn't want to give it another five or ten minutes, though, so I braced it with a foot and a hand and started pulling. I wasn't able to tear the door off, but I buckled it enough to be able to reach inside and get my wallet. I pocketed it then and walked out, taking a right on Washington Avenue.

"I continued along this until I came to the road to Hyde Park, where I turned and started to climb. I knew that it would eventually pass through a part of the National Forest. I could find myself a good place to hide out there before morning. And I did."

Croyd rose, stretched, returned to the cooler, came back with two beers. He set one before Hannah.

He backhanded a moth.

"End of story," he said, "except for an Indian ace I met who could change the patterns on rugs into whatever was selling best, just by running his hands over them. I got away. *Now* can I buy you a drink?"

"Yes, now I'm thirsty," she said, reaching out and holding the bottle as he opened it. "But how did you get out of town?"

"I lived on roots and people's picnic remains for over a week," he said. "Then, with a short beard and wearing a pair of sunglasses I'd found, I took a chance and hiked back to town and bought a load of food and took it back to the forest with me. Lived on that until I got sleepy. Sacked out then in a rocky shelter I'd set up. When I woke a couple of weeks later I was a slim blond guy with the ability to shout at ultrasonic levels and knock people out or just make them uncomfortable, depending on how high I raised my voice and for how long. I went down to town then, got a ride out to Lamy, took a train back to New York."

"And Rudo?" she asked, sipping the beer. "Did you ever see Pan Rudo again?"

"Yes," he said. "Looked him up when I got to town. Got into his apartment building one day and picked the lock to his pad, waited there for him."

"And?"

"Of course he didn't recognize me. He looked startled when he saw me, but he just said, 'If this is a robbery, take whatever you want. I don't need any trouble.'

"I caught hold of his shirtfront and pulled him forward till his face was within an inch of my own. At first I'd planned to kill him, but then I decided it just wasn't worth it. Hell, maybe he was even helping some of his patients.

" 'It's me, Croyd Crenson,' I said, and he must have thought I was going to kill him because he went pale as a bone. Then, 'Just tell me why you did it,' I said. 'Why'd you set me up?'

"I guess he figured he had nothing to lose if he was going to die. His lip curled then, and he said, 'You're genetic garbage, you and all of the others! I hate what you have done to the race! I wanted to disgrace the lot of you—publicly, seriously! You got lucky, though.'

"I hit him then, in the mouth, twice, and I split his lip. I threw him down on his couch and used my handkerchief to wipe the blood off my hand. But it kept coming. I realized then that I'd cut a knuckle on his tooth.

" 'I'm not going to kill you now,' I told him. 'But one of these days—Who knows?'

"I left then, and when I checked a bit later I discovered that he'd moved out. And that is the story of something that might have hurt me and led to a lot of bad will toward jokers and aces in general, what with all the HUAC paranoia that was in the air."

"Thanks," she said, taking a swallow and shutting down her recorder.

She cased the recorder and placed it in her shoulder bag, along with the clipboard.

"So much for business," Croyd said. "How's about having dinner with me?"

She slung the bag over her shoulder and moved toward the door.

"Sorry," she said. "I've got to organize a lot of notes tonight, and I'll be leaving fairly early in the morning."

"You prejudiced against guys with tails?" he said.

She removed a collapsible umbrella from her bag and opened it. She smiled then.

"No, Croyd," she said. "But I'll be keeping mine to myself. Good evening," and she turned and walked off into the shadows and the drizzle.

Croyd stood in the doorway, watching until she was out of sight. Then he turned back to the empty bar.

"Play it, Sam," he said softly, and racks of glasses began to sing. A horde of flies chose that moment to swarm about him. Cursing, he swatted at them. Their buzzing took on the sounds of a tune.

The Ashes of Memory

7

"I know you. You're Hannah."

The quiet voice spoke in the dark. Hannah turned. In the dim glow of the lamps hung from the porch's ceiling, she could see Quasiman's eyes looking at her. "Hi. You came back, huh?"

"Yeah. Sorry." He looked pained, frowning as if he had a migraine. "Hannah, it's so damned hard keeping it all together. Remembering you, remembering what we're doing and who's involved and why. I write it down every day, and I keep looking at it when I forget, but . . ."

"Don't apologize. I know you can't help it. Where were you?"

The hunchback shook his head. "I don't know. I heard a gunshot, and I was frightened. I saw you, but . . . but . . ." His shoulders sagged. His mouth twisted as his lips pressed together. "I've forgotten it. Already. The whole thing's gone now, and I don't know what it was or what it meant, but it was important. Damn it!"

Quasiman went silent. He stepped out onto the rude wooden planks where Hannah leaned against the railing, looking out to where Faneuil's grave lay invisible in the jungle night. Gently, as if he didn't want his nearness to trouble her, he halted several feet away. The gesture, so caring and self-effacing, touched her. She found herself smiling at the joker; he gave her a tentative smile in return. "Where's . . . ?" Quasiman asked.

"Croyd? He got himself invited to dinner at Ngo's."

"You didn't want to go?"

Hannah shook her head. "No. I just felt like thinking."

"Are you still having nightmares about the bomb?"

"No. But it's nice of you to ask."

Quasiman took a step toward her. His hand lifted as if he were going to touch her as he had after the bomb in Saigon, then halted in mid-motion. "You sound sad," he said. "Didn't you find out anything this afternoon?"

Hannah gave a soft laugh at that. She moved her hand away from his. "I found out nothing, and also more than I bargained for. I'm just not sure what it means. You've sure set me on a strange course, you and your talk. The trouble is, it's starting to scare me, too." Hannah looked up at the sky. She didn't know if she'd ever seen so many stars. Yet like the prejudice and hatred she was uncovering, they too had always been there, hidden but unseen. "I think we've hit a dead end with Faneuil," she told him. "No records, no problems. Nothing. Dead men don't talk."

"But they can," Quasiman replied, softly and earnestly. He was looking at the sky also. "With the right person they can. I know how, Hannah."

It seemed so easy in the old horror movies.

They took a pair of kerosene lanterns from behind the bar.

In the back of Croyd's jeep they found a medical kit, a crowbar, and a shovel. Thus armed, Hannah and Quasiman went out into the field behind the village. Quasiman was a tireless, powerful worker, but he had his own limitations. Twice they had to stop: once when Quasiman found that he couldn't lift either arm because a major muscle group in his back had phased out, and again when his left leg disappeared. Both times, the episode was short, and Hannah only had to remind Quasiman of what they were doing a few times. Even so, it was several hours before the shovel made a harsh *tchunk* as it struck wood.

In that time, they'd piled up an impressive amount of earth, made a fair amount of noise, and acquired an audience of villagers. Hannah found it blackly amusing: a circle of awed Asian faces watching a cliché in motion: the middle of the night, a hunchback digging up a grave in the light of a lantern held in the hand of a young woman. Croyd came up about the time Quasiman struck the casket, Ngo Dinh Yie in tow. Croyd stopped and let out a hoarse laugh. "Vell," he said, in an atrocious Germanic accent. "Haf you got ze brain for me, Igor?"

"As soon as you stop laughing at your own jokes, give us a hand with this," Hannah told him. "Bring that crowbar."

"*Ja*, Frau Frankenstein. Did anyone ever tell you you're lovely when you're macabre?" Croyd picked up the crowbar and walked over to look down into the hole, where Quasiman was standing on top of the rough wooden casket. "Mind if I ask what you're after? I mean, it's obvious enough what you intend to do, but why?" His tail brushed the length of her leg.

Hannah ignored it. "We need a ring."

"You could've asked me. There's a thousand jewelry stores back in Saigon. This is going about it the hard way."

Hannah glared at him. "All right," Croyd said at last. He hopped down into the open grave with Quasiman. Hannah came down after him with three handkerchiefs soaked in smelling salts. "Here," she said. "This is going to be bad."

It was. The smell of corruption hit them like a sledgehammer as soon as the lid was pried open. The handkerchiefs were little protection; Hannah, who at least had some small experience of decomposing bodies, gagged but managed to hold it down. Croyd struggled, then lost his supper to the side. Almost all the faces that had been looking down at them from above disappeared quickly. Quasiman alone seemed unaffected.

Hannah took a slow, deep breath into the handkerchief, then shone the light in. The face was unrecognizable, flesh rotting and peeling away from the bone. The wood had let in moisture: a green fuzz hung around the body's neck like a fur collar and mushrooms sprouted from his chest. The hands folded over the moldy suit were almost down to bone. In the lamplight, a ring glittered on the right hand: a class ring with a blue stone, inset with diamonds. "I'll do it, Hannah," Quasiman said.

"No," she told him. "I'll do it. Here, hold this." She gave the joker the lamp, then reached into the coffin with trembling fingers. She snatched at the ring, grimacing as the finger bones broke apart from dried tendons. She slammed the lid down again and let out a breath she hadn't known she'd been holding. "That was gross," she said. "I sure as hell hope this was worth it." She shuddered. "Let's get this done and over with. I have to take a bath."

She started to climb out of the grave. One face was still looking down at them, framed in stars: Ngo Dinh Yie. He was staring at the ring in Hannah's hand.

— — —

"Anything to declare?"

"A few articles of clothing," Hannah said. "Maybe a hundred dollars' worth. That's all."

The customs agent—his name tag said FIELDING—snapped shut her passport. He tapped it against his palm. Hannah's purse was still open before him, and Hannah tried to avoid looking at it, tried to pretend that it wasn't important. "Ms. Davis," Fielding said. "Would you please step out of line and follow me?"

"Wait a minute," Hannah said. Her stomach was suddenly knotted; her breath tight. She could feel sweat beading at her hairline. Her fellow passengers were watching, and she could feel the mixture of fascination and irritation coming from them.

"Please, ma'am. You're holding up the line."

Fielding led her to a small office, opened the door, and ushered her in. Another customs official, seated behind a desk, nodded to them. Her passport and purse were given to the man, then the door was shut behind them. The agent perused the passport. "Ms. Hannah Davis?"

"And you're . . . ?"

"Agent Stone. I need to ask you a few questions. You're returning from Free Vietnam?"

"Yes. Is there a problem? I had a personal invitation from Ambassador Ngu, Prime Minister Meadows, and President Moonchild to visit the country."

Stone smiled. "Yes, ma'am, we know. However, a Free Vietnam state official contacted us. They are investigating a report that a small group of Americans recently plundered an old grave in their country. Among the stolen items was a ring. We also had a tip from another source that someone of your description would be smuggling it in. I wonder if you have a receipt for the ring that Agent Fielding found in your purse?"

Hannah tried to keep her expression noncommittal. "No, I don't. I didn't buy it. It was given to me several years ago. As you can see, I wasn't trying to hide the ring or smuggle it past. The ring wasn't sewn in the lining of my coat or inside my shoe heel, Agent Stone. It was lying in the bottom of my purse. The ring's mine."

Stone reached into the purse and pulled out the ring. He placed it on the table in front of Hannah. "Yours?" he said. "Odd. This looks like a man's ring. Would you mind putting it on?"

Hannah didn't move. Her stomach churned and she fought not to show it. She looked at Stone blandly. "I don't have to; it won't fit. The ring belonged to an old lover of mine. He died in an auto accident. I keep it for its sentimental value, not to wear it. That's why it's in my purse."

"Ahh." Stone drummed his fingers on the table. "I'm afraid that I'll need to keep the ring for a few days, until we can verify with Saigon that this isn't the stolen item. We will, of course, give you a receipt."

"No!" Hannah protested. "You can't do that. That's not right."

Stone almost smiled. "I'm afraid that under the circumstances we both can and must, Ms. Davis. I can assure you that the ring will be returned to you just as soon as we hear from someone in Free Vietnam."

"Call Meadows, then. He'll tell you."

"We've done that. Unfortunately, he is unavailable at the moment." Stone smiled, and Hannah knew the man was lying. "I regret the inconvenience, but regulations . . ."

"Are you detaining me as well, until you talk to Mark?"

"No, ma'am. At the moment, no formal charges have been filed. I'm sure you'll keep yourself available to us if we have further questions, but since Mr. Meadows knows you so well,

I'm sure the whole matter will eventually be dropped. Still, I'm sure you understand why I have to do this."

"I understand," Hannah answered. "Actually, I think I understand very well." There didn't seem to be much else she could say. Stone was smiling politely at her. Hannah took a deep breath. "All right," she said. "I suppose I don't have a choice."

"I hate this," Hannah said. "I hate being suspicious of everyone I meet, and I hate even more the fact that it seems like the paranoia's justified. I hate being scared even worse, and that's what I feel all the time now. I'm frightened at what all this means."

"You want to quit, Hannah?" Quasiman asked.

Yes. "No," she said at last. "I guess not. I'm just, well . . ." Hannah frowned, then made a halfhearted attempt at a smile. "Where's the ring?"

Hannah hadn't thought the subterfuge necessary, but suspicion seemed to be coming more easily now, and she'd worried about the way Ngo Dinh Yie had been staring at them, especially since Ngo's son had disappeared along with Durand. Once back in Saigon, she'd asked Croyd to find them a ring similar to Faneuil's. In the crowded warrens of that city, it had been easy enough. Quasiman had teleported back to New York with Faneuil's ring, while Hannah carried the false one.

"Ring? What ring?" Quasiman said now. "Was I supposed to remember something about a ring?"

An invisible fist seemed to grab Hannah's lungs and squeeze. "Oh, no."

"It's a joke, Hannah," Quasiman said. He was smiling. "The ring's right here." Quasiman held out his hand. In the dim light of the nightclub, the blue stone and diamonds glittered.

"That wasn't funny. Not funny at all," she said, but she smiled back at him. Hannah breathed a sigh of relief. She was still exhausted from the flight in and the confrontation at customs.

Hannah had thought herself half-crazy for being that devious. She told herself it was only a little test, to prove to herself that she was being ridiculous. She'd told herself that she was going to feel absolutely silly when she got back to New York and nothing had happened. Now she wondered whether she'd been cautious enough.

She wished that this mysterious ace they were waiting for would hurry. Being in Jokertown was bad enough, but the Club Dead Nicholas wasn't exactly a place to inspire confidence. The Dead Nicholas had once been a crematorium. Hannah and Quasiman were seated at the table near the old furnaces, the walls of which had been taken out and turned into a large open grill, where a trio of demonic-looking jokers were grilling steaks and flipping burgers. Altogether-too-cute mechanical bats flapped and squealed through the dark recesses of the ceiling. Hannah's table was a glass-covered coffin, in which the corpse of a blue-skinned joker resided. Their waiter, a pale wraith wrapped in a gauzy shroud, had assured her that all the corpses were waxworks; Hannah hoped he was right. The blackened chicken she'd ordered had been tasty enough, but she'd only picked at it, her appetite gone.

Hannah suspected she was the only nat in the place. She felt out of place and a little threatened despite the mask she wore— a foam rubber feline half mask.

Masks, in and out of fashion in Jokertown since the fifties, had once again become chic in the wake of the Rox invasion, when the joker-ace Bloat, who could reshape reality, took over Ellis Island along with his joker minions and renamed it. The Rox had become a sanctuary for all jokers—even the violent and dangerous "jumpers," who could swap bodies with an unwilling victim, leaving them trapped in the jumper's body—but it was destroyed during an assault by government forces and aces. Or at least that's what Hannah had been told.

Hannah didn't care for the masks. The faces twisted by the wild card were bad enough, but masks hid entirely too much. There was too much hidden about Jokertown already for her taste.

"Your friend is ready for you." The waiter had drifted up to their table—literally. Hannah noticed that he had no feet underneath the ragged shroud. "If you'll follow me . . ."

Hannah and Quasiman followed the joker to the rear of the club and down a short corridor. He knocked on a door and nodded to them. "Go on in," he said.

Someone opened the door. Hannah could see a room decorated in red satin wallpaper, dimly lit by a few lamps. The corner of a low table was just visible in front of a worn sofa. Quasiman went in first. The woman who'd opened the door greeted the joker, then looked at Hannah inquisitively. Hannah took off her mask and nodded to the woman.

"Cameo," Quasiman said. "This is Hannah. We're—" He stopped and looked distressed. "I've forgotten why we came," he said, looking from Cameo to Hannah.

"It's okay," Cameo told him. "Father Squid told me most of it." Hannah could see how the woman came by her name: the cameo profile of a woman, white on black, hung from a black ribbon around her throat. She had a man's fedora hat in her hands; it looked too large for her: worn, stained, and dirty. "Hi," she said to Hannah.

Her voice was soft and, like Quasiman's, somewhat shy, but there was hardness underneath. An angry sadness hung about her like a psychic cloak, and her large, dark eyes looked as if they had seen too much. This was a woman who would follow her own agenda, Hannah decided. She wasn't sure she was going to trust this Cameo. "Father told me about what's happened," Cameo continued. "He said you think there's a group of people out to hurt the jokers. The fire was a horrible thing. I think nearly everyone in Jokertown lost someone close to them that night. I . . . Well, I'll do what I can." She sat on a small couch next to the table, and gestured for Hannah and Quasiman to take the two chairs on the opposite side.

"You really can do this?" Hannah asked. "You can talk with a dead man through his ring? I can ask you the questions I need to know?"

Cameo shook her head. "You ask him yourself. I *become* him."

"I'm looking for anything Faneuil knows about a man called Pan Rudo." Hannah stopped, her eyes narrowing. Cameo's mouth had opened slightly, as if she were about to speak, and she twisted the fedora in her hands as if it were a washcloth. Then the woman recovered, and an inner veil seemed to draw across her eyes. "You'll really be Faneuil?" Hannah finished.

"For as long as I'm wearing the ring. If he were an ace, I'd have his powers. That's why—" Cameo stopped, swallowing hard, and Hannah could see the pain again, closer to the surface. "That's why Battle thought I'd be so useful on the Rox."

"George G. Battle?"

"Yeah. That's him."

The same people, all the time. The fear that had haunted her in Vietnam returned to Hannah. "You were there working for him? You fought against the jokers?"

"I've been lots of people," Cameo said. The fedora slapped her thigh angrily. "Every last one of them had done something at some time that they weren't proud of. I guess this was my turn. Battle used me and lied to me, but I was still stupid enough to go along with him in the first place. It'll be a long time before I forgive myself."

"That's what someone who was still working for them might say."

"It might be." Cameo spat out the words, staring at Hannah. The woman held out her hand. "So where's this ring?" she asked.

Hannah was no longer sure if she wanted to go through with this. But before she could move or speak, Quasiman handed Cameo the ring. Cameo placed the ring on her finger and fisted her hand around it. She threw the fedora on the coffee table, sat heavily on the couch, and closed her eyes, leaning back. Hannah waited, not quite knowing what to expect. Would this Cameo change her appearance? Would she speak in Faneuil's voice like she was possessed? Quasiman and Father Squid had both been vague on the details of this summoning. Hannah shifted in her seat, uneasy.

Cameo's eyes opened. She uncurled her hand.

"Faneuil's not dead," she said.

Quasiman snorted. Hannah felt like she'd been kicked in the stomach. "You're sure?"

Cameo nodded. "There's a lot of personal energy in this ring. I can feel it. When you wear something all day, every day, when you use something so much that it becomes part of you, then some of your energy gets locked up in the item. That's not so unusual a belief, either; that's why a lot of so-called 'primitive' cultures are careful about how they dispose of hair clippings and even excrement: What was once part of you is *always* part of you. When a person dies, I can use the emotional matrix embedded in a physical object to bring them up. I think . . . I've kind of imagined that the ego barriers are gone then. But while they're still alive, the person is too strong, too connected to their body. I can't do anything with the energy, even though I can sense it. This is the same. Whoever wore this ring is still alive somewhere."

Hannah looked at Quasiman. The hunchback was looking at her, waiting, with a trusting gaze. "You knew that, didn't you, Hannah?" he said. "You weren't convinced he was dead."

"I wondered, yes. But . . ." Hannah frowned, looking at Cameo. "Pardon me, but how do we know you're telling the truth?"

"Why should I lie?"

Because you worked for Battle. Because even though my instincts tell me that you're genuinely sorry, I don't trust anyone anymore and my stomach's killing me and I can't sleep nights. Hannah didn't say it, she only stared. That was a standard procedure in interviewing: wait. Most people hate silence. Sometimes they fill the silence with things they might otherwise not have said. Cameo either knew that or was an exceptionally patient person. She returned Hannah's gaze openly, keeping the eye contact far longer than Hannah expected. Finally Hannah sighed and stood up.

"Thank you, Cameo," she said. "You've given us a lot to think about."

"You don't like me, do you?"

"I don't know you." Hannah held the woman's gaze without blinking. "But I don't trust you."

"I don't trust anybody, either. Except the dead." Cameo picked up the hat again, placing it on her lap.

"I prefer people when they're living. Come on, Quasi." Hannah started toward the door. Quasiman stared at Cameo for a long minute, as if he were seeing something in her face invisible to Hannah.

"*He* wanted to help," Quasi said to her, then limped after Hannah. Cameo reacted as if she'd been hit in the stomach.

Her face went as white as the cameo at her throat. Hannah reached the door and opened it.

"Pan Rudo," Cameo said behind them.

The name was like an incantation. Hannah shivered, as if someone had just brushed her spine with a finger. She turned.

Cameo's fingers crumpled the fedora's rim. "Pan Rudo. Card Sharks. They're what you're looking for, right?"

Card Sharks. The words sent an icy finger down Hannah's spine. "Yes," she managed.

"You going to see Rudo again? You going to tell him about what you know?" When Hannah didn't answer, Cameo smiled grimly. "Hey, it's a fair question. You asked me about Battle. And I don't care if you have Quasiman and Father Squid fooled, you're still a goddamn nat."

Hannah nodded. She knew that without Croyd's tale, she would have gone back to him. She would have told Rudo everything. But not now. Croyd hadn't seemed to be the most stable of personalities, but his reaction to Rudo's name had been genuine, and there'd been no reason for him to lie.

Just as there was no reason for Cameo to lie about Faneuil. "All right," Hannah answered. "No. That's your answer. Rudo may be the one responsible for the fire. So do you know him?"

"Not me. A friend. I brought the hat along because of that, because of what Father told me when he called. Kept me up all night, and I spent today trying to decide whether I was going to come here or not. Trying to decide whether I'd tell you or not. I'd even made up my mind that I wasn't going to." Her eyes were bleak, and Hannah had a sense of the frailness and vulnerability that lay under the woman's surface. "One of the side effects of my *gift*"—she said the word like it was a curse— "is that I experience vicariously everything the person I summon has experienced. I get to know my people very well. Too well sometimes." She picked up the fedora and placed it on her lap. "This is Nickie's hat," she said. "He knew Rudo. And he . . . he . . . ."

Tears had gathered in the young woman's eyes. Hannah waited. On the couch, Cameo took a deep breath. "I'll let him tell you," she said.

Cameo put the hat on her head.

Cursum Perficio

Kevin Andrew Murphy

It's kind of hard for me to talk about the
past. I mean, I *know* it's the past, that it's 1993, not 1962, but it's
hard to come to grips with, you know? Like being dead. And
waking up in a woman's body. And knowing the woman who
killed you is out there, somewhere, with your son.

But let me tell you my story. It all took place so far away
from here and now, you might as well think of it as an old
movie. Fade in. Superimpose title: Hollywood, California.
February 15, 1962. Orson Welles's office, the Fox lot.

I slipped inside, shutting the door behind me, and took off
my fedora. The one I'm wearing right now, though it was new
then. But even in '62, it was still the only thing about me that
looked the part of the private investigator. The rest looked like
central casting had got mixed up and sent out for a hero for
some Viking flick: six-three, blond hair, blue eyes, and a California tan. A Malibu Siegfried, and since it's bad luck to speak
ill of the dead, I'll say I was pretty darn good-looking, not that
it matters now. It would have been a liability any other place

than Hollywood, but snooping around the studios, everybody took me for just another nowhere actor and didn't give me a second glance.

Welles sat behind his desk, trying to grow a beard over his baby fat. He leaned over and stabbed the intercom with a pudgy finger: "Hold all calls, Agnes." His face had the same jaded and disturbed look he'd worn in *Citizen Kane*.

There was one of those nasal voices you only hear in movies: "Right-o, Mr. Welles." Central casting had done their job with the receptionist at least.

"Make yourself comfortable, Mr. Williams. This should take a while." He gestured to an overstuffed leather armchair and I sat down, perching my fedora on one knee. "Nice hat," he added. "Makes you look the part. Cigar?"

"Cigarette, thanks." I took one from the box he proffered and accepted a light, though passed on the burgundy he held up next. If I got tipsy, I'd start glowing with St. Elmo's fire; I said I preferred not to drink on the job.

I guess I can safely admit it now that I'm dead. I was one of those "hidden aces" McCarthy was talking about. Had been since my sophomore year in college when I stepped out of the pool and into the high voltage cord for the floodlights. I got electrified. It wasn't fatal, just permanent. Two days later, I found I could toss around balls of lightning and light myself up like a Christmas tree. I did my best not to, grounded my excess, and went on with my life, which led roundabout to detective work, though that's another story.

Welles took a swallow of burgundy and a long pull on his cigar. "You know Wally Fisk, Nick?"

I shrugged. "Not much. Good detective."

"Bit of a bastard, too," Welles finished my unspoken thought. "He was working for me."

"Was?"

He flicked his cigar ash to indicate the past tense. "He went mad."

I didn't bother to echo him this time, just waited until he filled in the rest. He was paying, after all.

"Stark, raving mad," Welles said finally. "Torched his apartment, burned his files, and ran around screaming that everyone was out to get him. They got him before he could top it off with a suicide. He's in the lockdown ward at County General.

"Yesterday he was sitting in the exact same chair you are now, saner than most people in this town."

Welles took a long pull on his cigar and let it out slowly.

He watched the smoke as it drifted toward the ceiling. "Will you take over?"

"Depends on the case."

Welles smiled. "Smart man. Wally was hired to protect my film. If he'd turned up dead, I'd at least have some of my suspicions confirmed. This . . . I don't know. I've never had a detective go mad on me before."

"I'm sure it wasn't anything he'd planned." I took a puff on my cigarette. "Did he find anything that would make him snap?"

Welles shrugged. "Who knows? He torched everything he hadn't turned in to me already."

"What was he protecting?"

"*Blythe.*" Welles said it more like he was invoking a goddess than saying the name of a woman or a film.

I just took a drag and waited until he continued.

"I got the script from Dalton Trumbo." Welles took a long sip of burgundy. "It's the story of the Four Aces, focusing on the House Committee on Un-American Activities. Picture it in all its sordid glory."

His voice was the showman's now, ringing through the office as he sketched pictures in the air with his cigar. "Dr. Tachyon as the Lost Prince. Black Eagle as Othello. Jack Braun as Judas and Senator Joseph McCarthy as Torquemada. And Blythe van Renssaeler as the beautiful, doomed madwoman."

I knew about as much as any wild card about the Four Aces. They'd been the few lucky ones the first Wild Card Day, and Archibald Holmes had got them together as the Exotics for Democracy. Black Eagle, who could fly. David Harstein, the Envoy, sort of a Shylock with a conscience, who could get you to agree to anything, no matter how bizarre. Blythe van Renssaeler, Brain Trust, who had the world's greatest intellects all within her own mind.

And then there was Golden Boy, the strongest man in the world, who'd told everyone's secrets to the Committee on Un-American Activities in exchange for a thank you and thirty pieces of silver. Black Eagle flew away, Tachyon was deported, Holmes and Harstein were sent to prison, and Blythe van Renssaeler went mad and died in an insane asylum a few years later.

And Jack Braun got to go on being an indifferent actor, in between busting heads for the government.

Welles swirled the burgundy in his glass, contemplating the color. "You come recommended as someone both thorough and discreet, and not overly worried about danger, so long as you receive adequate compensation."

It was a leading statement. "Who did you hear that from?"

"Kim Wolfe."

I know I blushed, and I was hard-pressed to keep from topping it off with St. Elmo's fire. A detective does a lot of questionable things in his profession, and I think the worst thing I ever did was take pictures of Jack Braun with his wife's pretty girl dermatologist. It got her a divorce and me a down payment on my house. In celebration, Kim Wolfe tried to get me into bed.

They should have stayed married. They deserved each other.

I didn't feel so bad about that case—believe what you will, it's standard for a PI—as I did about what came after. I got into the habit of taking similar photos and selling them to Braun's successive wives. There were enough for an erotic pin-up calendar and another brace of divorce suits. I told myself I was doing it to give the Judas ace a taste of his own medicine, but with 20/20 hindsight, I can say I did it for the money.

But back then, I *was* doing it for the money. "What sort of pay are we talking here?"

Welles named a figure that you'd never find anywhere outside the budget of a major motion picture.

I know I paused too long. "I need to know all of my duties before I accept anything."

"Smart man," Welles said again. "You'll be doing anything and everything to protect *Blythe*. If someone tries something, you'll stop it, and if possible get evidence we can use for PR." He tapped the ash off his cigar with a final gesture. I watched it fall. "And of course you won't breathe a word of this to Hedda or Louella."

Now, there's something you ought to know about Hollywood, or at least the Hollywood I knew: The gossip columnists ran the town. And the two biggest harpies in Hollywood were Louella Parsons and Hedda Hopper.

Louella, or "Lollipop" as she liked to be called, invented the business. She was a neurotic old biddy with a bald spot and a voice like a crow, but at least she could be reasoned with. She didn't have an axe to grind, only papers to sell.

Hedda was another matter. Hedda was a failed actress who

found that all the venom she'd built up over the years actually sold papers and radio spots. She was also a weird old lady who went around in these giant hats and hated everything outside of Middle America prewar, pre–wild card. She hated Reds, she hated Pinks. She hated lavender boys and foreigners and Charlie Chaplin and just about everyone else. But more than anything, she hated wild cards.

Her files must have pinned about half the people on the Blacklist. And if you were an ace-in-hiding, you didn't forget that she was thick as the Forty Thieves with J. Edgar Hoover.

She was also tight-knit with Willie Hearst, whose papers owned Louella, and the animosity between them and Welles was public knowledge. If anyone was to get the scoop, it wasn't going to be Hedda Hopper or the Hearst empire.

"Let me tell you something, Nick," Welles said. "*Blythe* is going to be big and it's going to piss off more people than *Citizen Kane*. But unlike *Kane*, I'm not keeping it under wraps."

I paused and took a drag on my cigarette. "You've done a pretty good job so far."

Welles poured himself another glass of wine. "That, Nick, is the problem. It isn't a secret, but short of taking out ads in *Variety*, no one knows what's being produced. And with the number of spies and rumormongers in this town, it doesn't take a genius to recognize a conspiracy of silence when he hears one.

"I hired Wally to see just how deep it went. This is what he found before he went nuts."

He gave me a sheaf of documents: letters, bills, newspaper clippings, insurance claims, unproduced scripts like *The Bowery Boys in "Jokers' Town,"* and scenes cut from *30 Minutes Over Broadway*.

What it added up to was that someone had it out for wild cards, and scenes that made aces a little too heroic had gotten the axe. And movies that showed jokers as anything but monsters terrorizing teenage beach parties invariably had set fires or other accidents.

Welles swirled his burgundy. "I was over at MGM when they were doing *Golden Boy*. From what I saw of the dailies, it looked to be a reasonably good film. What happened in the cutting room was criminal, probably in every sense of the word.

"Someone doesn't like wild cards, Nick," Welles said. "I want you to find out who. *Blythe* is going to go ahead and it's going to be the best damn picture I've done."

He gave me a copy of the script and filled me in. They hadn't contracted all of the players yet, and Trumbo was still doing a polish, but Zanuck had lent him Marilyn Monroe for the title. After her performance in *Cleopatra,* they'd have lines down the block.

I believed it. Blond Marilyn was nothing compared to raven-haired Marilyn. I was one of ten thousand men wanting to have been that asp.

I stubbed out my cigarette and Welles offered another before I had to ask. "Marilyn," he said, giving me a light, "is the risky bit. She's on the bottle, and that wouldn't be half so bad if it weren't for Paula Strasberg, her acting coach, and her new psychiatrist, Dr. Rudo. Between the two of them they've got her loaded down with more pills than any woman should be able to swallow." Welles scrunched down, mimicking the posture and accent of a New York matron: "Marilyn, darling, take one of your tranquilizers." He straightened up then, affecting a haughty look and an aristocratic German accent: "Miss Monroe, I prescribe a Damn-It-All. Take two, they're small."

I bit my cigarette to keep from laughing. "So you want me to pry Marilyn away from her bottle and pills?"

Welles was back to himself, trimming another cigar. "I don't care," he said, lighting up and sucking smoke like some sort of directorial dragon. "I don't care if she takes twice as many or goes cold turkey, just so long as she can act. The money for *Blythe* comes from people who're willing to bet on the combination of Monroe / Trumbo / Welles, not a bunch of philanthropists who'll pay for any actress to play a diseased schizophrenic the government's glad is dead."

He paused, leaning back in his chair, tapping the cigar with finality. "If Marilyn goes, *Blythe* is dead, too. And whoever doesn't like wild cards gets what they want."

I may have been a hidden ace, but I was still a wild card. There was no way I was letting this one go.

"I'll take it."

"Deal," Welles said and we shook.

The next day, I showed up at the lot, bright and early. I'd gone through the papers the night before and read Trumbo's script. It was still rough in places, but genuinely moving, with the mark of Hollywood: It may not have been exactly what *did* happen, but it was the way things *ought* to have happened.

I think someone once said that art wasn't truth, but a lie that made you realize the truth. That was the beauty of Hollywood, and *Blythe* was beautiful.

I'd asked Welles if there was some part he could make up that would give me an excuse to be on the lot, preferably near Marilyn. After giving me a director's once-over, he asked if I'd like to be stand-in for Golden Boy. I gave him my best Jack Braun *aw-shucks,-I-can't-act,-Colonel* grin and saluted, saying I'd be happy to stand wherever the committee wanted me to.

My name was at the front gate: Nick Williams, nowhere actor and Golden Boy stand-in.

I got to meet the cast. Costuming wasn't quite finished, but

James Dean had a hat from one of the old Robin Hood flicks. Add a red wig and he'd be Dr. Tachyon. Sidney Poitier, of course, was Black Eagle.

They hadn't contracted for Harstein yet, but Welles had another stand-in, name of Josh Davidson, from New York. He was a little chubby and didn't have a Jewish nose, but otherwise looked even closer to the Envoy than I did to Golden Rat. Everybody liked him, but Welles was looking for a name actor.

And then there was Marilyn. I know everyone has seen her pictures, but none of that compares to the reality. She was beautiful. The "iron butterfly" they sometimes called her. Small and delicate, but with this underlying strength, something that told you that, yes, this woman could be crushed, but not as easily as you might think.

Her skin was pale white and her eyes were blue. But her hair . . . In *Cleopatra*, most of the time she'd worn a wig, her real hair too damaged by the bleach. But now it had grown out, and it was dyed a rich, sable black. Ebony on snow.

It was *Cleopatra* all over again. Blythe van Renssaeler had been a beauty, but nothing compared to this. Marilyn *was* Blythe van Renssaeler, the way Blythe should have been. It was like a butterfly coming out of a chrysalis. A beautiful, fragile thing, destined to float briefly, then die.

Costuming had gone full stop. Her dress was sheer black silk with a silver fox wrap thrown over her shoulders, like the princess from a Russian fairy tale. And around her neck she had a triple string of pearls, clasped with an onyx square set with a diamond. It was the necklace Blythe van Renssaeler had worn during the trial.

She read her lines haltingly, almost childlike, while Paula Strasberg, her acting coach, watched from offstage, along with what could only be her new Svengali, Dr. Rudo. They observed her like butterfly hunters after some prized new specimen, but then, God, she was beautiful.

They were practicing the scene where Blythe comes to Tachyon's apartment after her husband throws her out. Marilyn was curled up against James Dean's chest, weeping, and those were real tears, not glycerin. And her words: "I don't know what's to become of me. What man could ever love a woman who knows all his secrets?"

"I would," Dean said, and I know I mouthed the line as he said it. That moment was magic. Marilyn stood there, the silver fox wrap sliding softly off her shoulders, like a chrysalis off a butterfly. And one by one her tears hit the floor.

That was the moment I truly fell in love with her.

Then there were people swarming around her, Paula Strasberg shrieking like some Jewish grandmother from Hell, alternately congratulating her and asking if she wanted one of her tranquilizers, Dean hugging her, then Welles swept through them, pulling Marilyn free of the knot. He gave her directorly compliments and she started to laugh and dried her tears, then Welles steered her and her admirers over in my direction and introduced me to the crew.

I don't know what my first words were to her. Probably something stupid and obvious like "That was wonderful" or "I've been a fan for a long time." It didn't matter. That was Marilyn's moment, and I think there's no way to do it justice. She was brilliant.

Then the tension was broken by Josh Davidson going, "How did you *do* that?"

Marilyn suddenly calmed down and started giving him a whole explanation of method acting, and Paula took them off into the corner.

And I found myself face-to-face with another hero from a Wagnerian opera.

The joke was, the voice matched. "She is very complex, yes?"

I think I sort of vaguely nodded as I looked at the owner, trying not to laugh: Welles's impersonation had been spot-on. Like I said, he was another blond-haired, blue-eyed type, and even had the same little Kirghiz fold to the corner of the eye as I did. He looked like my uncle Fritz.

The German extended his hand. "Miss Monroe's psychiatrist, Dr. Pan Rudo. You were very moved."

I suddenly noticed that a tear had escaped down my cheek. I brushed it aside and shook hands, saying something about how any actor would have been moved by that performance, but I know it didn't sound believable. I was scared. If I'd let go any more, I would have lit up like a ship in a rainstorm.

Rudo laughed and offered me a cigarette. I accepted and lit up in the more conventional sense. After all, without alcohol, I had to have some vice. Cigarettes were as good as any.

Dr. Rudo's cigarettes were expensive and French. So, I think, was his suit, and as I learned later, his tastes in wine.

We talked a while and I learned that he'd come to the States before the war, from Dresden. A Prussian aristocrat most likely, or maybe the air of fallen nobility just worked to his advantage as psychiatrist to the stars.

As soon as the rumors worked themselves free, I wanted to question him about Wally Fisk and just exactly what *might* have happened to him. But I wasn't going to broach the subject until I heard it from someone else, so I just made small talk.

Everything else was the usual preproduction wrangle, and somewhere in there I managed to link up with Flattop.

Flattop was an old friend, or at least a friendly informant. He was a joker ace. That's A-C-E, as in American Cinema Editors, not ace PI or ace wild card like I was. He was also a joker and an almost-deuce: You never noticed him except when you were looking right at him. But when you did, you wondered how you could have missed the guy, since his irises were candy-striped orange, yellow, and green, one inside the other, like a photographer's test pattern, his fingers were twice the length they should have been, and his toes were almost as long, and he had a six-ounce Coca-Cola bottle screwed into a socket in his left arm, right inside the elbow.

But he was a good-looking guy for all that, with a nice even smile; clean-cut, straight-arrow looks; a cross around his neck; and dark-brown hair cut in a conservative flattop.

Like most jokers, he was also pathetically happy to have anyone just treat him like a human being. I'll admit I used him shamelessly, but you could find out half of what was going down on any lot for the price of just fifteen minutes with Flattop.

"Ooh, Marilyn is pissed off, man," Flattop said as he fiddled with some editing equipment. I tried to ignore the fact that he used his prehensile toes for half the job. "Zanuck stuck her on this pic for the last spot on her contract, and I don't know what deal Welles made to get him to do it. She'd walk if she could."

"What's the problem?"

"Didn't you know, man? This is a wild cards pic and that old witch Hopper's declared war. She's been flying around the set trying to twist Marilyn's arm. I wouldn't be surprised if she hired a stunt plane and had it write *Surrender Marilyn!* over the studio."

It sounded like standard tactics for Hopper. First she gave you a friendly warning, then she blasted you in her column. Welles's "conspiracy of silence" might end quite soon.

It was getting late in the day, and there was a lot more information I wanted to pump Flattop for. I asked if he'd like to go out for beer after he finished up.

"But you don't drink, Nick," he pointed out. Like I said, Flattop was perceptive.

I shrugged.

"There's a party out in Malibu tonight. They actually invited me." He smiled and there was the strangest mixture of pain and happiness in his weird eyes. "This is the first one I've been asked to since . . ."

I clapped him on the shoulder. "Don't sweat it, Pete." That was his name, actually. Peter Le Fleur. Sometimes I was jealous of him. His wild card was out for everyone to see, so he didn't have to lie to anyone about who or what he was, including himself.

Then again, I didn't get the joker treatment.

He folded his elongated fingers over my hand and I made sure I didn't flinch. It wasn't as if there was anything I could catch from him. "Thanks, Nick. If you want to tag along . . ."

I thought of Marilyn. "Wouldn't miss it."

The party was at Peter Lawford's beach house in Malibu. It was pretty exclusive: cast and crew favorites, along with Rudo and Strasberg and some others. Poitier was absent, but that was to be expected. And Davidson had talked his way in, so I wasn't the only stand-in.

Lawford was there, of course, three sheets to the wind, riding on the fame of his wife's brothers, one of whom was actually present. Robert Kennedy, the attorney general, was in the pool, flirting with Marilyn, as was James Dean.

It was a moment to make an entrance, and I took it. I did a 360 off the board and the water cleft perfectly. I'd had an athletics scholarship to USC and Olympic hopes, but I had to give them up when they started testing for wild cards, not that being an electric eel shaved any time off me in the fifty meter.

Once I came up, there was some gratifying applause and I managed to insinuate myself into the conversation with Marilyn. It was light politics, Dean going on about getting Tachyon back into the country, but the pauses let me discover what I'd heard rumored: Marilyn and Bobby were having an affair.

It wasn't any part of my ace. A detective just gets a sixth sense for that sort of thing. It's a matter of ordinary animal magnetism and body language. Bobby Kennedy wanted Marilyn and acted like he'd had her before.

Marilyn's reactions were more subtle, with a note of anguish underlying the laughter, but I could tell that she wanted Bobby in more of a primal way, more like a little girl wants her father than a woman wants a man.

Dean was attentive, but didn't desire Marilyn in any manner beyond the general. He had a long scar down one leg, visible even through the ripples of the pool. I'd never seen it before, but I knew it was a legacy of the car crash that had killed Liz Taylor and nearly claimed him, back at the end of *Giant*.

He didn't drive quite so fast anymore.

Marilyn hadn't given Dean a second glance, but she looked straight at me.

There was chemistry there, and it wasn't the sort you got with the wild card. I made a total fool of myself; but then, that was the general idea. Once or twice I felt Welles giving me a look, but damn it, I was more than just being paid to stick around Marilyn. I wanted to be with her.

The party went all night and I ran into a number of other hangers-on, the youngest of whom was Tom Quincey, a freshman from USC who looked younger and kept babbling on about Aldous Huxley and his book *Destiny and the Doors of Perception*. It seemed Huxley had been at the party, but had left early, though Tom was more than happy to tell me all about him and showed off some white tablets he'd left behind. "They're LSD!" he said. "From the Swiss pharmacy. See— they're stamped with the Sandoz mark!"

I'd never seen LSD tablets, but Rudo came over and explained that they were perfectly legal, nonprescription.

"Similar to mescaline," he said. "They expand perceptions."

To demonstrate their harmlessness, Rudo and Tommy both popped a couple. I chose not to indulge, not wanting to see what they did with my wild card, but Marilyn and the Lawfords tried some, and so did another Tom—Douglas, I think—a musician friend of Quincey's. Flattop amused everybody by taking the half-empty Coke bottle from his arm and filling it up the rest of the way with the Lawfords' rum and a couple of Tommy's tablets before plugging it back in.

Flattop, of course, got the first effects and started staring at the pool lights, with the Toms joining in soon after. Rudo didn't say or do much out of the ordinary, so I concluded that it was just like fraternity brothers getting drunk for the first time and Flattop and Tommy and Tom were playing it up.

There was something about Tom Quincey that set me on edge, though I couldn't quite say what.

Marilyn, however, thought him amusing. She said he'd followed her here from New York and had refused to go away ever since. I knew they had a relationship, too.

Welles and Trumbo were at loggerheads over the direction of the script—pretty much whether it would be "Orson Welles's *Blythe*" or "Dalton Trumbo's *Blythe*"—and Trumbo went into a paranoid jag about capitalist interests wanting to subvert the proletarian heart of his story. Welles told him to get stuffed and that the heart of the story was the romance between a New York bluestocking and an alien prince, and it would be hard enough getting it to play in Peoria without holding out for Moscow, too.

Everyone at the party seemed generally enthused for the project, with the exception of Paula Strasberg, and even she loosened up after Josh went on about the evils of the HUAC and how brave it was for Bobby and the president to end the Blacklist by going to see *Spartacus*.

Paula got drunk then and started to demand McCarthy's head on a stick, but people had to remind her that he was already dead and his head would be a bit moldy.

After the requisite head-butting, Welles and Trumbo tried to figure out who to get for Golden Boy and Harstein. Pat Lawford then mentioned that Jack Braun lived down the street.

I should have remembered that. After the eight-by-tens I'd taken, that's all he had left.

Marilyn, very drunk by this point, and stoned on an interesting mixture of Paula Strasberg's tranquilizers and Tommy's LSD, suggested that everyone invite him to the party. Who better to play Golden Boy than Golden Boy? He'd already done it in one movie.

This notion was entertained in varying levels of seriousness, but Trumbo thought it could be useful to at least get Braun's input on the script, he being the only one of the Four Aces both easily accessible and living.

Marilyn and Tommy, bearing bottles of champagne and wearing nothing more than bathing suits, elected to be the ones to go be neighborly and invite him over. I, being the only sober person left, volunteered to shepherd them down the street.

I can't forget Jack Braun's expression. He had a bottle of cheap scotch in one hand and the door in the other and I knew he must think he was hallucinating. I mean, if you open your door at ten o'clock in the evening, you don't expect to see Marilyn Monroe in a bathing suit, accompanied by a teenager and the detective who'd taken pictures of you *en flagrante delecti*.

Of course, I'd made sure Braun never saw my face—I'm not suicidal, no matter what you might think—and you don't take candid pictures of the strongest man in the world if you expect him to know who you are. All he must have thought looking at me was that I was another Malibu Siegfried, even if I was half-Irish.

I don't know of any man who'd say no to an invitation from Marilyn Monroe. That man was certainly not Jack Braun. He and his scotch joined the party at the Lawfords', and everyone was still there except Paula and Josh.

Braun got a lot of attention, but didn't want to talk about the Four Aces, or the script. He said he'd had enough of playing Golden Boy and wouldn't take the part. That was probably a relief—I don't recall Welles ever offering it. "I'm not a hero," Braun said between drinks. "I just get paid to swing on vines and talk to chimps. I don't even do my own stunts—They've found it's cheaper to get an actor who doesn't glow when he slams into trees than to retouch all the negatives."

To demonstrate, he stood up and pounded his chest, flashing gold like a strobe light, then gave a yell as he jumped into the pool in his clothes. It may not have been part of the mystery I was paid to solve, but I at least knew why *Tarzan* always used the same closeup of Braun beating his chest.

The rest of the evening went by in a blur. I wasn't drunk or stoned, but everybody else was, and that helped. I played the sober gallant and drove everyone home who didn't crash at the Lawfords'.

Marilyn didn't do either. The next day I discovered that she'd spent the night at Jack Braun's.

Braun followed her to the set, as under her spell as any man, though he'd joined the circle who'd actually gotten to touch her. I hated him for it, but then there was a peculiar scene that made me wonder just what I had to hate.

Braun was drunk, as usual, and stumbled out of Dalton's trailer. He was shouting back at Trumbo: "No, you're right, I'm a scum and I betrayed my friends. Everything should stay except the last scene—I never got a chance to say goodbye to anyone."

Braun walked down the street, kicking rocks into Sherman Oaks, and a cloud of French cigarette smoke materialized next to me. "A very troubled man, don't you think? He is haunted by his past. He does not think himself a hero."

I looked over to see Dr. Rudo, smoking one of his trademark cigarettes. He offered me one and his lighter.

I lit up, figuratively, and passed the lighter back. "He's not a hero."

"He could be, Mr. Williams. That is his great lie. He cannot ever be close to another for fear of hurting them."

I wasn't sure whether he'd said that to gauge my reaction, or if he just got off on summing up people's lives in a couple of lines. I think it was a little of both.

That was the last I saw of Braun, but I saw a good bit more of Dr. Rudo.

Marilyn ran round the studio in a daze of alcohol and Paula Strasberg's tranquilizers. I knew, though not from experience, that if you mixed the two you got a feeling of euphoria.

If what Marilyn was going through was euphoria, you can have it.

In the next few days, they contracted Ron Ely for Golden Boy and Jeff Chandler for Harstein. I never saw much of either, Ely for the obvious reason, Chandler because what few scenes he had with Golden Boy, he practiced with Ron. Jim Bacchus, the eternal father figure, came on as Archibald Holmes and kept making *Rebel Without a Cause* jokes to Dean: "Well, I see you've gotten into trouble again. Now we've had to move across the *galaxy*. I hope you're satisfied."

I did a quick prowl around Wally Fisk's apartment, but his fire had been thorough, and I didn't find anything not already included in the notes I'd gotten from Welles. The only thing I'll say about Fisk's detective work is that he'd constructed an impressive case that *someone* was sabotaging pro–wild card films. The question of who was left open. And the question of how *Blythe* was going to be killed was up in the air, as well.

And the only man who might have a clue had gone mad.

However, the scuttlebutt had worked its way around and I heard about Wally from Flattop and about six others. Now that it was safe, I sought out Dr. Rudo.

He said he'd had only one or two conversations with Fisk, but could hazard a guess as to what happened.

"Conscience, Mr. Williams," he said, flicking his cigarette. "Conscience can be a terrible thing. A private detective must bury his very deeply, or else it may rise up and destroy him. I suspect that is what happened to the unfortunate Mr. Fisk."

He asked if I knew what case Wally had been working on, but I said I didn't know. I didn't say how close he'd come to my own reservations about my profession.

That done, I called up a contact in the press. Now, I know I was supposed to keep my investigation secret, but let me explain: A major Hollywood detective had gone mad, and if I wanted an interview for a case I was not *officially* working on, I'd need an alibi for a case I was officially working on. Bit actors wear a lot of hats, and it's hardly unusual for one to pick up a little extra money as a spy or journalist. I slipped my press pass into the band of my fedora and headed down to County General.

Hospitals were places I'd always hated, and the lockdown ward was always the worst. It stank of urine and pain and sedatives. The set designers for *Blythe* had tried to convey the dismal inadequacy of a state hospital, but none of that could compare with the reality.

I talked briefly with the doctors and asked about the blood

panels, but they didn't show any sort of drug or poison. Wally was as clean as the next man.

He was also completely insane. They had him in a strait-jacket and I don't think he even recognized me. In the movies, the madman sputters some sort of cryptic clue, or shouts a warning at the investigator. Wally only stared at the wall and drooled.

The doctors were slightly more helpful, but not very. They only confirmed Dr. Rudo's diagnosis: acute attack of con-science. Wallace Fisk was being tormented by his own per-sonal demons and so far no therapy had helped.

I asked to have a little time with him alone, playing the role of grieving friend, though I was really just a shocked former colleague. But I knew a bit about shocks, including that the electrical sort could sometimes knock people like Wally back into some form of sanity.

As soon as the nurse had left, I popped one of my little lightning balls into my hand. Will-o'-wisps, I called them, 'cause they just sort of floated and bobbed unless I kept a grip with my mind.

This one was only three inches across, just a shocker, not even enough to knock someone out. I let it ground on one of the buckles of his straitjacket.

He jolted, but didn't change expression. I tried a couple more, a little larger, then bobbed one in front of his eyes kind of like a hypnotist's pendulum. I'd usually never risk some-thing like that, but even if Wally remembered, I could explain it away as the hallucinations of a madman.

I called his name several times until he blinked and I saw his eyes focus on the will-o'-wisp, then I let it slip back inside me and waved my hand in front of his face. "Wally," I said, "what do you remember? What's the last thing you remember?"

His voice was hoarse from not having spoken, but I got him to describe a relatively ordinary day snooping around the Fox lot, checking for anything that might look like sabotage, but not turning up any more than I had. He'd blacked out everything since then, which was good.

Then I made a mistake and asked him if he remembered me.

He turned and took one look at my face and started screaming and raving, well, like a madman. It was just like the stuff in the movies, lots of "Stay away from me!" and "No!" and "I didn't mean to!" and thrashing around enough to make the bed lift off the floor.

I didn't know whether I should shock him again or just get away, but before I could do anything, the nurses rushed in. They listened long enough to realize he wasn't making any sense, then got out the sedatives. A minute later, the doctors cornered me and asked what had happened.

I told them everything except my attempt at electroshock therapy, and they let me go, not much wiser, and a little less sane.

I went back to the studio and watched throughout the week. The mystery, however, was not much closer to being solved. Wally had discovered evidence of a conspiracy against wild cards, then had gone insane, imagining that everyone he'd ever lied to or investigated was coming to get him.

It explained why he'd burned his apartment—destroy it and destroy his files. But Fisk's reaction to my face . . . I don't think I looked very demonic, and only knew Fisk vaguely from past cases.

However, there was another face very similar to mine . . . belonging to Dr. Pan Rudo. Did Fisk have Rudo on his conscience?

Of course, Wally might have started screaming if I'd shown him a hand puppet, but I wasn't about to investigate Kukla,

Fran, and Ollie. Dr. Rudo, however, gave me the beginnings of an idea. A psychologist with a knowledge of drugs, especially psychoactive ones, might be able to brew a potion that would drive a man mad, but that would be undetectable with the standard blood panels.

Motive, however, was a problem. Dr. Rudo was Marilyn's psychiatrist, and if he wanted to kill the film, he had enough influence to make her quit and let it collapse on its own. And so far as hating wild cards went, Rudo showed no more disdain for Flattop than he did for anyone, and was actually kinder to Jack Braun than anybody should be.

Then again, maybe he was just currying favor with a potential client. If there was ever a man in need of a shrink, it was Braun.

As for the movie, *Blythe* was proceeding without a hitch. Trumbo had polished the script with Braun's input, the filming had begun, and I was becoming closer to Marilyn.

Maybe I wasn't quite honest about why I was around her— Welles was paying me, after all—but it hurt to see her with men who just wanted her for their own status. Bobby Kennedy wanted her because his brother had had her, Jack Kennedy wanted her because he was the president and could have anything, and Tom Quincey wanted Marilyn because he was a randy little bastard and wanted everything.

After one of the Lawford parties, he even propositioned me.

I didn't know what to make of it. I'd met boys who liked boys before, but I'd never met one who liked both boys *and* girls. To make things worse, I double-checked his school records and found that while he was a freshman at USC, he was also sixteen, not eighteen.

I didn't know if Marilyn knew. I hoped no one else did, or it could have been used to blackmail her.

And in addition to the boy genius with the non-preferential

dating habits, there was Dr. Rudo. When I asked about him, Marilyn, in a more drunk than usual moment, confided that she'd slept with him as part of her therapy.

I'd seen the signs, but I'd refused to believe them. Rudo went to the top of my list of all-time bastards.

I had half a mind to sic the AMA on him and get his credential revoked, but I knew the scandal would wreck Marilyn and wreck *Blythe*.

I also didn't want to betray any confidences. I may have been a spy, but if someone entrusted me with a secret, I'd take it with me to the grave.

I think I would have even kept it beyond that, if it weren't for the way things turned out.

But right then, things were turning out great. Now that main filming had begun, we stand-ins weren't quite as much in demand and I had more time to myself. Flattop held court in the cutting room, showing everyone the best of the dailies. They were the most powerful pieces of film I'd ever seen.

Blythe would be amazing once she was complete.

I remember one day I was there with Josh Davidson, watching the scene where David Harstein was locked in HUAC's soundproof glass booth. In the flickery light of the projector, Jeff Chandler beat against the glass: "All right, you Nazis! When are you going to turn on the gas? That's what you did before, isn't it?"

Josh's lips moved silently as he watched and there were actual tears on his face. "That's just the way it happened. It's just the same."

I gave him a pat on the back. "I know. They cut out the Envoy's silver tongue, clipped the eagle's wings, and shattered the mind of the woman who knew too much. They couldn't stand for anyone to be different from them."

Josh sighed. "And they put pressure on the strong man until he bent."

Flattop nodded as the clip came to an end, the impassive faces of Nixon and his cronies taken straight from the news-reels. "This is going to do great things for wild cards. People are finally going to get a chance to see who the enemy really is."

The lights came on and Josh stood up slowly, looking a little pale and shaken. "I don't know about you two, but I could use a drink right now. Anyone want to join me?"

Flattop smiled a bit shyly and held up his foot-long fingers. "Not many places take jokers."

Josh smiled. "Then we go wherever you go. My treat."

The Santa Monica Pier was the closest thing LA had to a Jokertown. Everything was so spread out, and there were so few wild cards overall, it wasn't something that would come about. The few aces and jokers the city had to offer before the McCarthy witch hunts had set up in the old carnival booths and freak shows along the pier, though the mind readers and crystal gazers had long since been snapped up by J. Edgar—at least the real ones.

The jokers were the ones left, and after a day of entertaining the tourists, they mostly kicked back at the Menagerie, LA's single joker bar. It was on the pier, next to the merry-go-round, and the few nats in the place were the fuzzy sweater set. That made me nervous more than anything else. The only things I liked Greek were the letters on my fraternity pin.

Flattop introduced Josh and me around, and I smiled and tried my best not to stare. The two I remember in particular were Richie, who the wild card had turned into a sort of human aquarium, and Panda Bear, who spoke bad pidgin like she was auditioning for a Charlie Chan movie. Her accent was Mexican underneath, not that I'd point it out to a lady, especially one with fangs and claws.

Josh and Flattop seemed to enjoy the beer, and I got by with soda water like I usually did. The conversation mostly went around *Blythe*—Flattop had told his friends about the project and they were all excited, especially with the prospect of being extras—and Hedda's latest column, where she'd called the Menagerie a "cesspit of freakishness" and said the city fathers should clear it and "all the other rubbish" off the public pier.

This went over like you'd expect it would, but you had to give it to Hedda, she was at least consistent—she'd never voiced approval for the Exotics for Democracy, even when they'd been making the cover of *Life*. And as she always pointed out, she'd disapproved of Hitler long before the war.

Sometimes I wondered whether I would have been as well disposed to wild cards if I hadn't been one. Somehow I don't think so.

Everyone swapped Hedda jokes and threw darts at her picture in the corner and there was a big laugh when Josh put on Panda's hat and got up on the table to imitate Hopper doing her "This is my town!" speech from her television show.

I stepped outside for a breath of fresh air. Something had been itching me all the time I'd been in the Menagerie. How should I put this? I needed solid ground under my feet. My ace made me sensitive to the electromagnetic spectrum, and I could sense where things were: people, electrical wiring, metal, the ground. It wasn't anything really clear, not like sight or hearing. More of a prickling in the back of my neck and the hair on my arms. I was used to feeling the ground beneath me, both as a barrier and a sap to my power. It was gone, along with the clutter of metal struts and power lines, and I'd gone hypersensitive. The free ions were soaking into me like heroin into an addict.

And for the past hour, I'd felt something moving underneath me, under the pier. It moved too regularly for it to be coincidence, and it left metal behind, where there hadn't been any before.

Call me drunk or paranoid, it was probably some guys out crabbing, but I'd been twitchy around the studio with absolutely nothing happening that wasn't supposed to, and I couldn't figure out why crabbers would be hanging traps six feet *above* the waterline.

I dodged the few candy wrappers scudding around in the sea breeze and found a ladder leading down the side of the pier. I hesitated, wondering if I shouldn't just mind my own business, but then Flattop and Josh showed up.

"You okay, Nick?" Josh asked. "Anything bothering you?"

I had a sudden urge to tell him everything—and I mean *everything*—but I took a deep breath of the wind coming in off the ocean and the impulse passed. "I dunno," I said. "Just twitchy, I guess. I heard something funny under the pier."

"Probably sea lions," Flattop said. "They sleep on the crossbeams."

I knew it wasn't sea lions suspending crab traps above the water line. "Anyone care to play detective?" I didn't wait for an answer, just swung around onto the ladder and led the way down.

Josh was a little tipsy, and so was Flattop, but I was so hyped and paranoid that I didn't question the wisdom of taking a couple of drunks on a jaunt through the underpilings of a pier. As it turned out, I shouldn't have worried about Flattop, anyway, since those overstretched digits of his let him climb like a monkey. Josh got by by holding on to his belt.

I don't know if you've ever been under a pier, but halfway down there's a whole network of beams and cross-joists, sturdy enough to support almost anything, though it's generally just used by the sea lions who hop up at high tide. It was low tide now, a good twelve-foot drop to the water below.

I followed the prickling in my skin, avoiding the occasional sea lion, and soon heard the sound of an outboard motor. That was the main source of electricity. On one of the nearby pilings, a metallic circle gleamed in the reflected light of the water.

A boat had tied up to the pilings, and three men were busy affixing another to the tar-soaked wood with duct tape. From the size and shape, I knew exactly what it was—a film canister.

Maybe I should remind you, since it's generally known only in Hollywood, but film used to be made with nitrocellulose. That's half of what you make dynamite with, and any blast you see in a motion picture generally comes from a few old reels and a match.

I probably don't need to tell you that, but from what happened next, all I can say is that they don't breed for brains in New York. The outboard engine had covered the sound of our arrival and the men in the boat hadn't noticed us yet, but then Josh called out as loud as he could, "Excuse me! You don't want to be doing that, do you?"

They turned around and next thing there were guns out. Flattop pulled Josh to the planks, which was lucky for him since a moment later a bullet whistled through in the space where he'd been.

That was all the time I needed. My St. Elmo's fire was up and my will-o'-wisps were out. They went straight for the guns.

Honestly, I'd only thrown shockers, not enough to kill a person, just enough to zap them unconscious, but electricity has a mind of its own and it *likes* metal. You run a couple hundred volts through a loaded gun, well, all I can say is, you don't have a gun anymore.

You don't have a hand, either, not that it mattered, since

there were a couple strays, one of which went for the engine, the other for the stuff in the bottom of the boat.

The explosion would have looked good on film, if you like things like that. Bodies flew everywhere and I fell to the planks next to Josh and Flattop, struggling to pull my St. Elmo's back inside before I killed them, too. Salt water splashed over me and I felt the energy arc and sizzle.

Then there was a gurgling sound as the boat went under. In the distance, I could hear the barking and splashing as frightened sea lions jumped back into the ocean.

A moment later, everything was back to normal except for a few bubbles and bits of flaming debris on the surface of the water.

Josh was babbling something about there being too much wind, then Flattop looked at me and I almost gagged at the hero-worship in his weird eyes. "You're Will-o'-Wisp . . ."

I looked away. "Yeah, I guess so." The film spool taped to the piling glinted evilly, a white envelope stuck to its face, water dripping from the corners.

"Who's Will-o'-Wisp?" Josh asked.

I gritted my teeth, wishing Pete would take that note out of his voice. "Will-o'-Wisp's a hero. He's saved the lives of a lot of jokers. He's about the only one who protects us out here . . . but no one knows who he is."

I looked over at Flattop, now being supported by Josh. I shrugged. "I got an ace. I shocked a few people I saw beating up jokers, and no one seems to remember your face if you've got glowing eyes."

I lit them up with a little foxfire for demonstration. I'd done it a few times in the mirror, and I knew that under the shadow of a hat it could make you look pretty scary. More than that, it kept people from remembering my face, which is important if you're up the sleeve.

"'Who knows what evil lurks in the hearts of men . . .'" Josh intoned.

"Beats me, but it sure as hell isn't the police." I took out a cigarette and used a tiny will-o'-wisp as a lighter.

I didn't even have time to take a puff before the bomb's envelope went up in a flash of blinding white fire. We hit the planks just as a second explosion blew, louder than the first, without the water to cushion it.

Once my eyes cleared from the dazzle, I saw what was left behind: the piling, cracked through and bent sideways. Small flames licked at the tar-soaked wood.

"Oh, shit," Josh said.

Oh, shit was right. I totally lost it and my St. Elmo's went up like a beacon. I got to my feet, bristling with energy, and moved away from Josh and Flattop so I wouldn't run the risk of killing them, too. My mind went into overdrive as the pieces clicked together. The dripping envelope. The magnesium flare. The blast.

"The tide's the timer," I said. "We've got to disarm the suckers before the water gets high enough to finish the job." One of the things I'd learned was that bombs got a lot more powerful the greater the resistance around them. Anything that could crack a piling on the surface could shear right through underwater.

I could feel where the other canisters were taped to the pilings, but they were too far down for me to reach. But Flattop— I swear, the man could literally hang upside down by his toes. His X-Acto knife made short work of the duct tape, and he came back up with a bomb, the envelope-fuse thankfully dry.

It was hard, but I pulled the St. Elmo's fire back inside myself, then gingerly pried the envelope loose from the tape. Underneath was a strip of gray metal, the end leading to a hole drilled in the upper edge of the canister. The seam where the halves fit together was carefully tarred shut, waterproofing the ensemble until the tide did its work.

I slit the envelope with my penknife. Inside was some glittery powder. I dropped it into the water and it went up in a flash of white fire.

Pete touched the metal strip. "Magnesium."

I nodded. "In the powder, too." I carefully pulled out the wire, then got out my penknife and pried apart the halves of the canister.

Black and gray flecks drifted free, dancing in the ocean breeze. Just like I thought, someone had run film through a coffee grinder. Messily, since there were a few larger chunks and snippets mixed in.

I took out one of the largest and held it up to the Moon. The film was scratched, but the image was still clear: Jane Russell and her bosom got up in a western outfit. I slipped it in my pocket and closed the canister.

The fuse was simple stuff with a formula out of any chemistry textbook: three parts ammonium chloride, three parts ammonium nitrate, and three parts powdered magnesium. Stuff you could get at any hardware store, nursery, or chemical supply company. The same with the magnesium strip. Or the whole ensemble could be found in the special effects department of a movie studio. It was the Jekyll and Hyde formula: The mad scientist pours a vial of tap water into a beaker with a dusting of the powder in the bottom and a photogenic flare goes up. Add magnesium wire and some canisters of nitrocellulose and you could kiss the entire Santa Monica Pier goodbye.

Flattop collected the remaining film bombs and we took them back to the trunk of my car. While we did that, Josh used his jacket to beat out the flames on the one demolished piling. Do you find it suspicious that the police never came to investigate the explosion? So did I, which is why we didn't call them.

"Jesus, Nick," Flattop said as I locked up the trunk, bombs carefully defused. "I never knew you were an ace. And man, not just any ace . . . you're Will-o'-Wisp."

"Shut up," I snapped. "You don't know what you're talking about. You got rid of the bombs, and you didn't have to kill three people to do it."

"But Nick—"

"Let him be," Josh said, and Flattop shut up.

I was really rattled. I'd only killed once in my life—before I'd figured out how to measure my charges—and I'd sworn I'd never do it again. Guns and explosives were something I'd never really taken into account. A private detective doesn't make his living by getting in firefights, and the bastards I'd dealt with before had been into baseball bats and nailed boards.

And I'd just blown my cover. There were now two people who knew I was Will-o'-Wisp. And one of them was a nat and the stupidest blabbermouth I'd ever met. Josh's speech under the pier should have won the Oscar for idiocy.

"Josh, please. You can't tell anyone this." I fumbled with my keys, not making eye contact. "You've got my life in your hands."

"Don't worry." He patted me on the shoulder and helped me into the car. Ironic, isn't it? The drunk helping the sober man. "I was in New York the first Wild Card Day. I had friends infected with the virus. And I know what can happen to aces who get found out. Believe me, I know."

I don't know why I believed him, but somehow I did. And I didn't worry about it anymore. Maybe when you reach the breaking point, you find it's either that or go mad.

This is going to sound like the craziest thing, but it's what honestly happened next. Josh suggested we go to a party, never mind the load of bombs in the trunk, and Flattop and I thought it was the greatest idea in the world.

I don't know if we'd been invited to the Lawfords' that evening. It didn't matter—Josh talked our way in, we borrowed swimsuits, and it was like a dozen other parties. Marilyn and I flirted shamelessly.

Finally it got so late that everyone had to call it a night. Flattop and Josh hitched a ride with Trumbo, but someone needed to drive Tommy back to the dorms. I volunteered, being sober as usual, and Marilyn came along for the ride.

As soon as we left the party, my conscience and worry started back up, eating at my brain. I'd killed three men. Two people knew my secret. I was driving down the Santa Monica Freeway with the Goddess in the seat beside me and enough nitrocellulose in the trunk to blow up a pier. And to top it off, there was a sixteen-year-old sex maniac in my back seat giving a discourse on surrealism, metaphysics, and the need to break through mental barriers.

I think the effort it took to stifle my wild card was the only thing that let me keep my sanity.

Once we'd dropped off the boy genius, Marilyn said she wanted to go for a swim. Like I said, I'd gone to USC and had been on the swim team. I also had a key I'd never turned in and went and swam laps whenever I got stressed.

I'd kept myself in good shape.

The pool was in the basement of the athletics hall. It was like something from a DeMille epic, an old twenties aquatic gymnasium with green tile around the edges and heraldic dolphins at the corners.

The ceiling was high above the pool, with windows along the sides covered with wire grates, but the effect was more like stained glass than an athletics hall. And the light shone up through the water and reflected off the enamel, the patterns shifting and changing as you swam.

We were alone, and the pool was silent except for the echoes.

Marilyn took off her dark glasses and scarf and laid them on one of the chairs. I caught a whiff of her perfume—*Scandal*, I think—then she put an arm around my shoulders and I could smell the champagne on her breath. "Oh, Nickie," she laughed. "This is so silly. I forgot my swimsuit back at Peter and Pat's.

"Oh well," she said, "it's not as if we weren't born with swimsuits." Before I could stop her, she slipped away and stripped down to her bra and panties.

"Marilyn, no, you're drunk." I grabbed for her as she stepped back toward the pool.

I didn't get Marilyn. I got her bra.

She fell backward with a splash, then came back up, her famous breasts bare in the water. "You're wicked, Nickie."

"Marilyn . . ." I leaned over, holding out the bra, but next thing I knew she pulled me over into the pool, on top of her.

I came up sputtering, and she dunked me a second time, then swam away, laughing. But it's a mistake to turn your back on a would-be Olympic swimmer. I kicked off my shoes and followed.

Marilyn got to the edge of the pool and started to pull herself up on one of the dolphins, but I pulled her back in. We wrestled, and somewhere in there her panties slipped off.

"Ooh, Nickie, you *are* wicked . . ." Marilyn screamed with laughter and pounced on me. The panties went flying out of my hand.

I let her get her revenge and we played strip water polo, my shirt and socks and the rest drifting down to the bottom of the pool. It was one of the craziest and most wonderful moments of my life. We played tag, ducking and bobbing under the water, then came close, our arms around each other.

Marilyn gave me a long, slow kiss.

"Nickie," she said, drawing back. "You're always so tense. Dr. Rudo says you're keeping secrets. Lots of them."

It was that obvious, then.

"Tell me a secret," Marilyn said.

I was tempted to tell her then and there. I mean, she'd slept with Jack Braun. She wouldn't care if I were an ace or a joker or whatever I was.

But it was my life, and it was all I had. And no woman could ever love a murderer.

I gave her the old line: "If I told, then it wouldn't be a secret."

"You're crying, Nickie," she said. "Dr. Rudo says that tears are secrets trying to come out."

It was just the chlorine, but I held her then, her skin against mine, naked in the pool. I could feel the electricity flowing inside her body, and the tight core of energy coiled inside mine, wanting to come out. I knew if I said anything more, I'd lose control, so I kissed her.

She was the first woman I'd kissed in years, and I think I really did start to cry. I never let myself open to another person. Secrets are like that. Lies are like that.

And a relationship built on lies would never last. I knew that from experience.

And I knew it would be the same with her, and I think that was most of why I cried, but God she was beautiful. I wanted her so much, but the energy was boiling up inside me and I knew if I gave off a pulse too close, I would shock her to death.

I broke away and swam off, fast as I could, to the other end of the pool. I let my entire charge flow out and forced it through the bolts of the underwater light to ground itself in the wiring. The bulb popped like a strobe and all the lights in the hall went dark, but the charge was gone and I was safe and drained and crying like a baby.

Marilyn swam up beside me in the dark pool as I babbled something about faulty wiring and electrical danger.

"Shh, Nickie," she said. "Sometimes you've just got to let things happen. I want you, and if you want me, I'm here."

She floated there like some water nymph from an old tale, Lorelei or Calypso or Nimue. I reached out to touch her breasts and she drew back, then laughed and grabbed my arms, drawing me toward her.

We fit together, mouth to mouth and body to body, and her legs folded around me as my arms went around her.

We did it right there, in the pool, in the dark, with the shadows dancing off the ceiling and the echoes calling back to us from the corners of the gymnasium.

If there was anyone who saw, they never interrupted.

When it was over, we were both giggling with nervous laughter, Marilyn's intoxicated, mine drunk on fear and sobriety. And love.

She'd wanted me for me. And she knew I kept secrets and didn't care.

I think I could have loved her just for that.

I was in love, for the first time, really, and so, I think . . . at least I'd like to think . . . was Marilyn.

I was like a giddy teenager. It was like nothing I'd ever had, even before the wild card.

But you're probably wanting to know what happened with bombs and all that. The next day Flattop and I went through the larger snippets, but had trouble placing them. The breakthrough came from Marilyn.

Marilyn had been friends with Jane Russell ever since *Gen-*

tlemen Prefer Blondes, and she identified the first clip I'd found. "Oh sure, Nickie," she said. "That's from *The Outlaw* Jane did for Howard Hughes. But don't show Jane. The film was an absolute *bomb.*"

I gave Marilyn a kiss and she forgot about it, but I didn't. The rest of the snippets came from *The Outlaw* and other bad adventure flicks, all from RKO, owned and operated by one Howard Hughes.

Hughes's paranoia about disease was legendary, so it was likely he'd been behind the bomb attempt, not that there was anything you could prove.

The Hearst papers carried an article about a Japanese mine from World War II drifting into the Santa Monica Pier. How it managed to hit six feet above the water line was never explained.

The pier was closed for "structural damage" and the Menagerie was shut down, though in a much less bloody fashion than was no doubt planned. A check of public records showed the long arms of Howard Hughes and Willie Hearst pulling the strings. Hopper's column raved about the planned renovation, during which no doubt the Menagerie would lose its liquor license.

In an unrelated piece, the bodies of three men were found washed up on the beach. The corpses were identified the next day as belonging to three of RKO's special effects men. The obituary listed the cause of death as a "boating accident." Their names correlated with Wally's suspects for several sabotaged pics.

I had evidence, but nothing I could present to anyone, Welles included. And it was just more conspiracy work for the files—nothing about any particular plot against *Blythe.*

But Marilyn was the key to the whole house of cards. If she fell, the whole thing would collapse. I stayed close by her during the day, and at her house at night. There really wasn't anything else I could do.

She had a small place in Brentwood, with an inscription above the portico that read *Cursum Perficio*, "My journey ends here." Sometimes we dallied in the house, and sometimes in the pool in the backyard, memories of our first time together.

I felt like I had come home at last.

During the day, I escorted Marilyn around the set and played stand-in what little time I had to. And at night, back at her place, Marilyn told me her nightmares.

Sometimes she woke up from them screaming like a little girl and begged me to hold her until they went away.

Her nightmares . . . How can I describe them? In one she was Mary Shelley, talking to her husband about the baby she'd lost. Then he'd console her, and say that she was the mother of far more, since hadn't she created *Frankenstein* and given her nightmares to a thousand people?

And then there was the one where she was Cleopatra, and it was like the last scene of the movie, except the asp talked, and it said, "You are the Goddess. You are the Queen. And I am all men and I will have you. And I will kill you."

And then, trapped in the motions of the story, she dropped the asp down the front of her dress. But instead of biting her, it crawled inside her.

And she knew her body was not her own.

Then she was Guinevere from *Camelot*, singing "The Simple Joys of Maidenhood" just like Julie Andrews on Broadway. And as she did, the bodies of her admirers piled up around her feet, one after the other.

There were a dozen others, sometimes as many as three a night. Sometimes I did nothing but hold her, and sometimes we did nothing but make love until the nightmares went away.

And sometimes, during all that, I wondered if it were the LSD that had caused the nightmares, or perhaps something else.

And every afternoon, she had a session with Dr. Rudo. I didn't like to think of what they did together, or the trysts she had every week or so with either of the Kennedy brothers, but whenever I raised the subject, she just laughed. "Nickie, you're so old-fashioned," she'd say. "We're all sexual creatures. If I make love to another man, it doesn't mean I don't love you. And anyway, it's part of the treatment."

Dauerschlaf, that's what Rudo called it: the long sleep. Marilyn had first come to him for her insomnia, and then for her other problems. Sometimes she said she felt like a thousand women packed into one. *Blythe* was almost autobiographical.

Schizophrenia ran in her family. It had claimed both her mother and grandmother. She didn't want it to claim her.

Whatever the problem, I didn't believe that sex was a necessary part of any therapy. What did Dr. Rudo do with boys? But somehow, bastard that he was, Rudo's cure seemed to be working. Marilyn got better for all the bad dreams. She drank less, and slept more without tranquilizers.

And her acting became heartbreakingly beautiful. I wasn't the only one to cry when I saw her do Blythe's final scene. And her last coherent words:

"Tisianne, hold me. I can't bear them any longer."

Seeing her in the straitjacket as she descended into Blythe van Rensseaeler's madness, I was reminded of Wally Fisk. While Marilyn and I had made love, he'd swallowed his tongue and died in the hospital.

"A brilliant performance, no?" Pan Rudo stood next to me and lit another cigarette. The smoke curled lazily from his fingers. "You find it very beautiful, but very disturbing as well. Some personal meaning, perhaps?"

He shook forward a cigarette from his case, but I got out one of my own and used my own lighter. "Do you always state the obvious, Dr. Rudo?"

He tapped his unlit smokes back into line and snapped the case shut, slipping it into an inside pocket.

"Frequently." He took a lazy pull from his cigarette as the scene broke down and Welles called it a wrap. "There are so many lies and self-deceits abounding, it's often useful to remind oneself of the facts. 'To thine own self be true,' as Shakespeare put it. Wouldn't you agree?"

I blew some of my own smoke in his direction. "I've always been more of a 'Pay no attention to the man behind the curtain' man myself."

He laughed. "I never cease to be amazed by you, Mr. Williams. I always keep thinking I've found your heart, but all I get is another matryoshka doll. What's inside the last, would you say? Pins and sawdust? Clockwork springs? Or is there really a lion's heart of flesh and blood?"

I looked into his eyes, cold blue mirrors of my own. "Being that I don't wear it on my sleeve, Dr. Rudo, I don't think you'll ever have a chance to find out."

He leaned back on one heel, regarding me. "Perhaps, Mr. Williams. Perhaps."

He broke off the look abruptly. The witch had arrived, hat and all.

Hedda was wearing a salmon-pink linen skirt and jacket, with a matching hat: salmon felt decorated with silver applique waves and, I kid you not, an honest-to-God, life-sized gold-lamé fish lunging after the fly that dangled from the miniature rod stuck through the crown.

"Pan, darling!" Hedda cooed. "And dearest Nicholas! What luck to find you both here!"

Rudo paused and looked to me. "You know Hedda, Mr. Williams?"

It was the first time I'd ever seen him taken off guard. Hedda breezed right in between us.

"Oh pish, darling," Hedda said, "you know I have my little spies everywhere." She reached up and pinched his cheek, then linked arms with me and patted the back of my hand. "Nicholas and I go back a long way."

Rudo took a long drag on his cigarette. "I should never be surprised by anything you know, Hedda."

Hedda laughed and led me a ways off into the set. "So, Nick, what you got for me?"

How should I put this? Hedda owned a lot of people in Hollywood. One of the ones she owned was me. She'd given me a couple breaks early in my career—back when I was nothing more than a frightened young actor—and she made sure I knew I owed her. I was part of her spy network, and that, more than anything, was what got me to turn pro at it.

That press contact I'd phoned in the Wally Fisk story to? That was Hedda. The job for Welles had been a conflict of interests since the beginning.

I wondered what Flattop would think. His hero, the ace Will-o'-Wisp, was a spy for Hedda the Hat.

I sighed, recalling the list I'd prepared for her. "Well, Jeff Chandler has a new girlfriend. And I told you about Wally Fisk . . . he died this morning."

"Old news, dearest," she said, patting my hand. "I put it in this morning's column. Now, tell Mother what she wants to know: What's the job you're doing for Orson? Wally's old case?

"Now, don't look so shocked, dearest," Hedda said as I struggled to keep my St. Elmo's from springing up and killing the old hag. "Mother knows lots of things, and who do you think it was who got you this lovely job? The moment I heard about poor Wally, all I had to do was have dearest Kimberly drop a word in Orson's pudgy pink ear and voilà! Here you are.

"So now, my little Nicholas, tell Mother the dirt."

Have you ever been caught so off guard you can't speak? That was me. I was so good at deceptions, I'm surprised I didn't come up with one immediately.

"And no lies, Nicholas," Hedda said. "Mother can tell. And," she said significantly, "since I know Kimberly, if I find out you've lied to me, I'll be forced to tell the truth to Jack Braun. You know him—the glowing freak with the photogenic bottom and the hands that can punch through walls? You're considerably thinner than a wall, Nicholas, and I'm sure he'd have no trouble at all getting through you. And wouldn't that be a horrid scandal."

She smiled, as if relishing the possibility, and I swallowed. Electric ace or not, there was no way I could stand up to Golden Boy.

I wish I'd had the stomach for cold-blooded murder. Hedda had her arm around mine, and all it would take was one jolt to send the old harpy to Hell. But I knew the nature of the beast I was dealing with—upon her death, Hedda's lawyers would send packets to various addresses, and there was no way of knowing whether a sheaf of photographs would be her bequest to Jack Braun.

I settled for the simple truth and told Hedda the gist of Wally's investigation. All I said about my own work was that it had been fruitless—nothing about the little altercation under the pier, or the unprovable connections to Howard Hughes and Willie Hearst.

Hedda clicked her tongue. "My, my, how very interesting. You've done well, my little Nicholas. But isn't there something you're not telling Mother?"

I shook my head, smiling. It was hard, but I told myself that even if Hedda found out, I could hide behind J. Edgar. Golden Rat may have been the strongest man in the world, but the one thing he was frightened of was the Feds.

Hedda pinched me on the cheek. "Oh come now, Nicholas, don't be so shy. I've heard the rumors. You've been seeing Marilyn, haven't you?"

I blushed, feeling the strangest mixture of fear and relief. There was a reason why Hedda called her home "The House That Fear Built."

She crowed with laughter. "You're so wonderfully ingenious, Nick. I think that's why you've always been one of my favorites." Hedda extended her hand to be kissed.

I did it carefully, holding down my gorge and my ace.

"Thanks, Nicholas," she said. "You're a dear. But as they say at Disney, TTFN—ta-ta for now!"

Hedda left, the fishing fly on her hat bobbing like some satanic sound boom, and I slumped back against a piece of scenery. My life was swiftly becoming a nightmare.

But there's never bad without some good. That evening I lay in bed with Marilyn, just holding on. There was so much I wanted to tell her, but couldn't.

"Shh, Nickie," she said, stroking my hair. "Shh. You can tell me when you feel it's time. But I have something to tell you."

"What, Marilyn?"

"I talked with Dr. Rudo this afternoon. He's interpreted my nightmares, and says I have a choice: I can be all women to all men, or one woman to one man." She paused and I looked up into her blue eyes.

"Will you be my one man, Nickie?"

I began to cry, hugging her, holding her. "Yes."

She kissed me and we made love.

"There's one other thing, Nickie," she said once we were

done. "I'll never be whole until I have a child. I hope you like children."

"I love children, Marilyn."

A few days later, she told me she thought she was pregnant.

"And it has to be yours, Nickie," Marilyn said. "I've counted, and Jack and Bobby always use condoms, and Pan's had a vasectomy."

That satyr had an appropriate name, at least. I asked about Jack Braun and Tom Quincey.

Marilyn shook her head. "I gave Jack a blowjob and he passed out. And Tommy's sweet, but we were through months ago. It has to be you."

It was then that I realized that with all the pills she'd been taking, none of them had been birth control.

And I'd never used a condom.

She begged me to keep it a secret. With as many as I had, one more wasn't any trouble.

But, oh, God, what a dilemma. If Marilyn had a child conceived out of wedlock, the controversy would wreck the movie. Possibly her career.

"It's my career, Nickie. I can wreck it if I like," she told me. "I can do anything I want."

But I'd heard Marilyn's nightmares and her whispered confidences. She'd had abortions before, and I knew one more would destroy her.

There's an old legend that will-o'-wisps are the souls of unbaptized children. In Marilyn's dream, they were the souls of her abortions. They haunted her night by night, saying, "We are the dead and we are secrets and you will never know who we are. That is our vengeance and that is how we will haunt you."

She loved me, she said, but she could never marry a man who couldn't tell her his secrets. One more secret and she would die.

I didn't tell her any of mine, let alone my nickname for my little ball lightning charges. But I held her in my arms all that night and told her that the ghosts would go away if she would just name them. And one by one Marilyn named them, all seven, until she fell asleep in my arms.

I didn't sleep well at all, knowing all that. But we all make sacrifices for our careers, and Marilyn's had been her children. I know that the law makes her a murderess, but I couldn't bring myself to hate her for that. Maybe it sounds crazy, but as she fell asleep against my chest, I think I loved her all the more.

The weeks flew by and March passed to April. Marilyn was Blythe as she had never been and I was alternately stand-in or spy, but my heart wasn't in either. It was with Marilyn. Welles had hired me to save his movie, but I knew the greatest threat to Blythe was our love, and I wouldn't kill our child or destroy the woman I loved to save a strip of cellulose. It was none of his business anyway.

Hedda wasn't even a consideration. She'd discover everything in due time through her other spies. I'd even give her a refund if she complained.

Otherwise, everything was perfect. The conspiracy of silence had broken down of its own accord and there was some grudging press and commentary, spiced with Hedda's venom and Louella Parsons's treacle.

And then there was another party at the Lawfords', grander than the rest since it had a theme: Walpurgis Night.

It was the brainchild of Rudo and Quincey, a dress rehearsal for the May Day celebration they planned to hold on May second, a day late, when both Bobby and Jack Kennedy would be in town. Marilyn planned to spend the night with them. I wasn't pleased, but I knew that if you tried to hold a butterfly, you'd crush it.

Marilyn said it was one last fling, and I had to take that on faith. I tried to be open-minded.

But April thirtieth, Rudo explained, was a traditional time for the opening of the gateways of perception, and beyond that, a good excuse for a masked ball.

Nobody took it seriously aside from a few domino masks, with the exception of Tom Quincey. He'd got himself up in drag as Guinevere from *Camelot* and did an a cappella version of "The Lusty Month of May" as the Lawfords' grandfather clock struck midnight. Everyone thought it was amusing except Marilyn and myself.

Tommy danced around handing out Sandoz tablets like candy and Dr. Rudo had brewed up an Indian punch using peyote buttons. Marilyn wanted me to take some, but vomiting until you hallucinate wasn't my idea of fun, even if I weren't an ace.

She got me a Coke instead, and I nursed it along as everyone around me drank every variety of alcohol along with Rudo's mescaline punch. I hadn't gotten drunk since college. You don't know what it's like being a teetotaler in a fraternity.

The pool lights sparkled as they came on, and it was then that I noticed that I was glowing. My St. Elmo's fire was out, a crackling blue aura around me, sparking and making the lights flicker as I fed on the power.

I tried to damp it. I really did, but then I saw everyone looking at me.

No one said anything for a long while, then finally Tom Quincey went, "Wow, man! Colors!"

I ran off down the beach, trying to get away. My whole world had suddenly fallen apart. I had suppressed the power for so long, it had finally struck back. The wild card had played its cruelest trick on me and I knew I was going to die, I was getting so dizzy, and I fell down on the shoreline.

Then all my nightmares were around me. Everything I'd always feared would happen. Jack Braun standing over me, glowing gold to my blue: "You bastard. You think you're so much better than me. I only hurt people because I was scared and stupid. You did it out of spite, nothing else. Traitor ace."

Then Hedda Hopper: "I always knew you were a joker, Nicholas darling. But now that you know I know, I own you—unless you want everyone else to know." And I saw her smile. Then there was the Olympic committee taking away medals I'd never won, and J. Edgar Hoover with draft papers, a choice between prison or disappearing somewhere where I'd never see anyone I loved again.

And Marilyn: "Sorry, Nickie. I could never love a sparking electrical freak, so you might as well go, anyway."

Then she was slapping my face and shaking me. "Nickie! Nickie! What's wrong?"

"I'm an ace." I'd finally said it, admitted it to her, to myself, to everyone. "I was glowing. Everybody *saw*."

She splashed some water over me and I came to a bit more. "Nickie, nobody saw anything except you screaming and running off down the beach. Pan said you needed to loosen up, so I slipped some of Tommy's pills in your drink. I'm sorry. I didn't think you would have a bad trip." She paused and a look passed through her eyes. I still don't know how to describe it. "What do you mean about being an ace?"

I broke down then and I really did start to glow, and Marilyn did notice this time. Tears poured out of my eyes, glowing with foxfire, and I forced the charge out of myself and down the wet sand and into the ocean. For a moment, I think the sea glowed, though that may have just been my imagination.

Then I told it all to Marilyn. Everything I've just told you and more. All my nightmares and my tears.

I must have passed out at the end, since I didn't know where I was until I woke up on somebody's couch the next morning.

Marilyn was there. She said that after I'd passed out, I was still sparking, so she couldn't touch me. She'd run and got Jack Braun and he'd carried me up to his house, and his glow had probably covered mine, so she didn't think anyone else would know. Know that I was an ace.

Nobody but Marilyn and the greatest betrayer in the history of wild cards.

She was crying. I could never stand it when she did that. I think her tears were why I first fell in love with her. She said she was sorry she'd given me the pills, but she hadn't known I was an ace, and she said she never would tell. She said Jack promised not to, either.

Marilyn called in sick to the studio for both of us. I was so raw with nerves I could hardly move, so she drove me back to her house.

She left me by the pool while she went to fix lunch. But I had the beginnings of an idea, the product of nightmares and panic: LSD, whatever the stuff was, caused nightmares. I knew it. Mine had been living and waking. Marilyn's came at night.

And Wally Fisk? His had driven him mad.

But doctors know ways to determine the effects of drugs. Marilyn, though it was awful, was slowly getting over her problems. Maybe I would have, too, if they hadn't been so big, or if the LSD hadn't made me lose control of my ace. But Rudo, I was convinced, could make a far nastier mixture if he had a mind to. The connection was firm, if circumstantial.

And the motive? Rudo may not have hated wild cards, but there was someone who did. And there was Rudo's comment: "You know Hedda?"

You didn't *know* Hedda. You feared her, then either avoided her or worked for her. If I had to suspect someone in Hollywood of masterminding a conspiracy against wild cards, there was only one name that would be at the top of my list.

She was just so obvious, I'd never suspected her.

Rudo was the perfect pawn—he could be anywhere on the set, spy out anything she wanted him to, and at the end of production, one of his cigarettes in the film locker and *Blythe* would be as dead as the original, with no shame to Marilyn or her career, or Rudo's finances or reputation.

I kissed Marilyn and rousted her out of the house and off to work, telling her not to tell anything to anyone, especially Dr. Rudo. I then got on the phone to Hedda, dropped enough hints to leave her drooling, and said I'd be in late to give her the full stories.

She was interested. She'd wait up.

I spent the afternoon back at my place constructing a careful stash of rumors, then set out for Hedda's.

It was near midnight, but she was still there, alone in the office after everyone had left. In some perverse way, I always admired the woman. She worked harder than anyone I knew. It was what she worked at that I had problems with.

Hedda had composed herself for my entrance. That was one of the ways you could tell that she liked you. She had on a blue wool skirt and jacket and this huge hat with ostrich plumes and stuffed doves and ropes of faux pearls. I'd heard that the one time they'd met, Dr. Tachyon had kept after her to tell him the name of her milliner. She'd used that to pillory him in her column for months. The lavender boy from outer space—that's what she called him—and I guess that's the other thing I agreed with her on. People were dying of his virus and he was concerned about hats.

"Nicholas, darling," she said, smiling. "Let's see what you have for me." I gave it to her and she typed for a few minutes, then got on the phone and called in last-minute changes.

"Thanks, dearest. That was very useful. So, what favor would you like?"

I hadn't counted on her being that pleased, but as she'd said, I was one of her favorites. "You guess."

Hedda dimpled, cocking her head. "You'd like your little tryst with Marilyn to stay silent until you're both in . . . less embarrassing circumstances."

I nodded.

Hedda clucked her tongue. "Nicholas, dearest, you're going to ruin your career if you aren't wiser with your choice of jobs. And," she said, "you may tell Marilyn that associating with these wild card freaks won't do her any good, either. My husband had blue skin and not a hair on his body, and the only thing I can say is that it's a good thing for Wolfie that he died before this virus ever showed up. No good can ever come of it, no matter what anyone says."

I'd heard her stories about DeWolf Hopper and knew that an overdose of silver nitrate and a bout of rheumatoid fever could make a joker out of anyone. I think bad memories of Hopper left her ill disposed to any other "freak."

Hedda showed me out and locked up behind her, and then I played the next card in the game: I drained my own battery.

It wasn't hard. I was a good enough actor to fake my car not turning over, then once I'd flipped up the hood and put my hand on the negative terminal, the battery was well and truly dead. The trick was keeping the charge from making me glow.

Hedda came over and tried to start my car, but of course she didn't have any luck, either. She also didn't carry jumper cables and I'd made sure to leave mine at home.

In the end, I got what I wanted: Hedda let me into the office to use the phone to try to find an all-night towing service, and told me to lock up when I left.

Once she'd gone, I got out my camera and went into her

private files. Hedda kept great records and I'd taken impressions of the keys back when I'd worked for her.

Hedda really couldn't blame me. She'd taught me the trade.

There was the file: Rudo, Dr. Pan. I flipped it open and was immediately struck by the swastika stationery, but after I parsed through a bit and looked at the comments in Hedda's handwriting on the attached page, the reason for the hooked cross and the size of the sword over Rudo's head became clear: In 1938, Dr. Pan Rudo was in Vienna, experimenting on mental patients with his *dauerschlaf* technique under the auspices of the Nazi party. Five died before the Nazis felt it best for Dr. Rudo to leave for Switzerland. He'd gone to New York afterward, perfecting his technique all the while.

I thought of Wally in the hospital. The easiest thing to repeat is a mistake.

I took pictures of everything in the file, reading through occasional bits and glancing into related files.

Hedda seemed to have a whole clique of agents called the "Card Sharks." Dr. Rudo was one, helping her in her crusade against wild cards, not that I would expect a Nazi to have any compunctions about genocide.

Hedda's partner, or perhaps just contact with other sharks, was J. Edgar Hoover. The files were stuffed with FBI transcripts, courtesy of same. Likewise, money came from Howie Hughes and Willie Hearst, and they were responsible for some jobs. There was a copy of a letter from Hedda to Howie, blistering him for having bungled the job on the Santa Monica Pier.

There was also a file on Will-o'-Wisp, the ace vigilante. Hedda had got my height and build right, but the rest was wild speculation and frothing. I was a major priority for the sharks, either termination or conscription.

Then I got to Marilyn's file, sticking a little out from the others. There had been a recent addition.

It was an obituary. It isn't unusual to find obituaries in the files of celebrities. What is unusual is to find them postdated, describing the manner of death. It was scheduled for May 3.

I remember that column as if I'd read it last week. It was last week, for me.

The headline read: BRILLIANT CAREER CUT SHORT.

Hedda had written below that: Marilyn Monroe—brilliant life, tragic death. What happened? Ask Jack and Bobby! Pretty Marilyn was due to wish Jack "Happy Birthday" at his big fundraising bash in New York come the nineteenth, but evidently Jack wanted to have his present early. But he and Bobby played too rough and the pretty toy broke.

"Hedda told Marilyn never to go near that Lawford house. Marilyn paid the price for not listening to Mother, but let's see the Kennedy boys weasel out of this one! The Kennedys, the most famous crime family in America!"

It went on from there. The plot was simple: Tomorrow John and Robert Kennedy would be staying the night at Peter Lawford's. So would Marilyn, as I already knew.

Dr. Rudo would slip Marilyn just a few too many of Paula Strasberg's trademark tranquilizers, so the Kennedys would be sure to wake up with the corpse of Hollywood's greatest star.

The president and the attorney general would be politically ruined. Paula Strasberg would be implicated for manslaughter. And Marilyn would be dead before the filming of *Blythe* was complete.

I got it all, then carefully put the files back in order, my hands shaking all the while, and I know I was sparking from the stress.

I went to the outer office, made sure to move the phone book and the telephone slightly out of line, locked up, then went and recharged my battery.

It was 4 A.M. by the time I got home. I put the film in the

developer first thing. I wanted to call Marilyn, but for all I knew, J. Edgar had the phone bugged. Hedda had her spies everywhere. I should know.

But oh my God, I didn't know where to turn. I could tell Welles, but what would he do? Make a film of it? Likewise with Trumbo and the rest. And Flattop? I could trust him, but there are some things people are better off not knowing. It would be like telling Poitier about the KKK.

The police were out of the question. Even the ones I knew I could trust would have to hand it up, and J. Edgar would know about it before the day was out. Hoover had been Hedda's conspirator since before HUAC.

There was only one possibility: Marilyn. Marilyn Monroe was one of the world's greatest actresses, no matter what the critics said. If she could just elude the Card Sharks' snare without arousing their suspicions, she could live to deliver the negatives to the president.

I knew just the time: Jack Kennedy's "Happy Birthday" bash at Madison Square Garden. On a stage in front of a million people with a thousand flashbulbs popping, Hedda's Card Sharks wouldn't dare try anything. Marilyn could deliver the evidence into the president's hands without anyone the wiser and the sharks would all fry for treason.

I got the negatives and a double set of prints into an envelope and arrived at Marilyn's house just before seven. Her housekeeper, Mrs. Murray, let me in, and I surprised Marilyn in the middle of putting on her mascara.

I take it as a measure of her trust for me that she didn't do anything other than grab her makeup case after I got the overnight travel bag she always kept packed. My expression must have spoken worlds.

I don't know what Mrs. Murray thought. Maybe that we were eloping, I don't know.

I got Marilyn into the car. She took one look at my face, then silently paged through the stack of photographs I handed her. I headed west and we hit the Pacific Coast Highway.

It was either Northern California or Mexico. I headed north. I wasn't sure where we were going, but it had to be far away if we wanted to miss Dr. Rudo's May Day celebration.

At last, Marilyn put the photographs back in the envelope. "These are Hedda's, aren't they?" I think she said.

I nodded, then I couldn't take it anymore. I pulled to the side of the road by one of the beaches and poured it all out to her.

She just listened silently, then asked for the keys. She said she knew a place up the coast, the Brookdale Lodge, an old inn up in the Santa Cruz mountains. It had bungalows in back and the folks who ran it were very discreet about who was staying there, at least until after they left.

The iron butterfly. It was such an appropriate name. I'd just revealed a plot against her life, and she calmly went about finding a place to hide until the storm was over. Marilyn made me take one of her tranquilizers, and I slept in the car on the way up.

It was then that I realized I had told Marilyn my secrets, my fears, my lies, all of them. And she still loved me. It was the most wonderful day of my life. It was also the most frightening.

Marilyn took charge of the espionage game as if she'd been born to it. She got us a room, then went to the local bank, rented a safe deposit box and secreted one set of photographs.

Then we went back to our hotel room and she called Welles, laughing and apologizing about having stolen his Golden Boy stand-in for a quick jaunt. She asked him to convey her apologies to the Lawfords and the Kennedys, but she just couldn't stand the pressure. Still, she'd make sure not to miss the "Happy Birthday" bash later that month.

I was seeing a great actress at work: Pretend you've run away for a short fling, then call and apologize to everyone you've let down. The Strasbergs' Method served her well.

At the hotel gift shop, she bought a toy tiger. She ripped a seam in its neck and slipped the negatives inside, then stitched it back together with her sewing kit. It was the perfect thing to give the president as a present in front of a million people. I hid the last set of photographs under the carpeting in the trunk of my car.

The getaway was mad and beautiful. Marilyn took me out to dinner at the inn, which had a creek running through the old Victorian dining room. She said there was supposed to be the ghost of a priest or a drowned girl who walked through every once in a while, but we never saw it.

Funny, isn't it; a dead man telling ghost stories.

And then came the hardest thing I've ever done. We drove back down the next day, the day Hedda's column was supposed to run, and pretended that nothing had happened. Marilyn went on with her role, and Welles called me into his office and chewed me out. He'd hired me to protect his movie, damn it, not run off with the star, make them run a day over budget, and piss off the president and the attorney general in the process.

I tried Marilyn's Method, doing Lovestruck Swain Grovels Before Boss. I managed not to get fired, but mostly, I think, because Welles didn't want to upset Marilyn. If I'd become her pet, well, he'd dealt with bigger expenses, and at least she'd lightened up on the pills.

Marilyn had gone off them all cold turkey, in fact. She couldn't swallow even one, knowing that they were the intended murder weapon had the Card Sharks' plans for her succeeded. She drank more, though, and two days later fired Dr. Rudo. I got to watch the scene as she tore into him, calling him the most overpriced gigolo in Hollywood, and under-endowed to boot. She threatened to tell the AMA and Louella Parsons how many times they'd had sex on his psychiatrist's couch.

It was a spout of venom worthy of Hedda. Rudo glared at me the whole time, but I didn't say a word.

That evening I got a call from Marilyn. She wondered if I could come home a bit early. I didn't even question the reason; I knew how much pressure she was under. I think the only thing that held us together that week was holding each other in our arms at night. I hadn't gone to my own place except to pick up clothes.

I slipped into Marilyn's house, under the portico with its strange little inscription: MY JOURNEY ENDS HERE. I never thought of it as an epitaph. It sort of fits, you know.

I went inside the house and called Marilyn's name. Then I heard her voice from the backyard, stuttering like she always did when she was scared. "N-Nickie, could you come out here?"

I didn't suspect anything. I really didn't. When your nerves are that raw, it's either suspect nothing at all, or suspect everything and go mad. And I'd already seen enough of madness.

I stepped outside the house, and in the late afternoon light I saw the impossibly high hat stacked with a florist's shop of silk begonias, Hedda and a chromed pistol resting in the shade beneath. She sat in the deck chair as if she were a countess holding court, one leg crossed over the other.

Marilyn sat to one side in another chair, clutching the toy tiger, while Dr. Rudo sat a bit behind and kept a businesslike Luger pointed at her back.

"You see," Marilyn said then. "There's n-nothing to be shocked about. He'll do whatever I want."

I came closer, taking Marilyn's signal, and put my hands in

the air where both Hedda and Rudo could see them and where I could throw my will-o'-wisps.

"Hello, Nick," Hedda said as if it were nothing more important than one of her afternoon teas.

"You've always been practical, so please don't play the hero. You'll just get both yourselves killed."

She pulled back the hammer of her gun. "Stand by the edge of the pool, please."

"Your scheme's ruined, you know," Marilyn said.

Hedda bowed her impossible hat slightly. "I know, darling. You've really fucked things to a turn."

"I'm pregnant," Marilyn said.

There was a moment of dead silence. At last Hedda licked her lips. "Could you repeat what you just said, dearest?"

"I'm pregnant," Marilyn said it with the exact same tone and inflection. "Do you w-want to know who the father is?"

Hedda paused, the nature of her profession plain on her face. "Does it have any bearing on the present situation?"

"Most l-l-likely, since the father is either J-Jack or Bobby Kennedy. I f-found out last week."

"Are you considering an abortion, dearest?"

"No." Marilyn said it definitely, with force. "I'd decided I was going to h-have it, both for myself, and to spite all the m-men who've u-used me."

There was a look on Rudo's face I couldn't quite make out. "Which men, Marilyn?"

"Jack. Bobby," she said, and her voice became harder, clearer. "Zanuck. It would serve them all right. It was going to be the one thing I was going to do for myself. Darryl Zanuck stuck me on this lousy jokers pic for the last spot on my contract and there was nothing I could do about it. Except this."

She gripped the toy tiger in her lap, her knuckles turning white on the plush fur. "If I puff up without a husband, the protests will wreck any pic I work on. It'd serve Zanuck right to have to swallow the entire budget for gypping me on my contract. And the scandal would toss Jack and Bobby out on the street with the jokers they love so much. I planned to sink this filthy jokers pic myself."

Marilyn turned toward Hedda, slowly. "You don't believe me. But there's a lot about me you don't know, Mrs. Hopper. You want the exclusive? When I was nine, I was *raped*. By a joker." Her face contorted and tears began to run down her cheeks, smearing her mascara. "It was at my foster parents' house. One of them—you know I had four different sets. These ones rented out rooms, and one of their boarders was a joker. He had these furry green eyebrows that moved when you talked to him, but I'd been told he was a nice man, and I was too young to know what sort of monsters jokers were. So I went into his room and he took out his penis and it was all spiky. Sharp, green spikes, curving backward, like a foxtail, and he . . . he . . . stuck it into me."

She let go of the tiger and her head collapsed into her hands. "He r-raped me," she blubbered between her fingers, her voice quaking like a little girl's. "I bled for days. And I was so ashamed I never told anyone.

"It was years before I learned that normal men weren't like that. All green and spiky." She shook with sobs. "You know some of it, Dr. Rudo. I told you about Flattop following me around. I'm afraid of him. His penis is probably as stretched out and spiky as the rest of him. His diseased body makes me sick."

Hedda and Rudo looked as if they didn't know if they were hearing the truth or a Method actress giving the performance of her life. But I knew from Hedda's expression that Marilyn was offering a scandal that would both kill the movie and hang the Kennedys with rope to spare.

"Darling," said Hedda, testing, "I know you've spent the night with Jack Braun."

Marilyn shrugged, straightening back up and wiping some of the tears from her cheeks. "That was business. I've done a lot worse on the casting couch than just give a joker a blowjob to get help with a script. His dick's normal enough. And," she said, "a girl does what she has to."

I was the only wrinkle in the plan, but Marilyn was working to take that out.

"N-Nickie always wore a condom," she said. "I m-may be a little tramp, but I'm not going to have a love child by a no-body." Marilyn looked at me. "Sorry, Nickie," she said, "but you're nobody special."

I think that was a signal for me to use my ace, but God, I don't know. Hedda and Rudo had guns. And I knew from the encounter under the pier what happened when you ran a charge through one of those. The shrapnel from Rudo's Luger would kill Marilyn if the bullet didn't first.

But Marilyn looked at me, the tears running down her face. I never could bear to see her cry.

I focused my ace as hard as I could, large charges, kill-ers, but tightly bound so they'd go straight for Hedda's and Rudo's heads and avoid the guns. I hoped, I prayed.

My will-o'-wisps may have been lightning springing from my hands, but they didn't move that fast.

And Hedda's trigger finger was faster.

The shot hit me in the chest and the pain made me lose con-trol as I fell back into the water. My will-o'-wisps lost cohesion, dissipating harmlessly. And the blood flowed out of me along with the electricity, my ace sparking around me, grounding into the pool.

I struggled to keep my head above water and then I saw Hedda and Marilyn and Rudo standing there, looking at me.

"Oh my God," Marilyn breathed then in the most horror-struck voice I've ever heard, "he's a j-joker."

"Didn't you know, my dear?" Hedda asked.

Marilyn slowly shook her head, dropping the toy tiger. "N-no."

"Well," said Hedda, "then you shouldn't have any trouble killing him."

Hedda passed Marilyn the pistol. She looked at it for a second as if she didn't know what it was, but then she seemed to reach some sort of decision and slipped her fingers around it. I know Rudo must have had his Luger pressed into the small of her back, but I couldn't see, and God, she did it so fast and so easily.

Marilyn raised the gun, and one by one her tears fell into the pool. But I don't know whether they were tears of pain or hatred.

I can still hear her last words to me: "Goodbye, Nickie."

And then . . . there was an explosion and I felt the water close around me. And then I don't remember anything until I woke up here, with Ellen.

And I don't know. Don't you understand, I don't *know*. Ellen says Marilyn had our child, a son, but I don't know him, and I don't know if he knows about me.

And I don't know if his mother still loves me, or even if she ever loved me at all. She said she didn't care that I was an ace, but she never did like jokers, and then there was that story from her childhood.

She made things up and you could never tell the truth from the fiction. You just had to trust her. She was so many women. You never knew who was the real one.

She killed me, you know. It kind of makes you wonder.

The Ashes of
Memory

8

Emotions were warring within Cameo/
Nickie. Her shoulders lifted in silent, gulping sobs, mixing incongruously with Nickie's narrative.

"I've seen the birthday party clip a dozen times or more," Hannah said into Cameo's weeping. "Marilyn singing 'Happy Birthday' to JFK, blowing out the candles on the cake, and handing him a stuffed toy. It wasn't a tiger, though—I remember a penguin."

"Cameo told me," Nickie/Cameo said between sniffles. "Maybe she gave the stuff to the Sharks, maybe she just got scared, maybe she decided to tell Jack later. If she'd given all we had to him, everyone would know. There would have been a public scandal, high-ranking, wholesale firings in the White House staff and cabinet, an uproar within the FBI. None of it happened. Instead, Kennedy was assassinated. Makes you wonder about that, too, doesn't it?"

Hannah shrugged, but it didn't keep away the shivering

chill that crawled up her spine. "I'll have to look up *Blythe*. I don't remember seeing it."

"The picture was never released," Nickie told her. "Hedda got her way. Marilyn had a nervous breakdown and couldn't finish the shooting, and they didn't have enough in the can to edit around it. Welles tried to redo the picture with a different actress, but he couldn't keep the rest of the cast or the production staff together. Then the funding dried up."

"And he ended up doing wine commercials."

"Everyone has to make a buck. Welles never starved, not anywhere close, and at least he got to live his life. I don't exactly feel sorry for him."

Cameo had bowed her head forward, still sobbing between Nickie's words. The fedora slipped off. With that, some inner dam was rent. She brought her legs up and hugged them to her chest, burying her face as the tears came fully. "Ahh, Nickie," Cameo wept. "Why did you have to die?"

Hannah rose from her chair and went to the woman. Sitting alongside Cameo, she hugged her, and Cameo clung to her briefly before pulling herself away again. "I'm sorry," she said. "I'm sorry."

"It's okay. Thank you for letting us meet Nick. I know it must have been hard for you."

Cameo nodded, red-eyed. Hannah hugged her again, then picked up the fedora from where it had fallen to the floor. She set it carefully on the couch next to Cameo. Rising to her feet, she caught Quasiman's eye and nodded toward the door.

Hannah closed it softly behind them.

"I don't understand," Quasiman said. "Why is that woman crying? Who is she?"

"She's someone who fell in love with a ghost, a man who died before she was born." Hannah bit her lower lip. Suddenly the dreary decor of the Dead Nicholas seemed appropriate.

She slid her mask back over her face. "C'mon," she said to Quasiman. "I think we need a drink."

"I shouldn't have had that last drink," Hannah said. Her voice seemed to be coming from someone else. She frowned hard, trying to concentrate. "What a lovely list: Meyer Lansky, Henry van Renssaeler, both dead; Phillip, Baron von Herzenhagen, still around and moving in high circles; Dr. Faneuil and his kindly nurse, Margaret Durand, lurking around in the background; Zb . . . Zbag . . . Zbingniew Brzezinski—my, I sure mangled that name—making a fortune as a Washington consultant, no doubt; George G. Battle, last seen having fun wasting jokers on the Rox. Now we can add Hedda Hopper, William Randolph Hearst, J. Edgar Hoover, and Howard Hughes. At least they're all dead, everyone but Hughes, but then no one's seen him in years. Oops, I left out Marilyn. And did I mention Pan Rudo? I think I did, didn't I?"

Quasiman didn't answer. She hadn't expected him to, since he'd been sitting motionless at the table for the last half an hour. "I should probably put old Malcolm Coan on the lish . . . I mean list. You know, I do believe I'm just the slightest bit drunk," she said to the comatose joker. "Hope you don't mind."

Hannah downed her Rusty Coffin Nail. There were five empty glasses in front of her. The ghostly waiter drifted toward their table and whispered to her in a sibilant voice, "We all know Quasiman. He's all right here. If you need to leave . . ."

It seemed a good idea, somehow. Hannah, scowling in concentration, paid her bill and called Father Squid. "Don't worry about our friend," the priest said. "He has his own ways home. And, Hannah, I know it's just a few blocks, but please don't walk. Call a cab." Hannah did that; twenty minutes later, it still hadn't arrived. Hannah called again. "He's on his way, lady. He should be there any second." With a glance back at Quasiman, still sitting motionless at the table, Hannah went outside to wait.

Outside, the streets were only sparsely inhabited. It was Wednesday, hardly a party night, anyway, and Jokertown had lost much of its luster as a tourist attraction in the last few years. The first problem had been the jumpers: gangs of sadistic teenagers with the ability to take over someone else's body while imprisoning that person in theirs. Then the joker named Bloat had taken over Ellis Island and renamed it the Rox, proclaiming it to be a refuge for the jumpers and all jokers. The invasions of Ellis Island by the various authorities had been bloody and bitter, leaving behind a legacy of hatred between jokers and nats. Positions had polarized. Even with the masks, even in the "safe" streets around the edges of Jokertown, this was not a place where nats felt comfortable anymore. There'd been too many reminders that hatred was a sword that cut both ways.

A black and yellow–checked taxi idled at the light half a block up. Hannah stepped out into the street to wave at him, but when the light turned green, the fare light went off and the taxi turned right and away.

"Hey! Damn it!" Hannah looked up and down the street. No other cabs in sight. The bus stop was a block and a half down and the streetlight was out next to it. Hannah started back to the sidewalk. Her head was spinning.

A car pulled around the corner. Hannah didn't know why she suddenly felt fear that dissolved the fumes of scotch in her head. Maybe it was the way the car hugged the curb as it turned, maybe the fact that all the windows of the Lincoln were tinted so dark as to be almost black, or the slow way it approached. Hannah watched it, held for a moment like a deer in its headlights, then backed toward the curb. Tinted windows shushed down in the rear, and a head wearing an H. Ross Perot mask stared at her.

Hannah started to run for the entrance of the Dead Nicholas.

The Lincoln accelerated.

It was such a small sound. A cough. Something hot and fast slammed into Hannah and spun her around. She screamed at the pain, surprised to find herself sprawled face down on the sidewalk. Someone—she could only see the feet—came out from the Dead Nicholas and she heard the Lincoln squealing away around the next corner. Hannah tried to turn her head to follow the car, to see if she could see the license plate, but her head wouldn't turn and it seemed that the lights had gone out anyway. Even the entrance to the club was dim now and the pain and the wetness on her back seemed to be feelings experienced by someone else and there was yelling and a person was screaming but it all sounded distant . . .

. . . so distant . . .

The arms of the octopus coiled about her. Screaming, she ripped one of the sucker-laden arms away, tearing her flesh, but a tentacle still curled around her waist, another at her throat, yet another around her legs. The beast, an unseen, black presence just below the surface of the water, pulled her inexorably toward itself. Rising now above the waves, its great, lidless eyes glaring at her, the hooked beak of its maw clicking as it brought her nearer and nearer. She struggled, but it was useless. She could smell the creature now, and it smelled like the open door of a slaughterhouse. It smelled of sewers and piss and corruption.

It smelled of death.

"Hannah? I'm sorry, Hannah."

She opened her eyes. Quasiman was standing in the far corner of the hospital room, away from the hospital bed, like a child sent to his corner. An IV drip burned in Hannah's arm and her chest and shoulder were swaddled in gauze underneath the thin gown. Her lips were dry and cracked, and she'd scraped her face on the concrete when she'd fallen. One eye seemed swollen shut. "It wasn't your fault," she said, her voice cracking. Hannah frowned. There were vague memories: of an ambulance, of serious faces hovering over her and someone saying something about an exit wound. "Who did it?"

Quasiman snorted. He lifted his powerful shoulders. "No one knows. No one cares. The police came, wrote down their reports, and left." His fist pounded slowly against the wall: *Thunk. Thunk. Thunk.* "I had to have seen it before. I must have known. Why didn't I remember?"

"Quasiman." *Thunk.* He looked at her with bleak eyes. "Stop it. It's not your fault. No one blames you. You can't control when and where your mind goes." Without warning, then, the tears and the fright came. Hannah shuddered, gasping for breath, then fought back her control. She forced herself to breathe slowly, biting her lips. She sniffed, dabbing at her nose with a Kleenex from the box alongside her. "Ouch," she said, and gave a short laugh. Quasiman was watching her, her own anguish reflected in his gaze. "That's the second time someone's tried to kill me," she said. "Y'know, I don't really like the experience." She tried to smile at her joke and couldn't.

"You can give it up," Quasiman said. "I'd understand that."

"So would I."

The voice came from the doorway. Hannah turned her head. David was standing there, a bunch of carnations drooping from his hand. He seemed to remember the flowers at the same time. He held them up apologetically, then set them on the stand alongside the bed. "You look like hell," he said.

"You were always such a romantic, David." Hannah didn't know what to say or feel. *The last time I saw you I was leaving. You were telling me how stupid I was.* Not knowing how to reply, she retreated into polite nothings. "Thanks for the flowers."

"Uh-huh." He was dressed in the Italian-styled tailored suit he'd bought that summer, his expensive Hart & Dunlop overcoat on his arm. His hair was newly trimmed. "You going out, David?" Hannah asked.

"The governor's in town. There's a party. Lots of high muck-a-mucks will be there: the mayor, Judge Bradley, Brandon van Renssaeler . . ." The familiar last name gave Hannah a physical shock, but David didn't notice. He wasn't even looking at her. David was only too happy to be talking about himself. "In fact, Brandon's responsible for inviting me. I've been handling some litigation for the firm. There's talk that maybe President Barnett will come up from Washington, and—"

"I'm so happy for you."

David stopped in mid-sentence. His mouth clamped shut and Hannah saw him slip into his lawyer face, the noncommittal, oh-so-serious, and oh-so-rational mask. "I see you've worked on your sarcasm since you've been gone."

"Hey—" Quasiman said, and David nodded toward the joker without looking away from Hannah, frowning.

"The nurses tell me the hunchback's been in here since you were brought in. They don't like it. Why don't you tell your friend to take a hike? You and I have things to talk about."

Any remaining illusions Hannah might have had dissolved with the words. "I won't tell him that because he is my friend," she told him.

"Hannah," David began, but Quasiman cut in.

"It's okay, Hannah," he said. The joker shot David a glance that Hannah couldn't decipher. Some silent communication seemed to pass between the two men. "I'll be right outside," Quasiman added.

And the joker vanished, soundlessly. Hannah enjoyed the involuntary yelp that David let out. "Goddamn freak." Then the lawyer mask slipped back into place. "Hannah, I won't beat around the proverbial bush with you. I've talked with Malcolm, and believe me it took a lot of talking, but because of the good publicity the Bureau's received after you solved the case, he's agreed to ignore your little scene with him. The job's still yours." He smiled. *Like I'm a puppy being handed a bone: "Sit up, girl. Roll over, girl. Good girl."* Looking at him, Hannah knew that David expected gratitude, that he expected her to thank him, maybe even to cry in relief. Disbelief at his arrogance drove away her pain and she sat up in the bed, ignoring the pulling of torn muscles in her shoulder.

"I didn't solve the case. It was handed to me practically tied up in a bow. I'm still working the case."

"Hannah, the arsonist has been found. Please do yourself and everyone a favor and drop this paranoid joker fantasy of yours. There's no conspiracy. There's no hidden agenda. It was a psychotic's lone deed and it's over."

"Yeah," Hannah said bitterly. "That's why someone tried to kill me last night."

David leaned over the bed, his well-tailored bulk throwing a shadow over her. He shook his head. "No one tried to kill you, dear," he said softly. "Not this time. Believe me, if someone had actually wanted you dead, you would be dead."

Something in his tone made her stomach churn. "What are you saying, David?"

"I'm saying that if I had my pick of weapons and wanted to

take someone out, a .38 handgun wouldn't have been my choice. And even as few times as I've fired a gun, I'll bet I could hit something more than your shoulder at the kind of range you were hit."

"You're telling me this was some kind of accident? A drive-by shooting by someone out for thrills? Just another psychotic, right?"

"I'm saying that it might have been a warning, Hannah." He was a silhouette against the room's overhead light, but she could see his eyes, gleaming down at her. She chose her reply carefully.

"If it was a *warning*, David, then someone has something to hide. If it was a *warning*, then my fantasy plot exists. You can't have it both ways." It came to her then. She wondered how she missed it until now. "Are *you* part of this, David? Is that why you're here tonight, to make sure the message is delivered and I understand?"

David gave an exhalation of disgust and moved away. "You *are* getting paranoid," he said. "I meant a warning from God or fate or whatever. A warning that fooling around in Jokertown is stupid. Just listen to yourself, Hannah. You've gone totally around the bend on this. All I'm doing is trying to find some way to convince you, one way or the other, that it's over. Drop it, Hannah. Please. For your own safety and sanity, drop it."

"No." The quickness and vehemence of the decision surprised even Hannah. "I can't."

David was shaking his head, as if he were confronting a rebellious teenager. Then he waved his hands in disgust. "Then I give up. Have it your way, Hannah. I've tried to help you, but you won't let me." He put on his overcoat and started for the door.

"David?"

He turned.

"Take your fucking flowers with you. Give them to the governor for me. Better yet, stick them up your ass."

"That's cute, Hannah. Very cute. Almost a great exit line, but I have a better one for you." David smiled at her. "Goodbye, Hannah," he said, and left.

The nurse came in about an hour later. Hannah was drifting off to sleep; Quasiman was again at his post in the corner of the room, his eyes staring unfocused at some inward vision. "How are you feeling?" the nurse asked.

"About as well as I could expect, I guess. When can I get out of here?"

The nurse smiled. "Tired of the food already, eh? The doctor will be in tomorrow morning. We'll see what he says then." She went to the IV stand and checked the bag of saline. She adjusted the drip, then reached into her pocket for a large syringe. She opened one of the feed lines to the IV and inserted the needle.

"No," Quasiman said. He'd stirred and moved silently next to the nurse. His massive hand was around her, preventing the woman from pressing down on the plunger.

"Hey!" the nurse said. "Get off me!"

"No," Quasiman repeated. "Hannah . . ."

"What is that?" Hannah asked the nurse.

"It's just a sedative, to help you sleep." She struggled; Quasiman kept his grip and at the same time pulled the syringe from the IV. "Tell him to let go or I'm going to have to call security."

"It's a lie, Hannah. I saw it," Quasiman said stolidly. His other hand pried her fingers from the syringe; with a cry of pain, the nurse let go. Quasiman glared at the woman, then turned to the bed. "Hannah, we can't stay here any longer."

"Go! Now!" Quasiman yelling at Croyd, the explosion just behind them . . . "All right," Hannah said. She threw the covers aside. Grimacing, she ripped off the tape holding the IV and slid the needle out of the vein. "You can't do that," the nurse said in alarm as Hannah stuffed a tissue in the crook of her elbow to stop the bleeding and swung her legs over the side of the bed.

The nurse was very nearly right. The room did a lumbering waltz around Hannah and the stitches in her left shoulder screamed. Hannah gasped, then forced herself to stand. She nearly fell.

The nurse had gone to the wall and slapped a button. A red light flashed above the door and an alarm sounded distantly. Hannah started for the door and realized she wasn't going to make it.

"Hannah!" Quasiman was talking to her, one hand still holding the syringe. His arms were open wide, as if he wanted to embrace her. "Come here."

"No." Hannah took another step toward the door. The nurse was yelling, and she heard running footsteps from outside.

"Hannah!"

She looked at him. She was sobbing now, in hurt and panic and fright. "I never let you get near me," she said.

He simply held his arms wide. Someone appeared at the door and Hannah threw herself toward Quasiman. His arms closed around her. He smelled like anyone else, his skin felt like anyone's skin, and his embrace was strong yet gentle, like a lover's.

"Now, Hannah," he said. Hannah hugged the joker tightly, one-armed.

And they were gone.

— — —

Dr. Finn came into the bedroom of Father Squid's apartment. The centaur looked as if he'd had a hard night at the clinic. "Insulin," he said without preamble. "A nice heavy dose of it."

"What would have happened?" Hannah asked him.

"You'd have drifted into insulin shock. Considering that you've been shot, the resident's best bet probably would have been that the shock was due to some continuing internal blood loss they'd missed. Because of the shock and supposed loss of blood, the book response would have been to give you fluids. So the first thing they'd've done is crank your IV wide open, giving you even more insulin."

"And?"

"Convulsions. Then death." Dr. Finn sniffed. "In a busy hospital, they might never have figured it out, unless someone knew what to look for."

Hannah took a deep breath. She looked at Quasiman, sitting next to the bed. She found his hand, squeezed it. "Thank you again," she said.

"I should report this." Dr. Finn's tail lashed. "It makes me sick."

Hannah shook her head. "You can't," she told him. "We don't have any evidence. None. Anyone in the hospital could put the insulin in a syringe. For all we know, the nurse may have been entirely innocent; someone else could have prepared the syringe and told her to give it to me."

"Then what can we do?"

"Let me work. Let me figure this out. And . . ."

"Yes?"

"Could you leave us alone for a minute?"

Dr. Finn glanced at Quasiman. Shrugged. "Sure." With a graceful turn of his palomino body, Dr. Finn left the room. Hannah looked at Quasiman. "What's my name?" she asked.

"Hannah. I remember."

"I haven't been very nice to you. Do you remember that, too?"

"That wasn't important. I didn't write those parts down, and I never told Father."

"Quasi—" She stopped, her voice breaking. "Come here a second. Yes, that's it. Now, bend down . . ."

She grasped his head with her good arm. Kissed him. His lips were warm and soft, and they yielded slowly. "Why?" Quasiman asked when she released him. He remained stooped over her bed, close to her.

"I don't really know," she answered truthfully. "Just tell me that you'll remember it, okay?" She smiled at him, stroked his cheek. "I don't care if you forget the rest."

"I'll try," he said earnestly. "I'll try very hard."

Brandon van Renssaeler . . . *In fact, Brandon's responsible for inviting me . . .*

Van Renssaeler had an interesting history, Hannah discovered, almost as interesting as his father's. In the late sixties and early seventies, a rising young lawyer in a powerful firm, he'd also performed gratis work for the UN and WHO. Now established and well respected, blessed with his family's wealth, with looks, and with a brilliant legal mind, Brandon moved in high circles. Among his friends and companions were senators and representatives, corporate executives, and presidential advisors. He'd separated from his first wife in the late sixties, though they never officially divorced. He and his current paramour attended all the right functions and appeared regularly in the Society pages of the *Times.* They looked to be very happy.

Brandon van Renssaeler's marriage had not been so pleasant.

And it seemed his ex-wife lived in Jokertown.

- - -

"It's hot, Hannah," Quasiman said.

"Like Saigon, huh?"

"Have I been there?"

Hannah sighed. "Yes." The side parlor of the brownstone was at least 90 degrees inside, though the foyer had been cool enough. The person who escorted them in, an older man who looked perfectly normal, had begun sweating. "She needs the heat," he said and smiled. "You'll see. She's waiting for you in the rear room."

The man left them. The heat was quickly transforming Hannah's bangs into matted, dripping ringlets. Hannah had worn a coat against the early October chill; she took it off and loosened the first button on her blouse with her good hand. It didn't do much good; under the sling that held her left arm, her blouse was already soaked. Her pantyhose were sticking to her uncomfortably. "Let's go in," she said to Quasiman. He didn't answer. His legs were missing below the knee. Hannah touched his arm softly, squeezing. "Wait for me," she told him, even though she knew he couldn't hear, then called out loudly, "Hello? Mrs. van Renssaeler?"

"Come on in, my dear. Don't be shy." The voice sounded like that of a mature woman—a soft, pleasant alto.

Hannah followed the sound of the voice into the back room.

The room was dominated by a thick oaken branch, as if a tree had jabbed one of its lower limbs into the house from outside. The only other furniture in the room was a small couch with a coffee table on which sat a plate with pastries and a sterling tea service with a cup and saucer set alongside it. The couch was obviously a concession for visitors. Hannah knew that the woman in the room could never use it.

The joker's bald head and upper body was that of a human melded with a cobra. The skin was covered with bright, multicolored scales, and the folds of a fleshy hood hung on either side of her neck. The arms were human enough in appearance, but scaled like the rest of the body. Even the naked breasts were scaled, the nipples still faintly present as patches of darker color. Below the breasts, she was entirely serpent; the long, thick body coiled around the oaken branch. Hannah estimated that, stretched out, the woman might be fifteen feet long or more.

The head bobbed, swaying back and forth. The eyes were round like a human's and lidded, but with the vertical golden irises of a snake; from her scaled woman's lips, a long forked tongue darted quickly out and back. The hood swelled briefly, then subsided. "Aah," she said. "There you are. My goodness, what happened? Your poor arm, and the scratches on your lovely face."

"I'm much better than I was a few days ago," Hannah answered.

"I'm happy to hear that. Father Squid told me that you'd been injured helping find the awful person who burned down the church. Come in. Please, don't let my appearance alarm you, my dear girl, and call me Lamia. Mrs. van Renssaeler is too long and tiresome, and not really true anymore, after all. Sit down, sit down. The scones are cranberry; I had them delivered from the corner bakery this morning and they've assured me that they're absolutely delicious. Normally, I would go myself and pick them out, but I'm afraid that I become rather torpid in the cold. I'd fall asleep halfway there. Ahh, well. I'll be most upset if you don't try one. The tea's Earl Grey. Do you use cream? Some of us Americans don't, I know, but there's cream next to the service."

The woman smiled, and the tongue slithered in and out again. "Thank you," Hannah said. "This is, ummm, just fine." Under Lamia's intent gaze, Hannah one-handedly poured tea into the cup and took a scone. She took a polite bite and set it down on the linen napkin folded on the table. "Your baker was right," Hannah said. "They're delicious."

Lamia seemed pleased. Her smile went wider as Hannah took a sip of the tea. "Now then, what can I help you with? Father Squid asked that I tell you anything I know, but you were rather vague over the phone. I understand this has something to do with Brandon?"

Hannah set the cup down; the china rang delicately. Expensively. "I'm not entirely sure, Mrs. . . . Lamia. Maybe. Does the name Card Sharks mean anything to you?"

It did. Hannah could see it in the way the woman's head drew back, the sudden brilliant color that washed through the scales of her chest, and the spreading of the cobra-like hood. Hannah pressed the advantage. "It's possible that an organization by that name was responsible for the fire," Hannah continued. "They may also be responsible for many more acts of violence against wild card victims." Lamia had regained control of her body. The color faded, the hood collapsed around her neck. "The name van Renssaeler has come up several times in the stories I've heard, and I wondered—"

The end of Lamia's tail lashed. "Whether Brandon was part of it, you mean? I suppose his dislike of jokers is fairly well documented. May I ask you something? Will you be discreet if I tell you what I know? If they knew I were telling what I know, I'm afraid that they'd do something. I'm not so worried for myself, you understand, as for my daughter. They might harm her to harm me, and I couldn't bear that. I'd rather take this secret to my grave, as terrible a burden as it has been to me these twenty-five years."

"I don't know what I can do with anything you tell me yet," Hannah said. "But if you don't tell, these Card Sharks will continue to do what they've been doing. They'll kill and hurt and destroy, if not your daughter, then someone else's." Hannah shifted on the couch, and the healing wound pulled. She grimaced.

"Oh, look at you," Lamia said. "And listen to me. You've already put yourself in danger, haven't you? And you didn't need to. You look beautiful and normal; you're safe from them. Clara's safe enough, too; she's been safe since I left when she was five." The tongue darted: in and out. The scales glittered as she rearranged her long body on the branch. "I've been using Clara as an excuse for a long time. This is rather like lancing a boil, isn't it? The infection can't heal while it's buried beneath the surface. Everything has to be exposed to light and air to clean away the toxins. My God, the lives that were lost in poor Father Squid's church. I weep for those souls! If only I'd spoken sooner . . ."

Her voice was so pained that Hannah leaned forward and shook her head. "No. You couldn't have known about that. Even if you had, who would you have told that would have believed you?"

Lamia smiled at her sadly. "You're so kind, my dear. And you're right; I mustn't blame myself. This guilt I've carried, it's like a rock in my gullet or a meal that won't digest."

"Guilt because you didn't tell anyone about the Card Sharks?"

Lamia's head moved slowly back and forth. "No. Not that. You don't have any children, do you? When you do, you'll understand. There are joys to children that only a parent—a mother—can know. You love them sometimes more than you love yourself. And because of that, there are pains."

Lamia's body wriggled, the muscles rippling in a wave down the length of her body as she moved closer to Hannah. The joker sighed, the hiss of a serpent. "Let's get on with this, then . . ."

The Lamia's Tale

Laura J. Mixon

My true name is Joan van Renssaeler,
nee Moresworth, of the Philadelphia Moresworths. I was a hot
number back then, though you wouldn't know it to look at me
now. Here, hand me the large book on the mantel, the leather-
bound one. It's my scrapbook.

These pictures certainly take me back. I haven't thought
about Brand in years. A blessing, that. Our marriage wasn't a
good one. But some of the old memories can still make me
smile.

Now, there, that's a shot of me. This was taken in late May
of 1968, at a party the firm threw for Brand when he was pro-
moted to associate at Douglas, Mannerly, & Farsi.

No, no—I'm the willowy blonde with the sulky expression
and the Twiggy haircut. Look at all those sequins and feathers!
What we used to wear! I shudder to think how much I loved
that ghastly white lipstick. But it was positively The Thing
back then.

Funny how the things we value change, isn't it, my dear? I
look back and all those things I had, the money, the fame, the

social connections, they brought me such pleasure then but they mean nothing to me now. Even my looks, my young woman's body, which I had so little chance to enjoy before the virus took it from me—I was only twenty-three when this happened, you know—even for that I feel little more than a lingering nostalgia. The only treasure that has lasted is my Clara.

My dear Clara. How I loved to dress her in lace and ribbons and tiny patent leather shoes. I took her everywhere.

I have news of her now and then. She's brilliant, just like her father. I suppose you could say she inherited my looks and his brains. At least my pre-viral looks.

Here. Here is a photo of Clara when she was four, and these are of her at college. I hired a private investigator to take some pictures of her while she was an undergraduate at Rutgers back in the early eighties. Isn't she lovely, with those long legs? She resembles me a good deal; she has the same delicate facial features. And of course she looks rather like her grandmother Blythe, God rest her soul.

But I'm getting off track. Let me tell you about the doctor's appointment, where it all started.

Dr. Emil Isaacs was a leading obstetrician, a diplomat of some board of obstetricians, or some such.

Dozens of certifications and awards hung on the wood paneling behind his desk. He was a rather short man, as I recall. Nervous nature.

Dr. Isaacs had always been so kind to me, so gentle and wise, that I couldn't imagine going to anyone else. Most people weren't patient with me back then, with my sharp tongue and ill tempers, so I valued the few who were. I didn't even mind—had long since forgotten—that he was a Jew.

You look shocked at that. I can understand that; attitudes

are different now. Including mine. But, well, I'm determined not to distort this story to save face. Self-deceit is a terrible trap. I should know.

And there is no getting around the unfortunate truth. Jews, blacks, Catholics, Hispanics, Asians, wild card victims, the poor—I feared and despised them all. Anyone who wasn't in my little social circle, frankly, and even they weren't always spared.

Weakness enraged me, you see. It awakened a need in me to strike out. Perhaps I thought I had to keep others down so they couldn't hurt me. I don't know. Only Clara was safe from the predator inside me.

And to a lesser degree, such serene, gentle people as Dr. Isaacs.

But the most important thing was, he had slender hands. Between us ladies, my dear, you know how important slender hands are.

"You must have some important news for me," I said.

He sighed and looked reluctant. "I know how much you wanted another baby, Mrs. van Renssaeler. But I'm afraid your test came back negative."

I looked from him to Clara to a chart with my name on it that lay open on his big rosewood desk.

"I'm not pregnant?" I asked. He shook his head.

Tears welled up in my eyes. I'd been so sure.

Clara said, "Don't cry, *Maman*. It'll be all right."

I dried my eyes and gave her a big hug; she wrapped her arms about my neck.

"Sweet girl. We'll keep trying. You'll have a little brother soon. Or maybe a little sister."

Clara gave me a wet kiss and told me she loved me. Children give their love so freely. It was so long ago; it's remarkable that I'm tearing up about it now, isn't it?

Where was I? Oh, Dr. Isaacs. When I looked back up at him, the pitying expression on his face infuriated me. I thought he pitied me my failure to be pregnant. Gathering up my hand-bag and kerchief, I stood.

"Well. I certainly don't understand why you felt the need for an appointment to tell me *that*. You could have informed me over the phone."

The doctor grimaced and ran a hand over his face. He glanced at Clara. "Please sit down. That wasn't the only reason I asked you to come in. I need to discuss your pregnancy screening tests with you."

His tone alarmed me; I sat. "What? Tell me. Have I got can-cer? A venereal disease? The wild card? What?"

Something in his expression told me I'd guessed the truth. The world went strange and flat. I pressed my kerchief to my lips. Clara's hand was on my arm; her worried little face looked up wide-eyed at me, asking me what was wrong.

"Tell me which."

"Perhaps we should have Nurse Clifford take Clara out-side," he said.

Once we were alone, he told me what you must have al-ready guessed, that it was the wild card.

"It's a standard test for pregnant women. I'm sorry."

"Whatever are you apologizing for?" I had my composure back by then. "Obviously you've confused my blood sample with someone else's. I don't associate with those sorts of peo-ple. I go out of my way to avoid jokers. There's no way I could have been exposed."

Unless, it occurred to me, Brandon had been visiting houses of ill repute, or joker drug dens, or had a secret life as a "week-end hippie." Weekend hippies looked and acted normal during the week but then put on wigs and bellbottoms and love beads and peace signs at night or on the weekends, grew sideburns, and read bad poetry to each other and smoked marijuana cigarettes till their brains leaked out their ears.

And I knew he'd tried that marijuana stuff at a recent American Bar Association convention. He'd brought a marijuana cigarette home and I'd flushed it down the commode, terrified the police would break in and arrest us both at any minute, or that mere skin contact might be enough to tie my unborn children's chromosomes into pretzels. He'd laughed at me.

Brandon. Brand could have picked it up someplace disreputable and given it to me.

But Dr. Isaacs was shaking his head. "You could live alone on a desert island and it wouldn't make a bit of difference. The spores are all over the world by now and they aren't transmitted from human to human. They're airborne. Or genetic. Those are the only two ways you can contract it. And since we know you *didn't* have it while pregnant with Clara, you must have contracted it in the interim."

"But I feel fine!"

He was shaking his head again. "The virus is dormant in you right now. It could remain dormant forever, or it could express itself tomorrow."

I remained silent, just looking at him.

He went on, "There are things about this situation that you can't control, and things you can. You can't control the fact that you have the virus. But it's possible that the virus will never express itself in you. You could live out a very normal, fulfilling life.

"But I must strongly advise you against a second pregnancy. The child would be at high risk of being a carrier. And the stress of the pregnancy and labor would almost certainly cause the virus to express itself in you.

"The wild card is a life-threatening illness and I won't lie to you: The prognosis is not good if it is triggered. The vast majority of wild card victims die a very painful death, and most of the rest end up with severe deformities. I've lost a sister to the disease and I can assure you, it's not to be taken lightly."

"Doctor, this is absurd."

He leaned across the desk. "I know this is difficult for you to hear. But you must do everything you can to minimize all stress in your life. Stress is a key factor in whether the virus expresses itself. Here." He placed a business card down on the desk. "I'm sure you're familiar with Dr. Tachyon's work at the Blythe van Renssaeler Memorial Clinic in Jokertown. There's no one in the world with greater expertise in the wild card virus. I advise you to make an appointment to see him as soon as you can. Today, if possible."

I was familiar with Tachyon, all right. That odious alien had seduced Brand's mother, Blythe, away from her husband and children, had destroyed first her reputation and then her life—had brought Brandon such pain he still couldn't bear to speak of it, after all these years. I didn't pick up the card.

"Surely you jest."

"I'm quite serious. He's the best."

I said nothing for a moment, looking down at my handbag and the kerchief wadded up in my trembling fist. Then I looked at the doctor again.

"I can assure you there's been some mistake."

But he was giving me that look again, that unbearable pitying look. I stood.

"I'll want a second opinion, then, by a doctor I can trust."

Douglas, Mannerly knew how to throw a party.

Of course, the senior partners were up to something more

than just presenting Brand to New York society as their boy wonder after the big court case he'd just won. Sixty-eight was a national election year.

The papers and TV newscasts were cluttered with stories about the presidential and other candidates making their junkets around the country, and the city's power brokers were plotting for all they were worth.

I didn't know what their other motives were, and didn't care. The party was a major event and Brandon was at the center of it, which meant I was only a little right of center myself. The glow it gave me blotted out any lingering unhappiness from the doctor's appointment.

Remember that dress you saw in the photo, with the big blue sequins? Those sequins shivered and glittered like shiny coins when I walked. The dress had spaghetti straps and was sinfully short, with cobalt-blue silk stockings; squaretoed, sequined platform heels; and a garter that one caught glimpses of when I danced, or lifted my arms or bent over just the slightest bit. And I loved the cobalt-blue feather boa. My mother would have had to get out her smelling salts if she had seen me.

I'd done up my eyes in beatnik fashion. I had that sort of sultry, honey-blond, green-eyed beauty that captivates certain men. So I got a few admiring looks, I don't mind telling you.

Douglas, Mannerly had rented the two uppermost floors of St.-Moritz-on-the-Park, which has a spectacular view of Central Park, and had hired a top-notch caterer and a jazz band. Enormous arrangements of rare tropical flowers rimmed the tables and walls. Lace-covered tables displayed caviars and pâtés, finger sandwiches, crisp vegetables on ice with dip, shrimp and smoked salmon.

The bar served hard liquor and mixed drinks, as well as

wine and champagne. The musicians were colored, but I didn't care as long as they didn't mingle.

Brandon was supposed to have come straight from work, but I didn't locate him right away. Plenty of introductions kept me busy, though.

Mayor and Mrs. Lindsay came. Several rumormongers had been whispering it around that Mrs. Lindsay had a joker deformity, which she may have been hiding under that full gown of hers, but I scrutinized her closely and saw nothing except a tendency to obesity. Needless to say, I avoided her anyhow.

Gregg Hartmann gave me a dance. He was a city councilman then, not yet mayor, or senator. I can tell you, the man knew how to foxtrot. I also chatted with Asaf Messerer, the ballet master and main choreographer for the Bolshoi dancers, who were performing at the Met.

I tipped the photographer covering the party to get several shots of Brand and me during the evening—which is where the photos you're looking at came from. He promised to mail them to me within the week.

Eventually I found Brand seated at a table in a side room, an interior balcony lit only by votive candles, with a great view of the west side of the park. Brand introduced me to his companion, Dr. Pan Rudo, a noted psychiatrist. That's him right there, with Brand and me.

They definitely made an odd pair. Brandon cut an exquisite figure in his formal tails and black tie, his gold cuff links and silk shirt and kerchief. That night he looked his best: intense, excited, his dark auburn hair slicked back, his ruddy complexion aglow, hands moving in sudden, enthusiastic gestures.

His black eyes were all fiery with glory and dreams.

The doctor's appearance also commanded attention, but in a cooler, more exotic way. His hair was a blond so pale it looked white, his eyes a violet-blue that stared right past one's surfaces into the soul.

I remember shivering deliciously when he looked me over.

He stirred his drink with a paper umbrella swizzle stick and stroked his lower lip thoughtfully: pale ice to Brand's dark burning; serene age to Brand's youthful, barely suppressed impatience. He had the hypnotic patience of a cat.

That suit of his was a Nehru; do you remember those? The intelligentsia and other trendy types favored them back then. It was made of an expensive, cream-colored Irish Moygashel linen. About his neck was a thick silver chain with an ankh hanging from it. Very odd.

Despite his bizarre appearance, he emanated power and money; from Brand's demeanor I could tell the man was Someone Important. We chatted a bit, and the doctor seemed quite congenial.

Brandon's older brother, Henry, walked up shortly after.

Of all the people who made me wild with fury, Henry van Renssaeler, Jr., headed the list. He had accepted a scholarship to Juilliard, thwarting his father's wishes for him to pursue a political career, and had become a brilliant classical pianist instead. This had been all to the good, as far as I was concerned. But once he had completed his degree he'd grown long hair and a beard and taken up the acoustic guitar, of all things. He now spent all his time in little cafés or bars in the Village, playing folk rock, when he wasn't marching in antiwar protests. I considered it a hideous waste of talent.

Worse, he had spent this spring loudly supporting Bobby Kennedy for president, who was not only a little carbon copy of his older brother John, which was the last thing we needed in the White House again, but a Catholic to boot. In fact, Henry had a KENNEDY FOR PRESIDENT button on the lapel of his dinner jacket. A thoroughly tasteless gesture.

Henry kissed me on the cheek and slid into the chair opposite Brand, folding his lanky legs under the table.

"Where's Fleur?" Brand asked.

"Here somewhere. Have you caught up on your sleep yet? The papers are still talking about the coup you pulled off."

Brandon flushed and shrugged. I could tell he was pleased that Henry had noticed, despite their mutual animosity. A weirder love-hate relationship I'd never seen, unless it was their relationship with their father.

Brand introduced him to Dr. Rudo, who raised his eyebrows at Henry's campaign button and smiled. "Can you really back a man with Bobby Kennedy's platform? His position on jokers' rights and war only promise to divide the country further."

"Oh, I don't know. He beats Clean Gene hands down, don't you think?"

Brand flushed again, and not from pleasure. Brandon wanted Eugene McCarthy to win. For myself, I couldn't understand how *anyone* could vote Democrat after what they'd done to the country.

"Kennedy is a power-grabbing poseur who's simply trying to cash in on his brother's name," Brand said in a flat tone.

Henry gave him a sour look. "You're in fine form tonight, I see."

Another of their endless arguments was in the works; I excused myself and went in search of Patricia.

It was around then that one Miss Marilyn Monroe arrived.

She stood framed in the doorway for a moment and surveyed the party. The shy, vulnerable look on her face infuriated me. Whom did she think she was fooling? I'd read about what sort of woman she was.

A silence fell over the room when people first began to notice her. Apparently she had come unescorted. I wondered who had invited her.

She wore a dress even shorter than mine, and she certainly had the legs for it. Her dress was made of layers of translucent silk the red of candied apples, snug at the waist with a flaring skirt. Brilliant, heart-shaped diamonds made up a cluster of buttons at her waist, and more of the same were stitched into her plunging décolletage. The diamond teardrops at her ears and a matching pendant on a gold chain must each have weighed at least four carats. She had the pale skin and dark mole on her lip she was so famous for, and her hair was shoulder-length, and wavy. She had let the color return to its natural dark chestnut.

Several men rushed forward, including doddering old Thomas Mannerly, the firm's senior practicing partner. Patricia caught my eye and motioned me toward the ladies' powder room down the hall, where we spent a few minutes repairing our faces and remarking upon Marilyn's taste in clothes. Not to mention certain of her other characteristics.

"I feel so embarrassed for her," Patricia said, "wearing a dress like that."

I arched an eyebrow at her in the mirror; the dress I wore was similar to Marilyn's—at least in its length. Patricia sat down at one of the chairs and applied a little eyeliner, then caught a look at my expression.

"I mean, for a woman her age. Did you know she's supposedly at least forty-five? Well, forty, anyway."

"Did you see those diamonds?" I asked, dabbing a bit of powder onto a shiny spot on my nose.

"They're a bit overdone, aren't they? Someone should take her aside."

"What embarrassed me was that cleavage!" I said. "You could see practically everything. And her breasts, they are so enormous. I can't imagine they're real."

"Those Hollywood doctors can work miracles."

We both giggled.

Patricia was smaller in stature than me, with a round face and a tendency to pudginess. She was always dieting. Tonight she wore an empire-style black gown with black bead embroidery and pearls. More pearls were wound up her swirling hairdo, which she now teased with a comb.

She wore a more subdued style than usual because she was five months pregnant with her first child.

Looking at the curve of her belly I felt a tightness in my chest. The doctor's appointment came back to me; my hands curled into fists on my own, flat belly. I had to breathe deeply for a couple of seconds before my heart stopped pounding.

My face had lost color. I applied a bit of rose-tinted rouge and brushed more powder over it.

Patricia didn't seem to notice my reaction; she was applying a new Chanel color to her lips.

"Did you hear how she got invited?" she asked, squinting as she pursed her lips at herself. Looking at her expression, my anxiety passed. I suppressed a smile.

"For heaven's sake, dear," I said, "stop impersonating a fish and put your glasses on. We're alone here."

She gave me a rueful glance and slipped her rhinestone-rimmed, cat's-eye glasses out of her handbag.

She put them on and surveyed her appearance, dabbed at the corners of her mouth.

"I hate these things." She tucked the glasses back into the bag.

"You look fabulous. Tell me who invited her."

"Oh! Caroline's husband found out that she was going to be

in town, and went straight into old Douglas's office." Patricia laid a hand on my arm, leaned close enough to me that I caught a whiff of her spicy perfume, and continued with a conspiratorial tone. "They were holed up in there for *two hours*, his secretary told Caroline. And the invitation was hand-delivered by Douglas's private chauffeur."

I paused with my powder puff in midair, studied her reflection in the mirror. "Two hours, eh? Maybe they want to set up a Hollywood office."

"Who knows? They're always up to something." She gave me a meaningful look in the mirror. "It's going to be nothing but trouble while she's in town, you know, with the partners courting her influence. She'll sleep with anyone, they say. I'm keeping my George under lock and key and you'd be wise to do the same with Brandon."

I put my compact back into my handbag and gave Patricia a thin-lipped smile. "Brandon's too busy pursuing glory to waste time pursuing women. Especially an older, burnt-out woman like our dear Marilyn."

Still, on our return to the party, I had to admit she didn't look old and burned out. She looked pretty damned good for a forty-year-old, pardon my language.

Looking at her wide, innocent eyes, her winsome expression, my heart filled with rage. I wanted to bring her down. I wanted to see her humiliated.

Dr. Rudo had taken her hand and was saying how lovely it was to see her again; it'd been so long, etc. etc., as Brandon and I came forward to be introduced. But something about how they acted—the way she straightened almost to stiffness, something in his face—made me believe they loathed each other.

"How is your movie deal proceeding?" he asked. At her lifted eyebrows he added, "That is why you're here, is it not? That's what the papers say."

"Oh, I'd love to discuss it with you, Dr. Rudo," she said in a light tone, "but you know how these ventures are. The backers get jittery if we discuss too many details before the deal is closed."

"But of course. Pardon my prying." He smiled. But his attitude was aggressive, and he didn't take his eyes off her. It seemed to make her a bit nervous. Which suited me just fine.

Dr. Rudo's example emboldened me. When Brand and I were introduced I refused to take her extended hand, merely gave it a cool, quizzical glance. As if to say, *What should I do with that?*

A look of hurt and bafflement came into her eyes, but she simply gave me that smile she is so famous for, equal parts innocence and sensual languor, and nodded to me. She kept her hand extended, transferring it to my husband, who bent over it and kissed it, lingeringly.

I wanted to scream. As I pulled Brand away he gave her a charming little grin and a shrug, and I knew he'd seek her out later. Then and there I decided to glue myself to Brand for the evening.

"What is your problem?" he asked sotto voce, summoning up his courtroom smile, a parody of the one he'd given Marilyn. I suppose you could say he was more concerned about appearances at the moment than I.

"I don't know what you're talking about."

"Lower your voice. You know precisely what I'm talking about." Brand pried my hand loose from his arm and, folding my hand and arm under his in a deceptively tight grip, dragged me along toward the end of the room with the dance floor. He nodded a greeting at Councilman Hartmann, who stood nearby watching us.

"Let me go."

"I mean it. I have important plans for tonight. This may be

my big chance to make some important contacts and I won't have you interfering."

"Exactly what sort of contact did you intend to make, darling?" I asked, showing as many teeth as he, though his fingers were digging hard enough into my wrist to leave bruises. "And with whom?"

"Don't bait me."

"I saw how you looked at her."

"Someone had to show some courtesy."

"That woman is in no need of your courtesy."

He virtually dragged me out onto the dance floor, with that hateful, suave smile on his face, making pleasantries all around. The song was Louis Armstrong's "What a Wonderful World." He grasped me in a clutch with a hand around the back of my neck and an arm around my waist, and whispered in my ear, "This is my big night and I won't have you interfering."

"Stay away from her."

"Don't push me or I'll make you regret it."

His hand closed alarmingly tightly on the back of my neck; I started to become frightened. Councilman Hartmann still watched us over the heads of the crowd. He must have known something was going on, and was wondering whether he should intercede. A sudden impulse rose in me to struggle in Brand's grip, to hit at his face, to cry out for the councilman's help—for anyone's. Which would have been disastrous at a time like this. I knew how to handle Brand; why was I getting so panicked?

Besides, Councilman Hartmann had looked away by that time, so I was on my own. I took a deep breath and relaxed in Brand's grip. Wrapping my arms around his neck, I breathed a gentle breath in his ear.

"I can't help being jealous. You're such a powerful, attractive man that other women won't be able to resist your charms. I couldn't bear it if you got involved with another woman."

He loosened his grip a bit and drew back to give me a suspicious look, but I had my most sincere face on. After a moment he said, "All right, then, but no more public displays."

"You have my word."

He let me go, so suddenly I stumbled. "All right. Go get yourself a drink and find Patricia. I have business."

"I'll come with you."

"No, you won't." The *I can't trust you not to make a scene* was implicit in his expression.

Hurt, I turned my back on him and went over to the bar. I'd intended to drop a few hints into Councilman Hartmann's ear about my husband's inexcusable behavior, but he had wandered away.

By the time I found him he had become embroiled in a heated political discussion with the mayor, Governor Rockefeller, and several other men. When it became clear that nobody was going to take particular notice of me, I went in search of Patricia and my circle, to pass the evening with martini in hand, exchanging gossip about those of our circle not present, along with other unfortunates whose names arose in idle conversation.

Brand spent most of the evening with Marilyn. I comforted myself that the husbands of most of the women in my circle also paid court to her. But Brand was clearly a favorite, and they went off together at least twice, before I got too drunk to notice.

Patricia began throwing me pitying looks, which reminded me in an unfortunate way of Dr. Isaacs's expression earlier. I'd be a target for nasty rumors as soon as my friends gathered without me. I wasn't the only predator in my social circle.

The rest of that evening fades into obscurity in my memory,

but one other incident stays with me. New York politics and high society were always weird and paranoid, and one got used to not knowing what was going on. But this seemed different.

The party had thinned out so it must have been quite late. In the past couple of hours I had managed to sober up a bit. On my way out of the ladies' room I happened to hear Brand's voice, quite low but recognizable. It came from within a cranny around the corner, where the pay phones were.

I started to enter the cranny but paused at the corner when I heard Dr. Rudo's voice. He spoke in a soft and reasonable tone that nevertheless managed to sound as though he expected unquestioning obedience.

"It would be preferable for you to avoid her altogether."

Brand sounded a bit chilly. "Let's leave my personal life out of this, shall we?"

"Your involvement with her could complicate matters. It's easy to underestimate her, but I've known her a long time. She's seductive and she can be cunning."

Brand scoffed. "Oh, come now. There's not a ruthless bone in that lovely body."

"I don't think you understand me. She is one of ours."

Brand's voice was shocked. "She's a Card Shark?"

"Mmmm. She holds a key position in Hollywood and is an important player—even if she is inept."

"Then . . . if she's one of us, why the secrecy?"

Dr. Rudo's voice was sharp. "Think about it."

A pause, then a gasp. "Of course. She's compromised."

"Seriously so. We've kept her completely out of the picture. But it's my guess she's gotten wind that something's up. She'll learn eventually—she probably knows we're up to something right now—but it's important she doesn't find out what we're about too soon. Otherwise she might try to stop us."

Somehow, call it a woman's intuition, I knew that they were talking about Marilyn. And that Brand had fallen for her. The rest made no sense to me, but it all sounded so odd that I decided to take notes in my address book, in case I needed details for emotional blackmail later.

I wrote down *Card Sharks*. I thought they were playing one of those silly conspiracy games one hears about, played by men old enough to know better, who don silly hats and pass secret codes and handshakes back and forth.

"She'll need someone, then."

"Don't be a fool, van Renssaeler. She's using you. She knows you're involved. And if not now, afterward she'll certainly know."

"Nonsense. How could she?"

"I imagine my organization has sprung a leak. And I intend to locate it. In the meantime, I suggest you stay away from her."

Perhaps I should have taken some comfort from the fact that Dr. Rudo was warning Brand off Marilyn, but I knew Brand too well. He had never listened to his father, never listened to me, and he wasn't going to listen to this Dr. Rudo person, either, if he could help it.

A noise, like a chair bumping the wall, made me flee to the bathroom, heart racing. I put away my address book with shaky, sweaty hands, and then made a commotion coming out again. But they had already headed down the hall to rejoin the party.

Though I could have caught up with them, I didn't feel I could face Brand right then, so I went in search of friends— only to learn that Patricia and most of my social circle had left.

I headed straight for the bar and ordered a highball, and another. And another. But the alcohol didn't dissolve the indigestible knot that had formed in my stomach.

– – –

The sun was rising when Brand finally blurred into view and announced that it was time to go home. As he hailed us a cab I remember hugging myself, looking at Brand, wondering if he'd already taken her someplace and had her— someplace filthy like a stairwell. Or perhaps he'd thought to rent a room. A tear or two trickled down my face. I rubbed my belly again.

With that artificial clarity that comes as drunken euphoria collapses into toxicity and illness, I recall thinking as Brand bundled me into the cab that all I'd have to show for this night was a terrible hangover and a lot of trouble.

Incidentally, I can't help but notice that you're feeling the heat a bit. I would turn down the thermostat but you would find me talking ve-e-ery slowly.

Do feel free to remove as much clothing as you need to, to remain comfortable. It's just us ladies here tonight and as you can see, all I wear anymore are my scales.

Tuesdays, at promptly 9:30 A.M., Patricia and her car and driver would arrive at our apartment.

I would rush down, climb into the back of her gray Mercedes limousine, and we would descend upon the upper-class Midtown stores. Our sweep usually encompassed Chanel, Bergdorf's, de la Renta, Jaeger, and the higher quality Midtown boutiques along 5th Avenue. We'd hand our purchases to the driver as we went along, to dump into the trunk of the limo.

Afterward we would send him on his break and eat a late lunch at the Russian Tea Room on 57th Street near Broadway, where we would pull out some of our smaller, choice pieces to croon over, and look for Igor Stravinsky. The famous composer ate chicken-with-giblets soup at the Russian Tea Room every Tuesday afternoon. He was a friend of my parents, and it wasn't unusual, if we ran into each other, for him to join us for lunch. Often, though, Patricia and I got there too late. More rarely, we had a chance to dine with Salvador Dalí, as well.

The Tuesday four days after Brand's party was, in some respects, no different from most of our outings. Once the waitress had brought us our drinks and taken our orders, Patricia spread the *Times* across the table.

"Have you been following Dr. Spock's trial? They've selected an all-male jury."

I caught her cocktail glass barely in time to keep it from toppling; cloudy drops stained the newsprint.

She brushed the liquid away and went on. "It's simply shocking, isn't it? Him egging boys on to dodge the draft."

"I wish you'd wear your glasses, dear. You're terrifically clumsy without them."

"Oh, thank you very much I'm sure!" She turned to the inner pages and sat up a little straighter, studying the ink-sketched advertisements. "I *knew* we shouldn't have skipped Jaeger today. They're having a big spring sale. Listen to this. 'Nostalgic mists of organza silk. Café-au-lait, gentle gray, glade green.' Look at the cut of this dress. Perhaps we should have Rufus drop us by there on the way back."

I sighed and ran a finger slowly around the rim of my glass. It made a tone like a flute or a bell; I stopped, embarrassed, and folded my hands in my lap. "I'm all shopped out."

"You? Impossible. Besides, the glade green sounds perfect for you."

"I'm just not in the mood."

She folded up the paper with a sigh of mild exasperation

and looked at me. "What's the matter with you? You haven't been yourself all day."

The waitress brought our lunches. I leaned my chin on my knuckles, poked at my salad, and said nothing for a moment. Tears gathered in my eyes.

"He's having an affair. I'm sure of it. With that horrid Marilyn Monroe."

Her thoughtful nod told me she'd already known.

"Everyone knows, don't they?"

She nodded again, looking uncomfortable. "He's not making much of a secret of it, I'm afraid. Several people saw them leaving Tuxedo Park together yesterday. She met him there after the golf game."

My throat got tight and tears spilled down my cheeks. She took my hand and made several false starts.

"Look," she said finally, "he's swinging a bit, that's all. Free love, you know?"

"You're the one who told me to keep him under lock and key."

"And you were the one who said he'd never go for her." At my hurt glance, Patricia grimaced. "What I mean is that it's a little late to lock him up now. Why not let it run its course?"

"Thanks for the understanding."

"I mean it. She won't be in town long."

I shook my head, miserable, took my hand back. "This isn't just a fling. He's in love with her."

"You're exaggerating."

"I'm sure of it." I balled up my napkin, shook my head. A tear ran down my cheek. "He came home Sunday night smelling of her perfume and last night he didn't even come home. And with her, of all people. Damn him."

More tears came. Patricia shushed me, looking around. The

couple two booths down stared; I pointedly stared back till they looked away.

In a lowered voice I said, "He can't treat me this way."

"There's not much you can do, though. Really."

I was silent a moment, eyes downcast. Not because I didn't know how to respond or because I didn't know what I wanted; I'd given it plenty of thought. I hesitated because if I said what was on my mind it would be made too real.

But when I looked up, Patricia read my intent. "You know you can't. How would you survive?"

"I have my trust fund."

"That only gives you ten thousand a year! You'd live like a pauper, you'd have to get a job. And doing what?"

"I'll find something."

"What about Clara? You can't deprive her that way." She grabbed my hands again and held them. "Don't do something in haste you'll regret later. Brandon, you know, he's a fine catch. He'll probably be general counsel for Morgan Stanley someday. You'll have everything you ever dreamed of if you just stick it out."

I pulled my hands loose. "How can you say that? You know how miserable I've been. He doesn't care about me. I'm just an ornament on his arm. A hostess for his parties."

"It beats not having anyone." She paused, thinking. "Besides, Brandon will fight it. And he's a lawyer. They know all the tricks and they close ranks. You'll never win. At the very least he'd get custody of Clara."

Patricia must not have realized what was happening with me right then. Though the word *divorce* had never been uttered, the subject of how miserable I was with Brand had always been a favorite topic. Always before, her arguments had supported nicely my reluctance to act.

This time was different. This time he was in love, with something other than his dreams and ambitions. The pain was clarifying my thinking; this time I'd been pushed past my limits. And I knew what to do.

"I want the phone and address of your cousin Franklin. And I want your promise to say nothing about this, to anyone."

She didn't answer, merely looked distressed.

"Please promise me," I repeated.

"Franky doesn't do divorce investigations. He's not much more than a document hound for city councillors' aides."

"I want someone I can trust not to talk to Brand. Someone not connected in any way to Douglas, Mannerly."

"You're making a mistake."

"I'll call you when I get home. Have the information ready, all right?"

She bit her lip, looking forlorn. "I can't. George will kill me if he finds out I helped you find a PI to incriminate Brandon."

I shook my head. "Your name need never come into this. I'll tell Brand I had the information from the Yellow Pages, or something. In fact, if you won't help me I'll get the information that way anyhow, so you might as well help me. I promise I'll never tell."

"Promise?"

"Promise."

She sighed, and lifted her eyebrows in a shrug. "I still say you're making a big mistake. But okay."

I got the number, all right. I must have dialed it six times over the next day. And hung up before the first ring, each time.

— — —

Brand got home after eleven, smelling of perfume and sweat. We barely spoke a word to each other.

Wednesday morning I feigned a headache to escape an excruciating breakfast.

That night he came home at his usual time, and after dinner he played with Clara for a while. Then he retreated to his office.

The photographs from his party had arrived in the mail that day. Clara had been pestering me for a snapshot of *Papa* for her scrapbook; I had promised Clara a photo of Brand from his promotion party. But when I went through them after dinner, most of the ones with recognizable shots of Brand had Marilyn in them, as well.

Seeing them made me behave rather terribly to Clara. I shut the photos up in the rolltop desk, snapped at her when she asked for her photo, and put her to bed without a story. Which made Clara cry, which made Brandon spank her. Poor little dear.

So I sneaked in and rocked her till she stopped crying and promised her a better photo of *Papa* than those nasty old photos from the party. We'd take a snapshot of him for Father's Day in a couple of weeks. She seemed comforted; she stuck her thumb into her mouth and fell asleep in my arms.

Then I listened in on Brand's phone calls from the bedroom extension.

"Brandy." I'd have recognized the voice anywhere; I'd heard it in dozens of movies. "I've missed you terribly today."

"My darling." His voice quavered, for heaven's sake. I thought I'd be sick.

"Can you get away tonight?"

"No. She's getting suspicious."

"Poor woman. I feel bad for her."

"Don't bother. She's a bitch. Shallow and stupid."

"I wish you wouldn't talk that way about her, dearest. It makes me feel bad."

"Believe me, she won't care about us. All she cares about is whether I have enough money and power to keep her in designer clothes and the right social circles."

"Do you . . . really . . . think she knows?"

"Mmmmm. Don't know. It may just be a snit, but I'd best spend the evening here. And I have a business call at ten."

"I see." A pause. "Tomorrow, then. At Caffe Reggio, at four?"

"At the Reggio at four."

Another long pause.

"I love you," he said.

"Sweet Brandy. Not being able to hold you is torment."

I'll give you torment, I thought. *Slut.*

But she hadn't said she loved him. He'd said, "I love you" and she hadn't said it back. *She's using you, Brand. She's using you.*

"Tomorrow," he whispered. I slid the receiver back onto its hook.

"He's perfect for our needs," Dr. Rudo was saying. Brand's "business call." I scribbled furious notes at my bedside. "One of our inside people at the Jokertown Clinic tagged him immediately as a man with a mission. Seems he's into mind control, and hunted up Tachyon to see if he'd teach him some mentat tricks. Tachyon turned him away, of course, so he turned to the Rosicrucians."

"He sounds like a certified loon."

"By no means. I've had my people do a thorough check.

He's intelligent, well educated, dedicated, and has contacts in the Middle East—which should muddy the investigative waters nicely. He also has his own good reasons for volunteering, so no one is likely to come looking for us, if he talks."

"I don't like this. How can we trust him?"

"We don't have to trust him. How can he hurt us? Once you give him the schedule and hotel layout, pay him off, and turn him loose, all he'll know is that some man in a parking lot gave him money to do something he wants to do anyway. That's all he'll ever know."

"I still don't like it. He might be able to finger me later. We could use an underling just as easily."

"It's quite simple," Rudo replied. "You want to move into the upper tier. We need proof that you're willing to risk all before we allow that. Your reputation. Even your life. Consider this a rite of passage."

A pause. "If you insist on this, I suppose I'll have to do it. But if I go down, you'd better make sure of this: I'm taking you and a lot of other people with me."

"Look. It's up to you. You can do the payoff and come play with the big boys. Or you can refuse and stay right where you are, in the cozy middle of the organization, with the little boys.

"Don't worry; it's in our best interests to keep our people happy. The risks are minimal. And we'll protect you if anything goes wrong. But for now, it's your turn to prove yourself."

A longer pause. Brand sighed again. "When and where?"

"I'll give you the details tomorrow at lunch."

Thursday morning at breakfast, while Clara played with her oatmeal and blueberries and Brand read the *New York Times* Business section, I cupped my coffee mug in both hands and sipped at it, stared with burning, red-rimmed eyes out the window.

The housekeeper had put fresh-cut tulips in glass vases on the end tables in the living room, straightened up a bit, and opened the windows. Fresh air and sunlight streamed in through the picture window; the hyacinths and lilies-of-the-valley in the flower box outside were in full, fragrant bloom.

Too beautiful a spring morning can amplify one's misery.

Clara tugged at Brandon's arm and stepped on Frou Frou's, our Llasa Apso's, tail as he was lapping up the last of the oatmeal she'd dropped on the floor for him. Frou Frou retreated under the table, yelping.

"*Papa*, will you take me to the zoo on Saturday?"

Brandon didn't answer right away. Clara tried to scramble up into his lap, and in so doing tore a page of the Business section. Brandon scowled and started to chide her, but caught my warning glance. To assuage my own guilt, I had chewed his ear for quite a bit the prior night, over how he'd brutalized Clara.

At any rate, at my glance he laid his paper down, picked her up, and wrapped his arms around her instead, and kissed her curls.

"I have to work on Saturday. Sorry, Tookie."

"Please? Please?"

"*Papa* has to work," I told her. "I'll take you shopping with me instead."

"It's all right," Brandon said. "Maybe we can go to the park for a while on Sunday. We'll take Frou Frou along. Okay?"

She beamed, grabbed his ears, and gave him an excited shake. "Groovy! Then *Maman* and I can go shopping on Saturday, too."

"Where did you pick *that* up?" I asked.

"What?"

"The 'groovy.' "

"That's what Uncle Henry says. And Jessica says it all the time, too, when she talks on the phone to her boyfriend. She's hip."

"She's what?" I asked.

"Hip, *Maman*. In the groove."

I gaped at her, flabbergasted.

"That sort of slang may be all right for some people but it's not appropriate language for you, little lady," Brand said. To me he said, "You'd better have a talk with Jessica. And I'd better talk to Henry."

I might have felt the same way myself, if Brand hadn't suggested it first. But the slang did sound kind of cute, coming from her. "It's just a word, for heaven's sake. It's not an obscenity."

"Can we go shopping Saturday, *Maman*?"

"We'll see," I said, and smiled at her.

Brandon's and my eyes met over the top of her head.

"I'll be working late," he said. It occurred to me that I might as well have had Jessica set a place for Marilyn. She was right there at breakfast with us.

"Of course you will," I replied, and sipped coffee.

"I'm a friend of Patricia Wright's," I said into the phone. "Joan Moresworth van Renssaeler. We met last year at her Christmas party."

"Oh—yeah, yeah. I dig." Franklin Mitchell sounded as if he didn't have a clue what I was talking about. He also sounded like a flake. Not a good phone personality; he'd made a better impression in person. "How's Patsy doing these days? Has she, you know, like, dropped the kid?"

"I beg your pardon?"

"Has she had the baby?"

"Oh. No. Not for several months yet. Listen." Through the open bedroom door, I saw Jessica and Clara playing with Clara's Barbie dolls on the living room carpet.

Jessica had been helping me care for Clara since she'd been born. She was a strawberry blonde, at least forty pounds overweight, and had the most beautiful, freckled face. She was also Irish, but I didn't mind the Irish so much. At least they were Protestants, some of them.

I dried my palms on my skirt, lowered my voice.

"This may not be your usual type of job, but I need someone I can trust and you come highly recommended. I need you to follow someone and take some photographs. This afternoon. And possibly—well, the job may take a few days, before you get the chance to catch . . . exactly what I'm looking for . . . on film."

"Yeah? And what's that?"

My voice failed me for a moment. "Does it matter?"

"Well—yeah. Of course it does. How'm I gonna, like, know if I got what you needed, if you don't tell me what you need?"

"Oh. Well." I cleared my throat.

"*Maman, Maman,* look!" Clara came running in, holding up her Ken doll. She'd put a dress on him and was giggling. "He dresses funny."

"Amusing, dear," I said to Clara, and glared at Jessica, who entered behind her. "This is an important call; do you mind?"

A sullen look crossed Jessica's face. She scooped Clara up and carried her back out.

"Hello?" he said. "Hello?"

"My husband is cheating on me."

"Ah."

"I want you to get pictures of them together. Lots of them. In bed, if possible. I'll pay you well."

"I charge a hundred fifty a day, plus expenses. I'll get you all the pictures you need. Since you're a friend of Patsy's, you can pay on delivery."

"Don't be surprised when you see who it is."

He chuckled. "Man, nothing gets to me anymore. Not in this business."

Over the next few days life carried on in a travesty of its old routine: Brand ate breakfast with us, went to work, stayed late or didn't come home at all. Clara seemed to sense that something was wrong; she needed a lot more attention and reassurance than usual. Jessica and I had difficulty controlling her.

On Sunday after services, Brand stayed home all day. He paced the house like a caged wildcat. When I asked what was going on he told me to mind my own business. I grew afraid that he'd invited her over—that they were going to announce their intention to run away together.

That afternoon he surprised me by keeping his promise to take Clara and Frou Frou to the park.

Afterward, while Jessica and I helped Clara press the flowers and leaves she had picked in the park between sheaves of waxed paper and then glue them into her scrapbook, he spent a good deal of time in his office on the phone. I couldn't listen in because Jessica was around, and in the evening after she'd left he didn't make any calls. After we put Clara to bed he went out again, and didn't come back.

Franklin Mitchell called on Monday morning. "We'd better talk. Right away."

"I can't, not today. It's the babysitter's day off."

"I'll come there, then."

"You certainly will not! What's the urgency? Did you get the photos?"

"I got more pictures than I know what to do with, man. Something weird is going down."

"What are you talking about?"

"Listen," he said. His voice was strained. "Your old man is into some heavy shit. I don't know what it is, but this is more than I bargained for."

I closed my eyes, strove for calm. "Did you get photographs of him with Marilyn, or not?"

"I did. It was hot stuff, too. She's one sexy lady." He whistled.

"It'd be nice if you'd leave off with the commentary."

"Uh, right. Anyhow, you were right about them. It took till last night for me to get everything you wanted. You know," he cleared his throat, "them together in bed."

I couldn't bring myself to respond.

"They spent the evening in a room at the St. Moritz," he went on. "I got some great shots from the fire escape. And then he left. I was going to split but then the chick started tailing him."

His slang confused me. "What are you talking about?"

"I'm talking about *Marilyn*, man. She tailed him. You know—followed him. So *I* tailed *her*. We all took cabs to a deserted parking lot in Newark, where I lost her. But not your old man."

"Oh?" This didn't sound like Brand at all. He hated New Jersey.

"Yeah. He met a couple of dudes there. Heavy dudes, man. They went off and hid behind a wall, and then your old man stood around for a while under a streetlamp near this big graffiti wall mural. Then a fourth dude arrived and your old man gave him a big envelope.

"And while I was taking pictures, one of the other dudes spotted me. He tried to *kill* me. He shot at me and chased me for several blocks." He sounded indignant. "I think your old man is messing with the Mob, or something."

"Preposterous." But I thought about the odd conversations Brand had been having with Dr. Rudo. Card Sharks? A Mafia connection?

Brand's recent court case, the one that had earned him a big promotion, had been a Fourth Amendment case, and the newspaper involved had reputedly had connections with the Mafia. But Dr. Rudo had been so nice. And so—so Germanic. It didn't seem possible he was Italian.

"Look. No offense," Mitchell said, "but I want to unload these pictures, get my money, and say goodbye. You'll have to take them now, or I destroy them. I don't want any trouble with the Mob."

I looked down at Clara, lying atop big sheets of yellow, green, and red construction paper with her crayons scattered about her and her tongue poking out.

I didn't want her involved in this, in any way, no matter how urgent Mitchell felt matters were.

"Patricia will hold them for me. You have her address?"

"Of course."

"I'll call her now and tell her what to expect. Seal the photos and the negatives in an envelope with my name on it and drop it off at her place. She can pay you. I'll get the photos from her and reimburse her tomorrow."

— — —

Look at the hour. And I have to be at the Clinic at eight in the morning. I wonder if we could continue this some other time?

No, no. I understand. There's not much more to tell, actually. It's just, this is all rather painful to recount.

I'll make some sandwiches and coffee for you, then. I have a frozen pie in the freezer, too. And we'll get this over with.

The photos; I was about to tell you about those. Patricia dropped the sealed envelope off the next morning, with an accusatory look and a cool greeting. I repaid her the money she'd given her cousin, excused myself from our shopping spree, and asked Jessica to entertain Clara in her room. Then I spent a while looking at the photos and trying to think what to do.

Franklin Mitchell had indeed taken many photos. Brand and Marilyn at a café in the Village. Brand buying a diamond and sapphire necklace. A close-up of his hands putting it around Marilyn's neck. Brand and Marilyn eating a meal at I Tre Merli's. Marilyn, laughing, wrapping a scarf about Brand's head in Washington Square Park. And about two rolls' worth of Brand and Marilyn frolicking about in various stages of undress in a hotel room.

I had to give her credit; she had excellent taste in lingerie.

And then there were the "conspiracy photos," as I thought of them. A long shot of Brand talking to two sharply dressed men who loomed over him. Close-ups of each. A blurry shot of Brand standing alone under a streetlamp. Brand talking with another man—a short, dark-complected man, perhaps an Italian, with a thin, serious face. A close-up of Brand and the other man, with the envelope exchanging hands: the clearest picture of the bunch. A blurred human-shaped form in the foreground, with Brand and a piece of the big mural in sharp focus in the background. The blur presumably being the man who had chased Mr. Mitchell.

I had the photos spread all over the kitchen table when Jessica brought Clara out for some juice and crackers. The first I realized they'd left the bedroom was when Clara touched my arm and asked if those were the photos of *Papa* I'd promised her.

The thought that Jessica would see the pictures of Brand and Marilyn filled me with terror and rage. I swept Clara out of harm's way, held on to her arm as I came to my feet and shrieked at Jessica.

Blocking her view of the table, I ripped her to verbal shreds for bringing Clara out of the bedroom when I'd said they were to stay in there. She was disobedient, I said; slothful and incompetent. It was all in keeping with her scatterbrained, Irish nature.

She was no shrinking violet, was Jessica; she raised a few nasty welts herself, about my brittle, supercilious nature. I'm certain she used the *b* word at least twice, and she slammed the door on her way out.

Instantly I knew I'd been a fool. In spite of my ways, I trusted and needed Jessica. I told Clara to stay right where she was, then yanked the door open and caught Jessica before she got to the end of the hall.

She refused to be mollified. "I may not be some wealthy lady from Philadelphia, but that doesn't mean you have the right to insult me and treat me so poorly."

And when I offered excuses she said, "It's a wonder to me a girl like Clara could have a mother like you."

And she left.

— — —

To my relief, Clara was humming to herself in her bedroom when I returned. She was playing with her scrapbook and her Barbie doll and making up stories. I suppose she'd seen me like that often enough before. She told her Barbie not to be afraid, *Maman* sometimes just yells a lot. That brought tears to my eyes.

I'd tried, oh, I tried hard to be a good mother to her. But whatever it was inside me, some reptilian beast, ugly and hate-filled, it just got out of control sometimes. I rarely lashed out at her, but even when it isn't aimed at them, children get caught in the crossfire. Poor Clara.

Quickly, I gathered up all the incriminating photographs and hid them in the rolltop. Then I sat down on the couch and cried for a while.

I sure had my custody case. No court in the world would refuse me a divorce, nor grant him custody of Clara over me. The trouble was I didn't know what else I had. What was Brand involved in? I was frightened for him.

It can be hard to let certain feelings go.

That evening I reached Jessica by phone and begged her forgiveness. She finally agreed to return, for a raise in pay and the full day off on Sunday, instead of just mornings.

I took a sleeping pill and went to bed early, at the same time as Clara. I slept heavily. Brand must have come in during the wee hours. By the time I got up Jessica had arrived and was straightening Clara's room; Francine, our cook, was washing dishes; and Brand and Clara were eating breakfast.

Clara gave me a hug and a kiss. Brandon didn't even look up, just continued to read his paper.

On my plate was *The New York Times*, neatly folded open to page seven. I sat down and picked it up.

The article exposed said, "Private Investigator Killed in Crossfire." Franklin Mitchell's body had been found in the South Bronx, full of bullet holes. It was believed he'd been caught in the crossfire, in a shootout between the police and a roving mob of looters.

I looked up at Brand. He was watching me. All the warmth drained out of my body.

"Jessica," he called, without taking his gaze from mine.

She appeared in the doorway. "Sir?"

"I wonder if you could take Clara to her room and help her dress? Francine, you, too."

"I can dress myself!" Clara replied, indignant.

"Do as I say. Now." His tone was much sharper than it needed to be. Clara's face started to scrunch up, but Jessica murmured kind words as she and Francine hustled her away. Brand ate a bite of his toast and made a pretense of reading the Business section.

Numbed, I refolded the paper, then caught a look at the main headline on page one. I had a second shock. Bobby Kennedy had been shot.

I skimmed the article. The senator had been gravely wounded early that morning at the Ambassador Hotel in Los Angeles, upon winning the California primary. On an interior page they had a photo of the unidentified gunman who had been captured by Kennedy's supporters.

The man was the same young man as the one in the photos Franklin Mitchell had taken on Sunday, the swarthy man who had accepted an envelope from Brand.

I looked up at my husband. He was watching me now.

"I got an odd call at the office yesterday afternoon," he said.

"Oh?" I'd had years of practice disguising my own weaknesses; my voice didn't tremble.

"Mmmm. Patricia said you'd hired her cousin the detective."

Patricia knew where the real power lay, between Brand and me. She'd played it safe. Maybe even told herself she was doing me a favor. "Do tell."

"Mmmm. She said you hired him to take incriminating photographs of me, for the purpose of securing a divorce and custody of Clara."

"She certainly has an active imagination."

"Doesn't she, though?"

Jessica and Francine came out with Clara. Clara wore her peach corduroy dress. It had a felt poodle with blue rhinestone eyes on the bib over a white, short-sleeved blouse trimmed in lace. She also wore her white patent leather shoes and white stockings. Her dark hair was pulled back in white bows. I took Clara into my lap and buried my face in her dark chestnut-and-gold hair, which smelled of baby shampoo. I clutched her tight. She hugged back.

"Your hands are cold," she said.

"Go get dressed," Brand told me. I looked up at him, and my terror must have shown.

"*No.*"

"Yes. Now."

We both looked at Jessica and Francine, who knew something was up but not what.

"Are you going out, *Maman*?" Clara asked me. She'd put her hands on either side of my head and those beautiful, speckled green eyes were only inches away.

"Yes, she is," Brand said, lifting her out of my arms. He handed her to Jessica.

I should have fought him. I should have clung to her and

not let him have her. I could have run with her; maybe one of the neighbors would have helped me. Someone would have helped me.

I should never have let him take her like that.

Brand took me to an office in a skyscraper down in the Financial District. Dr. Rudo was there, dressed in a different Nehru suit, a black one that made his pale skin and hair and his violet-blue eyes seem luminous in contrast. He greeted me in a way that made me shiver and shrink away.

Brand said, "I believe you wanted to speak to my wife?"

The room looked like a doctor's office, with the requisite diplomas and certifications. An overstuffed couch and cubist paintings on the walls made it a little less medical-looking.

I thought about Dr. Isaacs's office, and what he had said about stress. I wondered if I was going to die.

Dr. Rudo put me in an armchair before his big desk, saying to Brand with a glance at me, "Yes, that would be charming. But a word with you first."

As soon as the door closed and the tumblers of the lock turned over, I dumped out the pens from a pen holder on the desk and rushed over to kneel by the door. The open end of the wood cup I pressed against the wood, and on the closed end I put my ear.

I heard Brand say, ". . . only wounded."

"Yes. It's a shame that the upper echelon's first impression of you will be how you failed at your first major assignment."

Brand sounded desperate, angry. "I was only the messenger. He didn't use a high enough caliber weapon. That's not my fault."

Rudo laughed. "Relax. It's a head wound. The senator will be dead before morning. And if not, we can send someone in to finish him off. Your wife is the more important factor. If her detective did get shots of you with our Palestinian friend, and she's passed them on, you're at real risk."

"The bitch . . ."

Their voices faded to murmurs as the floor transmitted to my shins and knees the trembling of their footsteps. They had moved away from the door. I stayed crouched at the door, shivering and sweating till I could smell my own stink, and thought about the photos in the rolltop desk back home.

A moment later footsteps shook the floor again. Dr. Rudo's voice said, ". . . I doubt her resistance is high; this shouldn't take long."

The tumblers turned and the door opened. They looked down at me. I tried to duck between their legs, but Brandon grabbed my arm and hauled me upright—virtually off my feet.

"My dear young lady, you're showing an alarming amount of initiative," Dr. Rudo said.

"What are you going to do with me?" I felt embarrassed, apologetic, at how my voice quavered. He smiled.

"Just ask you a few simple questions. Come sit down. Relax. Nobody's going to hurt you." He took me by the elbow and led me back to the chair.

Dr. Rudo made Brandon leave the room, and then we chatted. I should have been much more on the defensive; to this day I don't know how I could have relaxed around him, given what I knew.

But the questions all seemed so innocuous. I remember his cool violet eyes looking at me, and his head nodding . . . I went on about Clara, about myself and how much I wanted another child, about Brandon's ambitions. Memories and thoughts surfaced and spilled out of my mouth that I had thought were long buried.

And when he asked me about the photos, I should have been prepared but I—I don't know why; I must have been an idiot!—but I had become convinced that the photos Franklin had taken were harmless and pointless, that I had no reason to conceal them.

And, well, I told him where they were.

Do you know, it took me *years* afterward to realize that it was even odd I should have told him where the pictures were? Whenever I thought about the session my mind kept slipping and sliding off the memory of the pictures, every which way. I'm still disturbed by how I could have been so foolish, so easily fooled. I wonder if he hypnotized me?

Brandon came back in at some point and took me home. I don't remember that part too clearly.

When we got home, Clara and Jessica were nowhere to be seen. I had a high fever by then, and was freezing cold, quaking like an aspen leaf. My joints ached. Brand took the pictures out of the desk, then undressed me, put me in bed, and looked through the photos. He made a call on the phone, sitting on the bed.

"Pan? Brand. I found them right where she told us. Yeah, he got some shots of the exchange but nothing too incriminating. I think we can destroy them and leave it at that. I'll take care of them."

A pause. "I'll make sure she doesn't cause any more trouble.

Isn't that right, Joan?" he asked me, gripping me by my sweat-soaked hair. Pain spread inward from the loci of his knuckles. I moaned.

He released me and spoke into the phone again. "Okay. How about tomorrow evening? You can have supper with us." Pause. "Fine. Seven-thirty. See you then."

Next he set fire to the photos, one by one, and dropped them, flaming, into a crystal serving bowl. Except for several explicit ones of him and Marilyn. Those he waved at me.

"Perhaps I'll start my own scrapbook with these."

He eyed the photos for a moment, gave me a look, then threw back his head and laughed. I was struck at how honest and open that laugh sounded. He hadn't sounded so open in years.

"God, Joan. It's great to be free at last. Free to tell you how much I hate you. Your jealousies and suspicions, your pettiness, your clinging and complaining and prudishness and controlling, bitchy nature—you've made my life a living hell.

"But that's over now. From now on, you are Clara's mother and that's all. You have nothing to say to me, nor I to you. You'll be my wife to the public eye, but there's nothing between us anymore. And if you ever try anything like this again," he waved the picture at me, "I swear I'll kill you."

He put them in his wallet and then picked up the phone again.

"Hi. It's me." I could tell by how his voice grew husky and by how a bulge swelled in his trousers whom he'd called.

"I arranged for our babysitter to take Clara overnight," he said. "*She's* sick with the flu. I need a place to stay. I need to see you."

Pause. "Can't you find a sitter?"

Another pause. "I read about it in the papers. I'm so sorry. But, you know, he is a threat to our work, with his position on the wild card."

A pause. "Who told you? Wait—don't hang up. Damn it!"

He slammed the phone down and rubbed his face, looking at me. Anguish was stamped on his face like someone's shoeprint. He really loved her. I was curled into a tight ball, riding out the fireball of pain spreading through me, and couldn't focus on him, even to taunt him.

I don't remember him leaving.

That night, I became intimate with the virus. It was the longest night, the worst pain I have ever lived through.

The next morning I awoke to Frou Frou's yaps, welcoming Jessica and Clara into the apartment.

The night's agony was fading, though a thousand aches and twinges tormented me along my body. I had that light-headed, floating clarity one feels after a high fever breaks, and also a terrible, cavernous hunger. Morning sunlight streamed in through the sheer curtains. Jessica clattered about in the kitchen, making breakfast. Clara's voice rose and fell in a dialogue with Frou Frou in the living room.

Clara. I wondered if the prior day's torture had been a dream. I wanted Clara in my arms. I propped myself up on my elbows.

Great tufts of my hair lay strewn about my pillow. With a strangled gasp I touched my scalp and felt—baldness. Brushing backward, the skin was smooth and cool and dry; brushing forward it felt like sandpaper. My arms were covered in scales, in a pattern that vaguely mimicked the roses and dark green leaves twined on the comforter.

Throwing off the comforter, I meant to put my feet on the floor. But when I tried to swing my legs out from under the

sheets, nothing happened. My toes were down there somewhere; I could even wiggle them, but whatever was moving in
there wasn't my toes.

I strained to lift my legs again. Nothing happened except
the sheet moving. I was afraid to lift the sheet.

I heaved with all my might. My lower torso slid out from
under the sheet—and slid, and slid, and collapsed onto the
floor in a single looping, rubbery limb: a growing, sinuous
tangle. The weight of it pulled the rest of me off the bed.

I grabbed at the bedsheets to keep from striking my head on
the bedside table. Then I twisted around to see what I had become.

No legs. No toes. I felt them but they weren't there. My
torso, my navel, even my genitalia—or so I thought then—
gone.

From below my breasts, I was all snake, eighteen feet of
scaled coils about the thickness of one of my former thighs and
mottled now like our carpet, gleaming moonstone and sand.
Even the flesh of my nipples was scaled, a slightly darker
brown. My lips, too, felt scaled. How beautiful the scales were:
luminous, translucent, like semiprecious stones. Beautiful, and
horrible. My fingernails were long, horny claws, a lizard's
claws.

My lace nightie had slipped off my shrunken shoulders and
gotten tangled in the loops of snake flesh. I struggled with the
nightie, sliding it over the coils, heaving portions of myself
back and forth, till I could pull it off over my head. That small
exertion exhausted me and I had to rest for a moment.

Then, hand over hand, I dragged myself over to the mirror
by the door and propped myself upright, supported by shaky
arms. From the breasts up the thing in the mirror was mostly
me, though the wrong color, scaled and hairless, with an al-

tered nose, mouth, and ears, shrunken shoulders and arms. From there down, I'd become monstrous.

I reared back in horror and shock, and my lower body clenched into a mass of coils. The thing in the mirror bobbed like a cobra about to strike. Its color—and mine—went a brilliant parrot blue with yellow, black, and red striping, as a cobra hood spread behind its head. Its reptile eyes dilated. A bitter taste bled from my lengthened canine teeth as a milky substance leaked from the mirror thing's canines.

It wore my face. A scaled, reptilian face, but unmistakably mine. The colors were fading now to a softer, smoky blue as I studied it, with sand-, ash-, and rust-colored stripes.

I ran my tongue over my lips and saw it had lengthened and forked at the end. After extruding it, when I brushed the tongue against my palate, it could—taste the air, smell it; neither of those words is right, but it was a little like both. It could taste the scent of Brand's belongings and mine, and taste faintly the presence of Jessica and Clara and Frou Frou in the other room, of frying eggs and bacon and toast.

Hands over my face, I lurched away from the mirror with a soft cry.

First I thought, a dream. A nightmare spawned by my fever.

But I knew differently. What Dr. Isaacs had said would come to pass had come to pass. My body had been stolen from me during the night. Some malevolence had traded it for this mass of heaving, scaled coils. I'd become in body the predator I'd always had in my heart. I'd become a lamia.

One's priorities shift when survival is at stake. Hysteria was definitely called for; I felt it bubbling around the edges of my thoughts. But now was not the time. I couldn't be certain

Brand had gone for the night—he might have borrowed Clara's bed, since she'd been at Jessica's. And Clara, I couldn't bear for her to see me like this.

On the other hand, I couldn't bear to lose her.

Brand had always hated the wild card and its victims, as much as I had. He would never tolerate a joker wife. I didn't know what he would do when he discovered what had happened to me, but given that he had been involved in the murder of two men, I didn't want to find out.

But first things first. Food.

When I thought about eating, my tongue flicked, flicked again, tasting the air. The smells it detected made me writhe into knots of hunger and revulsion. The cooking eggs and bacon and toast turned my stomach. Raw animal flesh was what my body needed. A prospect equally revolting, but imperative.

Three prime, New York cut strip steaks were in the refrigerator. Those would do.

I lurched and slung and dragged my elongated self over to the door. It was exhausting work; slithering is not as easy as it looks, especially when one is starved, weakened by illness, and unaccustomed to the motion. Heart racing, I turned the knob, pulled the door open, peeked around the corner. The blue was fading from my scales and a dark brown with moonstone and sand mottlings, the combined colors of the door and carpeting, faded in.

My scales gave me protective coloring. With a sudden, faint hope that I could escape this situation unharmed, I slipped out onto the cool wood floor, my colors shifting as I moved.

Frou Frou's ears pricked up when the door opened. He looked over at me. I froze.

Clara had arranged Frou Frou and her dolls in a semicircle

beyond the couch. The circle included the dog, Barbie and Ken, the plastic Kathy Cry Baby, the fine, antique china doll my mother had given her for Christmas, and stuffed animals of assorted types, colors, and sizes. Clara told Frou Frou to sit down but instead he came around the end of the couch, suspicious and confused, with a growl rumbling in his throat.

I hurled myself toward the safety of the bedroom. But I was too long and clumsy to get all of me through the door and slam it shut before Frou Frou darted inside. Bristling, with little yips and growls, he backed me into the corner. I pulled myself into a tightly coiled mass, held out my hands.

"Frou Frou," I whispered. "Hush." My colors began to brighten, responding to my fear.

Frou Frou tilted his head at my voice, clearly confused, yipped experimentally.

"Hush." My voice trembled and my speech was slurred; I hadn't yet learned to form my words quite properly with my new mouth.

Frou Frou sniffed at my fingers, then made up his mind. I wasn't his mistress, I was an intruder. He snapped at my outstretched hand and started to bark. Jessica yelled at him from the other room.

I rose up above my coils. Colors blazed on my scales; my cobra's hood spread.

He darted at me, baring his teeth, and his teeth closed on my twitching tail. Pain lanced up my body.

With a cry I struck out and bit him on the left flank, behind his foreleg. While he struggled, yelping, glands in my palate emptied themselves, venom pulsed in my gums and through my teeth. Dismayed, I let him go.

He ran in circles, yowling, then staggered under the bed, fell on his side, and twitched. I worked my way over to him.

His eyes were glazing. I lay down next to him. His heart fluttered against the palm of my hand. Then the heart stopped beating.

Clara stood at the door.

"Clara," I said, propping myself upright with effort. Starvation and exertion made my head spin.

"You hurt Frou Frou."

"He attacked me, honey." I forced the words out. "I had no choice."

"You hurt Frou Frou! Bad snake!"

She came at me with both fists, struck at my face. One blow caught me on my nose, still tender from its transformation. At the pain, anger flooded me. I coiled and reared. My scales blazed blue with red, yellow, and black, and my hood fanned out.

Not Clara; *no!*

I forced down the urge to strike. The angry, brilliant colors drained from my scales. I caught at Clara's hands and held on to them till her rage passed. Without adrenaline I was so weak that it took all my strength to control a five-year-old.

"It's all right, honey. It'll be all right. It's *Maman.*"

She burst into tears. I put my arms around her and stroked her head. My arms were almost too weak to hold her. "I'm so sorry, honey. I'm sorry about Frou Frou."

Jessica had come into the room to see what the commotion was. She stood at the door, pasty white.

She must have seen me about to strike at Clara.

"My God," she said, "oh, my God."

Clara, nestled next to my heart, said, "Jessica, it's *Maman.*"

"Clara, come here." Jessica held out her arms. Her voice was shrill.

I didn't let go of Clara. "It's me, Jessica. It's all right. It's the wild card, that's all."

Jessica squatted. Her voice was tinged with hysteria. "Clara, come here *right now*."

I released Clara and gave her a gentle push. "We need to talk, honey. Go on out for a minute. Jessica—"

But she snatched Clara up, took her out, and slammed the door. Loud bumps and thumps told me she had blocked the door with the rolltop desk. I crept over and tested it anyway; it was blocked.

I collapsed on the floor and panted. I was ill from hunger, all but unconscious.

I moved back to the bed and flicked my tongue all up and down Frou Frou. He was dead and nothing I could do would bring him back. He smelled like what I needed to eat. Fresh, newly killed meat.

I dragged him out from under the bed, lifted his limp head, removed his collar with trembling hands, and then gave him a last caress. I shuddered. The dog was so big, I wasn't sure I could go through with it.

I forced his head into my mouth. My throat gagged but I kept pushing, salivating heavily, and my jaw unhinged as a snake's does, so he could pass more easily. The skin of my mouth stretched over him.

My throat expanded to take him.

He got stuck when his shoulders reached the back of my mouth. No matter how hard I shoved and punched at him, he'd go no farther. So I propped his hindquarters against the floor, struggled up atop him, and used my own weight to push him all the way in, fur, claws, and all.

It hurt a lot. I swallowed and swallowed. Tears streamed down my face. Eating him was a great labor. I swallowed some more and my powerful throat muscles carried him farther down my gullet, where he pressed hard against my rib cage and made my breathing labored.

The ache of famine was ebbing. The pain of an overlarge object stuck in my gullet remained but my body knew it had the right kind of sustenance.

Exhausted, still swallowing feebly, I lay on my side and looked down at myself. Frou Frou had lodged at about where my diaphragm tapered into the snake's trunk. My stomach—if that's what it was, though I guessed it was just a long tube with digestive juices; there didn't seem room for a set of intestines—growled and burbled. I looked pregnant.

At that thought I started to retch, and then couldn't stop. The same strong muscles that had swallowed him tried to force him back up my throat. But they were weakened now, and by concentrating and taking deep breaths I managed to keep him down.

Lethargy settled over me. I stretched out against the wall behind the bed, folding my tail double, and my scales faded to eggshell white, moonstone, and sand. I slept.

"Joan?" It was Brand's voice, and it roused me to semi-wakefulness.

The color and angle of the sunlight told me it was mid-afternoon. Jessica must have called him home early. I was in the throes of a massive, reptilian-grade digestive stupor, so I have only a vague memory of their voices, and of blurred images moving about the room, though I managed gradually to force myself to complete wakefulness.

Jessica said, "It was in here before. It said, 'it's me' in her voice." A moment later, "Where's the dog?"

They looked right at me at least twice. And then past.

"It *was* here," she repeated in a defensive tone. Brandon gave her one of his patronizing looks. "It killed the dog. It tried to attack Clara, too. I rescued her."

"I've never known you to be this excitable. I pray you'll do it on your own time next time, and not disturb me at work."

They were on their way out when Clara came in. *"Maman?"*

"Get back!" Jessica snapped, but Brand said, "There's no one here. Don't be a twit."

"Maman." Clara had a child's eyes, not as easily fooled by expectations. She saw me at the wall and came over, knelt beside me and touched my face.

I should have regretted her revealing me. But all I knew was joy at the relief and delight in her eyes and voice. She threw her arms about my neck and I enveloped her with arms and coils.

"I'm sorry I yelled at you about Frou Frou," she said.

"And I'm sorry," I replied. "I'm sorry that I scared you and hurt Frou Frou."

"He's not ever coming back, is he?"

"No, not ever," I said. "He's dead now. Gone. I'm sorry."

She gave it some thought. "You couldn't help it. I saw what happened. He was trying to bite you. You must have been really scared."

"Yes. I was."

"But I wish he wasn't gone."

"Me too, honey."

She pressed her cheek against my scaly breast. She stroked my skin, and as if her fingers were tiny paintbrushes, my scales changed color beneath their touch: silver, rose, amethyst.

She released a contented sigh. "You look pretty, *Maman.* Prettier than ever."

That brought tears to my eyes.

I heard a sound and looked up. Brand had a poker in his hand now, and was lifting it to strike a blow to my head.

My colors grew bright, blue / red / yellow / black, and dangerous. My coils curled up beneath me and my hood spread. I felt my glands taut and warm with venom, pressing against my sinuses and palate.

Brand hesitated.

But I was sluggish, and couldn't maintain my erect posture. My colors began to fade to smoke, rust, sand, and ash. I leaned against the wall with Clara in my arms, striving for fierceness.

"Put that thing down before someone gets hurt," I said. "Put it down."

He lowered his arm and regarded me. Then Jessica looked closely at my misshapen trunk, and her hand went to her mouth. "It ate the dog."

Brand winced. "My God."

"Leave us be," I muttered.

"Give me my child." Fear had entered Brand's voice. Fear for his child. "I'll let you go if you give me Clara."

I was shocked at that. "I'd never hurt her, Brand."

He dropped the poker and went down on his knees before me, folded his hands and held them out to me, pleading. A bead of sweat rolled from his temple to his chin.

"You were human once. You adored her. Swear to me that you won't harm her. Swear, or let her go."

I remembered, when she had struck me, precisely how close I had come to lashing out, poisoning her as I had Frou Frou. I remembered how the dog had thrashed when I'd struck him and I remembered the sensation as I'd shoved him down my throat. The thought turned me numb with dread.

I looked at Clara's trusting face, pressed against my chest, and sobbed. I'd just killed and eaten a pet I'd had since I was fourteen. I couldn't be sure of myself at all.

I handed her over to him and slumped back against the wall.

\- - -

I wouldn't have hurt her, you know. I would never have hurt her. If only I could go back, reassure that younger, frightened me. I'd tell her, *Take Clara, hold her to you. Trust yourself. She needs you. You can do it.*

I've never hurt a human soul since my changeover. Except to help the terminally ill on to a better life at their own pleading. And surely that's a gift, not a curse. I've forsworn bigotry and pettiness, and devoted my life to helping others.

I've killed animals, to be sure. Often. Famine drove me to eat Frou Frou that day, but it wasn't a human's hunger. This body needs the nutrients, the minerals and proteins in animal blood, skin, hair, and bones. That was why the craving was so strong. It's a part of my nature now, to require live, or newly dead, whole animals. Raw meat is as close as I can come to human foods, and it's not adequate to sustain me for very long. I'm not human anymore, in that way.

My eating habits are certainly less sanitary and more immediate than buying ground round at the grocery store. But it's not so different in concept, is it, after all?

Other animals, their intelligence is not the equal of ours. Yet they are still living creatures, and have more intelligence than we credit them with. They deserve life and respect, as much as we do.

But our very existence forces us to make hard choices. It forces us to prey on other creatures when the need is great.

I had always been a predator, by choice, without need. I had spent a lifetime preying on the weaknesses of others. The wild card made me a predator in truth, and gave me no choice in the matter.

I've learned from it. I learned that one must forgive oneself for what one has had to do to survive. And I can forgive myself everything. Everything but how I abandoned Clara that day.

I understand why it happened, don't mistake me. I'd spent

a lifetime being untrustworthy and shallow and hypocritical. And now I had become a creature whom I feared at least as much as Brand and Jessica did.

How could I know that all that had happened in the past few days would force me to find a strength I didn't know I had? Nothing in my past had prepared me to trust that I could protect Clara from the worst of what I had become.

I wish I could forgive myself for that failure of faith.

Brand kept his promise, to my surprise. They kept me shut up in the utility room for a couple of days, until my digestion had proceeded far enough along for me to stay awake for more than a few moments at a time. Then he let me go, with a suitcase stuffed full of personal memorabilia, a hundred dollars cash, and a check for two thousand dollars. I'm still grateful to him for that.

He held Clara in one arm and opened the door for me with the other.

"Where are you going, *Maman*?" she asked. I paused out in the hallway and looked back, but all the words lodged in my chest, the place where the rock was starting to form.

Brandon shushed her. "That's not your *Maman*. It's just an animal that looks a little like her."

She struggled in his arms, reaching out to me. "I want *Maman*!"

"Hush! *Maman* is dead," he said, and closed the door. Her rising wail, faint through the door, followed me down the hall.

I suppose that's all.

No, no. Please don't apologize. It was time for the story to come out. These are tears of release. Just let me be for a moment, will you? I'll be all right.

There, now. Much better, thanks. It's odd. I actually feel better for having told it. It's weighed on me so heavily for so long. I've kept that secret inside for so long, of how I abandoned my daughter.

Perhaps the key to forgiving oneself is through the telling of the tale.

My, it's three-thirty in the morning. Would you like to sleep on the foldout? My boyfriend is on call at the Clinic tonight, and this oak branch is quite comfortable for me. I only sleep when the temperature drops too low, or after eating a heavy meal.

No? Well. Certainly. No offense at all. Though you must take care out on the streets this late.

Here, before you go. I'd like you to have these notebooks; they contain the notes I made on what happened. I wrote everything down soon afterward so I wouldn't forget the details. They might help you in your research.

Oh. One last thing you should know. This may be paranoia on my part, but, well, it has returned to me over and over. As I related to you, Brand told Dr. Rudo on the phone that the photos the detective had taken weren't very incriminating. That closeup of him with Sirhan Sirhan, Kennedy's assassin, was damning. Perhaps he was lying to Dr. Rudo, but why?

And I remember how much Clara wanted a photo of her *Papa*, and how I had left her alone with the photos when I had that argument with Jessica. That photo was definitely the best shot of Brand's face, of the whole batch. I keep wondering.

But now I'm being paranoid.

Come, let me put on my electric sleeve and I'll escort you to the subway station.

The Ashes of Memory

9

"I'd like you to ring Ms. Monroe's room."

The hotel clerk looked at Hannah as if he had gas. "I'm sorry, but Ms. Monroe has left very specific instructions that she not be disturbed. What did you say your name was?"

"Rudo. Pan Rudo. R-U-D-O."

The clerk consulted his monitor, tapping at the keyboard. "Oh, I'm sorry, Ms. Rudo. Your name is on the list she left. You may use the white phone to your right. Dial asterisk, then 44."

"Thank you." Hannah went to the house phone and punched in the number. The voice that answered was still instantly recognizable: breathy, soft, and warm, not much changed despite all the years. "Hello?"

"Ms. Monroe, I must see you."

"Who is this?" The voice took on a touch of irritation. "Who gave you this number?"

"Nick Williams asked me to call, Marilyn. You remember Nick, don't you?"

There was silence on the other end. For a few seconds, Hannah thought that Marilyn had hung up, then the woman spoke again, and her voice sounded much older. "Where are you?"

"In the lobby of the hotel. I need to see you alone, Ms. Monroe."

"Give . . . give me a minute and then come on up. I'm in the Lindsay Suite. Seventeenth floor."

Riding the elevator, Hannah had time to wonder whether this was a mistake. In the three days since she'd spoken with Lamia—three days in which she'd found herself starting at every noise and peering suspiciously at every person that entered the apartment building—Hannah had come up empty. Clara van Renssaeler, who might or might not still have a photograph of her father with Sirhan Sirhan, refused to meet her the first two times she called. The third time Hannah reached her, there was such a strange tone in the woman's voice when she agreed to a meeting, Hannah deliberately missed the appointment. A friend of Father Squid's, known as "Blind Spot," went by the restaurant and reported back that the establishment was oddly deserted except for a table of three suspiciously attentive men. Hannah didn't try to call Clara again.

Much of Lamia's notebooks consisted of hearsay from friends, and none of them Hannah contacted cared to discuss what had happened back then. Most of them seemed to have put Joan van Renssaeler out of their minds entirely. "Her? She abandoned her daughter. Just up and left her family . . ."

It was Father Squid who read in the paper that Marilyn Monroe was in New York for a charity revue. Hannah had nodded, thinking it simply a mocking serendipity, but the mention had nagged at her. She knew already that there was little that the three of them could do. They had nothing, nothing but hearsay and a few interconnected names.

Marilyn, if Nick's story was true, had once had hard evidence: the copies of Hopper's files. Hannah wished she could have brought Quasiman with her, but Hannah had figured that there'd be enough trouble getting to the woman as it was; with an obvious joker accompanying her, there'd have been no chance at all. And as much as she hated to admit it, Quasiman was becoming a liability. He seemed to have reached the limit of his ability to maintain his focus on their problem. For the last few days, he'd forget her or Father Squid for an hour or more, then suddenly snap back to lucidity for a few minutes before drifting away again. "I want to come with you, Hannah," he'd said. "Please. Let me help you." But she'd said no.

"Just keep thinking about me," she'd told him. "Come and bail me out if you sense that I'm in trouble. Can you do that?"

"I'll try. I'll try."

The problem was that, even as she knocked on the door to Marilyn's suite, Hannah still wasn't sure what she was going to do. She saw the glass of the peephole darken as someone looked through.

"You're the one who called?" asked a voice through the door.

"Yes."

"Come in." The door opened just wide enough to admit Hannah.

Marilyn was in her late sixties, Hannah knew, but the woman who closed the door behind her looked at least a decade younger. She was dressed in an expensive silk robe, her lacy white chemise showing at the top. Her waist had thickened over the years, there was a network of fine wrinkles around the eyes and at the corners of the mouth, and the skin under her chin sagged, but the allure and the underlying hint of innocent sexuality were still there. Her hair was shorter now, and she'd allowed a touch of silver to accent her temples, but the rest was a gold-flecked brown, artfully disheveled as if she'd gotten up from a nap.

Hannah found herself feeling oddly plain alongside her, like a daisy in a vase with a rose.

"Who are you?" Marilyn asked. Her gaze was skittish, yet Hannah was certain that she'd been appraised and judged already. "Where did you hear about Nickie? If this is some kind of joke . . ."

"Nickie . . ." Hannah said. "You killed him. You put a bullet in his chest to save your career. He's the father of your child. He loved you, he saved your life and gave you a son, and you murdered him."

It was either great acting or genuine emotion—Hannah couldn't tell which. Marilyn's haughty demeanor crumpled, as if it were a paper mask Hannah had ripped off to expose a lost, frightened child beneath. Her whole body sagged, almost as if she were about to faint, then she caught herself. She took in a long, gasping breath and tears shimmered in her eyes. Her hand came up to her mouth, as if she were stifling a sob, and she turned and walked into the living room of the suite, collapsing onto the couch with her legs drawn up to her body. Hannah followed her in. From beyond the balcony, the towers of Manhattan thrust through afternoon haze. A tape deck sat on top of the television set in the corner of the plush suite, a video playing softly in it; Hannah realized that the movie was *Jokertown*. She wondered if that was coincidence or if Marilyn had set it running as a deliberate backdrop, a bit of added scenery.

As a much younger, agonized Marilyn told a glaring Jack Nicholson about the Lansky/van Renssaeler plot, the real Marilyn looked at Hannah with stricken eyes. "How do you know . . ." she began, then stopped. On the TV, Nicholson vowed to put an end to the plot. "I loved him," Marilyn said. "I did. They were going to kill Nick anyway. If I hadn't shot him, we would have both died that night. I thought . . . I thought that at least that way one of us would live. I thought I could find a way to pay them back . . ."

"But you never did," Hannah said sharply. Her voice sounded shrewish and shrill against Marilyn's polished tones. "You and Nick stuffed the files into a toy tiger, but that's not what you gave Kennedy during that birthday party. You gave him a penguin. You never gave the president the information Nick died for, did you?"

Marilyn stared at Hannah, her cheeks as red as if she'd been slapped. The woman tugged her robe more tightly around her neck, as if she was cold. She sniffed, visibly trying to rein in the emotions. "How much do you want?" Marilyn asked Hannah. "I don't care what your proof is, I don't want to know how you know. Name your price, I'll pay it. Just leave me alone."

"I want the evidence you never gave to the Kennedys. I want the prints that Nick took of Hedda Hopper's files. The ones that tell the story of the Card Sharks. There were three copies, or did you give them all to Rudo and Hopper?"

The gasp Marilyn gave could not have been faked. Her skin went pale, the hands that came up to cover her face trembled. She was crying now, rocking back and forth on the cushions. "Oh God, I've been so frightened." She wept for a long time. Hannah waited, as Marilyn sobbed and on the television Jokertown burned. Hannah had come here with no sympathy for the woman at all. She'd come prepared to threaten, to blackmail, to confront Marilyn with her guilt. But Hannah now found that while she might not be able to forgive what Marilyn had done, she couldn't hate the woman at all. She was a victim, too, as much as Nick. As Hannah had found with jokers, it was hard to blindly hate someone you understood.

"Ms. Monroe," Hannah said at last, softly.

Marilyn looked up, her face blotchy, her mascara now black streaks down either cheek. "Who are you? What are you after?"

"My name doesn't matter. What I'm after is the Sharks. What I'm after are the people who killed Nick and Jack and Bobby Kennedy and scores of others. I want to understand what happened."

"I was afraid," she said. "I knew Jack all too well; Bobby too. They would have tried to do something with the information. Jack wasn't perfect, he wasn't a saint, but he wouldn't have left that kind of rot alone, and there were too many powerful people involved. They already hated Jack and Bobby both, hated their idealism and their liberal 'softness' and their courting of minorities: jokers, blacks, anyone. I was aware that they were already working against Jack's reelection. I knew there were a few who were already talking assassination and I was afraid that if Jack moved against them, that would be the last straw. I thought that by doing nothing, I might at least save him." Tears had gathered in the corners of her eyes, rolling untouched down her cheeks as she gave a short, bitter laugh. "So I said nothing. And then Jack went to Dallas." Marilyn wiped at her tears angrily, defiantly. "You have no idea what you're facing, young lady."

"I'm facing you."

Marilyn took a sharp breath. "Me? I'm nothing," she said. "I never have been. Not to them. You want to know the truth? I hate them. I hate them more than I hate myself for never having the courage to do something about it." She sat up suddenly. "You have to go," she said. "You can't stay here."

"I'm not leaving until I have answers."

"Why?" Marilyn cried in that breathless little girl voice of hers. "What good is anything I know? Who can you go to? Who can you trust?"

"I don't know that yet. But I'll find out," Hannah answered. "I'll do something."

For several seconds, Marilyn just looked at her. "I'm not as flighty and reckless as the gossip says," she said finally. "Not really. They told me what I was to do if anyone ever confronted me. I was going to keep you here. I'd talk to you if I had to, pretend to give you what you wanted, until . . . Stay here a moment." Marilyn got up from the couch, moving now like an old person, and went into the bedroom of the suite, returning quickly. Hannah felt the breath go out of her when she saw what the woman held in her hands.

A bedraggled stuffed tiger.

"I kept this with me, all those years," Marilyn said. "The other sets I gave to Hedda. I had to, you understand. But these . . . I kept them, always thinking that one day I'd do something with them, that I'd pay them back for making me kill Nick. I must have started to do it a hundred times, even after the birthday party, but something always held me back. I was afraid of what they'd do to me, to my son. Every time I started to make the call, every time I wanted to call Jack or Bobby or anyone, I'd see Nick floating in my pool, the water going red around him and his open eyes staring at me, and I'd stop. After a while, I didn't even try. Everyone I might have trusted seemed to be dead and I didn't know anyone else. I was so scared, don't you understand? So scared."

She held the tiger out toward Hannah. "Here," she said. "Take it before I change my mind again. Now, please."

Someone rapped on the door, several quick knocks. "Marilyn?"

Hannah knew the voice. Marilyn put a finger up to her lips, then pointed to the bedroom. At the same time, she seemed to draw on some inward calm, inhaling deeply and rearranging the robe around her. Her demeanor changed, seeming to be that of someone younger and more vulnerable. As Hannah clutched the tiger and moved quickly into the bedroom, Marilyn rose from the couch and went to the door. "Pan!" Hannah heard her exclaim, and then the words came all in a rush: "Oh, Pan, I was so scared. The woman called me from the lobby, saying that she knew about Nickie . . ."

There was a door leading to the hall from the bedroom. Hannah turned the knob as softly as she could, listening to the conversation in the other room. "Where is she? Is she still here?"

"The woman banged on the door for the longest time. I was afraid to call Security. I didn't know what she'd say or do. She finally left . . . I don't know, ten, fifteen minutes ago. Come in, Pan. Hold me. Stay with me. I was so frightened . . ."

Hannah opened the door and slipped out into the empty hall.

She thought she was away and free, but as Hannah pressed the button for the elevator and watched the doors slide open, she heard the door to Marilyn's suite open again. She caught a glimpse of Rudo as she stepped into the compartment. There was a frightening moment of eye contact down the hall, then Rudo began to run stiffly toward her as the elevator doors closed. His fists pounded futilely on the door as she started down.

He can't get another elevator before I get downstairs. I'm okay. I'll have time.

The elevator stopped at 15. It seemed to take forever for the doors to open, for the elderly couple to shuffle inside and the doors to close again. They smiled at her, a young woman desperately clutching a stuffed toy tiger. Hannah gave them a quick, nervous smile back, then stared at the numbers:

14 . . .
12 . . .
11 . . .
10 . . .

They stopped again. And yet again at 6. Hannah was beginning to panic, hoping that Rudo would be having the same
problem. *He can't do anything in a crowd. Just stay with them. He
doesn't want any of this out in the open.*

They reached the lobby. Hannah slipped out first, looking
back at the numbered plate above the other elevator. As she
watched, the indicator light shifted from 3 to 2. She started
across the lobby with the older couple, trying to look as if she
were their daughter. Two dark-suited men were standing near
the street doors, one who looked like a movie version of a Sicilian thug, the other a tall and massive black man whose suit
seemed to strain to contain his sculpted body. Swallowing her
panic, Hannah turned to the woman. "That's such a nice
sweater," she said. "It's perfect for a chilly afternoon like this."

The woman smiled. "Thank you, my dear."

"I can't believe it's gotten so cold in the last few days. Fall's
definitely here to stay this time, I think." The men were watching the trio suspiciously. Behind them, an elevator chimed.
Hannah could feel Rudo's gaze on her back but she didn't dare
look behind her. A few more steps and they'd be outside.

"Ms. Davis," Rudo called loudly to her. "Such a lovely surprise."

The Sicilian and Muscles moved to intercept her at the same
moment. Her elderly escorts looked as if they were about to
protest, but Hannah, an icy resignation settling in her stomach,
gave them a rigid smile. "He's a friend," she said, giving them
what she hoped was a convincing smile. She kept the smile

cemented to her lips until the couple left the hotel; the expression vanished as she turned to confront Rudo. He was dressed elegantly and expensively, as always. His neatly trimmed gray hair was slightly mussed; disturbed, she thought inanely, when he ran down the hallway after her. He brought a hand up and smoothed down the errant strands.

"Rudo," she said. Rudo's men flanked her on either side, silent.

"I see you've dropped any pretense of politeness, Ms. Davis."

"You've lost any right you had to it," she answered. "Card Sharks—such an apt name for your little group of murderers."

"Shut up, lady," Muscles snarled in her ear. His voice matched the body: low and powerful. "Don't make yourself sound more like a fool than you are."

"Mr. Johnson, please," Rudo said. He smiled at Hannah. "Name-calling will get us nowhere," he said. "I won't bore you with justifications or the philosophy. My friend is right, however. You fail to see the larger scope of the problem we're facing. You have something of ours, and we'd like to have it back. That's all I care about; then we'll even let you go your own way for now."

Hannah clutched the tiger closer to her as Johnson grabbed her elbow. The lobby was busy, though no one had noticed them as yet. People were passing, going in and out on their way to the rooms or the street or the bar. "We're in public, Rudo. You really want a scene?"

The corner of Rudo's mouth lifted. "Someone used my name at the desk to gain access to Ms. Monroe's room. That same someone stole an item from her bedroom and then ran, as I am certain Ms. Monroe will testify. Fans steal things like that all the time. A scene, Ms. Davis? I assuredly don't want one. It would be a shame for you to be arrested—jail is such a dangerous place." He held out a hand. "The stuffed toy, Ms. Davis, if you please . . ."

Behind Rudo, a familiar form was suddenly there.

"Quasiman!"

The hunchback looked as if he were about to rush headlong at Rudo. His slablike hands were fisted, muscles bunched up all along the massive forearms. The Sicilian was already reaching inside his jacket. Hannah knew that if the joker attacked, no matter how strong or quick he was, they would lose. Quasiman was fast, but he couldn't move faster than a trigger could be pulled, nor was he any less vulnerable than anyone else to a bullet. And if Hannah just happened to be shot in the attack . . .

"Here!" she shouted, and tossed Quasiman the stuffed tiger before either of the goons could stop her. "Go!" she shouted as Quasiman caught the toy. "Go on!"

But Quasiman only glanced at the stuffed toy dangling by one leg in his massive hand, and the sudden vacancy in his eyes terrified Hannah. His aggressive stance relaxed, his body slumped. He gaped at Hannah as if seeing her for the first time, drool running from the side of his slack mouth, and she knew they were lost. The cavalry had come, horns blowing and flags flying, but it had forgotten why.

Rudo snatched for the stuffed animal. At the same moment, Hannah tore loose from Johnson. She shoved Rudo aside as Quasiman stared at her quizzically. Hannah felt movement at her back and half-expected to feel a bullet tear into her from behind. Desperate, she took Quasiman's ugly head between her hands, hugging him as she whispered. "Please, Quasiman. You've been holding it all together for so long. Don't forget now." She kissed him, but his lips didn't open to her. She might have been kissing marble. "Damn it, remember!"

"How touching." Johnson's fingers dug furrows in her biceps, dragging Hannah back. Quasiman just watched, a faint scowl on his face as if he were trying to make sense of what he was seeing. Rudo put his manicured hand on the tiger. "It's mine," he told Quasiman. "You will give it to me now." He pulled the toy from Quasiman's yielding grasp.

"Quasi!" Hannah cried desperately, and in that moment, there was the barest flicker of recognition in his eyes. Quasiman moved in a blur, snatching the tiger back before Rudo could react.

"Hannah," he said. "I remember." In the next moment, Quasiman and the toy vanished.

Hannah let out a breath she hadn't known she was holding. Relief coursed through her, molten. Rudo whirled around to her, glaring. "Where?" he said.

"I don't know," Hannah told him defiantly. She tried to pull her arms away from the Suits. They held her tightly. "It's a lovely day for a ride, don't you think?" Johnson said in Hannah's ear, beginning to pull her toward the door. People were staring at them, and the desk clerk was talking earnestly with a security guard, pointing in their direction.

"No," Rudo said sharply before Hannah could shout. "Not here. Not now." Johnson released her at Rudo's shake of his head. Hannah grinned triumphantly, rubbing her arms. Rudo leaned close to Hannah before she could step away, so that only she could hear what he said. "Listen to me." In the face of her triumph, he was almost smiling, a smile made of dry ice and stone. "You win this round, but nothing else. Nothing. The information will do you no good. No one's going to believe you, no one's going to listen. If you go to the media with this, they will think you are paranoid or even deranged. That is, if you even get the chance to speak. The fact is, Ms. Davis, you are dead. Maybe not today, but very soon. You are already dead and rotting in your grave."

His words caused the grin to vanish from Hannah's face. She felt sick. Rudo's proximity raised the goosebumps on her flesh and brushed icy hands down her back. Then Rudo straightened and smiled again: at her, at the desk clerk, at the security guard who had stopped halfway to them, at the people watching the confrontation from around the lobby. He began walking away with a casual stride.

"Rudo!" Hannah called out.

The man stopped and turned. Alongside Rudo, Johnson glared back at her, scowling.

"It was a mistake, wasn't it?" she asked him. "The fire, I mean. It had to be. That's not the way you people work. You just recruited the wrong person with Ramblur, someone who echoed your hatred and bigotry in the simplest, most direct way. Tell me. I deserve to know."

"We all make mistakes, Ms. Davis," Rudo answered softly. He regarded her with his cold, light eyes. "That one was rectified. As will be the others," he added.

With that, Rudo left the hotel, nodding politely to the doorman as he passed, the two guards in tow. The Sicilian opened the door of the limousine outside for him; Johnson watched the street carefully. Rudo paused, staring back into the lobby. He nodded to Hannah before getting into the car.

She found Quasiman by the kitchen window, staring out into the Jokertown dusk, his twisted, deformed body slumped against one of the cheap metal chairs. A streetlight flickered on, smearing dirty light over the streaked glass. The stuffed tiger sat on the kitchen table, wedged between a catsup bottle and the sugar bowl. Hannah picked up the toy and cuddled it to her chest.

"Quasiman?"

His face turned toward her. His eyes narrowed. "I don't know you," he said. "Am I supposed to know you?"

"I'm Hannah. You saved me again, not many hours ago. You'll remember soon. Just wait a few minutes."

"I'm not sure," Father Squid spoke behind her. Hannah looked at the priest quizzically. "Hannah, I've known Quasiman for many years. In that time, I have never—*never*—seen him hold on to reality this long or this coherently. I don't think we can understand the strain that was for him: trying to keep you in his head, trying to maintain coherency and some semblance of why any of this was so important. You saw him over the last several days; he was getting worse, losing more and more of what had happened and what you were doing. The poor man . . . It was a valiant effort, but it was also a battle he was doomed from the start to lose." Father Squid sighed, the tentacles over his mouth quivering. "He's been like this since he came back. I guess I've been expecting it. I don't foresee his mental state changing. Not soon, maybe not ever. I'll be surprised if he manages to come back to us for that long again."

Quasiman had been listening, his head cocked as he stared from the priest to Hannah. For all he reacted, they might have been discussing someone else. "It's not fair," Hannah said.

"It's the way the wild card remade him," Father Squid answered.

Hannah shook her head. "Quasiman." The joker looked at Hannah. "What's my name, Quasiman?" she asked again. "You can remember it. I know you can."

Quasiman's mouth opened. His brow furrowed. "I don't know you. I don't remember."

"I just told you, a few minutes ago. Try."

Quasiman shut his eyes. Opened them again. "I can't. It's not there. Who are you? I want to remember." He looked at her desperately. His hands were fisted, beating uselessly on his thighs.

Hannah knelt down in front of him. She placed the stuffed tiger on his lap and took his hands in her own. She kissed them softly: one, then the other.

"I'm Hannah," she told him. "Your friend. And I'll remember for you."

"Who can you *trust?" Marilyn had asked me.*

"No one's going to believe you," Rudo had said.

Funny . . . I'd solved the case, after all. You'd have thought that I'd have felt some sense of satisfaction, of closure. I didn't. I felt soiled and dirty and still very scared. Maybe the way Marilyn had felt for years.

I convinced Father Squid that we had to leave his apartment and stay somewhere else that night. We were lucky, because that same night, someone broke in and trashed the place. If any of us had been there . . . well, you can figure that out as well as I can. I figured that each day we held on to our little treasure trove of tapes and notebooks was just one more day they had to find us. I knew we had to make our decision and act on it.

I had the evidence in my hands. Hard evidence, real evidence. Right there. With my tapes and the transcripts, with what Marilyn had given me, I had enough to make people take us seriously if, if the right person brought it forward. The very fact that Rudo wanted it so much told me how valuable it could be, no matter what he claimed. But in one sense, he was right. Who to give this to? If we chose the wrong person, if this material landed in the wrong hands, it would all get buried. There might be a series of new deaths, more accidents and suicides, and everything we'd brought into the light would be lost again, maybe permanently this time.

Burned maybe. Cremated in another convenient fire. That'd be poetic justice, wouldn't it?

One thing all this has taught me is paranoia. For a long time, I

*couldn't think of anyone I felt certain had the power and the inclina-
tion to do something about this. Father Squid and I talked about it,
endlessly. Quasiman . . . Well, Father Squid was right. Even when
we told him everything that had happened, he'd forget it all again an
hour later. The Sharks had been willing to kill me in Vietnam, where
Quasiman and I would have been "innocent bystanders" slain by an
act of political terrorism. Here, they tried to be more subtle until it
was obvious that we were going to keep digging. Now they'll use the
sledgehammer approach, and none of us are big enough to dodge that.
We can't go to the police or the FBI or the CIA; in one way or another
all of them are compromised. We need to give this to someone with
the same kind of clout the Sharks have. This is bigger stuff than any
of us realized when we started. It needs someone bigger than me to
handle it. I can't go any further than I have, not alone. Rudo's still
out there, with Faneuil and Durand and Battle and van Renssaeler
and God knows who else . . .*

Then I realized . . .

*I'm not exactly a wild card historian, but you're one person who
has always come down squarely in the jokers' camp, even when it
wasn't to your advantage to do so. You're one person who has always
tried to bring some sanity to all this, to make peace. You've spoken
out against the violence; you've been visibly shaken by it. I mean, my
God, you lost your hand to the wild card and you're still fighting for
the rights of those infected by the virus.*

*In the end, we had to trust someone. That's why I've spent so
much time talking with you about this and giving you the whole
story. I feel good about you. I don't think you have any evil in you at
all.*

*So I'm handing all this to you. Please, look it over carefully. I
know you'll see the same things I've seen. And then do something
about it. Do what none of us have the connections and power to do.*

Don't disappoint us, Senator Hartmann.

About the Editor

George R. R. Martin is the #1 *New York Times* bestselling author of many novels, including those of the acclaimed series A Song of Ice and Fire—*A Game of Thrones*, *A Clash of Kings*, *A Storm of Swords*, *A Feast for Crows*, and *A Dance with Dragons*—as well as related works such as *Fire & Blood*, *A Knight of the Seven Kingdoms*, *The World of Ice & Fire*, and *Rise of the Dragon* (the last two with Elio M. García, Jr., and Linda Antonsson). Other novels and collections include *Tuf Voyaging*, *Fevre Dream*, *The Armageddon Rag*, *Dying of the Light*, *Windhaven* (with Lisa Tuttle), and *Dreamsongs Volumes I* and *II*. As a writer-producer, he has worked on *The Twilight Zone*, *Beauty and the Beast*, and various feature films and pilots that were never made. He lives with his lovely wife, Parris, in Santa Fe, New Mexico.

georgerrmartin.com
Facebook.com/GeorgeRRMartinofficial
X: @GRRMspeaking

About the Type

This book was set in Palatino, a typeface designed by the German typographer Hermann Zapf (b. 1918). It was named after the Renaissance calligrapher Giovanbattista Palatino. Zapf designed it between 1948 and 1952, and it was his first typeface to be introduced in America. It is a face of unusual elegance.